Fetch Nurse Connie

Fetch Nurse Connie

JEAN FULLERTON

First published in Great Britain in 2015 by Orion Books,
an imprint of The Orion Publishing Group Ltd,
Carmelite House, 50 Victoria Embankment
London, EC4Y 0DZ

An Hachette UK Company

1 3 5 7 9 10 8 6 4 2

A CIP catalogue record for this book is
available from the British Library.

ISBN (Mass market paperback) 978 1 4091 5112 8
ISBN (Ebook) 978 1 4091 5113 5

Typeset by Input Data Services Ltd, Bridgwater, Somerset

Printed and bound by CPI Group (UK) Ltd, Croydon, CR0 4YY

The Orion Publishing Group's policy is to use papers that
are natural, renewable and recyclable products and made
from wood grown in sustainable forests. The logging
and manufacturing processes are expected to conform to
the environmental regulations of the country of origin.

www.orionbooks.co.uk

To my writing buddies and dear friends who
have been with me through good times and bad,
Fenella, Janet and Rachel.

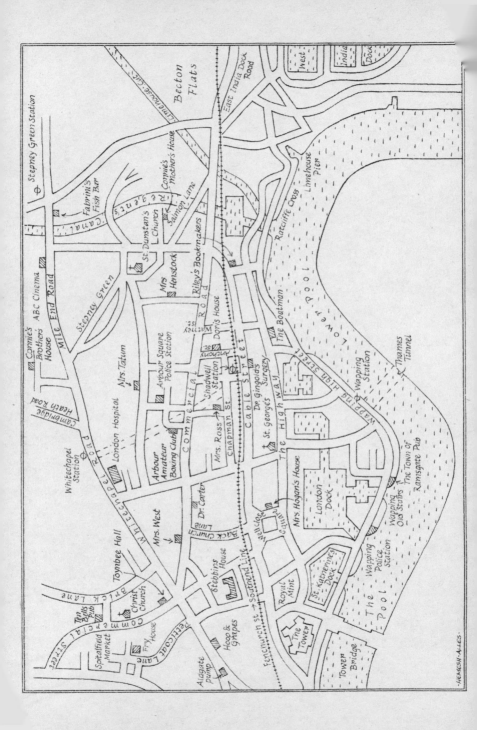

Chapter One

Connie Byrne, the Queen's Nurse, midwife and district nurse sister responsible for the Highway and Ratcliffe Cross area of the St George's and St Dunstan's Nursing Association, secured the bandage with a safety pin.

'There we go, Mr Bullock,' she said, surveying her handiwork. 'That should hold until I come on Friday.'

'Thank you, Nurse,' he replied twisting his leg back and forth to look at the toe-to-knee bandages through the thick lens of his glasses.

Stan Bullock, a heavyset individual with a florid complexion and an unfailingly jovial disposition, was one of Connie's diabetic patients, whom she visited twice daily. He and his wife, Peggy, lived in one of the many one-up-one-down eighteenth-century cottages crowded around the Shadwell Basin, which had somehow managed to avoid the Luftwaffe's attentions. Stan and Peggy were considered posh in the street because they lived by themselves, whereas most of the other houses were home to at least two if not three families.

Stan had been a painter and decorator until his eyesight started to fail and now he worked as a nightwatchman at Crossman's brewery. It was at work three weeks ago that he'd stepped on a broken bottle that had gone straight through the sole of his shoe. If it had been anyone else, it would have healed by now, but because of his unstable blood sugar, Stan was a slow healer.

Connie would usually have done the dressing after giving him his insulin before breakfast, but as one of the student Queenies, Annie Fletcher, was off with tonsillitis, it meant she had to do two of Annies morning insulins as well and they needed to be done before the patients had breakfast.

She straightened up to relieve her aching back. She'd been awake since 5.30, after the phone in the hall of Munroe House

Nursing Home had rung to summon the midwife on call. Even though it wasn't her turn to attend and she'd still had an hour before her alarm went off, Connie had been unable to get back to sleep. Instead she had lain awake listening to the slow plod of the horse's hooves and the bottles rattling in their crates as the milk float rolled over the cobbles outside. As Churchill was due to announce later that the war with Nazi Germany was well and truly over, she had reckoned she wasn't the only one in the street too full of anticipation to sleep.

She picked up the dirty gauze and dropped it on to the pages of the *Daily Sketch* by Stan's feet, then started to collect her galley pot and scissors.

The door opened and Peggy, Stan's wife, came in. She was carrying a bowl and had a hand towel over her arm. A stout woman in her early fifties, Peggy worked as a cleaner at Tate & Lyle in Silvertown, two miles away. She was dressed in a faded wrap-around apron with her hair tied up in a scarf, having just finished her morning chores.

'Are you all done?' she asked, giving Connie a friendly smile.

'Just about.'

'Is it any better?'

Connie smiled professionally. 'A little. I've left you a present.' She indicated the tangle of soiled dressings. 'If you can put them in a boil wash for—'

'Five minutes,' chipped in Peggy with a tolerant smile. 'I know.'

'Of course you do,' Connie replied apologetically. 'I must say "boil for five minute then leave to drain" in my sleep.'

'I'm not surprised,' said Peggy, putting the bowl and folded towel on the table. 'What with delivering babies all night and doing bed baths and dressings all day, you nurses at Munroe House must be run off your feet.'

'It could be worse,' said Connie, taking her instruments and rolling them in a dressing towel. 'We could still have bombs dropping on our heads.'

Stan and Peggy nodded their agreement.

'Can I get you a cuppa, Sister?' Peggy asked. 'The water's already in the pot.'

Connie glanced at the watch pinned to her chest. 'Oh, all right, a quick one then.' As you had to wipe your feet on the way out of some of the houses she visited, the usual reply to such an offer was 'Thanks but I just had one'; in Peggy's spotless house, however, a cup of tea was always welcome.

Peggy left the room and Connie stood up and brushed down the skirt of her navy uniform. As Stan put his sock on and rolled down his trouser leg, she wrapped the dirty gauze in newspaper ready for the fire then packed away her equipment into the outside pocket of her nurse's bag so it could be cleaned and sterilised back at the clinic. Within a few moments Peggy returned with a tray carrying three cups, which she set on the table.

'Sugar?' she asked, holding up a bowl decorated with roses and the word *Broadstairs* painted along the side.

'One, please,' Connie replied.

Peggy pursed her lips. 'Good, it'll put a bit of meat on you. Why, a strong wind would blow you away.'

Although six years of rationing had taken their toll, with a twenty-four-inch waist and at eight stone three Connie could hardly call herself a featherweight.

'And you want to put on a bit of flesh before you stand next to Charlie Ross in front of the vicar,' Peggy added for good measure.

Connie looked astounded. 'How . . . ?'

'Stan's sister Vi – you know, her whose husband breeds budgies – well her cousin lives two doors down from your sister,' explained Peggy.

'Maureen or Bernie?'

'The one with three boys,' Peggy replied.

'That's Mo,' said Connie.

'Vi's cousin told me your sister said that to her mind, you should have done what everyone told you to do and tied the knot when he was home on leave four years ago,' continued Peggy.

'Well, our Mo was ever the one to speak as she finds,' said Connie, almost hearing her eldest sister's voice in her head.

Peggy nodded. 'She said it was a crying shame as you could have had your own baby by now instead of just delivering them. And that your mum can't wait to be a gran again.'

Connie drank the last of her tea and returned her cup to the tray. 'Well, she won't have to wait long. Bernie's due her third in two months.'

Peggy's mouth formed into a perfect O. 'Goodness, your mother had a basketful.'

Connie gave a tight smile. 'Yes, five of us. Three girls and two boys.' She snapped her bag shut and stood up. 'I ought to be off. I've got another half a dozen visits before I'm done this afternoon. I'll be back just after five for Stan's afternoon injection.'

'And I'll have those dressings boiled and ready for you,' Peggy replied.

Retrieving her lightweight blazer from the back of the chair, Connie left Peggy to put the room back in order and, as she tried to decide whether to pop into the chemist before or after her next visit, let herself out.

A murky, damp start had turned into a very pleasant afternoon, and although it was only just after 1.30, there was a barely contained bubble of excitement and anticipation in Mercer Street. Without the fear of V-2 rockets raining down on them, people were milling around. Women sang as they whitened their front steps or laughed with neighbours while children played around their legs.

Unusually for a Tuesday afternoon there were as many men as women in the street because a number of the factories and offices had given their workers the day off. The sounds of the BBC Light Orchestra playing upbeat tunes drifted out from a number of open windows as everyone tuned into the Home Service ready for the Prime Minister's broadcast. Of course, the warm air meant the smell from the Thames less than half a mile away was a little more noticeable than usual, but even that didn't mar the carnival atmosphere.

Plonking her bag in the basket on the front of her cycle, Connie tucked a couple of wisps of her golden-red hair back under her hat before unchaining the front wheel of the bike from the boot scrap set in the wall. Rolling off the pavement, she placed her left foot on the corresponding pedal and pushed down before swinging her right leg across the seat as she bounced over the cobbles. A couple of people waved as she dodged between the boys playing cricket in the middle of the road, an upturned orange crate serving as the wicket.

4

Ringing her bell, she turned into Cable Street. The stubborn curls around her temples escaped again and whipped around her cheeks as she sped westwards between horse-drawn wagons and lorries. A group of young men outside the Old House at Home raised their glasses as she swung right into Watney Street and headed towards the railway arch.

'Come and have a drink with us to celebrate, sweetheart,' one lad called, his flat cap almost sliding off the back of his head.

'Sorry,' Connie laughed. 'Some of us have to work, you know.'

The men chuckled and jostled each other.

'You and your pretty nurse friends going up to the Palace later?' called another as she whooshed past. 'They say the King and Queen will be there with Churchill.'

'Just try and stop us,' Connie called over her shoulder as she entered the cool darkness of the arch.

Of course, she and the others would have to get a night pass from Miss Summers, the superintendent in charge of Munroe House, but that shouldn't be a problem.

Letting her feet rest on the pedals, Connie coasted into the bottom end of Watney Street, where the stalls and barrows on both sides of the road were already kitted out with patriotic red, white and blue bunting. Both the Britannia in Chapman Street and the Lord Nelson in the main thoroughfare were spilling over with people who had already started celebrating.

Unable to ride through the crowd, Connie hopped off her bike. There was a two-toned whistle and she turned to see Little Freddie Berry, the greengrocer, beckoning her over.

'Oi, oi, Sister,' he bellowed in a voice that could keep ships from foundering.

Little Freddie, who was built like a bulldog and was as bald as a billiard ball, was one of the old-time costermongers, whose family had hauled their large, brightly painted barrow from under the railway arch for over a century. He'd taken over from his father, Big Freddie, who now, unable to stand for long, made himself useful by sitting beside the stall with his cane discouraging children from pinching the apples. In late spring, with the new season's veg in full supply, Freddie's barrow was a feast of colourful delight, as tomatoes and beetroots nestled alongside spring greens and newly dug onions.

Gripping her handlebars firmly, Connie wheeled her cycle over to his stall. 'Morning, Freddie. How's your mum's legs?'

Freddie's pancake-shaped face lifted in a resigned smile. 'The ulcer on the left leg ain't weeping as much, but the right bugger's much the same. That cream you gave 'er has stopped the itch, though.'

Connie smiled. 'I'm pleased to hear it. Tell her I'll call by on Friday and take a look.' She started to walk on, but Freddie put his hand on her handlebars.

'Wait up a mo.'

He tore a brown paper bag down from the hook and picked up two Cox's Pippins in one enormous hand.

'There you go,' he said, slipping them into the bag and swinging it around. 'For you and your mate Sister Sullivan.'

Connie took the bag and placed it in her basket. 'Thank you.'

Carefully rolling her bike through the women and children queuing beside the barrows, Connie carried on to the top of the market, where she hopped back on and pedalled home to Munroe House.

Mrs White, the housekeeper, had just trundled the tea trolley along the hallway to the nurses' lounge when Connie walked into Munroe House, which served as both a clinic and the nurses' home.

It must have been a very grand family home when it was first built. The accommodation was spread over five floors, and a basement beneath – where the main kitchen had once been – was now the equipment store. The ground-floor rooms at the front of the building housed the nurses' and superintendent's offices and also the treatment room. What was once the boot room was now a sluice that drained into the back yard. There was also an airing cupboard for the linen and a dressings storeroom. The family dining room and parlour were now the nurses' refectory and lounge respectively. The morning room, where the lady of the house once met with her housekeeper to discuss the day's business, had become the superintendent's bedroom.

The nurses were allocated rooms on the floors above. The senior nurses like Connie had what had once been the family bedrooms on the first floor; the juniors and assistant nurses were on the next floor up and the trainee Queenies in the old servants' accommodation in the attic.

Hooking her jacket and hat on a free peg on the hall stand, Connie saw the letters from the 2 p.m. delivery sticking out of the postbox on the sideboard. Her hand automatically reached for the safety pin that secured her engagement ring to the strap of her brassiere. Satisfied that it was still there, she sifted through the half a dozen letters. Not finding the one she was looking for, she put the post back on the sideboard, then made her way to the sitting room.

As it was just after 3.30, most of the nurses were already lounging in easy chairs with a cup in one hand and a tea plate in the other. Three of the student Queenies were huddled on the bay-window seat overlooking the front of the house, while Connie's friends Sally, a curvy brunette, and Beattie, a tall, slender young woman with ash-blonde hair, were crowded around the Bush wireless on the sideboard.

'There you are,' said Sally, as she spotted Connie come in. 'We thought you were lost.'

Connie tucked her bag under an empty chair by the piano. 'I got held up at Mrs Dixon's, then I had to wait for Mr Letterman to make up Ken Feldman's dyspepsia medicine.'

'Never mind,' said Beattie, twiddling with the large knob in the centre of the wireless. A loud whistle cut through the lounge and Connie winced. Several other nurses gave Beattie a cross look and covered their ears.

Sally nudged her playfully out of the way. 'Let me try.'

Connie went to the trolley and poured herself a cup of tea, then picked up a flat round object from the three-tiered cake stand.

'What's this supposed to be?' she asked, holding it aloft.

'Jam tart, I think,' Beattie replied, fine-tuning the marker on the radio dial for the Home Service.

'Looks more like an old bath plug with iodine smeared across it.' Connie tutted. 'No butter at breakfast and a bit of grey pastry for tea. It's a disgrace. I don't know what Mrs White does with our rations.' She rested the jam tart on her saucer and joined her friends. 'Any word from Millie about her dad?'

Sally shook her head.

'Perhaps he's just taken a tumble in the garden,' added Beattie.

Connie didn't think so. It was rarely good news when you were called urgently to a hospital because your mother needed you.

'Have you had a letter from Charlie?' asked Sally.

A knot of unhappiness tightened in Connie's chest, but she put on a bright smile. 'No, but I'm not surprised. The papers say the whole of Europe's in turmoil, but now it's all over, I'm sure I'll hear something soon.'

The wireless crackled into life and the room fell quiet, all eyes focused on it.

'We are now going live to the Cabinet Room at Number Ten for an announcement by the Prime Minister,' the broadcaster's plummy voice told them.

Connie, Sally and Beattie smiled excitedly at each other.

'Yesterday morning at two forty-one a.m. at Headquarters,' said the resolute tones of Winston Churchill, 'General Jodl, the representative of the German High Command, and Grand Admiral Dönitz, the designated head of the German state, signed the act of unconditional surre—'

'It's over, it's over,' cried Beattie, jumping up and down on the spot and hugging the other two.

'Hostilities will end officially at one minute after midnight tonight, but in the interest of saving lives, the ceasefire—'

'We've won!' someone screamed. 'We've bloody well won.'

The room exploded with shrieks of joy and hysterical laughter. Everyone hugged everyone else. One of the student Queenies opened the piano and started bashing out 'Roll Out the Barrel'. They all linked arms and did a circuit of the room, looking more like Tiller Girls than state registered nurses.

After ten minutes of dancing and singing, Connie stepped out from the general mayhem to catch her breath. Letting go of the conga line, Beattie came to join her.

'I can't believe it's finally over.'

Connie smiled. 'Me neither.'

'No more dodging bombs,' said Beattie.

'Or damp air raid shelters.'

Beattie pulled a sad face. 'No more GIs.'

An image of Charlie in full battle dress, waving goodbye to her four years ago, flooded into Connie's mind.

'And our boys can come home!' she said softly.

Beattie slipped her arm through Connie's. 'I know. So could you ask the old girl for a night pass so we can go up West and celebrate?'

Connie knocked on the superintendent's door. After a few moments, she knocked again. She studied the antiquated oval sign with *House Superintendent* written in Victorian copperplate for a couple more seconds, then opened the door and peered into the room.

Miss Summers, the St George's and St Dunstan's Nursing Association's chief nurse, sat behind her mahogany desk with her fingers laced together on her bosom and her three chins resting on her white collar, asleep.

Her half-moon spectacles were perched at an unusual angle on her nose and a thin trail of spittle ran from her slack lips down to her chin. A couple of the buttons on her 1920s-style nurse's uniform were undone, while those that were fastened were in the wrong holes. Wiry strands of grey hair sprang out from under her frilly white hat like the legs of some enormous spider. The cap itself was at an odd angle and had twisted so that the two long tails of the traditional matron's bonnet, instead of running down her back, gathered over her right shoulder.

On the desktop was a jumble of papers, ledgers and work rotas. The inkwell was all but empty, but that didn't matter, as none of the four pens scattered across an old copy of the *Nursing Mirror* had a nib.

Connie stepped into the room and closed the door behind her. 'Excuse me, Miss Summers.'

The woman responsible for the Munroe House clinic and thirty-plus Queen's Nurses and midwives snorted and woke up. Her chubby hands grabbed at the order book in front of her.

'How dare you creep up on me like that, Sister . . .' she peered blearily at Connie, 'Wright. I was just—'

'It's Sister Byrne, Superintendent,' said Connie, with the sweetest smile. 'I'm sorry to disturb you, but I thought you'd like to know that Churchill has just declared the war over.'

Miss Summers stared vacantly at her for a couple of seconds, then blinked. 'Well that's all well and good, but some of us have work schedules to complete,' she huffed, picking up the infectious disease notification ledger. 'So if there's nothing—'

'Everyone in London will be out celebrating, and we – that is, me, Sister Scott and Sister Topping – were wondering whether, as it's such a special occasion, you'd be issuing some night passes,' Connie said.

Miss Summers burped, and a faint smell of spirits wafted across the desk. 'Special occasion? What special occasion?'

'The war,' repeated Connie. 'It's over.'

Miss Summer's gaze wavered. 'Is it?'

'Churchill just announced it.' Connie replied. 'And we would like to have some night passes.'

'Why?'

'So we can celebrate with the rest of London,' Connie told her. 'I don't know about that. I . . . I . . .'

'We'd make sure the required number of midwives were on call, and,' Connie crossed her fingers in the folds of her skirt, 'we'd all be ready for duty as usual tomorrow morning.'

Miss Summers chewed her lip for a few seconds, then spoke again. 'I suppose a little latitude in the rules might be in order just this once.'

Connie stood up straight. 'Thank you, Miss Summers.'

The superintendent shuffled the papers on her desk. 'I don't seem to be able to find the night ledger . . .'

'Let me help you,' said Connie, stepping forward.

Miss Summers slammed shut the desk drawer, and what sounded like a couple of empty bottles rattled together.

'Here it is,' said Connie, pulling the brick-red ledger out from under the layers of papers and documents. She opened it to the page for 8 May 1945.

Miss Summers secured her spectacles on the bridge of her nose. 'Who is it who needs permission to return late?'

Connie pulled out the sheet of paper with the list of names and handed it to Miss Summers. 'We thought it fairer to draw lots.'

The superintendent held the note at arm's length. 'I can't read . . .'

'Would you like me to write the names in?' Connie asked.

Miss Summers thrust the list back at her. 'You will really have to improve your handwriting, Patterson.'

'Yes, Superintendent,' said Connie, not bothering to correct her again.

Turning the ledger to face her, Connie perched on the chair on her side of the table and took the fountain pen from her top pocket. She quickly wrote down the dozen or so names and then turned the book for Miss Summers' signature.

'Nurses gadding about enjoying themselves.' The superintendent snatched the pen from Connie. 'Staying out to all hours!' she muttered as she scrawled a wiggly line across the bottom of the page. 'I don't know what the profession's coming to.'

'Thank you, Miss Summers,' said Connie, retrieving the ledger and her pen.

'Now if that's all, perhaps you'll leave me to get on with the mountain of work on my desk.'

'Yes, Miss Summers,' said Connie.

The superintendent waved dismissively. 'Out then,' she snapped. 'But note this. I'll only agree to this sort of thing once, so I don't want you coming back in a few days asking for more night passes because the Kaiser's been captured.'

Leaving the superintendent's office with the night ledger tucked under her arm, Connie crossed the hall to the sideboard where the telephone was situated. She stared at it for a few seconds, then picked up the receiver and dialled the seven-digit number of the Northern Star public house in White Horse Street. It rang half a dozen times and then the line connected.

'Hello, the Star,' a woman at the other end shouted over the singing and laughter in the background.

Connie turned her back on Miss Summers' office door and cupped the mouthpiece. 'Hello, Olive, it's Connie Byrne.'

'Hello, luv. Did you hear old Winston?'

'Yes, we had the wireless on at the clinic.'

'We bloody showed 'em, didn't we, those poxy Germans?' Olive screamed down the phone.

'We certainly did,' Connie replied, in as loud a voice as she dared.

'It's a pity we didn't get hold of Hitler before he topped 'imself,' Olive continued. 'But we'll have the rest of those bloody Nazis. String 'em all up's what I say.'

A cheer went up behind her and Connie held the receiver away from her ear until it subsided.

'I know you're busy, Olive, but—'

'Busy!' yelled the landlady. 'I'd say. At this rate we'll be out of beer by six. What can I do for you, ducks?'

'Is my mum or dad there?'

'I ain't seen your dad yet, but your mum's somewhere,' Olive replied.

'Would you mind if I had a quick word with her?'

'Course not, luv. Just you hold on a tick.'

Olive put the phone down, and Connie listened to full-throated renditions of 'My Old Man Said Follow the Van' and 'Run Rabbit Run' before it was picked up again.

'Wotcha, sis,' said her younger brother's chirpy voice.

'Bobby, what are you doing there?' Connie asked.

'Having a knees-up like everyone else,' he replied. 'You coming down?'

'I can't,' Connie replied. 'I've got a dozen visits then I'm up to the Palace with a few of the girls.'

'Can't you and your chums come here?' Bobby asked. 'Especially that little blonde nurse with the big blue eyes.'

Connie suppressed a smile. 'Hannah is already walking out with someone, and besides, she's almost six years older than you.'

'So?' he replied. 'I'm eighteen next month, and some women prefer a younger man.'

She laughed. 'Is Mum there?'

'I think she's popped off to fetch Mo and the nippers,' Bobby replied.

'Blast.'

'Did you want her urgent, like? 'Cos if you did I'd—'

'Not really,' Connie replied. 'It's just that on a day like today I wanted to say . . . well . . . you know.' A floorboard creaked upstairs and Connie hunched over the mouthpiece. 'Look, I'd better go. Just tell Mum I phoned, will you?'

'Sure thing,' Bobby replied. 'The street's having a party tomorrow. Can you come to that?'

'Yes, when I've finished work,' Connie told him.

'Right you are,' said Bobby. 'And see if Hannah Blue-Eyes wants to come too. Bye.'

'Bye,' whispered Connie and returned the handset.

'Making private calls, tut tut,' said a sharp voice behind her.

Connie turned and saw Gladys Potter, the nurse in charge of the Ben Jonson end of Mile End Road, standing on the stairs. Although she was chalked up on the duty boards until seven o'clock, Gladys was dolled up in a box-shoulder navy dress, a matching jacket with feature buttons, and high heels. She had finished her outfit with a small felt hat perched on her ginger hair, which was rolled up Betty Grable style.

'You're a bit overdressed for the teatime insulins, aren't you?' Connie replied, casting a critical eye over her.

'I've told the student to do them,' Gladys replied, clomping down the stairs.

Connie frowned. 'That's not fair. Doreen's already got Annie's four and three of Millie's.'

Gladys shrugged, checking her hat in the hall mirror, and strolled out of the front door, letting it bang behind her. As Connie stared after her, the phone rang.

She picked it up. 'Munroe House, Sister Byrne speaking. How can I help you?'

'Thank goodness it's you, Connie,' sobbed her friend Millie down the line. 'Dad's . . . Dad's gone.'

Connie hooked her fingers under the telephone's receiver bar and pulled the lead free. 'I'm so sorry,' she said, walking over to the stairs and sitting on the bottom step. 'What happened?'

'I think someone's coming on to the balcony,' yelled Sally, bobbing up and down on tiptoes to see over the heads of the three sailors in front of them.

'No,' said Beattie, shielding her eyes from the glare of the lamp above. 'It's just the curtains moving.'

Connie, Beattie and Sally were squashed against the railing on the top plinth of the statue of Queen Victoria that faced Buckingham Palace. They weren't alone: at least three hundred other Londoners were standing on the monument, all waving Union Jacks and singing at the top of their voices.

Having divided up the essential evening calls between them, the three friends had dashed around the streets, finishing their rounds on time despite the impromptu parties and intoxicated revellers.

They'd managed to walk out of the front door of Munroe House, dressed to the nines, just after 7.30. The buses travelling west were packed to the gunnels. People stood squashed between the seats both upstairs and down, while others clung on to the platform at the back.

The three girls had finally squeezed on to a number 15, singing along with their fellow passengers as they bumped towards the City. The bus ground to a halt on the Strand, so Connie and her friends had got off and walked past the boarded-up fountains in Trafalgar Square, under Admiralty Arch, and joined the ocean of people heading up the Mall. The crowds around the Palace railings were already twenty deep by the time they'd arrived. Some daring individuals had even clambered up and were perched on lamp posts, and every light in the street was fully ablaze, which seemed very odd after a six-year blackout. Some merrymakers had even brought instruments and had set up a spontaneous orchestra on the grass.

From behind them, the opening phrases of 'The White Cliffs of Dover' started, and the people around the statue took up the refrain. Connie linked arms with her two friends and swayed to the rhythm as they sang along.

'It's fantastic,' shouted Sally as the song ended.

'I don't think I'll ever forget it,' Beattie called back.

'Me neither,' agreed Connie.

'We want the King!' The crowd started chanting, shouting with one voice.

'We want the King!' screamed Connie, jumping up and down.

Sally and Beattie joined in the chorus, as did everyone else, and very soon the cry was echoing off the palace itself.

'There they are,' yelled a woman just below them, pointing up at the balcony.

Connie and her friends stood on tiptoe and peered across the packed roadway.

The curtain moved, then the double doors swung open and a roar of 'The King!' went up from the crowd. Connie stared transfixed as King George, his wife and the two princesses, Elizabeth and Margaret, stepped out on to the balcony. Without missing a beat, the crowd moved effortlessly into the first few bars of 'God Save the King'. As the familiar tune swelled to a roar, a shiver ran up Connie's spine. She closed her eyes and drew a deep breath, then joined in with the million voices around her.

'Long live our gracious King,' she sang with all her voice.

The King and Queen and the two princesses waved to the crowd and a roar went up. The people pressed into the road, hanging off the railings and lamp posts and piled up along the Mall sang the national anthem twice more. Then someone started on 'Land of Hope and Glory'. Grown men and women wept and hugged each other, friends and strangers alike.

Overwhelmed with emotion, Connie slipped her arms around her friends and embraced them. It was over. No more screaming bombs or casualties dug from the rubble, no more soldiers with missing limbs, no more Ministry of War telegrams delivered to mothers, wives and sweethearts.

Another cheer went up as the royal family waved their farewells and left the balcony to go inside, then the mood became more sober. The opening refrain of 'We'll Meet Again' drifted up into the warm spring evening. The girls linked arms as they sang the much-loved tune. Then a couple of conga lines started by the railings, and the merrymakers changed the song to 'Roll Out the Barrel'.

'We made it,' Sally whispered, her chin wobbling just a little.

'Yes, we did,' Beattie replied, with more than a hint of moisture in her eyes.

'I'm so glad I'm here with my best friends in the world,' sobbed Sally, squeezing their shoulders.

Looking up to save her mascara from running, Connie hugged her friends. 'I wouldn't want to be with anyone else tonight.'

Beattie gave her a wry smile. 'Oh yeah! You wouldn't say that if Charlie was around.'

'Neither would you if your Colin was back,' Connie replied, playfully smacking her friend's arm.

'Nurses, some decorum, please,' Sally said. 'Haven't you heard? Hostilities are over. Now let's join in the fun.'

Giggling, the three girls plunged into the melee and joined a circle doing The Lambeth Walk. Arm in arm with Sally and Beattie, Connie hopped forward and back, then hooked her thumbs in her blouse collar and wheeled left with everyone else. She laughed, knowing that after the long years of waiting, very soon she would finally become Mrs Charlie Ross.

Chapter Two

It was just after 4.30 according to St Dunstan's clock tower, and Connie could hear that the party in Gordon Street was already in full swing as she walked across the church graveyard. Waving to Olive's husband, Tom, a jolly, rotund man in his mid-forties who was standing outside his pub with a group of regulars, she turned the corner into her mother's road.

Like all the other streets that ran off White Horse Road, Gordon Street was lined on both sides by late-Victorian terraced houses, each with a minute front garden surrounded by a brick wall. Her mother's house was halfway down on the left, which suited her very well, as she could see up and down the street just by standing in the front bay window.

With just the milk float in the morning and the coal wagon once a week, Gordon Street was usually a quiet place. Children could play untroubled from morning till night while their mothers caught up on the local gossip. Today, though, it looked like the circus had come to town.

Her mother's neighbours had clearly been hard at work since they'd heard the news of Hitler's death. Home-made bunting was strung from bedroom window to bedroom window all the way along the street. In addition, every house had a Union Jack on a broomstick or washing pole jutting out above the front door. There couldn't be much furniture left in any of the houses, as running down the middle of the street was one enormous table draped with tablecloths made from bleached bed sheets. Not that you could see much of them, as the table was covered with plates laden with sandwiches, cakes and jellies, all of which were being consumed with great gusto by the children of the street. Apart from mothers supervising smaller children, the adults were all milling around and chatting. Some had even gathered to sing around a piano that had been dragged from someone's front parlour.

Next to the enthusiastic choir, Olive was standing behind an improvised bar, opening bottles of pale ale for all she was worth. The landlady of the Northern Star was serving PC Mills, the local bobby; clearly neither of them was too concerned about the licensing laws.

Scanning the street, Connie saw her father, Arthur, at the far end of the road. He was chatting to Mr Willis from number 40, probably comparing notes on their respective allotments. He was wearing his best suit and had a glass of beer in his hand. Her eyes travelled on until she spotted her mother, Maud, arms folded across her considerable bosom. She was sitting outside her house surrounded by a handful of women her own age, all of them keeping a sharp eye on proceedings.

'Wotcha, sis!'

Connie turned to see her brother Bobby hurrying towards her. With the same golden-red hair, grey-blue eyes and high cheek-bones, Bobby, of all her siblings, was the most like her to look at. He was the unexpected youngest of the family. Following weeks of pain and cramps in her stomach, Connies mother had been forced to visit the doctor. After she'd parted with two and six for the consultation, the doctor had told her that the baby was fine and would make an appearance in about eight weeks. This was a bit of a shock for Maud, who at forty-seven had put her lack of monthlies down to starting the change. It was more of a shock to Arthur, who to this day swore he couldn't understand how it had happened.

'Hello, Bobby,' said Connie, hugging him and kissing him on his downy cheek.

He wriggled out of her arms and glanced behind her. 'Did you bring Hannah?'

Connie suppressed a smile. 'I told you, she's courting.'

Bobby let out a long sigh of relief. 'Thank goodness for that.'

Connie looked confused. 'But I thought—'

'Oh there you are, Bobby,' called a girlish voice.

Connie looked around. Tottering towards them in impossibly high heels was a girl with springy black curls; she was dressed in a cherry-red dress and wore lipstick to match. She wound her arm through Bobby's and gave Connie the once-over.

'This is Patsy,' Bobby said. 'She and her family have just moved in around the corner in Maroon Street.'

'I'm Bobby's sister Connie.'

'Oh, the nurse who lives along Commercial Road,' said Patsy, looking a lot happier.

'That's me,' said Connie.

'You're getting married to Charlie Ross, aren't you?'

'I am when he comes home, though there's no knowing when that will be. How do you know him?'

'He played in the Shadwell Dock eleven with my cousin Dicky,' Patsy replied. 'They used to go regular to West Ham.'

'Oh, Charlie and his blasted football team,' Connie laughed. 'I wish I had a tanner for every time I've stood frozen on the touch-line watching him play. I'd be a rich woman by now.'

Pasty smiled. 'I bet you can't wait to 'ave him home.'

'No,' said Connie, feeling the ache of longing in her chest. 'But I don't suppose I'll have to wait too much longer now.'

Patsy looked at Bobby and a dreamy expression crept over her pretty face. 'Isn't it romantic?'

Bobby shrugged.

'Well, I'd better go and say hello to Mum,' Connie said.

'Yeah, she's been wondering where you are.' Bobby smiled at the girl on his arm. 'Let's go and grab ourselves a bit of grub.'

Patsy nodded and trotted off towards the table.

Bobby caught Connie's elbow. 'Do us a favour, sis.' He glanced over to where their mother was holding court. 'Me and Patsy want to have a bit of time on our own, so if Mum starts looking for me, tell her I'm just helping Tom in the Star.' He winked and sauntered after Patsy, who was already sitting at the table.

Connie watched him for a moment, then, skirting around a couple of boys playing tag, went to the tea table and got a cuppa from Mrs Pratt, who in honour of the occasion had discarded her full-length cross-over apron in favour of one that tied around her waist.

Taking a sip of her tea, Connie looked across at her mother. Now in her late sixties, Maud Byrne had dressed up for the occasion too. She was wearing the mulberry drop-waisted suit she'd bought for Connie's cousin Pete's wedding five years ago, just a week before he'd left for basic training. Her dad had once remarked that when he'd married Maud he could have encompassed her waist in his hands, but five children had spread her girth to more matronly proportions. She shunned the practical wartime bob, and her shoulder-length hair was combed back into a bun. The light copper colour that Connie had inherited was now so interlaced with white that it gave the appearance of a pale golden halo framing her face.

Maud and Arthur had moved into number 12 from Green Bank in Wapping just after Maureen had been born thirty-seven years ago. This meant that she knew everyone's history and no event in the street escaped her notice.

Now she spotted Connie and waved her over to where she was sitting with her long-time friends Ruth Brown and Dot Wilde, and another woman Connie didn't recognise. Ruth, the mother of four lively boys, and Dot acknowledged Connie with a friendly nod.

'Hello, Mum,' she said, squeezing between them to give her mother a peck on the cheek.

'I was wondering where you'd got to,' Maud said.

'Churchill might have given us all a bank holiday, but women are still having babies and I still have a full list of poorly patients to get through,' Connie replied.

Her mother sniffed. 'Well, better late than never, I suppose. I don't think you've met our new neighbour,' she added, turning towards the newcomer, a swarthy, narrow-faced woman with unnaturally dark hair. 'Mrs Silver has—'

'Oh, you're the nurse,' cut in Mrs Silver.

'Has just moved in to Old Ezra's place on the corner,' her mother said, giving the newcomer a stern look.

'Nice to meet you,' Connie said with a friendly smile.

Mrs Silver's arm shot out, causing her collection of heavy bangles to clatter. 'Lovely to meet you too,' she said, grasping Connie's hand. 'Your father's told me so much about you, like how you delivered a baby in the middle of the street while there was an air raid on.'

'Well, the baby wouldn't wait,' said Connie.

Mrs Silver laughed, setting her bosom and stomach shaking. 'I always wanted to be a nurse.'

'Did you?' said Connie.

'Yes, but oi!' She threw her hands heavenward. 'The sight of blood . . . You young girls today are so lucky and have so much freedom.'

Connie's mother heaved her bosom up with her forearms and gave her new neighbour a cool look. 'A bit too much, I'd say.'

Mrs Silver laughed again. 'Oh really, Mrs Byrne. After all they've been through, let them have a bit of fun, I say, before they get tied down with a house and kids.'

'My Connie has done her bit these last few years,' Maud said. 'And me and her dad are right proud of her, but now she can't wait to marry her Charlie and give up work. Can you, luv?'

'Well, I can't wait to be Mrs Ross,' said Connie. 'But as the Association has just changed the rules so married women can stay on, I'm not too sure I'll be giving up work right away—'

'Of course you'll give up,' interrupted her mother. She adjusted her bosom again and her mouth pulled into a tight bud. 'Unless you want people to say your Charlie can't provide for his wife.'

'Well, no, but we're already a dozen nurses down at the clinic and—'

'And I'm sure you'll be in the family way soon after and that'll be an end to it,' her mother added, waving Connie's words aside. She smiled at Mrs Silver. 'Have you got any grandchildren?' she asked sweetly.

'Yes, two.'

'Two. How nice.' A smug smile spread across Maud's face. 'I have seven, four boys, three girls, and another on the way.' She took Connie's hand. 'And I'm sure my Connie will be adding to the number before the year's out.'

Dot Wilde touched Connie's arm. 'Have you set a date for your wedding yet?'

Connie shook her head. 'I can't book anything until I know when Charlie's being demobbed.'

'I heard they were going to let men go as quickly as they could ship them back, so it might only be a few weeks,' said Ruth. 'I expect you'll get a letter from him any day now telling you when.'

'I'm sure I will,' said Connie, feeling excitement start to bubble.

Maud patted her hand. 'Don't fret. Your Charlie's no shirker so he's probably been in the thick of it, but I expect he'll put pen to paper now the fighting's done. And as soon as we hear, we'll book St Martha's and St Mungo's social hall and you can make an appointment to see Father Gregory.'

Connie forced a smile. 'Perhaps we should wait until Charlie's actually back so he can have some say in—'

'It ain't the groom's job to organise a wedding,' her mother said firmly. 'All he has to do is turn up, and didn't his last letter tell you to get the wedding sorted out for when he got back?'

'Not exactly, Mum. He said we'd be married when he returned,' Connie said.

Maud waved impatiently. 'Same thing.'

'I think your mother's right about getting your name down as soon as you know,' said Dot. 'After all, you won't be the only one wanting to be wed once the troops start coming home.'

Connie bit her lip uncertainly. 'Perhaps you're right.'

'You'll be such a beautiful bride, Connie,' said Ruth.

A sentimental expression crept across her mother's face. 'She will, and as I say to any that ask, if ever a couple were made for each other it's my Connie and Charlie Ross. Don't you worry none.' She patted Connie's hand. 'Me and your sisters will make sure you have a day to remember.'

Connie skidded to a halt in the back yard and, hopping off her bike, jammed the front wheel in a vacant space in the rack.

Not that you'd know it from incessant rain for the past three weeks, but it was now the 15 August and although it had been three whole months since VE Day the Japanese had finally surrendered. Despite the fact that there were men in ill-fitting demob suits spilling out of every train coming into London, she'd had no news of when Charlie would be one of them.

Still, no matter, it couldn't be much longer, and then ... A saucy smile lifted the corners of Connie's mouth. Well, then they would have to make up for lost time.

Connie had had a busy morning. She'd managed to complete her breakfast insulins in just under an hour. But unfortunately, as she left the last house, a neighbour called her in to see an old lady who'd fallen out of her chair. There were no broken bones but Connie had needed to find someone to help her lift the woman off the floor. The men in the street had gone to work so she had flagged down one of the Maguire coal wagons and asked the two coalmen for their assistance. This meant that now, just after ten o'clock, she was over half an hour behind herself. And she'd have to make that up by midday because she was in charge of the afternoon antenatal clinic, which started promptly at two.

Mentally running through her other morning calls, Connie grabbed her bag and headed for the back door. Shoving it open, she strode into the hall and met Annie Fletcher clutching her nurse's case in one hand and a bed cradle in the other. Annie, a pretty young woman with a soft smile and curves in the right places, was Millie's Queen's Nurse student.

'Oh, Connie,' Annie said as she spotted her. 'Dr Carter rang and asked for a nurse to call.'

'Have you put it in the book for Sally?' asked Connie.

Annie shook her head. 'He asked for you.'

'Did he say what it was about?'

'No,' Annie replied. 'But he asked for you in particular.'

Connie sighed. 'All right. I'll pop in on my way to the chemist after I'm finished doing the treatment room's weekly order.' She wondered if she'd ever get to the four patients she still had to visit before lunch.

The phone sitting on the hall table rang.

'I'll get it,' said Annie, changing the bed cradle to the other hand and picking up the receiver.

'Munroe House, Nurse Fletcher speaking. How can I help?' She raised her gaze and looked at Connie. 'Yes. She's right here.' She offered Connie the phone. 'It's your sister-in-law.'

Holding her nurse's hat in place with one hand and her bag in the other, Connie dashed along Ernest Street praying the leaden sky above wouldn't open. She reached the five steps to the familiar front door just as the first fat raindrop plopped on her nose. She pulled on the string dangling from the letter box and burst into the house.

'Where is he?' she shouted.

'We're in the front,' her sister-in-law Sheila yelled back.

Dropping her nurse's bag on the nearest chair, Connie hurried through to the front room. Her mother was sitting in the alcove chair with a cuppa in her hand, while Sheila was at the window table presiding over her best china.

But Connie barely noticed anything, her eyes fixed on the man sitting in the armchair beside the hearth. Her brother Jim.

As she walked in, he stood up and grinned. 'Wotcha, sis.'

'Jim!' she shouted.

He caught her and hugged her in his bear-like embrace, and Connie closed her eyes and clung to him, taking in the familiar smell of cigarettes and Brylcreem. Thank God!

At just a shade under five foot nine and with an elongated face, her brother James was almost a carbon copy of their father. The last time she'd seen him, four years ago, just before he'd embarked to who knew where, he'd had the beginnings of their father's paunch too, but not now. His demob suit hung from his shoulders and there was a touch of grey at his temples, but the merry eyes were the same even if they had tired lines around them. As his birthday was just two days after hers, Jim was exactly ten years older than Connie.

After a moment or two, he let her go and sat back in his chair. Connie perched on the arm.

Jim and Sheila rented the top two floors of number 7 Ernest Street. And although they had to share the outside toilet with the older couple who lived in the basement below them, they were better off than some. Ernest Street, which was just behind Charrington's brewery in the Mile End Road, was pleasant enough as long as the vats weren't brewing. If they were then the whole area was blanketed with the sour smell of steaming hops.

'You want a cuppa, luv?' asked Sheila, holding up the teapot.

'Just a quick one,' said Connie. 'I'm still on my rounds but I dashed around as soon as you rang. How are you, Mum?'

Maud pulled a face. 'Me joints are giving me gyp and I haven't had a wink of sleep with the pains in me arms, but I mustn't grumble.'

'Well at least you've got Jim home safe and sound,' said Sheila, as she poured Connie a cup.

'Praise be to Mary,' said Maud, crossing herself.

'So what time did you get back?' said Connie hastily before Sheila could speak.

'Me and a couple of lads caught the milk train this morning from Southampton to Waterloo, so I got here just after eleven,' Jim replied.

'And I had the fright of my life when he walked in, I can tell you,' said Sheila, giving her husband a plate with a huge slice of cake on it.

Husband and wife exchanged a private smile and she smoothed her fingers through his hair.

'I did think you might have saved your old mother the walk and dropped by the house first, Jim,' said Maud, putting her poor-neglected-old-lady face on.

Sheila gave her mother-in-law a withering look and opened her mouth to reply, but once again Connie cut in.

'It's a pity you missed Lawrence and Janice,' she said to Jim.

Sheila turned her back on Maud and smiled sweetly at Connie. 'Yes. If I'd known, I'd have kept them home from school.'

'I can't wait to see them,' said Jim. 'I bet they've grown.'

'You'd hardly know them,' said Sheila.

Sadness flitted across Jim's face. 'They were only a couple of tots last time I saw them, so I just hope they recognise me.' He forced a cheery smile. 'But never mind about me. What about you, Connie? Mum said you've got the wedding all set up ready for Charlie as soon as he sets foot on land.' He grinned. 'I don't know. Out of the army and into wedlock. The poor bugger!'

Connie nudged her brother playfully. 'Watch it or you won't get an invite.'

Jim laughed.

'I've got the dress fabric – my friend Millie's helping me make my dress, and the bridesmaids' outfits too,' continued Connie, who'd spent her last two days off running around organising things. 'Plus Pat on the market has got the flower order ready to go and Father Gregory said he'll read the banns straight away so we can be married within the month.'

'That's good of him,' Jim said.

Maud's lips pulled together. 'After the amount of money I've put in the collection over the years, there'd be trouble if he hadn't.'

'And your dad's found them a place,' added Sheila. 'On the Chapman estate. He's been decorating some of the old houses and asked the governor.'

Jim looked impressed.

'It's just one of the old cottages in Anthony Street,' explained Connie. 'But a couple of the girls at the clinic are going to give me a hand sprucing it up so it'll be ready for Charlie when he gets back.' She frowned. 'Whenever that might be.'

Sheila gave her a sympathetic look. 'Still no word?'

Connie shook her head. 'I met his mother in the market the other day and she's not heard either. I'll give him a right telling-off when I see him, keeping me waiting like this.'

'It ain't his fault,' said Jim. 'The blooming army postal service couldn't organise a piss-up in a brewery. I wrote Sheila three letters from Baden-Baden two months ago and not one's arrived. I bet Charlie's written dozens of times and they're in a sack in some army transport depot.'

'That's what everyone says.'

'And don't forget,' continued her brother, 'at least you're at home. Charlie's kicking his heels in an army camp in the back of beyond waiting for some pen-pusher to sign his discharge chit.'

'You're right,' sighed Connie. 'Charlie never was one to wait patiently. He must be tearing his hair out.'

Her brother winked. 'So don't be too hard on the poor chap when he does pitch up.'

Connie laughed. 'I won't. In fact I'll probably sob so much I won't be able to speak.' The longing rose in her again and tears shimmered on her lower eyelids. 'I just want him home. That's all. Home where he belongs.'

Jim smiled and placed one of his paw-like hands over hers. 'I know, luv. Charlie's a lucky man having a girl like you waiting for him.'

Connie laughed . 'Yes, he blooming well is, isn't he? And I shall tell him so, don't you worry.'

Jim and Sheila laughed.

'So where were you, Jim?' asked Connie.

He gave a weary sigh. 'Tunisia, then France and finally Germany.'

'Goodness,' said Connie. 'You must have some stories to tell.'

He gave her a sad smile. 'A few.'

'But now it's over and he's back where he belongs,' said Sheila, giving Connie a meaningful look.

Connie took the hint and stood up. 'I ought to get on, but make sure and give Lawrence and Janice a kiss from me, Jim, and welcome home.'

He smiled. 'Thanks, sis. I suppose you and the girls at the clinic are out celebrating VJ night later.'

'We are, we're going to the Regency,' Connie replied.

Her mother frowned. 'Do you think you should?'

'Why ever not?'

'Well, with Charlie on his way home and all,' Maud replied.

Connie laughed. 'We're just going to dance.'

Her mother didn't look convinced. 'And we know what that can lead to.'

'Didn't you say you met Dad at a dance?' asked Jim innocently.

Sheila turned away and smiled.

'Yes,' Maud replied. 'But it was at St Martha and St Mungo's, and old Father Flaherty – God rest him – kept a sharp eye on things, I can tell you. Not like today with that jitterwotsit those darky GIs brought over. Indecent jungle music is what I call it.'

Crossing the room, Connie gave her mother a peck on the cheek. 'Don't worry, Mum. I'll behave myself.'

The hall was full of the mouth-watering smell of mutton stew when Connie opened Munroe House's front door, but instead of the usual sound of music from the wireless drifting out of the kitchen and the pattering of stockinged feet upstairs as the nurses prepared for supper, it sounded as if a meeting of the Billingsgate fishwives was taking place in the rooms above.

As she unpinned her hat and hooked it on the hall stand, Sally, Annie and Joyce rushed out of the treatment room.

'Oh Connie, where have you been?' asked Joyce, hurrying towards her.

'At my brother's.'

'Well,' said Sally. 'You've missed all the fun.'

'Fun?'

'Yes. Miss Summers,' said Joyce hopping up and down on the spot. 'She's gone.'

'Gone? Gone where?'

Sally pulled a face. 'Who cares, but—'

'You know Mrs White didn't turn up this morning to do the breakfast?' cut in Joyce.

'Oh no,' said Connie. 'She didn't have one of her turns again, did she?'

'No,' shrieked Annie. 'She's been nicked.'

Connie pointed at the kitchen. 'But—'

'Oh, Millie organised Marge and Nancy to do supper,' explained Sally.

'And Alfie boy's been nabbed too,' added Joyce.

'What's Alfie White got to do with anything?' asked Connie.

'He's been done for racketeering,' Sally replied. 'I heard in the market that the cops burst into his house at dawn and found loads of restricted stuff.'

'Me and Millie were packing the dressing tins for tomorrow in the treatment room when the Association's chairman Mrs Harper walked in,' continued Annie excitedly. 'They looked very serious and asked Millie to go with them.'

'They all went into Miss Summers' office and shut the door,' explained Sally. 'Then half an hour later Miss Summers slammed out and went to her room. About ten minutes after that, she marched out again in civvies carrying a suitcase.'

'And that's the last we've seen of her,' added Joyce.

'Then Mrs Harper and Mrs Roper came out with the clinic accounts books under their arms and faces like thunder,' added Sally.

Connie looked puzzled. 'But how is Miss Summers involved in this?'

Sally shrugged. 'Millie wouldn't tell us, but . . .' she grinned and slipped her arm through Connie's, 'I'm sure she'd tell *you*.'

Her three friends looked eagerly at her.

Connie laughed. 'Honestly. You lot.'

Joyce nudged her. 'Go on.'

A wry smile lifted Connie's lips. 'Where is she?'

'In the super's office,' Sally replied.

Connie gave an exaggerated roll of her eyes then headed for the room at the end of the corridor.

Millie was sitting behind the long oak desk, still wearing her navy uniform, with a stack of patient record cards on one side of her and the daily record book on the other. Spread in front of her was the blank allocation rota for the following month.

She looked up as Connie walked in. 'I suppose you heard about Miss Summers,' she said wearily.

Connie took the seat on the other side of the desk. 'What happen?'

Millie hooked a stray lock of hair behind her ear and leant back. 'It seems Mrs White had an early-morning visit from a detective inspector from Arbour Square police station. His officers found no end of contraband, but they also found tins of corned beef, condensed milk and powered egg from Munroe House's larder, as well as a number of our ration books.'

Connie's jaw dropped. 'No!'

'Yes,' replied Millie. 'Mrs White confessed that she'd been stealing stuff from Munroe House for ages.'

'Well I suppose that explains why we're always out of butter and sugar,' said Connie. 'Was Miss Summers in on it?'

Millie shook her head. 'But Mrs Harper and Mrs Roper dismissed her on the spot for gross negligence of her duty.'

'Goodness,' said Connie. 'No wonder the house is buzzing.'

Millie sighed. 'I know Mrs Harper and Mrs Roper didn't want to broadcast it, but I suppose as the Senior Sister I'll have to say something at supper.'

'I think the girls have pretty much added two and two together,' said Connie. 'But it would be better if they heard what actually happened from you rather than reading it in the local rag.'

'You're probably right,' said Millie.

'So,' said Connie picking up an old dog-eared note with Miss Summers' scrawl across it and tossing it in the bin. 'Who's in charge of Munroe House now?'

Millie gave her a baleful look. 'Me.'

Chapter Three

Connie's partner swirled her around in a flourish as the last chord of 'In the Mood' blared out. Then he let go of her hand and clapped. 'Good band.' He was a young man with sandy hair and had only trodden on her toes once.

'Yeah, they're not bad,' Connie replied.

It was 15 August, VJ night, and the Regency ballroom in Stratford was packed to the rafters.

After a mad rush to scrub the treatment room, clean the instruments and set them to soak in Dettol, pack the bandage drums and fill the Little Sister pressure steamer, Connie, Millie and Beattie had dashed upstairs. They must have set some sort of record, because forty minutes later and dressed to the nines they had jumped on board a bus for the three-mile journey to the Regency in Stratford Broadway.

They weren't alone. It seemed as if everyone east of the City had decided to celebrate the end of hostilities, and the old music hall, which had long since lost its rows of seating and chandeliers to a sprung dance floor and a rotating mirror ball, was heaving. They'd been very lucky to find a table.

The band leader called the musicians to order and announced the next dance.

'Do you fancy another spin?' asked the young man.

'Thanks, but I ought to rejoin my friends,' Connie replied, nodding at Beattie, who had just returned to the table with another round of drinks. 'Perhaps later.'

He took her elbow and led her off the floor.

'Seven out of ten?' asked Beattie when he was out of earshot.

'Six,' Connie replied. 'He works for the gas company, or was it the electricity board? Anyway, I now know what happens when you put your half-crown in the meter.'

Beattie laughed. 'I got you and Millie another G and T.'

Connie took a sip of her drink. 'Where is she?'

A wry smile spread across Beattie's face. 'Still dancing with that chap.'

Connie's eyes opened wide and she scanned the room. Sure enough, there was Millie, a slim brunette, still in the arms of the dark-haired man who'd walked her on to the floor four dances ago.

Connie and Millie had been firm friends since the day they'd met, just before the war, as wet-behind-the-ears pupil nurses at the London Hospital. They had been staff nurses together on the evacuation of the wards at Brentwood, after which Connie had gone to Woolmer Park in Hertfordshire to study for her part one in midwifery while Millie went to Queen Charlotte's to do hers. They had reunited in the London for their part two and had worked together as sisters of the St George's and St Dunstan's Nursing Association ever since. More importantly, Millie was also going to be Connie's chief bridesmaid.

'I bet she's glad you persuaded her to come instead of staying in with a mug of cocoa,' said Beattie.

Connie laughed. 'It's nice to see her with a smile on her face.'

'Yes, she's had a tough three months, what with losing her dad and now having to step into Miss Summers' shoes,' agreed Beattie.

'Do you think she'll apply for the superintendent's job?' asked Beattie.

'I think so,' Connie replied. 'Although if you ask me, I don't see why the Association doesn't just give her the post and save themselves a lot of time and trouble.'

Connie, Beattie and Millie were among the last to leave the Regency, just before 10.30. Although tomorrow was a working day, outside on Stratford Broadway the partying continued, with people carousing up and down the market area and around St John's church.

'Look,' said Millie pointing down Romford Road. 'There's a 25 coming. If we're quick, we'll catch it.'

The three girls waited for the Woolwich tram to pass, then dashed across the road just as the bus rolled to a stop outside Marks & Spencer. The crowd at the bus stop surged forward and the vehicle rolled on its wheels as the weight inside increased.

Connie grabbed her friends' hands. 'Come on or we'll miss it.'

'I'm running as fast as I can,' shouted Beattie, wrenching her heel free of a tramline.

With her lungs burning and her calves aching from sprinting in high heels, Connie grabbed the upright rail at the back of the bus and jumped on. Millie leapt on too and collided with her. The conductor pulled on the cable strung along the roof of the cabin to ring the bell, and the bus jolted into action.

'Jump!' screamed Connie and Millie.

Beattie launched herself on to the platform. The other two grabbed her as the vehicle bounced along towards Bow Bridge.

Beattie wriggled her foot. 'Ouch, I think I've twisted my ankle.'

Connie stretched on tiptoe and spotted a space just behind the driver. The bus was overloaded, with double the number of recommended people standing in the aisle.

'There's a seat at the front, Bea,' she called over her shoulder. 'You take it and me and Millie can stand.'

People shuffled aside to let Beattie limp through, leaving Connie and Millie hanging on to the rails on the footplate.

'Sorry, girls, but I can't have you standing there,' said the conductor, a lean young man with a toothy grin. 'There's a couple of seats upstairs, darling.' He winked at Connie and leant into the curve of the metal stair rail leading to the seating above.

Tucking their clothing tightly around them to prevent him looking up their skirts, Connie and Millie climbed to the top deck. As expected, there were several couples canoodling at the back, so the two girls made their way to a seat halfway down.

'So?' said Connie when they were settled.

Millie looked puzzled. 'So what?'

'So who was that chap you were dancing with?'

Millie tried to look innocent. 'Which one?'

'Don't give me that, Millie Sullivan,' chuckled Connie.

Millie grinned. 'Alex. Alex Nolan.'

'And what does he do?'

Millie shrugged. 'I didn't ask. It was just a dance, that's all.' A little smile lifted the corners of her lips. 'And he was just what I needed to get my mind off the mountain of clinic paperwork on my desk.'

The conductor came up to collect the fares. Millie gave him sixpence for them both.

'Are you going to apply for the superintendent's job?' Connie asked once he'd gone back down to the lower deck.

Millie nodded. 'The application doesn't have to be in until Friday week, so I thought I might start it this weekend.'

'Just shout if you need me to read through your letter or anything,' Connie said.

Millie gave her a considered look for a few moments and then spoke again. 'You know, if I did get the promotion to superintendent, there would be my senior post going.'

Connie's eyes stretched wide. 'What, me?'

'Why not? You're a Queen's Nurse, like me, with the same length of service and experience.'

'Yes, but I'm getting married soon.'

'So? London's so short of nurses, some hospitals are already allowing women to stay on after they're married, and I read somewhere that schools, banks, even the civil service are doing the same. With three nurses leaving this month and two at the end of the next, I'm pretty sure the Association will be forced to follow suit before too long.'

Connie was taken aback. 'I've never really thought what I'll do after me and Charlie get married. I suppose I haven't had to. Although we've been engaged for almost four years, he's been away all that time and I've always had it in my mind that when he returns we'll be married and starting a family pretty soon after.'

'And I'm sure you will, but you and I both know that babies don't always follow right after a wedding. I can't see you being happy stuck in a house all day cooking and cleaning.' Millie gave a sweet smile. 'It's just something to think about, that's all.'

An hour later, holding their shoes in their hands, Connie, Millie and Beattie tiptoed up the main stairs of Munroe House to their bedrooms on the first floor. Mouthing good night to her two friends, Connie slowly unlocked her door and let herself in. She put her shoes on the floor and switched on the light. The four-watt bulb glowed for a moment as it warmed up, then popped into life.

Softly humming 'You Made Me Love You', she put her

handbag on the dressing table, then took off her dress and hung it in the wardrobe. She unfastened her suspenders, then carefully unrolled her stockings and, folding them together, slipped them into the corner of the top drawer. Stepping out of her underslip, she draped it over the dressing table chair ready for the morning. She padded over to the small sink in the corner of her room, turning on her bedside lamp as she passed. After a quick wash, she brushed her teeth, then, pulling on her nightdress as she crossed the room, switched off the central light and slipped into bed.

Reaching over, she opened the drawer in her bedside cabinet and took out Charlie's letters. She untied the white ribbon holding them together and took one at random. It was dated 26 June 1942 and had a British Forces in Egypt stamp in the top right-hand corner. It also had 'Released by army censor' stamped in black next to her address. Propping herself against the headboard, she pulled out the page and read the familiar lines.

Dear sweetheart Connie,

I hope you are well and that things are well with you. I'm sure you're busy with babies and things like you told me in your last letter. I had a letter from Mum last week telling me about how she is helping with the church dinners and knitting for the merchant navy. She also said you'd dropped around to see her and I'm glad about that as she is all alone.

I'm not busy here as we have had weeks of sitting around while the top brass get things organised. It's not bad as me and a couple of the lads here have got together a football team. We are the Hammers Exiles and we had a match with a team who call themselves the Tyne Wanderers. You couldn't understand a blooming word of what they said but they were a good bunch and we got a draw which meant we all was happy.

But although it was a right laugh I'd rather have been sitting with you in the Ship downing a pint of mild any day. I showed your picture you sent me to the boys in my tent and they all said I was a lucky bugger having such a pretty girl waiting for me at home. And I know I am.

I can't wait until I get home to see you again and I think
about you all the time, especially in bed at night. I hope
you think of me too, Con.
Hope it will all be over soon and we can get hitched.

Love and kisses from Charlie

When she got to the bottom of the page, Connie refolded the letter, slipped it back in its envelope and put it with the others. Retying the ribbon, she placed the bundle back in the drawer and closed it. Her gaze travelled up and rested on Charlie's photo sitting beside her bedside lamp.

It had been taken at Charing Cross station when he'd last been home on leave. They hadn't had much time together but had squeezed on to the train at Whitechapel for a day in London. Although it had been early March, it had been unseasonably warm, and they'd strolled along the Embankment and then up to Horse Guards and into St James's Park. They'd found a free bench beside the lake and had chatted about their family and school days. Connie confessed her girlhood crush on Mr Taylor, the music teacher, and Charlie told her how he'd kissed Winnie Freeman for a bet behind the bike sheds. They talked about what they would do when the war was over, and about the children they would have. Charlie wanted two boys and a girl and Connie said she'd be happy with whatever they were given, and in the end Charlie agreed. They had tea in the Lyon's Corner Shop on the Strand, then walked down to catch the District Line. They'd cut down the side of Charing Cross mainline station when they spotted a photographer offering concessionary rates for soldiers. Charlie had mucked about in front of the camera, as he always did, but the photographer finally got a couple of decent shots.

Charlie had shipped out the next day and the photograph arrived a week later. It had been on her bedside table ever since. It was the last thing she saw when she closed her eyes at night and the first thing she saw when she opened them in the morning.

Her gaze ran over her fiancé's laughing eyes and cheeky grin for a moment, then she picked up the frame and kissed the cold glass briefly before setting it back and turning off the light.

*

Three weeks later, after saying goodbye to her last morning patient, Connie was heading back to Munroe House when she was stopped in her tracks by the gas board drilling up the carriageway in Tarling Street. Jumping off her saddle, she rolled her bicycle along the pavement, but as she passed the roadworks someone called her name.

'Connie! Connie Byrne.'

She turned and saw a young woman in a green suit and a scarf tied into a turban on her head running across the road towards her. She stared at her for a moment, then recognised Frances Unwin, her old school friend.

'Hello, Fran,' she said, smiling warmly at her. 'Long time no see. How are you and your family?'

'Mum's got a touch of hip trouble and Dad's still on the docks, but me, I'm over the moon. Aren't you?'

Connie looked puzzled. 'Well, I'm rushed off my feet at work, and Mum's—'

'I mean about Charlie coming back,' laughed Fran.

'Charlie's coming . . . ?'

'Yes, on the twenty-ninth,' Fran continued. 'I got a letter from my Gordon last week saying he and the rest of the regiment had just landed in Hastings. They'll be arriving on the three thirty at London Bridge.' She laughed again. 'Oh Connie, don't tell me you've forgotten.'

'I . . . I . . .' Connie stammered as Fran's words whirled in her head.

'They've just shipped back from Italy. I'm surprised you didn't know.'

'I haven't had a letter from Charlie in two years,' she said in a small voice.

Fran looked sympathetic. 'I've only had two myself. I expect Charlie's letter telling you he was coming home got lost. Freda Cross didn't get one either.'

'Freda . . . ?'

'Yes, you must remember her. Frizzy hair and big ears,' Frances explained. 'She was in Miss Swann's class and married Harry Lowry from Bigland Street. He's in the same company as Gordon and Charlie and she never got a letter either. But I saw her scrubbing her smalls in the municipal baths last Monday and now we're going to meet them off the train. And you didn't know either?'

'No,' said Connie.

Frances rolled her eyes. 'Blooming army. I don't suppose it's easy getting post out of Italy, though, after our boys bombed the roads and railways to smithereens.'

'I suppose not,' Connie replied, picturing Charlie traipsing over mountains in the blazing Mediterranean sun. 'Although his mother hasn't heard either. Its a bit odd for both our letters to have gone astray.'

Frances looked at her blankly for a couple of seconds and then grinned. 'Unless he wanted to surprise you so wrote to his ma and told her not to let the cat out of the bag.'

The worry and anxiety that had threatened to suffocate Connie for months evaporated in an instant.

'Of course,' she laughed, feeling a little light-headed at the thought of having her fiancé in her arms again. 'That's my Charlie all over.'

'Yes, he was always a joker,' Frances agreed. 'Don't they say all Charlies are wags?' She looked at her watch. 'I'd better get on. I'll see you around, Connie.'

'You certainly will, Fran,' Connie replied. 'At London Bridge station on the twenty-ninth for a start.'

Back at Munroe House, Connie all but skipped up the stairs to her room. She hurried to her wardrobe and carefully took out her wedding dress. Closing the door, she slid it out of its paper cover and hung it on the outside of the closet.

It had a square neckline with home-made beaded decorations, a tight fitted bodice with a peplum and long sleeves with pointed cuffs. Connie had scrimped and saved her precious clothing rations and had bought the six yards of ivory rayon from a stall in Wentworth Street market. She and Millie had spent the last few weeks cutting out the pattern and sewing it together on Munroe House's old treadle machine.

She gazed lovingly at it for a moment, then went over to the bow-fronted three-drawer chest under the window. Sitting down cross-legged on the floor, she pulled out the bottom drawer and smoothed her hand over the crisp cotton tablecloths, pillowcases, sheets and towels she'd been given as presents since her engagement. She imagined the home she would soon be making with them. Then she shifted them aside and pulled out a mock-leather photo album. Placing it on her knee, she opened it and smiled.

On the first page were school photos of her and Charlie aged about six or seven. They were both in their Greencoat uniform and sitting at a desk. Her hand rested on an open book that had been provided by the photographer and Charlie held a protractor and compass. While she was all pigtails and shy smiles, Charlie had a skew-whiff tie and a missing front tooth.

There was a knock on the door.

'It's not locked,' she called, flipping over to the next page.

The door opened and Millie walked in holding two cups of tea.

'I thought we could both do with a cuppa.' She smiled. 'Having a look to see what you've got in your bottom drawer?'

Connie took her drink from her friend and laughed. 'I don't have to. I know exactly what's there down to the last face flannel and tea towel.'

Millie settled on the floor beside her. 'Is that on Southend Pier?' she asked, turning her head sideways.

Connie nodded. 'August Bank Holiday Monday 1938, a few months before we started our training,' she replied, turning the album so Millie could see better.

'Looks a bit blustery,' said Millie, taking a sip of her drink.

'It blooming well was. At one point we nearly got blown into the sea. The papers the next day said there had been a force nine gale all down the east coast.' Connie smiled. 'But it didn't matter. We had a great time in the Kursaal, though Fran Unwin, who I bumped into this afternoon, was sick when she got off the Cyclone, and me and my best friend Martha' – she pointed to the girl she was linking arms with in the picture – 'screamed ourselves hoarse in the ghost train. A whole gang of us got the District Line to Barking and picked up the Westcliffe train from there.'

'Who's Charlie wrestling with?' asked Millie.

'Tommy Timms.' Connie smiled. 'They were always larking about, those two.'

Millie gave her a querying look. 'Timms? He's not one of that rowdy lot down by Limehouse Cut, is he?'

'Yes,' said Connie. 'They were one of those families who had a child in every class and they all looked the same. Charlie and him were thick as thieves and always getting into scrapes.'

She turned the page to a picture that her sister Bernie had taken of them in her mother's back yard the last time Charlie had been home, and a pang of longing rose in her. Charlie was coatless, with his collar open and sleeves rolled up, showing off the muscles of his forearms. He had his arm around her waist and they were laughing.

'You know, Millie,' she said, her heart aching with love. 'If I'd married him then as everyone told me to, I might have our son or daughter with me now to meet their dad.'

'But you were in the middle of your part one midders,' said Millie.

'I was, and that seemed important at the time, but . . . I just love him so . . .' Tears sprang into her eyes. 'Look at me.' She pulled out a handkerchief.

'I'm not surprised you're emotional.' Millie put her hand on her chest and pulled a comical face. 'I was all of a-flutter too when you told me the news earlier and Charlie's not even mine, so goodness knows how you feel.'

Connie laughed and wiped her eyes. 'Stupid, isn't it?'

'Of course not,' said Millie in her nurse-knows-best voice. 'You've both been through a lot. We all have.' She put her hand over Connie's. 'But I bet by the time Charlie's been home a week, it will be like he's never been away.'

The girls exchanged a fond smile, then Connie's eyes drifted to the dress hanging on the wardrobe.

'Do you think he'll be all right about the plans for the wedding?' mused Connie as she finished the last of her tea.

'I don't see why not. In fact, I think he'll be blooming pleased that all he has to do is turn up,' Millie replied.

'I'm sure you're right. I'd just be a bit happier about it if I'd been able to tell his mother what we've planned, but every time I call she's either not in or she's just hurrying off on church business.'

'Well, she can't complain about it on the day then, can she?' Millie replied.

Connie wound her arms around herself and took a deep breath.

'I can't wait. I'm sure I won't sleep a wink between now and the twenty-ninth.' She looked at her friend. 'And thanks for saying you'll come with me to the station.'

Millie raised an eyebrow. 'I'm still not sure about that. After all, I don't want to be a gooseberry—'

'Don't be silly,' Connie cut in. 'Isn't it the chief bridesmaid's job to wait on the bride?'

Millie laughed. 'I suppose it is.'

'Good,' said Connie, closing the album and sliding it back into the drawer. 'And who knows, I might be doing the same for you one day soon.'

A wistful expression stole across Millie's face. 'Yes, I suppose you might.'

Chapter Four

As the driver's mate jumped down from the green-and-yellow-liveried Southern Railway engine in the siding opposite, Charlie Ross tilted his face to the pale autumn sunlight to enjoy the warmth of the early-morning air on his skin. Seagulls stretched above, and as his gaze ran over the ornate wrought-ironwork of the Victorian station, a sense of well-being swept over him. He was home.

It was probably a little after seven now, and he was standing on the London-bound platform of Hastings railway station surrounded by the men he'd fought and bled with for the past four years, and the memories of those who'd been left in early graves.

But he wouldn't dwell on the living hell of chasing Rommel across the desert or the hand-to-hand carnage recapturing Italy from the Nazi stormtroopers. Not now he was back on English soil. Tonight he would sleep in his own bed without fear of a night attack or a forced march to the next battle in the morning.

He watched the steam billow out from the train's engine box as the massive pistons of the locomotive ground forward a couple of hundred yards before squealing to a halt. The fireman hopped down from the cabin and changed the points with the trackside lever, then climbed back on as the train reversed.

Charlie pulled a packet of army-issue cigarettes from his pocket and took one out. He struck a match, lit the cigarette and took a long drag. Out of habit, to hide the glow from enemy snipers, he curled it in his palm.

They would have to live with his mother for a while, but only until he found his feet, and then it would be a place of their own, a family place with a garden and hot and cold water. Somewhere you couldn't hear the neighbours having a barney and they couldn't hear you having a bit of 'ow's-your-father. Perhaps somewhere a bit posher, like Stratford or Leyton, near enough to keep up with mates and family but away from the stink of the dockside and the old streets.

The scrape of metal on metal sounded along the platform as the train and its tender recoupled to the carriages ready for the journey to London. The engineer checked that all was in order and signalled to the stationmaster, who blew his whistle.

Clamping his cigarette between his lips, Charlie slung his kitbag over his shoulder and then picked up the small tan-coloured suitcase from the platform beside him. Surging forward with the rest of the demobbed soldiers, he yanked open a carriage door and deposited the kitbag on the seat nearest the window to save it, before stowing the suitcase in the net luggage rack overhead. Others piled in after him, and those who couldn't find a seat went out and sat in the corridor. When the carriage was full, Charlie stood up again and, releasing the leather strap, pulled the window down. Sticking his head out, he looked along the platform towards the entrance gate.

A heavily pregnant young woman with jet black hair and wearing a crumpled raincoat pushed her way through the crowds boarding the train. The doors slammed and the stationmaster stood with his whistle ready in his mouth. As the young woman reached his carriage, Charlie opened the door and stepped off the train.

'Come on, luv,' he said, as the stationmaster tooted a warning blast. 'Or it'll go without you.'

He offered her his hand to help her on to the train, then climbed in after her. There was a long rolling whistle and the train jolted forward. Charlie moved his kitbag and she sat down, her hand on her chest as she caught her breath.

'You shouldn't be running in your condition,' he said, taking a last drag on his cigarette and flicking it out of the window.

'*Si*, I know, but I needed the . . .' She gave him an embarrassed look as he heaved his kitbag up next to the suitcase.

The corridor door opened and a portly guard stepped into the carriage. 'Travel passes, please.'

Charlie shoved his hand inside his jacket pocket and produced the travel chit given to him at the demob centre. When the guard reached him, he handed it over.

'It's for both of us,' he explained, indicating the woman at his side. 'Mr and Mrs Ross.'

Try as she might, Connie's eyes strayed back to the station clock on the other side of the station's main concourse for the second time in as many minutes.

London Bridge station was a heaving mass of women dressed in their best, rushing towards platform gates dragging bewildered children behind them. The station was also busy with soldiers bidding farewell to comrades before continuing on their journeys and porters wheeling handcarts stacked high with first-class passengers' suitcases. But Connie was barely aware of the hustle and bustle before her as her gaze fixed on the dial.

Ten past three!

Just twenty minutes, twenty small movements of the wrought-iron hand and Charlie would step off the train and into her arms.

She was sitting in the station tea room opposite Millie. Her friend was explaining how Alex, the chap she'd met on VJ night, who she was very keen on, was in fact a local villain. Connie managed to chip in the odd word here and there, but in truth, with the blood pounding in her ears and her heart thumping in her chest, she was amazed she hadn't passed out.

Her gaze moved from the clock to where a station official on the gantry was putting up the notice for Charlie's train on the arrivals board. Dizziness and nausea swept over her. She took a deep breath and the room stopped spinning.

She snatched up the bill. 'We have to go,' she said, rising unsteadily to her feet.

Outside, Connie could barely make herself heard above the tannoy announcements.

'What platform does it say?' she shouted.

'Five.'

'Oh, quick. I don't want to be late.' She grabbed Millie's arm and dragged her towards the gate. They stopped at the barrier and Connie opened her handbag and took out her compact. She flipped it open and with a shaking hand reapplied her lipstick before tucking the compact away again.

'Is this all right?' She straightened her skirt. 'Maybe I should have worn the blue one.'

'It looks just fine,' Millie laughed. 'And I'm sure that after four years Charlie won't even notice the colour.'

The train puffed into sight around the bend.

'It's coming!' Connie shouted, her head swimming with excitement and anticipation. 'Charlie's train's coming.'

Heedless of the cold metal, she pressed against the rail as the train, with a squeal of brakes, ground to a halt. Doors banged open and Connie gripped Millie's hand.

'Oh Millie, I can't believe he's actually here.'

'It might be best if I wait by the newspaper stand,' Millie murmured.

'No, don't be daft,' Connie replied as laughter bubbled up. 'Charlie won't mind.'

Bobbing up on the balls of her feet and with her heart pounding in her chest, Connie peered through the smoke and scanned the people alighting from the train.

'I can't wait to see the look on his face when he . . . There he is! Charlie!'

The people and sounds faded around her as her gaze fixed on the man she loved and had waited four long years to wed. Feeling exhilaratingly light-headed, she took in Charlie's tall, raw-boned frame, long legs and straw-coloured hair. He stood like a rock in a sea of people, with the steam from the engine billowing around him as though he was in some Hollywood movie.

The whole world paused for a moment, then sped on at breakneck speed as she squeezed past the ticket collector and dodged through the throng of passengers, dashing along the platform. She slowed as she reached the first-class carriage, and was just about to call Charlie's name again when she saw him turn back towards the open carriage door. A heavily pregnant young woman with black hair appeared holding a small suitcase. Charlie took her hand and helped her down.

Connie's heart lurched painfully as she watched her fiancé slip his arm around this expectant young woman and kiss her. They exchanged a private smile, then Charlie threw his kitbag over his shoulder, took the small suitcase from the woman beside him and led her towards the platform gate.

With her head spinning, Connie stumbled towards them.

'Charlie!' she said, as the couple passed within an arm's length of her.

Charlie dragged his eyes from the woman on his arm and turned. He looked puzzled. 'Connie! What are you doing here?'

Fury surged up in Connie. 'What the bloody hell do you think I'm doing here, Charlie Ross? And who the bloody hell is this?' she screamed, jabbing her finger at the raven-haired woman clinging to his arm.

'Calm down, Connie,' said Charlie, a flush spreading up his neck and jaw. 'This is Maria, and—'

'We are married. At the army base,' said the young woman, shooting a triumphant look at Connie. She clenched her fist against her chest. 'I am Mrs Ross, Carlo's wife.'

The ground shifted under Connie's feet. 'Wife!'

Maria smoothed her hand over her swollen stomach. 'And I have 'is *bambino* here,' she said, smiling lovingly up at Charlie.

'Let me handle this, ducks,' replied Charlie with an adoring glance at his wife.

Just then Millie pushed urgently through the crowds and put her arm gently around Connie's shoulder. 'Let's go, Connie,' she said softly.

With tears burning her eyes, Connie shrugged her off. 'But you wrote and told me that we were to be married as soon as you came back. I've booked the church and everything.'

Charlie gave her a pitying look that cut her to the marrow. 'For goodness' sake, Connie, that was two years ago. I'm sorry, I really am, but,' he smiled dotingly at Maria, 'I fell in love. And . . .'

A roar filled her head and black spots started at the corners of her vision as Charlie continued to speak. As she felt herself sway, a comforting arm slipped around her shoulders again. 'Come away, Connie,' she heard Millie say as she led her back along the platform.

With her eyes raw from weeping, Connie stared blankly at the flowery wallpaper on her bedroom wall. Draped across her legs lay the wedding dress she'd spent her hard-earned money and fifteen clothing coupons on, not to mention the hours of sewing she and Millie had put in. She ran her fingers over the beadwork at the corner of the neckline and the tears flowed again.

Out of the corner of her eye she caught a glimpse of the framed picture of Charlie that had sat on her bedside cabinet for the past four years. She grabbed the frame, removed the back and took out the photo. Ripping it in half, she threw it in the bin. She twisted back around and opened the bedside cabinet's small drawer, pulling out the bundle of letters. With tears swimming across her vision and a knife cutting deep into her heart, she tossed them on top of the photo then flopped back against the headboard, feeling as if some great beast had reached in and clawed out her very being.

There was a knock at the door but Connie didn't move. After a pause, the handle turned and the door slowly opened.

'I've made us a nice cup of tea,' Millie said, balancing a tray as she entered the room. She closed the door with her foot and placed the tray on the dressing table.

Connie ran her hands over the beading around the neckline. 'It's so beautiful.'

'It is,' agreed Millie, handing her friend a mug. 'Let me hang it back in the wardrobe in case it gets tea on it.'

'It doesn't matter,' Connie replied, 'because I'm never going to wear it now.'

'Even so, it would be a shame to ruin it,' Millie replied.

She took the dress gently and slipped it on a hanger, then hung it in the wardrobe next to Connie's uniform and her going-away outfit.

Connie looked at her bleakly. 'How could he do it?'

Millie sat on the bed. 'I don't suppose he meant to.'

Connie frowned. 'You don't get married by accident.'

'No,' replied Millie quietly. 'But these sorts of things happen to men during a war.'

'In films, but not to ordinary blokes like my Charlie.' The yawning ache in her chest rose again. 'But he's not my Charlie any more, is he? He's her bloody *Carlo*.'

She covered her face with her hands and sobbed. Millie reached across to give her a fresh handkerchief from the dressing table.

Connie took it and blew her nose. 'I'll never forgive him.'

'Of course you won't.'

'Even if he were to crawl in here on his knees and beg me to marry him, I wouldn't. And when I think of all the men I've turned down,' Connie went on, wiping her nose again. 'Do you remember that big American who came from Indiana, or was it Idaho?'

'Illinois.'

Connie snapped her fingers. 'That's him. Pleaded with me, he did, to be his gal, but I said no.' The pain in her chest gripped her again. 'I bloody wouldn't have if I'd known my sodding fiancé was making *bambinos* with that skinny Eyetie. I tell you, Millie, I've been a right bloody fool.'

'No you haven't,' Millie replied, putting a comforting arm around her.

Connie blew her nose again. 'It will be the talk of every street corner tomorrow.'

'And forgotten by next Saturday.' Millie smiled fondly at her friend.

The thought of the whole family waiting in her mother's house to have Sunday tea and welcome Charlie home loomed into Connie's head. 'And what about my family?'

'They'll rally around you, tell you that they always knew he was a rotter.'

Connie sniffed. 'They will, won't they?'

'To a man.'

'I'll have to let the priest know too.' Connie's shoulders sagged. 'And I'd better drop in at the Chapman estate office so they can . . . let the house to someone else.' She covered her face with her hands again, and Millie hugged her as she sobbed uncontrollably. 'I was going to make it a snug little home,' she said, wiping her eyes.

'Connie,' Millie said in a thoughtful tone.

Feeling exhausted and empty, Connie raised her head. 'Yes.'

Millie gave her an awkward smile. 'I hope you don't think I'm being selfish in asking, but . . . could I come to Chapman's office with you when you go?'

Connie looked puzzled. 'Why would I think you're being selfish?'

Millie looked sheepish. 'Because Mum's got to find somewhere else to live and Anthony Street is just around the corner from Munroe House. It would be perfect.'

Connie forced a smile. 'Why didn't I think of that?'

Millie hugged her again gratefully, then caught sight of Connie's alarm clock on the bedside table. 'Goodness, is that the time? I've got to iron my dress for tomorrow.' She gave Connie an apprehensive look. 'Will you be all right if I quickly pop down and do it?'

Connie blew her nose. 'Of course.'

When Millie had gone, Connie picked up her mug of tea. As she took a sip. she caught a glimpse of Charlie's letters in the waste-paper bin. She regarded them thoughtfully for a few seconds, then, putting her drink on the table, she reached down and snatched them back.

As Connie walked towards her mother's house along the path between the headstones in St Dunstan's graveyard, her pace slowed. Although it was the last day of September, the sun was warm on her face, as if it were still the middle of August. She wasn't the only one taking advantage of the Indian summer: there were at least a dozen families, dressed in their best clothes, taking the short cut through the church ground to visit relatives or catch a bus up West for an afternoon stroll followed by tea and cake. How often had she and Charlie done the very same thing on a pleasant Sunday afternoon?

The pain gripping her chest tightened as the scene on the platform played over in her head yet again. She cut it short and, squaring her shoulders, picked up her pace. After all, the sooner she got it over with the better. Within a few moments she was standing outside her mother's door. Knowing that as always it was on the latch, she pushed it open and walked in.

'Hello,' she called in an overly cheery voice.

'We're in here,' came the chorus of voices from the front room.

Leaving her handbag on the coat stand, Connie took a deep breath to steady her racing heart, then walked into the lounge.

The room was wall-to-wall Byrnes. Her mother sat with her arms folded, like an Eastern potentate, with her family ranged around her. Mo was perched on the arm of the sofa, with her husband Eddy, who had been demobbed a month earlier, on the seat next to her. Sheila and Jim sat in the same arrangement at the other end, while Bernie, who was a smaller, darker version of Mo, was squashed between them holding her ten-week-old baby,

Betty. Her husband, Cliff, perched uncomfortably on the upright chair by the window next to Bobby, who was leaning against the piano with a roll-up dangling from his lips.

The children of the family, Mo's three boys, Jim's two children and Bernie's other two daughters, who had all clearly been threatened with dire punishment if they misbehaved, were sitting cross-legged in front of the adults. They rested their chins on their hands and stared longingly at the white-draped tea table in the bay window, which was laden with sandwiches, sausage rolls, a blue and white bowl of jellied eels, pickles and fairy cakes.

Connie's father, who was wearing a tie in honour of the occasion, had sensibly tucked himself out of his wife's direct sight and had taken refuge in the chair by the china cabinet. He gave Connie a sympathetic smile as she walked in alone. Everyone else just stared.

Mo looked concerned. 'What's the matter with your eyes, Co—'

'Never mind that,' cut in her mother. 'Where's Charlie?'

'He's not coming,' Connie replied bleakly.

'Is he ill?' asked Bernie.

Connie shook her head as tears pinched the corners of her eyes.

'Is he coming later?' asked Jim.

'No, no, he's . . .' The lump in her throat stopped Connie's words.

'What's happened then?' asked Bobby.

'I'll tell you what's happened,' Maud cut in again, her face scarlet. 'That bloody stuck-up mother of his got wind we were putting on a spread for him and—'

'He's not coming because he's already married,' Connie cried.

Her mother's mouth dropped open. 'Married!'

'Yes, married,' Connie repeated, slumping on to the piano stool. 'To some Italian girl, and she's about six months pregnant.'

As her family stared incredulously at her, Connie recounted the events at London Bridge. They listened in total silence, and when she had finished, her mother stood up.

'Right, get your coat!' she said, turning to her husband.

Connie's father looked puzzled. 'What for?'

'What for?' her mother exploded. 'I'll tell you what bloody for. So you can go and teach that bastard Charlie and his pigging

48

mother a lesson or two.' Her dentures clicked as she ruminated on the situation. 'We'll show them they can't treat our Connie like that.'

'You're telling me to go and give Charlie Ross a pasting?' her father said.

Maud's eyes flicked over her husband. 'The boys will go with you.'

Bobby smacked his right fist into his left palm. 'Don't worry, sis, I'll show him.' Jim didn't look so certain.

Connie's mother crossed her arms and glared at her husband. Several moments passed, then Arthut grasped the arms of the chair and stood up.

'You're not going to fight Charlie, are you, Dad?' Connie asked.

'Course not. I'm going up to the allotment until your mother's off the warpath,' he said, giving his wife a meaningful look. He took his cap from his pocket and flipped it on to his head.

'That's it, leave me to deal with everything as usual,' screamed Maud as he strode out. 'My mother was right. I should have married Harold Kirby. He wouldn't have let his daughter be overlooked for a bit of Eyetie skirt.'

The front door slammed and the sound echoed around the house.

'There's nothing to deal with,' said Connie wearily.

'We were fighting the Wops not a dozen weeks ago, so perhaps we can report him for treason and get him shot,' her mother said, quite buoyed up at the prospect.

'They were married on an army base, Mum, all above board,' Connie replied.

'Well, she must have tricked him into it,' Maud replied.

'By the oldest trick in the book, by the sound of it,' observed Mo, lighting a cigarette.

Bernadette and Sheila nodded in agreement.

Pain cut through Connie again and she looked down.

Sheila stood up. 'Why don't you kids go outside and get some air into your lungs until teatime.' The children jumped up. Sheila scooted them out and the front door banged again.

Eddy rose to his feet and arched his back. 'I need to stretch me legs.'

49

'I'll join you, Ed,' said Jim, getting up from the sofa and giving his brother-in-law a pointed look.

'Me too,' said Bobby. 'I think the Star might still be open for afters.'

The men stamped out.

'Now,' said Sheila, 'what say I put the kettle on and make us girls a nice cup of tea?'

The women nodded and Maud sat back down in her chair.

'Look, Mum,' Connie said as her sister-in-law left the room. 'Charlie's married and that's that.'

Her mother looked bewildered. 'But we've got it all arranged.'

'Well we'll have to unarrange it,' said Connie. 'I've swapped my day off, so I can pop in first thing on Father Gregory to let him know. And Millie wants to put in for the house in Anthony Street, so she's coming with me to the Chapman estate office.'

Her mother gave her a sour look. 'I wonder if she'd jump in your grave as quick. I didn't even know she was courting.'

'She's not,' Connie replied. 'It's for her mum. She's had a rough time of it since her husband died, and Millie wants to have her living a bit nearer.'

'Well I suppose I can't fault her for that,' said Maud.

'Exactly. And what you've forgotten is that I put Charlie's name on that rent agreement, so I want to let the house go before he gets wind of it. I can just about cope with people laughing at me behind my back and pitying me for a blind fool, but if he sets up that bloody Italian woman and her *bambino* in my little house, I'll swing for him.'

Chapter Five

Chaining her bicycle to the lamp post outside the Duke of Brunswick on the corner of Gardener Street, Connie lifted her nurse's case from the basket and pushed open the newly painted red door that led to the living quarters above the public house.

'District nurse, Mrs Dance,' she called as she entered the minute hallway behind the bar.

'Come on up, ducks,' called Minnie Dance from the top of the narrow stairway in front of her.

Danny Dance and his wife Minnie had run the pub just off Stepney Green for as long as Connie could remember. The accommodation above spanned two floors and comprised a spacious front room the same size as the main bar beneath and a kitchen at the back overlooking the yard. The main staircase continued to the floor above, where there were three other rooms and a bathroom.

Although downstairs, from its etched glass windows to its polished mahogany counter, the pub was solidly Victorian, upstairs the decor looked like something out of a glossy magazine. Even though the country was in the grip of wartime austerity, Minnie Dance insisted on all the mod cons, including a refrigerator, a top-loader washing machine and a matching set of saucepans with coloured lids. Danny, too, had embraced the modern world and owned not just the only motor car in the street, a Singer Super 10, but also a Bush radiogram, which was encased in a lacquered veneer cabinet in the corner of the lounge.

Stifling a yawn, Connie headed upstairs.

It was over two weeks since she'd gone to meet Charlie from the train, and what with the restless nights arguing with him in her head and the pain cutting through her chest every time she thought of Maria's bulging stomach, she was beginning to wonder if she would ever feel right again. She'd finally given up on sleep once the grandfather clock in the hall chimed five, and after getting dressed, she'd nipped down to the treatment room and swiped a bottle of atropine sulphate eyedrops from the lotions cupboard. But even they hadn't helped, and her aching eyes still looked like two boiled eggs that had been soaked in beetroot juice.

'Morning,' she said as she walked into the lounge.

Danny, sprawled in a leather armchair wearing his dressing gown and holding a tumbler of whisky, chuckled. 'Heavy night, Sister?' He was six foot if he was an inch, with a barrel chest, arms like steam hammers and curly black hair over every inch of his body except his head. He'd been a boxer in his prime, as testified by all the faded photos showing him holding various title belts.

'I don't know what gave you that idea,' said Connie, putting her case on the straight-backed chair next to the unlit fire.

'Min, fetch Sister a large G and T,' Danny shouted.

'Thank you, but it's too early for me,' said Connie, taking off her jacket.

'Nonsense!' he said, waving away her protest. 'Hair of the dog is just what you need. Min!' He started coughing and punched his chest. 'Bloody gherkins. I said they tasted off.' He belched, and the sour smell of digested spirits wafted around the room.

Although it was unlikely to happen in the Dances' spotless home, Connie slipped her jacket into the brown paper bag all the nurses carried with them to prevent parasites such as bedbugs from creeping into their clothing.

'I've got most of your bits ready, Sister,' said Minnie, as she tottered in carrying a battered saucepan. 'The gas was a bit slow so these took an eternity to boil.'

In contrast to her husband's bear-like appearance, Minnie barely scraped five foot and looked as if a puff of wind might carry her away. She too was in her nightclothes, but instead of the shapeless candlewick dressing gown most people wore, she had a pink quilted rayon one with a lacy collar. She also wore a pair of kitten-heeled black velvet mules with fluffy pink pompoms and was fully made up, including false eyelashes and blood-red lipstick that didn't quite sit within the boundary of her lips.

She put the pan on the table, which had already been covered in pages from the *Sporting Life*. 'And your dressings are in the tin.' She indicated a circular Peek Freans tin with a faded image of a Christmas tree and a robin on the lid.

Patients or their families were expected to get the room in order before the nurse arrived. This entailed cleaning a suitable table and covering it with fresh newspaper. They also had to boil any equipment needed by the nurse, in this case the three pairs of tweezers, two small bowls and the scissors Connie had left on her initial visit. They were also expected to sterilise gauze by baking it in the oven. Every night all over the area, battered tins containing squares of white gauze sat in the oven beside the family's evening meal in readiness for a nurse's visit.

'Where's Sister's little tipple?' asked Danny.

'I can't carry everything,' snapped Minnie. 'That was Angelica that just phoned. She said she'd be back later.' She smiled at Connie. 'She's been invited up West to some swanky party in Mayfair, with champagne and everything.'

Connie looked suitably impressed. Angelica was Minnie and Danny's daughter, who had been the recipient of her parents' lavish and costly attention for eighteen years and consequently expected the world to follow suit.

'What you having to drink, luv?' asked Minnie solicitously.

'I'm all right, thank you.' Connie laughed. 'I don't want the beat officer arresting me for being drunk in charge of a bike.'

'I wouldn't worry about PC Nott,' said Danny. 'He's one of our regulars. You can find him any time of the day or night propping up the bar in the snug.'

'Under a table in the snug, don't you mean?' said Minnie.

Danny threw back his remaining drink and smacked his lips. 'Top us up, luv.'

Minnie frowned. 'You sure? You've already had three since breakfast.'

'So?' laughed Danny. 'And when did you ever see me drunk?'

Minnie took the glass from her husband and he slapped her bottom. 'That's me girl. Make it a double to save yourself another trip. And don't forget to fetch Sister her bowl.'

Quickly unpacking her bag, Connie spread more newspaper on the floor for the dirty swabs before placing surgical spirit, safety pins and a bottle containing half-and-half Dettol solution on the table. Then, folding another sheet of newspaper into an improvised bag for the dirty gauze, she placed it on the floor under the table

Minnie returned with an enamel bowl and a towel, which she put beside the rest of the equipment. Connie took out her nail-brush and soap and scrubbed her fingernails, then put the three pairs of tweezers to soak in Dettol. Meanwhile, Minnie handed her husband the bottle of whisky she'd brought in, then perched on the arm of his chair and took a Ronson lighter and a packet of Benson and Hedges from her pocket.

Connie dropped the used bandage in the bag and cast an experienced eye over the gash running the length of Danny's ankle. 'A few more days and it should be healed. Just make sure you don't walk into a broken beer crate again.'

Using the last pair of tweezers, she replaced the dressing, then bandaged Danny's foot and fastened it off with a safety pin.

'There you go,' she said, sitting back on her heels and surveying her neat work. 'It should hold until tomorrow.' She stood up and pulled her accounts book from her bag and took her pen from her top pocket. 'I'm afraid that'll be two shillings.'

Danny rolled to one side and shoved his hand in the pocket of his dressing gown. 'There you go, luv,' he said, handing her half a crown and a florin.

'This is too much,' she said, holding out her hand so he could see.

He waved away her protest. 'Buy yourself something nice with the rest.'

'Thank you.' Connie took the money, resolving to put the extra one and six in the Northern Star's British Legion box when she was there next. She marked off the payment, then packed away her equipment.

Slipping on her jacket, she picked up her bag. 'It'll be Sister Green tomorrow and I'll be back on Friday.'

'You sure you don't want a little something for the road?' Danny asked, holding the bottle aloft.

Connie smiled sweetly and snapped her case shut. 'Honestly, I'm fine.'

The door at the bottom of the stairs banged. 'Are you decent?' screeched a woman's voice from below.

'Never!' Minnie shrieked back.

There was a clatter of high heels followed by the heavy tread of a man's feet, then a woman wearing a snugly fitting dress and a musquash fur stole, and who couldn't have been anyone other than Minnie's sister, tottered in, followed by a man in a broad-striped suit and a fedora.

'Oops, sorry, Sister, we didn't mean to interrupt,' said the woman as she spotted Connie.

Connie smiled. 'You're not. I'm just finished.' Picking up her bag, she made her way out. As she reached the top of the stairs, Danny's voice boomed down the hallway after her.

'Right. Let's open another bottle and have a drink.'

The nurses were only just filing into the refectory by the time Connie finished her last morning patient and got back to Munroe House. Since the new cook, Mrs Pierce, had arrived, there was always plenty of food, so there was no reason to rush. Connie decided to find Millie so they could have lunch together for once.

Hanging her coat up and picking up her bag again, she made her way to the superintendent's office at the far end of the corridor. When she was within a couple of strides of the door, it opened and the Association's chairwoman, Mrs Harper, came out, dressed in a tailored suit and porkpie hat with matching veil.

She spotted Connie. 'Good afternoon, Sister Byrne.'

'Good afternoon, Mrs Harper.'

The chairwoman gave her a brittle smile and strode past.

Wondering why Mrs Harper was visiting in the middle of the day, Connie knocked on the office door. There was a pause, and then Millie called, 'Enter.'

Connie went in. 'What's Mrs Harper doing . . .' She stopped and stared at her friend's desolate face. 'What on earth has happened?'

Millie's lower lip trembled for a second or two, then her face crumpled. 'I didn't get the superintendent's job.'

'I hope they don't close the doors before we get there,' Millie said, standing on tiptoes to see the front of the queue.

'It's a Wednesday night. I'm sure they won't sell out that quickly,' replied Connie.

It was their regular weekly visit to the cinema, though in fact, what with frantic fathers-to-be ringing at all hours of the day, and having to take extra shifts to cover holidays, the two girls hadn't been to see a film for weeks. However, in view of Mrs Harper's earlier visit, Connie felt that a trip to see Robert Donat and Deborah Kerr in *Perfect Strangers* might cheer Millie up.

Millie looked dubious. 'I don't know. Mrs Lamb told me she and her husband got turned away last night and the night before.'

'Well let's keep our fingers crossed,' Connie said. 'I don't fancy making do with a cup of cocoa and an early night.'

'When are you going on the date with what's-his-name from the printers?'

'Harold. And I'm not.'

'Oh Connie, why not?' asked Millie. 'He seems a nice chap and very keen on you.'

'I'm not ready to start meeting men yet; in fact, after the way Charlie treated me, I might actually give up men altogether.' A resolute expression fixed itself on Connie's pretty face. 'Perhaps I could become a missionary or something. I'll ask Father Gregory at confession on Friday.'

Millie laughed. 'Oh Connie, I wouldn't give up on—'

Something caught her eye over Connie's shoulder and her smile vanished. Connie turned, and her heart plummeted as she watched Charlie guide his very pregnant wife, wrapped up against the chilly evening air in a black and mustard block-checked overcoat, between the crowds milling at the front of the picture house. Charlie himself was dressed casually in fawn slacks and a tweed jacket, with a trilby sitting rakishly on the back of his head, allowing the light from inside to illuminate his face.

As if he felt her gaze on him, Charlie turned. Their eyes locked for a moment or two, then Maria said something and he replied. She looked at Connie with a smug expression on her face, and the two of them strolled over.

'Hello, nice to see you, Connie,' Charlie said pleasantly as they stopped just in front of her. 'And Millie too.'

'Hello, Charlie,' said Millie with an icy smile. 'I haven't seen you since . . . oh, let me see . . . since you stepped off the train at London Bridge.'

Maria's eyes narrowed for a second and she slipped her arm through Charlie's. 'Yes, when we come 'ome.'

Connie smiled pleasantly. 'And how are you keeping, Mrs Ross?' she said, in what she hoped was a conversational tone.

'I'm well.' She looked lovingly up at the man next to her. 'Carlos 'e look after me sooo good. Don't you, darling?'

Darling Carlos glanced uncomfortably at Connie.

'Look, people in upstairs seats are walking inside,' Maria chirped as the more expensive gallery queue started to move forward. She gave Connie a syrupy smile. 'You have nice time with girlfriend while I have nice time with my 'usband.'

'Good to see you, Connie,' Charlie said in the low tone that always made her shiver. His gaze ran over her face again before Maria dragged him towards the throng of people heading for the box office. As he opened the door for her, he looked back.

Connie's heart gave an uncomfortable lurch.

' "You have nice time with girlfriend while I have nice time with my 'usband",' Millie mimicked. 'Blooming cheek.' She slipped her arm through Connie's. 'Don't you worry. There's someone out there waiting for you who's ten times the man Charlie will ever be.'

'I know,' Connie forced out through the thick lump of unhappiness lodged in her throat. 'Look, we're going in.'

Connie sat glumly through the Pathé news report on the Royal Engineers restoring the water supply to a village in Celon, knowing that somewhere above her, in the one-and-nines, Maria Ross was sitting with her ''usband'.

Propped up against the carved wooden headboard, Charlie watched as Maria, illuminated by the bedside light beside him, combed her hair in front of the dressing table mirror. Below them in the scullery he could hear the muffled sound of the National Anthem signalling that the Home Service was closing down for the night. He could also hear his mother washing up their empty cocoa mugs before putting the bottles out and locking up.

His mother had tried to be welcoming, and had even managed to get a double bed and some new curtains for the bedroom, but as soon as Maria had put the statue of the Madonna, a wedding gift from her own mother, on the mantelshelf, the atmosphere had turned decidedly chilly. It had gone from wintry to glacial when his mother put a bowl of swede on the table and Maria declared she wouldn't eat pig food, to which the older woman had replied, 'People who sided with Hitler should be grateful to be offered anything at all.'

Watching his wife tease out a tangle in her straight black hair, the image of Connie's red-gold curls as she stood in the cinema queue materialised in his mind.

A bit awkward that. Meeting her again with Maria. And her turning up at the station all dressed up and ready to welcome him home with open arms. He thought she would have got the hint when he stopped writing. And now all that business with the wedding she'd put together. Everyone was talking about it. Perhaps he should have taken the time and sent her a letter.

His eyes returned to his wife. She lifted her hand to pull her hair around to the front and he caught sight of the soft curve of her breast. Still, there was no point crying over spilt milk.

'You going to be much longer?' he asked.

Maria stopped mid-movement and regarded him in the mirror. 'Why?'

He raised an eyebrow.

Laying the brush aside, she stood up and came towards him, the fine cotton of her nightdress hugging her body as she moved. Charlie pulled back the bedclothes and she slipped in beside him.

He rolled towards her. 'Happy?'

'Always 'appy to be with you, Carlos,' she replied, placing a small hand on his upper arm.

'Good.' He puckered up and lowered his head.

'But,' she said, as his lips were about to touch hers, 'your mama is still doing thing I no like.'

'Of course she does,' he said, letting his hand wander down to her hip. 'You've just got to get used to her, that's all.'

Maria pouted. 'But I'm your wife, Carlos,' she said, twirling his chest hair in her fingers. 'She should get used to me, no?'

He kissed her. 'She will.'

Maria ran her hand over his stomach and Charlie's groin tightened. 'You tell her?' she asked.

'Yeah, all right.'

She wound her arms around his neck. 'Oh Carlos, I must be zee luckiest wife in zee whole world.'

Charlie grinned. 'And just you remember it.'

She giggled, and he reached out to turn off the side light, but Maria caught his hand.

'No,' she said, giving him a lascivious look. 'You so 'andsome, Carlos, I like to see.' She kissed him.

Thinking that this was a bit more like it, Charlie raised himself on one elbow and let his fingers make their way up over Maria's swollen stomach. Cupping her breast, he grazed his thumb over the nipple, and Maria sighed. Sliding his foot over, he pushed her legs apart.

'Charlie?'

He looked up. 'Huh?'

'Connie?'

He looked puzzled. 'What about Connie?'

'You say you wrote to 'er,' Maria said.

'I did.'

'So why was she at the station?'

'I don't know,' he replied. 'Someone must have told her I was coming home.'

Maria's eyes narrowed. 'Your mother, she tell her?'

Charlie mustered up a tender expression. 'Why would she?'

'Maybe your mother more happy if you had old girlfriend as wife, not fat Ita—'

He pressed his lips on hers and she relaxed beneath him.

'Now, Mrs Ross,' he raised his head, 'forget about "old girlfriend" and concentrate on "so 'andsome" me,' he said, mimicking her accent.

Maria snuggled into him. 'Yes, Carlos.'

Charlie rolled over her again and his hand returned to her breast. After a few moments of fondling, he reached down to her hip again, under her nightdress and up the inside of her thigh, but just as his fingers were within an inch of their goal, Maria put her hand on his chest.

'You no say she was ginger like my mama's cat.'

'Who?' said Charlie.

'Her. That Connie.'

Charlie took a deep breath. 'She's not ginger, Maria. She's a strawberry blonde.' He rubbed his erection against her hip. 'Now, sweetheart, can we—'

'You think she's more pretty than me?' asked Maria.

'The word's "prettier",' said Charlie, surprised that it had slipped his mind how eye-catching Connie was. 'And no, I don't.'

'But she's thin and I . . .' She ran her hands over her stomach. 'I like a sow.'

Actually, Connie wasn't thin; she was slender, with curves in all the right places.

Charlie caught his wife's hand and kissed it. 'Don't be daft.'

He shuffled between her legs, lifting her nightdress again. Sliding his hand down between them, he tugged the tie of his pyjama bottoms and pushed them down to release his pent-up member. He licked his fingers and was just about to delve down once more when Maria spoke again.

'Perhaps now you see old ginger girlfriend at the station you wish she be Mrs Charlie Ross,' she said petulantly.

'For fuck's sake.' Charlie rolled off and sat up. 'Perhaps I would if it meant I could have a bit of 'ow's-your-father instead of the bloody third degree,' he shouted.

Tears welled up in Maria's doe-like brown eyes. 'You shout at me.'

He raked his fingers through his hair. 'Do you blame me?'

'I no like you shout, make me unhappy,' she continued as a fat tear rolled down her cheek. She put her hand on her bump. 'Make baby unhappy.'

'I didn't mean to. It just—'

There was a knock on the door.

'Is everything all right in there?' his mother called.

'Yes, Mum,' Charlie called back, trying to keep the annoyance from his voice.

'It's just that I thought I heard shouting, that's all,' she persisted.

'Go to bed, Mum!'

The bedroom door next to theirs opened and closed. Through the wall he heard his mother's footsteps thumping about as she got ready for bed. He rolled towards Maria again, but before he could resume his previous position, she grabbed the sheet and blankets and pulled them up to her chin.

'I tired,' she informed him conversationally. She turned away, taking the bedclothes with her.

Charlie stared at his wife's huddled form for a moment, then threw himself back in a sitting position against the headboard. Reaching across, he grabbed the packet of cigarettes from his bedside table and lit up. He closed his eyes, inhaled deeply a couple of times and then, to take his mind off his rigid penis, started listing West Ham players in alphabetical order.

Chapter Six

Connie stifled a yawn.

'Keeping you up, are we?' said Sally, who was sitting on her left.

It was a little before eight o'clock, and Connie and the rest of the girls on duty were squashed into the nurses' office expectantly waiting for morning report. Perhaps 'apprehensive' would have been a better word to describe the mood in the room, as it wasn't Millie but the new superintendent who would be portioning out the work this morning.

In actual fact, Miss Dutton had arrived on the last Monday in October, but had promptly announced that she would need at least a week to settle in. Seven days had turned into ten, after which she'd moved into the newly refurbished superintendent's quarters above the storeroom in the back yard. Now, on the Monday of her third week in residence, she was about to take her first daily report. Millie, mercifully, had been called out to a delivery first thing so didn't have to watch the woman given the job that should have been hers take up the reins of Munroe House.

'Sorry,' Connie replied. 'I didn't sleep very well.'

'I'm not surprised, with Potter and her crew crashing up the stairs after midnight,' said Sally, looking across the room to where Gladys, Trudy and Marge were gossiping together.

Connie gave a wan smile. Of course she'd heard Gladys and her friends larking about on the stairs, but since running into Charlie a week ago she'd been unable to sleep, and thinking about him was the real reason for her wakeful hours staring at the ceiling.

The door opened and a slender ash-blonde in her late thirties with chilly eyes marched in. The chatter in the room ceased immediately as the girls around the central table stared at their new senior nurse.

'What on earth is she wearing?' whispered Sally.

Connie didn't rightly know. It was a nurse's uniform, that was true, but rather than the Queen's Nurse-approved navy A-line dress that everyone else in the room wore, Miss Dutton favoured a matron's outfit that wouldn't have looked out of place in a Great War field hospital. It had a snugly fitted bodice and leg-of-mutton sleeves that narrowed to starched cuffs. The long skirt flared more than was permitted by clothing rations, and swished around her legs as she walked. A broad belt fastened at the front with an ornate silver buckle, and an elbow-length cape was attached to the stiff upright collar. The whole ensemble was topped off by the frilliest matron's cap Connie had ever seen, complete with trailing tails.

Miss Dutton paused briefly, then swept past them to the chair at the head of the table where the clinic diary and message book were. She scrutinised them all with her icy blue eyes for a second or two, then clasped her hands.

'Shall we pray?'

Connie wove her fingers together in her lap and bowed her head. As Miss Dutton droned through the Lord's Prayer, an image of Charlie and his cheeky smile flashed into Connie's mind and cut deep into her heart. Her eyes snapped open and, mercifully, the picture disappeared.

Miss Dutton's high-pitched voice said, 'Amen,' and Connie looked up.

Taking out a pair of half-moon spectacles from her top pocket and perching them on her nose, Munroe House's senior nurse opened the diary. Connie and her fellow nurses took out their pens and pocket books as the new superintendent read through the list of patients needing visits, and then allocated tasks such as the collection of loaned items of equipment that were no longer needed. Finally she moved on to the weekly clinics.

She glanced over the rota Millie had written out, then picked up her pen and scratched a line through it. 'We don't need two sisters to cover each clinic. Scott and her student will cover the Tuesday antenatal clinic and Potter and . . .' She pointed at Hannah. 'Who are you?'

Hannah stood up. 'Nurse Green, Superintendent.'

'Well, you're doing the Thursday one.'

Gladys raised her hand. 'Excuse me, Superintendent, I know you're very busy getting things in Munroe House organised properly,' she said. 'But if you recall, you did say I could have that day off to visit my sick mother.'

'Sick mother my eye,' hissed Sally out of the corner of her mouth.

'Off to see her fancy man more like,' agreed Beattie.

The corners of Miss Dutton's mouth lifted a fraction. 'Thank you for reminding me, Sister Potter.' She scrubbed out Gladys's name. 'Then one of the trainees can help Green.' She scrutinised the four student nurses at the far end of the table. 'You. The blonde one.'

Annie stood up. 'Nurse Fletcher.'

'You're doing the antenatal clinic on Thursday,' Miss Dutton informed her. 'Now the dressing clinic—'

'Begging your pardon, Superintendent,' interrupted Connie. 'But Nurse Green can't be in charge of Thursday's antenatal clinic because she's not a midwife.'

Miss Dutton's chilly gaze fixed on Connie. 'You're Sullivan's friend, aren't you?'

Connie straightened and looked the superintendent in the eye. 'Yes, Sister Sullivan and I have been friends since we were students together at the London.'

'Well then perhaps you've forgotten that your *friend* is no longer in charge and that I am,' the superintendent barked. 'As such, I'll say who does what in Munroe House.'

'No, I haven't forgotten, Miss Dutton,' said Connie in a conversational tone. 'But according to the Queen's Nurse's Institute regulations, all Association antenatal clinics have to be supervised by a midwife who is also a fully qualified Queen's Nurse. It's all there in the procedural manual, which is the large green leather-bound book in your office.'

A scarlet flush splashed up Miss Dutton's neck and her thin lips all but disappeared as she pressed them together. She and Connie stared at each other for a few seconds, then the superintendent scribbled on the rota again. 'Well then, Byrne, as per regulations, you are now the supervising Queen's Nurse for the Thursday clinic.'

Connie was stunned. 'But I'm doing the health check at St

64

Katherine's. I won't be finished with that until twelve, and the antenatal starts at two.'

Miss Dutton smirked. 'Then I'd advise you not to dawdle over your lunch.'

'Right.' Connie plonked her bag on the public bar of the Duke of Brunswick. 'What's happened this time, Mr Dance?'

Danny was sitting propped up in one of the corner booths with a grubby-looking bandage wrapped around his head, a face like a plate of offal, and, although it wasn't yet noon, a glass of spirits at his elbow.

'You should see the other chap, Sister,' he chuckled. Connie raised an eyebrow. 'All right, I had a bit of a tumble at Min's birthday bash last night,' he said, giving her a sheepish look.

'A bit of a tumble! Done ten rounds with Rocky Graziano more like.' Connie gave him a severe look.

With a handful of regular patients, a school visit to St Katherine's and now this afternoon's antenatal clinic to supervise, she'd been less than amused by Minnie's phone call just as she was leaving Munroe House.

'As you're walking wounded, I should really make you go to the dressing clinic.' She gave a sigh and picked up her bag again. 'Let's go upstairs and see if I can patch you up.'

Danny grinned, revealing a broken tooth. 'Ta, Sister. But do you mind sorting me out here? Min's got the carpet fitters in upstairs.'

Connie opened her bag. 'No, that's fine. Can I use the sink behind the bar?'

Danny nodded and then winced. 'There should be a towel there.'

Once she'd washed her hands, Connie removed Danny's bandage revealing a deep gash running from his shining scalp to his bushy right eyebrow.

''Ow's it look, Sister?' he asked.

'Deep,' Connie replied. 'You're lucky you didn't knock yourself out cold. How on earth did you do it?'

'Like I said, we cracked open a couple of bottles after hours last night for Min's birthday, and I was leading the conga.'

'And you tripped?'

'I fell off.'

'You were dancing on the bar?' said Connie.

Danny gave her a roguish smile. 'We'd all had a few, but as any of my regulars will tell you, I can down ten pints and a couple of chasers and still walk in a straight line. But I lost my footing.' He took another mouthful of his drink. 'And hit a bar stool and the footrest on the way down.'

Resisting the urge to roll her eyes, Connie dropped the bandage in the rubbish bag at her feet.

The bar door swung open and Minnie came in. She was wearing ankle boots with three-inch heels and a smart new black coat with an astrakhan collar and cuffs. It had probably been sold as second-hand to get around rationing, but coupons or not, it still must have cost an arm and a leg. Behind her came Minnie and Danny's only offspring, Angelica.

If the fates had been kind, Angelica would have favoured her father's dark colouring and her mother's slight build. Instead, nature had perversely endowed her with her mother's sallow complexion and mousy hair and her father's bull-like physique. She had been in Connie's brother Bobby's class at secondary school, so he knew her well – him and the rest of the boys in his year, and the year above that too, if rumours were to be believed.

Minnie, who had been on the stage herself as a young woman, had early on discerned the showbiz star her daughter was destined to become, and had enrolled Angelica in every dance and acting class she could find. She had passed on to her adored child her dress sense, which was why at 10.30 in the morning Angelica had squeezed her size sixteen body into a size twelve red and white polka-dot dress, which barely skimmed her knees, and was tottering about on a pair of black patent peep-toe wedges.

She spotted Connie. 'That was very quick. Mum only telephoned an hour ago,' she said in a voice honed from years of elocution lessons.

'You're on my way to St Katherine's,' Connie replied. Dabbing iodine on Danny's wound, she covered it with a clean square of gauze from her supply, then wound a crêpe bandage over it.

'How's the patient?' asked Minnie.

'He'll live,' said Connie, securing the end with a safety pin just behind Danny's ear.

A pitying expression moved across Angelica's made-up face and she tottered over, bringing a cloud of heavy perfume with her.

'And how are you, luv?' she asked, putting a manicured hand on Connie's arm.

Connie's heart thumped. 'Me?'

Angelica's Paris Pink-tipped fingers squeezed. 'How are you holding up?'

So much for Millie's 'forgotten by next Saturday'.

Connie forced a bright smile. 'Not so bad.'

Minnie tutted. 'I said to Doris who runs the fish stall on the market, I don't know how Charlie Ross has the nerve to show his face around here. Not after the way he treated you.'

Tears pinched the corners of Connie's eyes and she turned away.

'Well, what's done is done,' she said, making a play of tidying away her equipment.

'I saw her in the market the other day,' Angelica added, slipping back into cockney. 'Bold as brass, with her belly sticking out, asking Little Freddie for some foreign muck called garlic.'

With a lump forming in her throat, Connie recorked the bottle of sterile water and shoved it in her case, throwing her tweezers and scissors in after. She snapped the clasp shut and picked up the bag. 'I'd better get on. I'll be back tomorrow about the same time.'

'Cheers, Sister,' said Danny, draining his glass. 'And remember, there's plenty more fish in the sea.'

Connie forced a smile, and with tears blurring her vision headed for the door.

'And don't you worry,' Angelica called after her. 'As I told all our customers and everyone in the market, Charlie Ross will regret the day he left you standing at the altar.'

Connie stepped out into the school hall and surveyed the last few fourth-year children sitting cross-legged on the varnished parquet flooring. She gave them a bright smile. 'And last but not least . . .' The ten-year-olds stood up and lined up along the half-tiled wall beside her.

St Katherine's Junior School had been built in the 1890s to replace the original church school that had stood on the site. It was made of solid red brick and was three storeys high. Each floor had a hall where the children had their twice-weekly music-and-movement and PE lessons. The classrooms were accessed through half-glazed doors, while the climbing apparatus was locked flat against the opposite wall. There was a stage at one end of the hall, and staircases on either side leading to the various staff rooms and offices, with the school kitchen on the ground floor. The headmaster, Mr Cuthbert, swept around the classrooms like a gangly crow administering six of the best to any pupil who wasn't applying themself sufficiently to their studies.

'Doctor won't be long,' Connie said as she went back to the ground-floor classroom that had been given over to the health checks. It was used by the first-year children, and the walls were covered with pictures of cheery farm animals and bright flowers all labelled in big letters. There was also a sluice adjoining the room in case of any little accidents, which was why Connie had commandeered it for her monthly visits, along with the fact that it had a cast-iron stove in the corner that kept the room warm for examinations.

Dr Carmella Davenport, an elegant woman in her late thirties with a high forehead and calm grey eyes, looked up as Connie shut the door. 'Many more?'

'Seven,' Connie replied.

The doctor scanned the list in front of her. 'Well, so far we have ten children with head lice.' She looked at Connie over her glasses. 'Have you enough Lethane oil to treat them all today?'

'Yes, I brought two bottles,' she said. 'And Nurse Fletcher will be here at ten thirty, so we should be able to do them all by dinner time.'

'Good.' Dr Davenport slipped a record card into the back of the wooden file box, then extracted a cigarette from a slim gold case. 'We've also got three with conjunctivitis, and one with suspected ringworm, which needs referring to the hospital so the hair can be removed by X-ray. But only three children with bedbug bites.'

'That's encouraging,' said Connie, moving the ashtray a little nearer for the doctor's convenience.

'Don't get too optimistic, it's just the cold weather,' the doctor said, blowing smoke upwards from the corner of her mouth. 'They'll soon come creeping out again in the spring.' She rested the cigarette on the side of the ashtray and pulled out the next batch of records. 'When you're ready, Sister.'

Connie went to the door. 'In you come,' she said cheerily. The children trooped in. 'Now quickly strip down to your knickers and vest but keep your jumper wrapped around you and sit quietly until you're called,' she said, tickling the nearest child.

With a great deal of giggling the three boys and four girls struggled out of their uniform and plonked themselves down on the half-size chairs Connie had set out for the purpose. Connie beckoned forward the first boy, a wiry lad with a mop of unruly hair.

'Hello,' said Dr Davenport, taking a fresh tongue depressor from the box. 'What's your name?'

'Sydney Melrose,' he replied, sniffing a bead of snot back up his right nostril.

Having shone a torch down Sydney's throat, peered into both his ears and listened to his chest, Dr Davenport asked him to touch his toes so she could check that his spine curved in a regular manner. Everything looked fine, so she passed him and his record card to Connie while she started the next child's examination.

Connie led Sydney over to the table she'd set up ready for the head lice treatments she and Annie would be doing later.

'Right, Master Melrose,' she said, shaking off the blue antiseptic from the metal nit comb. 'Let's see if you have any unwanted guests.'

The boy stood patiently while Connie parted his hair and scrutinised his scalp. After a couple of passes over his head and a quick check behind his ears, she put the comb back in the jar.

'Now give me a big smile.'

He grinned, showing that his top front teeth were correctly positioned over the bottom ones, but in doing so revealed very inflamed gums.

'Do you clean your teeth before you go to bed?' Connie asked.

'Yes, miss, if the lights are on. Mum won't put a shilling in the meter after supper, so if they go off that's it.'

Connie nodded. 'And do you have your own toothbrush?'

Sydney shook his head. 'Me and Freddy share.'

Connie reached into her supplies box under the table and took out a blue toothbrush and a red one.

'One for you and one for Freddy,' she said, handing them to him.

Sydney's face lit up. 'Fanks, miss . . . I mean Sister.'

'Now just let me have a quick look at your hands.' She took hold of them and turned them back and forth. The nails were bitten to the quick but were clean enough for a schoolboy so she let them go.

She ruffled his hair. 'You pass muster. Get dressed and off you go back to class.'

Sydney scooted back to the line of chairs as Connie quickly filled in her part of the school medical records.

Dr Davenport had just finished with the next child, so Connie beckoned her over. The little girl walked gracefully across the room. She had beautiful green-gold eyes and light ash-blonde hair that lay in a thick plait down her back. It was clear she would be a stunner when she matured. Also, whereas almost every other child Connie had seen that day wore washed-out underwear, her vest was as white as the day it was bought, without frayed edges, and her knickers were still navy, not grey through constant washing.

Connie glanced at the card, seeing that Dr Davenport had given her a clean bill of health. 'Grace Phyllis Tatum?'

The girl gave her a dazzling smile and stood up a little taller. 'Yes, Sister.'

'I'm afraid I'll have to unplait your hair,' said Connie.

'I don't mind,' Grace replied, turning around. 'Mum redoes it every night before she goes to work.'

Connie slipped off the ribbon at the end and placed it out of the way on the table. 'Does your mum work in a factory?' she asked as she unwound the girl's silky tresses.

Grace laughed. 'No, she works up West in a posh club with lots of rich people. Sometimes she brings me the cream cakes and fruit that isn't eaten.'

'That sounds nice,' said Connie, who couldn't remember the last time she'd had a cream cake.

She took the narrow-toothed comb from the antiseptic and parted the child's hair. It was clear, so she put the comb back into the glass beaker and checked the girl's teeth. As she had expected, there was no need to give Grace one of the Mothers' Union toothbrushes.

'Can I have a look at your hands?'

Grace held them out.

'You've got very long fingers,' Connie remarked.

'That's what my piano teacher says,' Grace replied, stretching her hand as if to span a chord. 'She says if I practise hard I could be a concert pianist.'

'Is that what you want to do?' asked Connie as she took the child's fingertips.

Grace shrugged. 'I'm not sure. I did think I might like to be a teacher or work in a bank.'

Connie smiled and turned the girl's hand over, noting neatly trimmed nails as she did so, but as she ran her thumb over the knuckles, Grace pulled her hands away and furiously scratched at them.

'Sorry, Sister, but it's so itchy,' she said apologetically.

'That's all right.' Connie took Grace's hands back, and as she looked closer she noticed a couple of red spots between her fingers. 'How long have you had these?'

'A couple of days.' Grace looked worried. 'Is it something bad?'

Connie smiled warmly. 'I don't think so, but the doctor needs to have a look.' She walked Grace over to where Dr Davenport was looking in the ears of a little girl with very wiry red hair and oatflake-sized freckles across her nose. 'Excuse me, Doctor.'

Dr Davenport put the auroscope down.

'Would you mind having a look between this girl's fingers, please,' Connie said, holding out Grace's hands for the doctor to see.

Dr Davenport studied them for a moment, then looked at Grace and smiled. 'I'm afraid, my dear, you have some unwelcome visitors, but it's nothing to worry about and we'll soon sort you out.'

Grace looked alarmed. 'Will I have to have an injection?'

'No, nothing like that,' Dr Davenport replied, taking a puff of her cigarette before putting it back on the ashtray. 'But Sister will have to talk to your mother today. Is she at home?'

'Yes, but she will still be asleep,' Grace replied.

'That's all right,' said Connie. 'I'm afraid you can't go back to class until I've visited your mother, but you can be my assistant here until I'm finished. How about that?'

Grace considered for a moment, then nodded. 'That might be fun. Perhaps I'll decide to be a nurse instead.'

Ten applications of Lethane oil and two hours later, Connie stepped out of the main gate of St Katherine's with Grace Tatum walking beside her. Dr Davenport and Annie had left half an hour earlier to continue their calls, leaving Connie to tidy away. As she had Grace with her and Mrs Tatum's house was just three streets down from Munroe House, she decided to leave her bicycle in the staff bike rack and collect it later.

During the past week, the weather had given up all pretence of being a chilly autumn and, with little over a month to go, was now preparing to deliver a full-blown white Christmas. Coal lorries that had sat idle during the summer months were now working double shifts to fill the neighbourhood coal holes and cellars before the north wind rattled windows and whistled under doors.

During the brisk walk to the Tatum home, Connie learnt that Grace's best friend at school was Hilda, her special cuddly animals were a teddy called Mr Blue and a stuffed rabbit called Miss Snowy, her favourite book was *Heidi* and she was hoping to get the latest *New Adventures of Rupert* for Christmas. Connie was surprised, firstly because most children only had one soft toy, if they were lucky, and also because, as the cost of a Rupert the Bear annual was approximately three hours' wages, Father Christmas didn't leave them in many stockings.

Within half an hour of leaving the school, Connie was standing on the front step of Grace's home in Albert Square, just off Commercial Road. A short walk from Limehouse Basin, the late Victorian square had once been home to shipwrights and master mariners. Like many of the squares in the area, it had a small ornamental garden planted with roses, a diagonal pathway running through it.

Although the houses nearest the main thoroughfare had been given over to small businesses such as tailoring sweatshops and wholesale haberdashers, the dwellings at the far end still retained some of their former gentility. The ornate ironwork around the doors and upper windowsills had disappeared, melted down to support the war effort, but the classical brickwork along the eaves and the stone door surrounds were still intact. Grace's house was one such, with a freshly painted black door and lace curtains at the windows.

'I hope your mummy is up,' said Connie as she reached for the lion's head knocker.

Grace smiled. 'Don't worry. She gets up before I come home for lunch.'

When the door opened, Connie could see clearly where Grace got her looks from. Mrs Tatum was wearing a long, silky lilac dressing gown, and it was obvious that she had only just got up, but even without a trace of make-up and her hair loose around her shoulders, she looked better than most women ready for a night out. She was probably five or six years older than Connie but at least four inches taller, and slim, with extraordinarily high cheekbones, startlingly blue eyes and a wide mouth. A man would have to be lying on a mortuary slab not to give her a second look.

When she saw her daughter standing next to Connie, a frown creased her forehead and her gaze ran anxiously over Grace. 'Is something wrong, Sister?' she asked.

'Nothing serious,' Connie replied, giving her a professional smile. 'But if I could just step in for a moment . . .'

Mrs Tatum looked relieved. 'Of course.' She moved aside. Grace trotted in and Connie followed. Mrs Tatum closed the door. 'Why don't you pop up and have a read while I talk to Sister?'

Grace nodded and led Connie through into the front lounge before heading upstairs.

Connie looked around at the immaculate parlour. Although the room had many of its original features, like the wrought-iron fire surround with tiled side features, the moulded cornices and the ornate plaster ceiling rose, the furniture was contemporary. Instead of a sofa with ill-matched armchairs, Mrs Tatum had an oatmeal-coloured three-piece suite with wide curved arms and low backs. The rug in front of the fireplace was russet and had sharp black lines running across it at odd angles, interspersed with lime green and mustard blobs. There was a long walnut sideboard, and Connie could hear the sound of *Workers' Playtime* drifting out from the fabric grill of a radiogram, which had a box of records next to it.

On the shelf above the glowing fire was a baby picture of Grace and a full-length portrait of her mother with a man. Connie walked over to get a better look. A younger Mrs Tatum gazed out of the portrait with the same confident smile she'd greeted Connie with a few moments ago. By the cut and design of the long evening dress and the man's top hat and tails, Connie guessed the photo must have been taken at least ten years earlier, when Grace's mother would have been just short of her majority. The man beside her, prosperous and nudging towards portly, was at least two decades older.

'Now what seems to be the problem?' Mrs Tatum asked as she shut the door.

'The medical officer carried out one of the routine health inspections required by the Education Department, and although Grace passed with flying colours, we found she has scabies.'

Mrs Tatum looked horrified. 'Scabies!'

'Yes, but there's nothing to worry about,' said Connie reassuringly.

'Do I have to burn my sheets?' asked Mrs Tatum.

'Not any more,' Connie replied. 'Doctors have recently found that the mite doesn't live in bed linen. Scabies is only caught by skin-to-skin contact. Children catch it very easily, especially girls, as they tend to hold hands with their friends, but there is a chance you might have it too. Would you mind if I took a quick look.'

Mrs Tatum gave a brittle smile. 'No, of course not.' She held out her hands and Connie took her fingertips.

'As the infection is only between Grace's fingers, she probably caught it recently, so it's unlikely that you—' Connie broke off as she spotted the rash around the woman's wrists.

'What's wrong, Sister?'

'I'm sorry, Mrs Tatum, but I'm afraid to say I think Grace has caught it from you,' said Connie, releasing her grip.

Mrs Tatum went white.

'As I said, it's very easily passed by day-to-day contact,' Connie added hastily. 'And it's nothing that a couple of visits to the treatment centre in Valance Road won't cure. It's open each morning and the nurse there will—'

'Couldn't you do it?' Mrs Tatum cut in. 'The treatment, I mean.

After all, Valance Road is two bus rides from here, and morning appointments aren't easy for me.'

'Grace said you work into the small hours in a nightclub,' Connie laughed. 'It sounds very glamorous.'

Mrs Tatum gave a sad smile. 'I'm afraid it's anything but, and I'm often not home until four in the morning. I happen to be awake now because I got home at two last night and had a full five hours in bed for a change, but usually I doze on the sofa until I have to get Grace up, then once I've seen her off to school I go to bed until she comes home. So you can see why I would be very grateful if you could treat us here.'

'Who looks after Grace while you're out?' asked Connie.

'Mr and Mrs Stein's eldest, Rebecca, who's nineteen,' Mrs Tatum replied. 'The Steins are my neighbours; they have both sets of parents living with them, as well as Mrs Stein's sister and her four, so Rebecca sleeps here each night. She's very sensible and I think she's glad of the peace. Will she have to be treated too?'

Connie smiled. 'I'll have to check her, but it's unlikely. I can treat you here but I'll have to charge for the visits and you'll have to get the lotion from the chemist.'

Mrs Tatum's shoulders relaxed. 'I'm very happy to pay if it saves me a trip to a council clinic.'

'Who's your GP?'

'Dr Gingold in Cable Street.'

'I'll pop in and explain the situation to her this afternoon,' Connie said. 'She'll send a prescription over to Letterman's in the market for you to collect later. I'll be back at six and you and Grace will both have to have a hot bath before I get here. It shouldn't take too long to paint you both, but you'll have to leave it on for a day, so it's no school tomorrow for Grace, I'm afraid, and I don't think you'll be able to go to work tonight either.'

The door opened and Grace came in dressed in a royal blue flared skirt and a pink jumper with a Peter Pan lace collar. The sort of outfit most mothers would have kept for Sunday best, not for playing around in the house.

A soft expression spread across Mrs Tatum's face.

'Come here, darling,' she said beckoning Grace to her and hugging her. 'I'm afraid we both have something on our skin, so the Sister is going to come back later and paint us from head to toe with some special liquid to make us better.' She squeezed her daughter. 'After which I'll be snuggling up with you on the sofa for an evening by the fire. Won't that be nice?'

Grace's young face lit up. 'Oh Mummy, that will be the best.'

Having left mother and daughter planning their evening in together, Connie decided to call at Dr Gingold's surgery on her way back to collect her bicycle. In a stroke of good fortune, the doctor was still at her desk when Connie arrived and wrote out the prescription for benzyl benzoate there and then, and Connie dropped it in at the chemist. Pleased to have successfully completed her morning tasks, she stepped out of the shop and continued on her way. She was just walking past the bookmaker's on the corner when the door opened and Charlie emerged.

The low winter sun highlighted the angular planes of his face, and his cropped fair hair had regrown enough to show the curls, making Connie want to run her fingers through them. Dressed in rough corduroys, a casual jacket and a collarless shirt, he was her Charlie again, just as she remembered him.

All the emotions she'd grappled with since she'd met him and Maria on the platform evaporated, and the urge to throw herself into his arms almost overwhelmed her. Thankfully, she held herself in check.

Pulling a tobacco tin from his top pocket, Charlie took out a roll-up and stuck it in his mouth. As he went to strike the match, he spotted her.

'Hello, Charlie,' she said, finding it difficult to say his name.

He drew on his cigarette and shook out the match. 'Hello, Connie, how are you?'

'Very well,' she said, noting the fine sprinkling of golden bristles on his chin. 'Never better in fact. And yourself?'

'Can't grumble.'

'Did McGuire's give you your old job back?'

'I didn't ask for it,' he replied. 'I didn't spend four years fighting the bloody Germans just to come back and hump coal.' He blew smoke from the side of his mouth. 'I'm working at Crow and Sons. You know, the big paint factory on Albert Dock Road. It's a good job, with opportunities for a fella like me.'

'Sounds like you've really landed on your feet,' she said, forcing a bright smile. 'Aren't you working today?'

Charlie shook his head. 'I felt a bit Tom and Dick when I got up. I've just popped out for some aspirin and a couple of apples for Maria.' He tapped his bulging right pocket. 'She had a fancy for them and I said I'd pick up the chap next door's winnings while I was about it.'

'I did wonder,' said Connie.

He laughed. 'What, me putting money on a horse?' He winked. 'My mum would tan my hide.'

Despite herself Connie smiled.

Charlie took a step nearer and the all-too-familiar feeling of excitement rose up in Connie.

'Look, Connie,' he said, meeting her eyes. 'I'm really sorry about everything. Honest I am. Perhaps I should have written and—'

'I ought to get on.' The happy bubble inside Connie burst. 'Nice to see you, Charlie.'

'It was nice to see you too, Connie.' His gaze ran slowly over her as a familiar look crept into his eye. 'Very nice indeed.'

Connie's stomach fluttered but she gave him a cool look. 'And do give my regards to your wife.'

Charlie's mouth opened, but before he could speak, Connie hurried past him, tears blinding her vision.

Sitting up, Connie turned her pillow and plumped it into place for the umpteenth time since she got into bed. She switched on the bedside lamp beside her and glanced at the clock.

Eleven fifteen!

She flicked the switch off and shut her eyes.

With her lips pressed firmly together, Connie lay still for a few moments then sat up and switched the light back on. Reaching down beneath her bed she pulled out the Dolcis shoebox. She drew out the last letter she'd received from Charlie. It was dated March 1943 and she knew now, he must have been waiting to be shipped over to Italy when he wrote it. Unfolding the wafer-thin blue sheet she read through it as she had at least a dozen times in the past few weeks.

No, there was nothing. Not one odd word or peculiar phrase that might indicate that anything had changed between them.

As the empty chasm in her chest stretched wider a tear rolled down her cheek. Connie brushed it away.

There was a knock on her door.

Dropping the letter in the box, Connie shoved it under the covers and turned off the light.

'Come in,' she called drowsily

The door opened and Millie popped her head around. 'Are you awake?'

'I am now,' Connie feigned a yawn and turned on her bedside lamp. 'What time is it?'

Millie closed the door. 'Just after eleven-thirty. I know it's a bit late, but I wanted to tell you about what happened at the police station.'

Pushing the box further under the covers with her knee, Connie sat up. 'I'm guessing by your jolly smile it went all right.'

Millie nodded as she pulled Connie's pink boudoir chair out from her dressing table and over to the bed. 'Yes. They'd arrested one of the gypsy girls from Beckton Flats and she went into labour in the police cell. And—'

'Could you save the rest until morning?' Connie cut in, turning the light off. 'We have to be up at six.'

She snuggled under the covers.

'And Alex Nolan was there,' Millie said.

Connie sat up and switched the lamp back on. 'Was he under arrest?'

Millie shook her head and laughed. 'No, it turns out he's the section sergeant on B Relief.'

Connie stared at her. 'He's a policeman!'

'And you could have knocked me down with a feather when the canteen door opened and he strolled in,' said Millie.

'I bet! What does he look like in uniform?'

'All right,' she replied. 'Well, perhaps a bit more than all right. But I felt so embarrassed. You know, thinking he was a rogue when actually he's the complete opposite.'

'Oh, I wouldn't go that far,' said Connie. 'I've seen the glint in his eyes when he looks at you.'

'Don't be silly,' Millie replied, a slight flush colouring her cheeks.

'So what did he say when you told him you had him down as Wapping's answer to Al Capone?' Connie asked.

'Funnily enough I didn't mention it,' Millie laughed. 'He only had time for a quick cup of tea before he had to leave on patrol, and I had to get back too, so there wasn't time.' Millie straightened an imaginary crease in her uniform. 'Perhaps I'll drop it into the conversation when we go out next week.'

Connie's jaw dropped. 'You're going out with him? When?'

'Saturday,' Millie said, a dreamy smile spreading across her face. 'They've brought some of the paintings back from storage, so he suggested the Portrait Gallery, and then we're going on for a meal somewhere.'

'Well, you be careful. You know what men are like. All lovey-dovey and sweet kisses until some other woman wiggles by,' Connie said, her knee scraping the cardbord box containing Charlie's letters as she moved.

'For goodness' sake, Connie, we're just visiting an art gallery.'

'I know, I know,' said Connie, in a kinder tone. 'I'm just saying.'

'Anyhow, it will be a nice afternoon away from Miss Dutton's prying nose, if nothing else,' replied Millie.

'And speaking of the new superintendent,' said Connie, reaching for the lamp again, 'I, for one, don't want to suffer her bad temper for being late for report in the morning.'

'Me neither,' said Millie, standing up. 'Give me a knock if I'm not stirring, will you?'

Connie nodded and switched off the light as Millie left.

Connie lay there in the dark until she heard Millie's door close then she sat up and switched on the light again.

Retrieving the shoe box from under the blankets, Connie leant over to put it back under the bed but then sat up again and took out another of Charlie's letters.

Chapter Seven

Connie lifted the set of forceps out of the disinfecting fluid, shook off the excess and then set them alongside the rest of her instruments on the sterile paper. Folding the paper into a neat package around her equipment, she carefully stowed it in the pocket of her case ready for her first visit. Just as she put the lid back on the metal tray, the street light outside went off.

She glanced up at the clock above the door. Five to seven. Just enough time for a leisurely breakfast before morning report.

She suppressed a yawn and opened the half-glazed door of the dressing cupboard. Inside, like a wall of battered metal bricks, were neatly stacked tins of gauze for new patients. Each evening the nurses rotated the duty of preparing the next day's dressings by cutting gauze into squares and packing it into unpainted tins ready to be baked in Munroe House's old-fashioned black-leaded range until the edges were brown. The on-call evening nurse would remove them from the oven when they'd cooled and replenish the stores each morning before she went off duty.

Selecting three tins for her morning calls, Connie packed them alongside the cleaned instruments. She closed the cupboard and was just about to fasten her bag when she heard a car door slam in the street outside. An engine revved and there was a screech of wheels as the vehicle sped away. The gate into the back yard creaked open. As she peered through the sheen of early-morning ice covering the rear window, Connie's mouth pulled into a firm line. Snapping her case shut, she slipped it under the chair at the top of the table and marched out into the hall. The faint sound of singing through the half-open kitchen door indicated that Mrs Pierce, the new cook, was already at her post.

Clasping her hands in front of her, Connie stood in the middle of the carpet runner with her eyes fixed on the back door. After a couple of seconds the brass handle turned slowly. The door edged open and Gladys slipped through the gap. She was dressed in a royal blue satin evening dress with open-toed court shoes, and had a short fox fur shrug around her shoulders. Her russet hair was gathered into an untidy bird's nest on top of her head, with only a feather grip holding it in place, and her mascara and lipstick were smudged.

'Good morning, Sister Potter,' Connie said pleasantly. 'Or should that be good night, since you look ready for bed rather than a full day on the district.'

Gladys blinked and screwed up her eyes. 'You what?'

'Where have you been?' Connie asked.

'Out.' A scornful expression spread across Gladys's heavily made-up face. 'Not that it's any of your business, but my fella took me to the Sunset Club in Carnaby Street, and a right posh place it was too, though I don't expect you've ever been there or even heard of it.'

'I have, actually,' Connie replied. 'But you wouldn't find me in such a sleazy dive.'

Gladys's assurance wavered. 'Yeah, well, my Raymond's friendly with the owner. In fact, everyone knows him up West.'

'That doesn't surprise me,' Connie replied, regarding her coolly.

Gladys gave her a belligerent look and headed for the stairs.

Connie stepped into her path. 'You do know you're supposed to be on call from eight, don't you?'

'And I'll be ready as soon as I've got my uniform on,' Gladys replied, breathing liquor fumes in Connie's face.

Connie moved her head away. 'You can't visit patients like that.'

'Like what?'

'Drunk.'

'I ain't drunk,' Gladys replied, wobbling on her shoes.

Connie raised an eyebrow. 'Well you're certainly not sober. And look at the state of you.' Her eyes ran over the laddered stockings and creased dress, then rested on a love bite just peeking out from Gladys's collar. 'You're a disgrace to your vocation.'

An angry flush reddened Gladys's face. 'Who the bloody hell—' One of her clip-on earrings slipped off and bounced on the floorboards. She scrabbled after it.

Connie gave her a contemptuous look. 'Why don't you just go

upstairs before the others see what a sorry excuse for a nurse you really are? Go on. I'll tell Miss Dutton you're sick.'

For one moment she thought Gladys was going to argue further, but then the other girl staggered backwards, catching the banister to steady herself. 'As it happens, I don't feel all the ticket.' She swung around on the bottom post before tottering precariously up the stairs to her room.

Connie watched her until she disappeared, and then walked back into the treatment room. She went over to the duty blackboard and, picking up the rag, wiped Gladys's name off the on-call rota and wrote her own instead.

Connie perched unsteadily on the edge of the chair. She had to, because most of the seat was taken up with back issues of the *Lancet*. On the floor to her left and almost at the same height as her knees was another pile of dog-eared periodicals, but this time it was the *British Medical Journal*.

The Redmans Road surgery was just a stone's throw from Charrington's brewery on the Mile End Road and occupied the downstairs rooms of an old printworks, upstairs being a secretarial employment agency. Dr Carter had moved into the present site only a few weeks ago, after an unexploded bomb left by the Luftwaffe decided to get on with the job and blew the best part of Redmans Road to kingdom come. The old surgery that the Carters, father and son, had occupied for almost half a century was among the casualties. What surrounded Connie now was what the locals had salvaged from the rubble.

'Would you oblige me by running through the list thus far, Sister?' asked Dr Carter the younger, who had taken over from his father before the war.

Weaving his fingers together across his fob chain, leaning back in his old leather chair he contemplated the far wall where his medical certificates were displayed.

William Rutherford Carter must have been nearer fifty than forty, but with a surprisingly full head of golden-brown hair, he looked younger than his years. As ever, he was wearing his tweed jacket with the leather-patched elbows, and worn corduroy trousers, as if he were taking a prize pig to the country fair rather than inspecting boils and haemorrhoids.

Connie glanced down at her notebook. 'I have Mrs Smith, Ogleby, Shaw and Hollis for maternity; Mrs Cornell, 48 Sydney Street, for a soap and water enema until we get a result; Mr Emery, 12 Cressey Place, for a morning wash and weekly bath, and Mrs Aster for a right leg ulcer.' She turned the page. 'And six-year-old Clifford Grant to teach his mother how to set up a vapour tent for his asthma.'

Dr Carter pulled his pipe from his top pocket and tapped it out on the ashtray at his elbow. 'Young Master Grant is turning into a delicate child; a referral to the Invalid Children's Aid Association might be in order.'

'Yes, Doctor.'

'And perhaps you could let the do-nothings at the council know he'll need a bit of supplementary teaching at home because of his wheezy lungs.'

Connie bit her lip. 'I thought they needed a letter from you?'

A lordly smile lifted the corner of Dr Carter's lips. 'I'm sure they'll waive the formalities for a pretty little thing like you.'

Feeling her cheeks start to colour, Connie looked down at her notebook. 'Is there anyone else you'd like me to visit?'

'Oh yes, I almost forgot. Mrs Cottrell's being sent home from Guinness Ward tomorrow.'

Connie looked astounded. 'Nelly's still alive?'

'Apparently so.' Dr Carter shrugged. 'It seems to fly in the face of all reason, not to mention Darwin's theory of the survival of the fittest, but it seems that double pneumonia and septicaemia still aren't enough to shuffle Nelly Cottrell off this mortal coil.' His gaze ran over her face. 'Do you know, Sister Byrne, you have very pretty eyes.'

'Thank you, Doctor,' Connie replied, somewhat taken aback. 'Er . . . what would you like us to do for Mrs Cottrell?'

Dr Carter brushed a speck of dust from his sleeve. 'Whatever you like, Sister. At eighty-nine, there's not much more modern medicine can do for her, so I'll leave it in your very capable hands.' He tossed curled-up notebooks, prescription pads and leaflets aside until he found a sheet of flimsy pink paper on his roll-top desk. 'You'd better have a copy of her hospital letter.'

He held out the carbon copy to Connie. As she took it, his fingers brushed over hers, and a lazy smile spread across his face.

Connie looked down at her notes. 'Is that all?'

'For now, although no doubt I'll have another dozen pregnant women asking for maternity services when I next see you.'

Connie closed her notebook and slipped it into her pocket.

'I don't usually listen to patient gossip, but I couldn't help but overhear recently that you've been disappointed,' said Dr Carter, his chair creaking as he shifted towards her.

'Disappointed?'

'In love?'

'Oh!'

His gaze searched her face. 'Well all I can say, Connie – you don't mind if I call you Connie, do you?'

'I suppose not . . .'

'All I can say is this fiancé of yours must be a very foolish young man.' He shifted forward again. 'Very foolish indeed.'

'He's not my fiancé,' Connie replied, a lump of desolation in her throat. 'Not any more.'

Her eyes felt tight so she looked away.

'I'm sorry to cause you pain, and I wouldn't have spoken except, you see, I know what it feels like to be rejected,' he said, his face the epitome of misery. 'My wife . . .'

'I didn't know.'

'Yes. Two years ago.' Dr Carter's wretched expression lifted a little. 'Of course, we hadn't really been a couple for years, but . . .' He rested his hand on Connie's knee. 'You know, if you ever need a shoulder to cry on . . .'

'You're very kind.'

'Perhaps we could go for a drink. I know this little place in Cheapside.'

Mercifully, the black telephone on his desk sprang into life.

'Thank you, Doctor.' Connie jumped to her feet. 'I'm sure you have at least a dozen important things to do, so I won't take up any more of your time.'

Before he could reply, she had picked up her case and dashed out of the room.

'Hold still,' laughed Connie, as she wiped the gauze laden with benzyl benzoate over the sole of Grace's right foot.

'I can't,' giggled Grace. 'You're tickling me.'

She was back in the Tatums' front lounge, helping Grace and her mother to apply the second scabies treatment. The first, a week ago, had probably done the trick, but the second treatment was standard practice. It was the end of a very long day. The afternoon clinic had been worse than usual, with the arrival of two emergency cases – a woman from a nearby sweatshop who had been scalded by steam, and a man who'd somehow managed to get his hand caught in some machinery. Thankfully, Beattie and her student were back early so they'd helped out, but Connie still hadn't managed to send the last patient on their way until gone 5.40.

The door opened and Mrs Tatum strolled in wearing her silky dressing gown, her blonde hair whirled up into a topknot.

'All done?' she asked

'Yes, we are,' said Connie, dropping the used gauze on the newspaper by her side. 'But it wouldn't have taken so long if someone wasn't so ticklish.' She gave Grace her severe matron look and the young girl giggled again.

Mrs Tatum smiled fondly at her daughter, who was also in her nightdress and dressing gown. 'What do you say to Sister Byrne?'

'Thank you, Sister Byrne.'

'My pleasure,' said Connie, popping the cork back in the brown bottle containing the lotion and stowing it in her bag. 'It's all in a day's work.'

'No, really,' said Mrs Tatum. 'You've put yourself out and saved us an awkward journey. I am very grateful.'

Pushing her feet into her slippers, Grace rose and went over to the fireside chair. She picked up the copy of *Black Beauty* lying on the seat, then snuggled back against the cushions and opened the book.

Connie stood up and arched her back to ease the tightness in her spine.

'Are you rushing off, Sister?' Mrs Tatum asked as she tidied away her last few bits.

'Not really,' Connie replied.

'Well then, why don't I make us both a nice cup of coffee?' asked Mrs Tatum.

Why not? Connie thought. She had her instruments to sterilise and restock for tomorrow, but as she had managed to get out of the evening's trip to the Regency, she had plenty of time to do that.

'That sounds perfect,' she said.

Mrs Tatum smiled approvingly. 'Good. You put your feet up and I'll be back in a jiffy.' She stoked up the smouldering coals in the grate, then left the room.

The fire crackled, and from the back of the house 'Begin the Beguine' drifted out. Taking her bag with her, Connie walked over to the sofa and sat down to write up her notes. Having completed the entry, she slipped the notes into the side pocket and leant back. Her eyes drifted up to the large portrait of Mrs Tatum and the older man on the mantelshelf.

'That's my dad,' said Grace.

'I guessed as much,' Connie replied.

'He died when I was a baby.'

'Oh dear.'

'Yes,' continued Grace in a matter-of-fact tone. 'He was knocked over by a bus in Aldgate on his way to work.'

'I'm sorry.'

'It's all right,' said Grace with a little shrug. 'That picture was taken before I was born. I don't remember him but Mummy's told me all about him.'

Connie smiled. 'I'm sure she has.'

'He worked in a bank in the City and . . .' a frown wrinkled Grace's brow, 'I think he worked with people in other countries or something. I'm not too sure but he was very high up.'

Given the comfortable house Grace and her mother lived in, Connie wasn't surprised to hear this. Whereas most families made do with a couple of rooms, Mrs Tatum had the entire house to herself, not to mention the small bedroom on the half-landing that had been turned into a bathroom. No zinc bath in front of the fire for Grace and her mother, and each room had a fire in the grate, which must have cost a pretty penny in coal each week.

'Do you think I look like him?' asked Grace.

'Maybe a little bit,' said Connie tactfully. 'But perhaps you take after your mother more.'

The door opened and Mrs Tatum walked in carrying a tray with their coffee, a glass of milk and a plate of something Connie hadn't tasted for five years: chocolate digestives.

'There we go,' she said as she put the tray on the low table in front of the sofa. 'Sugar, Sister?'

'One, please,' Connie replied.

Mrs Tatum handed her a cup, then offered her a biscuit. Connie took one and tucked it on the side of her saucer. Mrs Tatum put a gentle arm around her daughter's shoulders.

'Perhaps you'd like to take your milk and biscuit into the dining room and get on with your homework while Sister Byrne and I have our coffee.'

'Yes, Mummy,' said Grace, putting the book aside. She slid off the chair, collected her drink and snack and walked towards the door.

'And don't forget it's not long until the entrance test, so make sure you learn the extra spellings I gave you,' Mrs Tatum called after her.

'Yes, Mummy,' Grace called behind her as she closed the lounge door.

Connie took a bite of biscuit. 'Goodness, that's delicious.'

Mrs Tatum smiled and sipped her coffee.

'Which school are you trying to get Grace into?' Connie asked when the chocolate in her mouth had finally dissolved.

'Coborn School for Girls, in Bow,' Mrs Tatum replied.

'My friend Millie went there,' said Connie. 'It's a good school, but I've heard it's even more difficult to get into now, as there are only a few scholarship places each year and there've been double the applicants since the return of the evacuees. Although, from what I've seen of Grace, I'd think she'd sail through the entrance test.'

A worried look clouded Mrs Tatum's face. 'I do hope so. I want her to join a profession, like teaching or nursing. Since she met you, she's set up a hospital ward with her dolls.'

Connie smiled. 'I'm sure she'd be an excellent nurse, but nursing is a vocation, not a profession. I went to Raine's, and lots of my class became personal secretaries and teachers, but I've felt called to be a nurse since I was Grace's age and never considered doing anything else.'

'Well at least with a good education she will be able to stand on her own feet financially,' said Mrs Tatum.

Connie smiled. 'Perhaps she'll go into banking like your husband.'

Mrs Tatum looked blank for a moment, then a dazzling smile spread across her well-favoured face.

'Ah yes, dear Gerald.' She stood up and walked over to the mantelshelf. 'Such a wonderful man,' she said, picking up the portrait.

'You both look very happy,' said Connie.

'We were,' she said, gazing adoringly down at the photo. 'This was taken at the Café Royal just after Grace's first birthday and only a week before he stepped out in front of a bus in Piccadilly.'

'Piccadilly?' said Connie. 'Grace told me her father was killed at Aldgate.'

Mrs Tatum's cheeks flushed. 'Aldgate! Oh . . . yes . . . yes.' Her assured smile returned. 'Aldgate. Of course it was. Silly me. How could I have forgotten?'

Leaving mother and daughter to their quiet evening in, Connie cycled the half a mile back to Munroe House. She was more than ready to tuck into her supper, but as she turned the corner of Roland Street, her heart leapt into her throat.

Leaning casually against the wall was Charlie, dressed as if he was going out for the night, with a cigarette dangling from his right hand. When he spotted her, he took a last drag on his cigarette and stood away from the brickwork.

With the blood pounding through her ears almost deafening her, Connie rolled to a stop and stepped off her bike.

'Hello, Connie,' he said, in that warm, honey tone guaranteed to melt her bones.

Although she shouldn't have let them, her eyes roamed freely over his face, noting the contrast between his soft cheeks and harsh bristle, the golden flecks in the blue of his eyes and the bluntness of his chin.

'What are you doing here?'

'Waiting for you,' he replied, flicking his spent cigarette into the gutter. 'I just wanted to talk to you, Connie.'

'What about?'

'Well, seeing you the other day made me think that perhaps you and me could straighten things out.'

With something akin to a millstone pressing down on her chest, Connie tore her gaze from his face.

'I'm late for supper.'

'I just want to have a little chat with you, Connie, that's all,' he pleaded, raking his fingers through his hair in that oh-so-familiar way. 'To say I'm sorry. Properly.'

Connie gave a harsh laugh. 'Don't you think it's a bit late for that?'

'Maybe, but . . . Look, I'll be in the snug in the Rose and Punchbowl at eight on Friday—'

'Goodbye, Charlie, and give my regards to Maria,' said Connie. Concentrating on the spinning spokes of her front wheel, she rolled her bike past him and into the back yard of Munroe House.

'I'll be there until closing if you change your mind,' he called after her.

Although the melodious strings of the BBC orchestra drifted out across the nurses' lounge, Connie was no more listening to the music than she was reading the book propped open on her lap. How could she? The image of Charlie waiting for her outside the back gate materialised in her mind for the umpteenth time, but she cut it short and glanced at the clock. Almost nine, and with a bit of luck Millie would be back soon; in fact Connie was surprised she wasn't home already.

'Good book?' called Beattie from the other side of the room, where she and Sally were playing draughts.

Dragging her mind away from her feckless ex-fiancé, Connie forced a smile. 'Yes, very romantic.' She looked down at the title printed across the top of the page, only to find she'd picked an Agatha Christie novel from the shelf. She turned a page and pretended to be engrossed.

The music recital came to a close, and just as the plummy tones of the presenter announced the following quiz programme, the door opened and Millie walked in. Her fatigued eyes searched the room until she spotted Connie, and then she made her way over.

Connie put the book aside. 'How's your mum?'

Millie flopped next to her on the sofa. 'So-so.'

'These things take time,' said Connie.

'I know,' Millie replied. 'And now that all the shops are getting decked out for Christmas, she's thinking about what it will be like without Dad.'

The door opened and Mary, the evening maid, still in her pinafore and white cap, pushed in the trolley loaded with a dozen mugs of hot milk, Ovaltine and cocoa.

'You stay put. I'll get it,' Connie said, standing up. 'What do you want?'

Millie rallied a weary smile. 'Ovaltine, thanks.'

Leaving Millie with her head resting back on the lacy sofa cover and her eyes closed, Connie went to fetch their bedtime drinks.

'There you go,' she said when she returned clutching two mugs in one hand and a plate in the other. 'And I've got us a couple of digestives to soak it up.'

'So what have you been up to today?' asked Millie.

'Oh, this and that.' Connie took a sip of her drink. 'Charlie was waiting for me at the gate when I got back.'

Millie's mouth dropped open. 'He's got a nerve!'

'Said he wanted to have a little chat,' explained Connie.

'About what?'

'Getting things straight between us.'

'It's too late for that, isn't it?'

'It was too late the moment he stepped off that train,' agreed Connie. 'He even had the cheek to ask me to meet him in the Rose and Punchbowl on Friday. I told him to give my regards to his wife.'

'Good for you,' said Millie. She reached down and retrieved a copy of *Woman's Weekly* from the magazine rack beside the chair.

Cradling her cocoa, Connie raised it to her lips. 'He said he'd wait until last orders in case I changed my mind.'

Millie's head snapped up. 'You're not thinking of going?' she asked, scrutinising Connie's face.

'Really, Millie!' Connie laughed, not quite able to look her friend in the eye. 'What sort of idiot do you take me for?'

Chapter Eight

Staring at the faded candy-striped fabric of the portable screen, Connie worked her way down the six-month bulge of Freda Johnson's stomach as she tried to visualise what was beneath her fingertips.

It was the third Thursday in November, and as usual the antenatal clinic was packed with pregnant women and fractious toddlers. Connie, Hannah and Pat, the new student Queenie who was assisting them, had all bolted down their lunch so they could get the treatment room in order before the first expectant mothers arrived. The three antiquated fabric screens had been wheeled out and lined up either side of the two examination couches in readiness. They were supposed to provide privacy, but as they were almost transparent with age and washing, they were of little effect. Added to which, the two rows of chairs were set out so close to the screens that those waiting could pass the time by listening in on the consultation only a few feet from them.

The rain had been lashing against the windows since dawn, so not only was there the usual odour of cigarettes and full nappies in the cramped clinic but also the smell of damp wool. If that wasn't enough to give you a headache, then the screams of babies wanting to be fed and the shouts of protesting toddlers were guaranteed to.

Stretching her hand wide, Connie grasped just above Freda's pubic bone and found the baby's head immediately.

'He's head down,' she said, smiling at the round-faced brunette with her petticoat pulled up under her chin and her well-washed knickers tucked beneath her bump.

Connie had delivered Freda's first baby – a bouncing ten-pound boy – in an Anderson shelter during a night raid in June 1940. Young William had been an easy delivery, as had John, Ruth and

Marge who'd followed, so Connie was confident that number five would be much the same.

'That's all fine, Mrs Johnson,' she said, reaching for the Bakelite instrument on the stainless-steel trolley beside her. 'But if I could just listen to baby's heart.'

'Course you can, luv,' said Freda.

Pressing her ear to the narrow end of her foetal stethoscope, Connie watched the second hand on her watch turn for half a minute while counting the heartbeats. She doubled the number in her head before straightening up with a smile.

'Spot on. You can get up now.'

As Freda adjusted her clothing and got off the couch, Connie wrote up her observations.

'I'd like to see you on the third of January, and then every two weeks.'

'Right you are, Sister,' said Freda, winding a long knitted scarf around her neck and taking a pack of ten Woodbines from her pocket.

Connie smiled and handed Freda her notes. 'Could you give these to the nurse at the desk?'

Once Freda had gone, Connie poured some surgical spirit on to a gauze square and wiped her stethoscope and tape measure, then replaced the antiseptic paper on the couch. Satisfied that everything was in order, she stepped through the gap between the screens.

'Next,' she called above the hubbub of voices.

A young woman with blonde hair cropped becomingly around her ears, wearing a fitted brown coat and a bright red felt hat with matching handbag, stood up.

'That's me, I think,' she laughed, beaming around at the women surrounding her. Sensing a first baby in the offing, they smiled indulgently as she picked her way between the children and push-chairs towards Connie.

'This is all new to me,' she giggled, handing Connie her notes. 'It's my first.'

Connie smiled and glanced at the name on the top. 'Mrs Valerie Webb?'

The young woman nodded. 'That's me, and call me Val.'

'I'm Sister Byrne,' said Connie, closing the curtain behind her. 'And you've come to book in with us today?'

'I have,' said Mrs Webb. 'I might be a bit too soon, but my Ron said I ought to come to make sure everything's all right.'

'That's very sensible of him,' said Connie.

A fond look stole over Mrs Webb's pretty face. 'He's like that. Ever since he got back, he can't do enough for me. He even hung out the washing yesterday before he went on shift so I didn't have to stretch up.'

Connie smiled politely. 'Please take a seat.'

Mrs Webb tucked her skirt under her and settled in the straight-backed chair beside the couch, putting her handbag on the floor beside her.

Connie reviewed her medical history, noting that her blood pressure was normal, that nothing untoward had shown up in her urine and that her last period had been approximately nine weeks before, making her due date the end of May.

'I see you've been married for four years and your husband works at Crane Wharf,' said Connie.

'That's right,' said Mrs Webb. 'The manager gave him his old job back without a quibble. Well, they had to or he'd have had them all down tools. He's a shop steward, you see.'

Connie nodded. 'And you live in Smithy Street.'

'Only until we can get a place on the new estate in Dagenham.' She put her hands on her stomach and glanced down. 'Ron and me want our baby to be brought up in the country.'

Connie perused the notes again. 'I can see we've got a full history of your family's health but not very much about your husband's.'

'His mother's as fit as a fiddle, more's the pity.' Mrs Webb looked apologetically at Connie. 'I know I shouldn't say it, but we live with her and it's not easy. She has family in Hackney, I think, but they could be dead for all I know. There was an almighty bust-up years ago, before I met Ron, and his mother has had nothing to do with them since. Sorry.'

Connie put Mrs Webb's notes on the trolley next to her equipment. 'Oh well, never mind. If you just take off your coat and hop up on to the couch. I probably won't be able to feel anything much until at least three and a half months, but I like to do a quick examination, if you don't mind.'

'All right. That's fine with me,' said Mrs Webb.

She stood up and slipped off her coat to reveal a stylish burnt-orange button-through dress with padded shoulders and a pencil skirt. Connie's eyes flickered over the seams pulled tight across her stomach. Draping the coat over the back of the chair, Mrs Webb stepped out of her shoes and, placing them beside her handbag, climbed on to the couch.

'If you could just wriggle your skirt up to your waist and your knickers down to your hips, I think that will be fine,' said Connie.

Mrs Webb eased her slimline skirt up to reveal a pair of very lacy French knickers and a suspender belt holding up her nylons.

'My Ron brought them back from France,' she explained.

Connie smiled. 'I'm just going to run my hands over your tummy, so I want you to relax.'

Mrs Webb nodded and lay back.

Like the rest of the population after six years of food rationing, there was very little fat on Mrs Webb's body, and in repose her stomach was concave except for a slight swelling just below her waistline.

Connie rubbed her hands together. 'Take a deep breath and hold it.'

Mrs Webb breathed in and clamped her lips tight.

Splaying her fingers, Connie grasped just above Mrs Webb's pubic bone, then cupped her other hand and placed it below the woman's navel. She pressed down and felt an egg-sized hardness in the palm of her hand.

'Have you had any sickness?'

'A bit, but that stopped a month ago,' replied Mrs Webb.

Connie removed her hands and picked up Mrs Webb's record. 'When did you say your last period was?'

'Thirty-first of August,' Mrs Webb replied. 'I remember because Ron came home on the Friday after VJ day, the seventeenth, and it was exactly two weeks after that.

'And what was it like? Your period, I mean. Was it less than usual and did it last as long?' Connie asked.

Mrs Webb looked puzzled. 'Come to think of it, I usually go for five days but this came and went in two and it was a lot lighter than usual.'

'Have you had any bleeding since?'

Mrs Webb shook her head. 'Why?'

'Because, Mrs Webb,' Connie replied jollily, 'you must have been very welcoming to your husband when he returned, because you're actually four months pregnant, not three. What you thought was a period was in fact just a bleed. It happens sometimes in the first few months. It's to do with the hormones.'

'The what?'

'The body's chemicals that keep your insides balanced,' Connie explained. 'It takes a couple of weeks for your body to get used to having a baby inside it, and that's why some women are sick to start with. I suspect that in your case the baby hadn't quite fixed itself properly so there was a little show when your period was due. But don't worry, it's quite common. In fact one woman I looked after bled every four weeks up to her sixth month and still delivered a healthy baby at the end of it.'

Mrs Webb's hand closed over her abdomen. 'Are you sure? I mean, couldn't I be carrying twins?'

'Are there any in your family?'

Her shoulders slumped. 'Not that I know of, but there might be in Ron's.'

'Well, perhaps, but since your morning sickness stopped when you reached your third month, and as a twin pregnancy doesn't make much difference to the womb size at this early stage, I'd stick to my original thought. Now,' Connie put on her professional smile, 'we run a clinic on Tuesday and Thursday afternoon and you can come to either, but I'd like to see you again in a month's time, just before Christmas. I see you're one of Dr Richards' patients, so I'll visit you in the New Year to advise you how to get your home ready for baby. You can get dressed now.'

After a slight hesitation, Mrs Webb adjusted her clothing and got off the couch.

Connie handed the young woman her notes. 'If you go back to the nurse on the desk, she'll give you a form to take to the local food ministry office so you can get the green ration book. It allows you extra milk and meat during your pregnancy and while you're breastfeeding. And don't worry, you're in good company. You won't be the only woman around here having a VJ baby next May.'

'VJ night . . .' muttered Mrs Webb, staring at the file in her hand.

The rusty wheels squeaked as Connie pushed the screen aside. 'And if you have any problems, such as bleeding or cramps, we're only at the end of the phone.'

Mrs Webb gave her a vague smile and left.

Connie cleaned her instruments again, laid out another paper sheet, then opened the screen and stepped out.

'Who's next?' she said, scanning the dozen or so women in the treatment room. Her heart started to thump painfully as her gaze fixed on Charlie's wife, Maria, in the back row. Their eyes locked for a second, then Maria Ross rose to her feet and slowly ran her hands over her distended stomach. The shard of pain lodged deep in Connie's chest twisted as a self-satisfied expression spread across the other woman's face.

The patient in the cubicle next door emerged, followed by Hannah who, sensing something was wrong, stepped in front of Connie.

'If you'd like to come this way,' she said, beckoning Maria forward.

Maria gave Connie a pitying look, then made her way to the front before disappearing behind the screen. There was some sniggering as a couple of the local gossips explained the awkward situation to their neighbours, then the room fell silent.

Connie took a firm grip on herself and turned to the waiting women. 'So, ladies,' she said, forcing a jolly smile. 'Whose turn is it now?'

Connie shoved her needle through the next stitch, then looped the pink three-ply wool over her left knitting needle and hooked it through.

She was alone in the nurses' quiet room at the side of the house, overlooking the small garden and the perimeter wall. Of course she could have gone upstairs and joined the others in the main lounge, but tonight she didn't feel in the mood for company. It was Friday. Although she had promised herself not to, she glanced at the clock on the mantelshelf again. Twenty past eight. By now Charlie would be sitting in the bar at the Rose and Punchbowl.

She lowered her eyes and slipped her needle through the next stitch. The door opened and Sally walked in.

'Oh,' she said, looking surprised to see Connie sitting in the window. 'I thought you'd gone out with Beattie.'

'I was going to, but I've got a bit of a headache,' Connie said.

'Well, knitting in this light won't help,' said Sally, flicking the light switch. The suspended glass bowl hanging by three stout chains from the ceiling rose glowed as the light bulbs inside warmed up. 'What are you making?'

'A jumper for my sister Bernadette's new baby,' said Connie. 'I want to get it finished so she can wear it for our cousin Mary's wedding at the end of March.'

'A spring wedding, how lovely,' said Sally.

'Yes,' said Connie, in a tone that said otherwise. She was pleased for Mary, of course, but given her own recent experience, the prospect of a family wedding didn't exactly fill her with delight, especially with her mother close at hand.

She shoved her dispiriting thoughts aside and smiled. 'You look nice. New dress?'

Sally nodded. 'I made it myself.' She turned back and forth. 'Do you think it's all right? I mean, not too dressy for a first date. And are my seams straight?'

'No, it's not too dressy for a first date, and yes, your seams are perfectly straight. You look lovely, and that cornflower blue really brings out the colour of your eyes. Who's the lucky man?'

'His name is Tony Crisp. He owns Tony's Motor Shop in Globe Road,' Sally replied.

The door opened and Gladys strolled in, a fur wrap slung around her shoulders. In contrast with Sally, whose simple day dress and understated make-up enhanced her natural good looks, Gladys had gone to town for her night out. A heavy application of panstick and face powder had given her ruddy complexion an unnatural flat tone. This in itself wouldn't have been so bad if she'd used muted tones for her eyes, but instead she'd gone for an aquamarine shadow. The coloured beads encrusting the shoulder pads of her black dress put Connie in mind of an American general, while the French pleat in her curly russet hair was held in place by a diamanté comb.

Her scarlet mouth pulled into a tight line when she saw Connie and Sally. 'Oh, I thought you were upstairs.'

The mantelshelf clock struck the half-hour, and Sally jumped. 'Crumbs. Is that the time? I'm supposed to be at the bus stop at quarter to. Bye.' The door banged closed as she left the room.

Gladys adjusted her stole, then sidled over to the window and gazed out.

'You're a bit done up for darts at the Duck and Drake, aren't you, Gladys?' said Connie, resting her knitting on her lap.

'Very funny,' Gladys replied, not taking her eyes from the street outside. 'I'm going up West.'

'What, with that tall chap in the expensive suit who owns the Ford?' said Connie.

Gladys's head snapped around. 'How do you know about him?'

'I was in the kitchen the night before last making myself a hot drink when I saw you get out of his car,' Connie replied.

'What, at two in the morning?'

'I couldn't sleep,' Connie replied.

Gladys glanced at her watch, then returned to her contemplation of the road outside. 'If you must know, I *am* waiting for Wilfred. He's got a bit of a drive from St John's Wood but he'll be here any moment now.' She stroked the fur draped over her shoulder and a satisfied smile spread across her face. 'He's got such class and sophistication.'

'And a wife.'

Under the layers of make-up, Gladys's cheeks flamed. 'How . . . ?'

'Come off it,' laughed Connie. 'Only a mistress gets a mink stole like that.'

A car drew up and gave two blasts on the hooter. Gladys pulled back the lace curtain and waved excitedly. She hurried over to the mirror above the mantelpiece and checked her lipstick. Then she adjusted the fur and made her way to the door.

As she reached for the brass handle, she turned. 'Anyway, even if Wilfred is married, at least I'm out there having a bit of fun, not sitting by myself knitting for other people's babies.'

The door slammed, shooting a dart of wretchedness though Connie's heart. She looked down at the little pink garment on her needles, and tears welled up in her eyes. Then she glanced at the clock again, shoved her knitting aside and stood up.

Connie stood on the corner of Jubilee Street and Redmans Road and regarded the front door of the Rose and Punchbowl thoughtfully. Contrary to what she'd thought four days before, she found she actually had a great deal to say to Charlie. But now that she was outside the down-at-heel pub, she wondered if she should go in after all.

The faded red door swung open and two men stumbled out. Connie took a deep breath, then, without giving herself the opportunity to change her mind, strode across the road and through the door.

The Rose and Punchbowl was a spit-and-sawdust kind of pub – well, spit and stained carpet would be nearer the mark. It had discoloured non-descript wallpaper, low lighting, and a bar running along the left-hand wall. The small room was crammed with beer-stained tables around which men huddled clutching pints. They looked at Connie and nudged each other as she walked in, but she ignored the muttering and smirks and scanned the sea of faces until she spotted Charlie at a table by himself at the back of the room. He smiled, and despite the furious argument racing around in her head, Connie's lips threatened to rise at the corners.

He hurried through the throng of drinkers to meet her.

'Hello, Connie, I didn't think you'd come,' he said, taking her hand.

Connie snatched it back. 'Neither did I.'

He took her elbow and guided her towards the table. 'Well, you're here now, that's all that matters. Let me get you a drink. What do you want?'

'Just a tonic water,' Connie replied, tucking her skirt under her and sitting down.

Charlie went to the bar, returning within a couple of minutes. He set their drinks on cardboard coasters advertising Double Diamond and then sat down beside her.

Connie took a sip and pulled a face. 'I said just tonic.'

Charlie frowned. 'Sorry. I thought you said gin and tonic.' He took a packet of Benson & Hedges from his pocket and flipped

99

open the lid. 'I meant to say it when you walked in, but you're looking good and that colour really—'

'What did you want to chat about?' Connie put her glass down.

Charlie looked put out by her interruption, but his smile rallied.

'Well, Connie,' he said, striking a match and drawing on his cigarette. 'As me and you have been pals since—'

'We weren't *pals*, Charlie,' Connie cut in. 'We were engaged to be married. I had the ring to prove it.'

'I know, and that's why I owe you an explanation.' He took her hand. 'I don't like us being at odds with each other so I want to put the past behind us. You know, clear the air.'

'Do you?' said Connie brittly.

His smile widened. 'Yes, and to say I'm sorry.'

'Sorry for what exactly?' spat Connie. 'Sorry for stringing me along? Sorry for having me organise a whole wedding? Or perhaps making me a laughing stock on every street corner? Is that what you're sorry about? Well let me tell you, I'm sorry too. Sorry I spent the last four years worrying about you and counting every second until you came home, but most of all I'm sorry I was too stupid to realise that when your letters stopped arriving it wasn't because of the army post but because you'd changed your mind.'

'It wasn't like that,' said Charlie. 'You don't understand. You don't know what it was like over there, living in bombed-out buildings with the enemy shelling you, dropping bombs on you day and night. Never knowing if the next one had your name on it.'

Connie raised an eyebrow. 'I think as the Luftwaffe visited London every night for five years I might have a pretty good idea.'

'I know, I know,' Charlie replied. 'But at least you were here with your folks, not stuck in some godforsaken place with no one. After I went back last time, I spent a year trudging across North Africa, up to my armpits in bloody sand and scorpions, and if that wasn't bad enough, just when we've cleared the pigging Germans out of Alexandria, we're herded on to a troop carrier and shipped over to Italy.'

'Well poor you,' she said flatly.

His sad expression deepened. 'Honestly, Connie, I didn't mean to hurt you, but things happen.'

'I could see that when Maria's coat flapped open,' Connie replied.

'I don't expect you to understand,' said Charlie, looking hurt. 'No one would unless they were there, but war sort of makes you do things that would never have entered your head before. The places and people make you feel different somehow, and a lot of the fellas I was with said the same.'

'And these fellas, the ones who agreed with you, did they all come home with Italian wives too?' asked Connie, as the image of Maria smirking at her in the clinic flashed through her mind.

'No, no they didn't, and fair dos, Connie, I let you down, let you down badly. I know I should have written, but I tell you this.' That rare, tender smile of his lifted the corners of his mouth. 'There were times, when we'd been shelled for weeks on end and when I hadn't slept for days, that the thought of you was the only thing that kept me going.'

She held his gaze. 'That was, of course, until you clapped eyes on Maria.'

Charlie took another drag on his cigarette. 'It wasn't like that. I was in the middle of a war zone, under constant fire, and my platoon were holed up in a village just outside—'

'Look, Charlie, I don't care about the whys and wherefores of how you met Maria. The fact is, you're married now.'

Charlie's handsome face dropped and he raked his fingers through his hair. 'You don't know how hard it is, Connie. It started the moment we turned up at my mother's house. Nothing suited Maria. Mum did my washing like she always did and Maria did it again. Mum accidentally knocked one of her pictures of the Virgin Mary off the mantelshelf when she was dusting and Maria went mental. Screaming like a lunatic.' He ground the butt into the ashtray in the centre of the table. 'Looking back, perhaps I'd be a lot better off now if I had kept you in mind. And what with you looking so pretty in that dress and sitting beside me just like old times, it makes me wish it even more.'

Before she could stop it, the love she'd held deep in her heart all these years rose in Connie's chest. She stamped it down firmly and took another mouthful of her G and T.

'Well, as you say,' she gave her ex-fiancé a dazzling smile, 'probably best to put it all behind us.'

Sitting up in bed, Connie pummelled the pillow a couple of times, then lay down and resumed her study of the light fixture above her head in the darkness.

I let you down, Charlie's voice repeated yet again in her head.

Too blooming right you did, thought Connie, glaring at the fringe around the bottom of the lampshade.

The thought of you was the only thing that kept me going, he said.

Pull the other one, she continued the mental argument. *And don't sit there whining to me about how unhappy you are! You made your bed with Maria, now you have to lie in it, Carlos.*

She sighed heavily and closed her eyes again. This would not do. She had a full day's work in front of her, and at this rate she'd be lucky if she got any sleep at all. And it was all Charlie's fault.

She took a deep breath and forced herself to think of something else. She ran through the list of patients she had to visit in the morning and the supplies she'd need from the dressing cupboard, and then she moved on to what to buy the family for Christmas. Leaving the adults aside for the moment, she decided on *Boy's Own*, *Champion*, *Dandy* and *Beano* annuals for Mo's three boys and Jim's son and thought Bernie's two elder girls would probably like some new socks, while her niece Janice, who was mad about sewing, would be happy with a knitting kit. That only left baby Betty.

An image of Maria with her heavy stomach, holding on to Charlie's arm, flashed through Connie's mind again. She sat up.

And how dare he say I looked pretty?

She attacked the pillow again, but before she could lie down, a floorboard creaked on the landing and someone giggled. Letting out an exasperated breath, she flung back the blankets and got out of bed. If that was one of the trainees mucking about, she'd give them a piece of her mind. Taking her dressing gown from the end of the bed, she thrust her arms into the sleeves, padded across the room and yanked open the door.

Instead of it being one of the four student Queenies, it was Millie who was out on the landing, wearing her dressing gown too and holding open the window to the fire exit. Alex was with her. They stared adoringly at each other for a moment, then he drew her close and kissed her before ducking through the window. Millie gazed after him, then, with a last wave, silently lowered the sash window. As she turned away, she saw Connie and hurried over.

'Oh Connie, you'll never guess,' she whispered, her eyes bright with excitement. 'Alex proposed.'

'Did he?' asked Connie in the same hushed tone.

'Yes, I know we've only known each other a few months, but . . .' Millie clasped her hands together and looked upwards. 'Oh Connie, I love him so much.'

'I should hope so,' said Connie, looking pointedly at her friend's night attire.

Millie blushed. 'Yes, well,' she shrugged. 'You know . . .'

Thankfully Connie didn't, which saved her the worry of having to explain that to any future husband.

'When?'

'I'm not sure, but May or June we think,' Millie replied. 'Alex has applied to join the Palestinian Police Force and—'

One of the bedroom doors on the floor above opened and footsteps sounded across the landing.

'I'll tell you all about it at breakfast,' she said, lowering her voice. 'But not a word to anyone. We've got to tell my mum yet.'

Connie nodded and hugged her friend. 'I'm so pleased for you,' she said under her breath. 'And I'm sure you'll both be very happy.'

'Thank you,' said Millie.

Back in her room, Connie shrugged her dressing gown off and laid it across the foot of the bed. She got in, pulled the sheets and blankets up to her chin and snuggled down. After a second or two, she rolled over and buried her face in the pillow, sobbing as if her heart would break.

Maud took a sip of her brandy and orange and dabbed the corner of her eye with her handkerchief. 'I remember the day he was born,' she sniffed. 'And now he's leaving . . .' She blew her nose noisily.

'He's only going to do his National Service, Mum, he's not off to the moon,' said Connie.

It was just after midday on the first Saturday in December, and the family were gathered in the corner of the Northern Star. It was a typical East End Victorian pub, with a flock-wallpapered L-shaped public bar, an upright piano – almost in tune – a dartboard with a rubber mat in front of it, and a collection of dour-faced elderly regulars who seemed to be permanently glued to the polished mahogany counter.

Maud was flanked by Mo and Bernie, with four-month-old Betty asleep in the pram next to her. Sheila was working, so she had been excused from attending the gathering to wave Bobby goodbye. The children of the family were there too, but as they weren't allowed in the bar, they were playing outside, popping their heads through the door from time to time to badger their parents for a bottle of lemonade or a packet of crisps.

Maud put on her wounded look. 'When you've had one of your own, you'll understand.'

Connie rolled her eyes and Mo and Bernie gave her a sympathetic look.

'Seventeen hours in labour I was,' her mother continued. 'He was ten pound too. Almost tore me in half. I'm surprised I'm here to tell the tale.' She looked across at her youngest child, who was propping up the bar with the men of the family. 'But I'll tell you this and I'll tell you no more: he's worth all the agony.' A maudlin expression lifted her heavy features.

Bobby was dressed in his best suit and tie and had a small suitcase next to him on the floor, a pint in his hand and a grin as wide as the Blackwall Tunnel across his face. Doubtless the older men were instructing him not to drink too much and to avoid the young women who hung around the army camp. Probably the two things about National Service he was looking forward to most, Connie thought.

Maud sniffed and dabbed her dry eyes again. 'I hope he don't get sent to Germany with all those Nazis still running around.'

'He's got basic training first before he's sent anywhere, and the war's over, Mum,' said Connie.

'Even so, those Krauts are a sly bunch,' her mother continued. 'I wouldn't put it past them to start it all up again.'

'Honestly, Mum, I don't think there's much chance of that. The papers say the whole country's a pile of rubble, and I expect ordinary Germans are as tired of the war as we are.'

'Connie's right, Mum. The *Sketch* says they're starving in the streets,' said Mo.

'Let them starve,' snapped Maud. 'Serves them bloody well right for starting it, and after what they did in those camps!'

'You don't mean the babies too,' said Bernie, putting her hand on the handle of the pram.

Her mother crossed her arms and adjusted her bosom. 'What sort of woman do you think I am? Course not the babies. They should be adopted by people over here who can't have any themselves.'

'Right, ladies,' said Jim, with his arm around his younger brother's shoulders. 'I'm afraid time's moving on and our Bobby has to get himself to King's Cross, so we're going to have to say ta-ta.'

Cliff and Eddy shook Bobby's hand and slapped him on the back.

'Be good,' said Cliff.

'And if you can't be good, be careful,' added Eddy.

Then it was Jim's turn. 'Good luck, squirt.'

'Thanks, big bruv.'

They had a couple of manly shakes before Jim caught Bobby in a bear hug for a second .

'That'll do,' he said, breaking free. 'Don't want people thinking we're a couple of nancies.'

Everyone laughed, then Mo and Bernie stood up and squashed Bobby between them in a hug.

'Make sure you eat properly,' said Mo, planting a noisy smacker on her brother's freshly shaved cheek.

'Yes, Mo,' said Bobby.

'And keep your socks dry,' added Bernie. 'You don't want to get foot rot.'

'I will, Bernie.'

Maud struggled to her feet and held out her arms. 'Ain't you forgetting someone, son?'

'Course not, Mum,' he said, extricating himself from his two oldest sisters. He moved around to his mother and embraced her.

'You look after yourself, do you hear?' she sniffled, clinging on to him.

'I will,' he said, kissing the top of her head.

'And make sure you write as soon as you get to the base so I know you've arrived safely.'

'I'm only going to Catterick,' laughed Bobby.

'Well you never know,' she replied. 'Some funny people travel on trains.' She reached up and ruffled his hair.

'Mum . . .' he said, twisting away and looking around self-consciously.

'Seems a shame to cut all those lovely curls off,' she sighed. 'I remember when you were just a nipper how I—'

'He needs to be on his way, Mother,' cut in Arthur.

Bobby turned to face his father. 'Bye, Dad.'

Arthur grasped his hand. 'Good luck, son.' A twinkle of something lit his eyes and his usually sombre expression lifted a little. 'I know you'll do us proud,' he said gruffly.

They shook hands again, and then Bobby picked up his suitcase and looked at Connie. 'Walk us out, sis?'

'Try and stop me,' she replied, slipping her arm through his.

Once the pub door had swung closed, Bobby turned to her.

'So are you going to tell me to keep my nose clean, or make sure I get enough sleep?' he chuckled.

'I'm sure you'll do neither,' laughed Connie. 'I'm just going to tell you to enjoy yourself and to grab any opportunity that comes your way. And' – she placed her hands on either side of his face and scowled at him – 'if you don't write me at least one letter a month, I'll . . . well, never mind what, just make sure you do.'

Bobby laughed and hugged her with his free arm. 'I promise.' He kissed her loudly on the cheek, then released her, saluted with a boyish smile and marched off down the street.

Tears pinched the corners of her eyes. Not for Bobby, of course; she was sure he'd have a whale of a time. As she watched him, suitcase in hand, heading off to join the army, it wasn't her brother she was thinking of, it was Charlie.

'This will do,' said Maud, barging past a woman with two small children. Leaning over the table, she spread her shopping along one bench and herself on the other. 'Get me the usual and I'll keep our seats,' she called over the hubbub.

Putting their shopping bags that were bursting with Christmas presents alongside their mother, Connie and Mo exchanged a weary look then made their way to queue at the counter.

With its cream, brown and sage Victorian tiles decorating the walls, wooden benches either side of the polished marble-topped tables, and steaming vats of stewed eels behind the counter, Cooke's pie and mash shop had served up the cockney fare for well over half a century. Like the decor, the menu hadn't changed in fifty years and remained a choice of either stewed eels or a steak pie served with mashed potatoes – with the traditional lumps – smothered in opaque liquor. This pale gravy was in fact parsley sauce but made from the water used to boil the eels, which gave it a unique flavour and a green tinge.

Situated on Stratford High Street, next to the bus stops either side of the road and opposite the tram station, Cooke's was always busy on a Saturday lunchtime, with shoppers coming from as far afield as Ilford and Whitechapel and all stops in between. However, today, the last Saturday before Christmas, the place was positively heaving with red-faced women and fractious children doing last-minute Christmas shopping.

'I don't see why we have to come here every time,' said Mo as they shuffled forward. 'Lyon's is so much nicer.'

'Because if we didn't, we'd never hear the end of it,' Connie replied. 'Don't you remember last time in Boardman's?'

'Will I ever?' Mo screwed up her face. '*The tea's stewed. There's a thumbprint on the plate. Cucumber repeats on me.* But honestly, there must be somewhere else to eat.' She waved a hand in front of her face. 'And the smell of those eels.'

Connie suppressed a smile. 'So how far gone are you, then?'

Her sister looked at her in amazement. 'How did you know?'

'I've got eyes, Mo,' she said, glancing down at her sister's belt, which had been let out two holes. 'And because whenever you're carrying, some smell or other always upsets you.' She looked her sister up and down. 'Almost four months, I'd say.'

'Give or take,' her sister replied.

'That was quick,' said Connie. 'Eddy only got back at the end of August.'

A private smile lifted the corners of her sister's lips. 'Well, you know.'

'May baby, then,' said Connie, running through the familiar calculation. 'Have you told Mum?'

'Not yet,' Mo replied. 'I thought I'd wait until the new year, just to be sure.'

Connie nodded. 'Eddy wasn't the only one who got a warm welcome home, so make sure you get booked in to the clinic soon.'

The person in front of them picked up her loaded plates and moved aside. The woman behind the counter, wearing a red scarf tied into a turban, and enormous hooped earrings, took their order and returned a few moments later with three plates loaded with pie and mash. Mo paid while Connie carried hers and Maud's back to the table then returned to fetch their mugs of tea, by which time Mo was ensconced in the opposite bench.

'Perfect,' said Maud as she sprinkled vinegar across her food. 'You can't beat a nice bit of pie and mash to warm your cockles.'

Connie and Mo picked up their cutlery and didn't reply.

As they worked their way through their dinner, the three women came to the conclusion that children nowadays had far too many toys to play with, that until prices came down they'd make do with the old tree decorations, and that men were so-and-sos to buy presents for. They finished their discussion by divvying out the cooking tasks for Christmas Day.

'So now that's all sorted, I have to tell you who I ran into yesterday by Morrie Levi's pickled herring stall along the Waste.' The Waste was the open market that ran some half a mile between Cambridge Heath Road in the east and Valance Road in the west. 'Only Mrs snooty-nose Ross, that's who,' Maud continued, her eyes twinkling with mischief.

Connie's heart lurched. 'You didn't say anything to her, did you, Mum?'

'Course I bloody did,' Maud snorted. 'Surely you don't expect me to keep shtum after what that two-faced son of hers did to you.' She folded her arms. 'And you know me, Connie, I speak as I find . . .'

'And without fear or favour,' said Connie, finishing her mother's favourite phrase.

'At least people know where they stand with me, which is more than can be said for some,' her mother added. 'Anyroad, Ada Ross was just coming out of that posh hat shop next to Whitechapel station when I spotted her. She saw me too and tried to dodge behind the wet fish stall but I marched right up to her. "I don't know how you've got the nerve to show your face around here," I said to her. "Not after what your good-for-nothing son did to my girl." She started making excuses for him as I knew she would, but I told her straight, "If you had an ounce of decency in you, Ada Ross, you'd never have let him and his greasy wife over the threshold." And everyone agreed with me, saying it was a shame how Charlie had let you down with the wedding booked and all.'

'Did they?' groaned Connie, imagining her mother shouting at the top of her lungs in the crowded street market.

'Yes, they did,' Maud replied. 'Some didn't know that we'd shelled out on the whole thing and that Charlie all but left you at the altar.'

'But they do now,' said Connie.

'Too right they do,' her mother replied.

They'd been advertising for nurses to work in Kenya in last week's *Nursing Mirror.* Connie wondered if she applied tomorrow how long it would take her to get there.

'I told her straight,' continued her mother. '"With all your bloody churchgoing and lah-di-dah ways you like to think you're a cut above the rest of us, Ada, but I remember when you had to sit on the kerb outside the Town of Ramsgate until chucking-out time 'cos your father was too drunk to find his own way home."'

'And what did she say?' asked Connie.

'What could she say?' Maud snorted. 'But I tell you, her face went so red I thought her hair would catch fire.' Her eyes darted over her daughter. 'Of course, if you'd married him when he was home on—'

'For God's sake, Mum, do we have to go through all that again?' Connie snapped.

'There's no point biting my head off, Connie,' her mother replied. 'I know the truth hurts, but you have to face it.'

'I am,' Connie replied. 'But I don't want to keep going over and over it.'

A syrupy expression spread across her mother's face. 'Of course you don't,' she said, patting Connie's hand. 'All I'm saying is if you'd listened to me and got that ring on your finger back in forty-one, he wouldn't have been able to marry that Italian scrubber and it would have been me looking forward to holding a new grandchild, not Ada flipping Ross.'

Perched on a rickety stool next to the counter, Charlie listened to the race commentator bellowing out the progress of the two o'clock at Haydock Park. Having decided not to bother with going to work that morning, he had planned, after a couple of pints in the Lord Nelson at lunchtime with some mates, to spend a quiet afternoon kipping in front of the fire, but Maria had put paid to that when she started squabbling with his mother about Christmas decorations.

Standing on the other side of the wire grille from him was Paddy Riley, dressed as ever in a damp shirt with his sleeves rolled up, and his wife Marge, the usual sour sneer on her blood-red lips. They were taking bets as fast as they could gather in the sixpences and shilling and scribble out the slips.

Riley's was a one-man show run out of a dilapidated shop under the railway arches at the bottom of Watney Street. The decor, if you could call it that, consisted of drab olive emulsion to shoulder height with grubby grey above. There had been a foot-high wooden kick guard running around the walls, but this was mostly missing now, so beneath the narrow benches fixed to the walls, where the men wrote out their betting slips and stubbed out their fags, countless hobnailed boots had knocked out great chunks of plaster and scraped deep groves across the floorboards. The place always smelled of old fags and working men.

The radio commentator screamed out the winner and Charlie tore up the ticket in his hand and threw it with the remnants of his other half a dozen on the floor. Then, peeling himself off his perch, he strolled over to the newspaper pages pinned up on the wall and perused the runners and riders for the 2.30 at York. He'd just decided on a promising-looking filly when someone shoved him from behind. Balling his fist, Charlie swung round ready to deck his attacker.

The man, dressed in a smart American-style pinstriped suit and an angled fedora, blocked his blow with an arm and grinned.

'So they let you out then, Ross?'

'Stone the crows,' laughed Charlie. 'Timmsy, you old bugger.'

Tommy Timms, a swarthy individual with thick black hair, a physique like a bulldog and hands like shovels, was two months older than Charlie and, at five foot eight, three inches shorter. He put up his fists and they air-boxed for a bit, as they had since they were ragged-arsed kids running around the streets.

'I heard as 'ow you came home with some foreign skirt in tow,' said Tommy when they were done.

Charlie told him about Maria.

'You dirty old dog, you.' Tommy looked around surreptitiously. 'I've heard women from those 'ot countries like a bit of the, you know,' he winked, 'naughty stuff.'

Charlie smiled smugly. 'Be fair, Tommy, you know a gentleman don't tell.'

Tommy roared and slapped him on the back. 'You don't change, do you, Charlie? Always the ladies' man.'

Charlie didn't disagree.

'So where were you shipped out to?' Charlie asked, when Tommy's laughter subsided.

'Nowhere.' Tommy placed his hand on his barrel-like chest. 'Dicky heart.' He winked. 'That's what I bunged some Harley Street quack a fiver to write, if you get my drift. But don't you get to thinking I didn't do my bit for the war effort, 'cos I did. As much as anyone in the army and probably more, if the truth were told.'

Thinking of the dozens buried under the North African and Italian soil, Charlie doubted it but thought it better not to say so.

Tommy pulled out a packet of Mayfairs. 'Fag?'

'Don't mind if I do.' Charlie looked impressed.

'I only smoke cork-tipped now,' explained Tommy, taking out a chunky Ronson lighter and striking a flame.

Charlie drew on his cigarette, savouring the smoothness after years of rough army-issue tobacco.

'So what are you up to at the moment, Tommy?' he asked, blowing a stream of smoke towards the nicotine-stained ceiling.

'This and that,' Tommy replied. 'Domestic supplies mostly. Someone wants somefink and I gets it for them. Supply and demand it's called.'

'Well it must pay all right. That's a nice bit of schmutter,' said Charlie.

'Yeah, it ain't bad,' said Tommy, smoothing a chubby finger down the crease of his lapel. 'Maxie Cohen's in Aldgate. Next to the bus station. You want to get yourself along there. Where you working?'

'In Crow and Sons paint factory down by Albert Dock,' Charlie replied. 'But I didn't feel like it today.' He squared his shoulders. 'In fact I'm on the lookout for something else. Something that pays better.'

'Good for you,' said Tommy. 'Kowtowing to some bloody foreman would stick in any bloke's gizzard, let alone a smart chap like you.'

'Too right,' said Charlie, glancing at the gold cufflink on his friend's wrist.

Tommy flicked his cigarette butt on the floor and ground it under his polished shoe. 'Anyway, nice to see you, Charlie boy.'

'You too,' Charlie replied.

Tommy turned to walk away, but then clicked his fingers and turned to face Charlie again. 'Come to think of it, I might be able to help you find something that'll put more money in your pocket.'

'Oh?'

A benevolent smile lifted Tommy's bullish features. 'We're mates, ain't we?'

Charlie grinned. 'Always were.'

'Well, you can find me in the Blind Beggar most nights. Why don't you drop by and we can talk business.'

'I will,' replied Charlie, already picturing himself in a sharp made-to-measure suit.

Tommy leant forward conspiratorially. 'Dark Lady in the four thirty at Towcester,' he whispered, then tapped the side of his nose knowingly and strolled out.

Charlie turned back to the racing programme on the wall behind him. He located the horse Tommy had mentioned. A fifteen-to-one outsider! He might as well just throw his money down the drain! He chewed his lip and stared at the creased newspaper page for a moment, then he pulled a half a crown from his jacket pocket and went back to the counter.

Marge looked up at him with uninterested eyes. 'Yes?'

'A tanner on West Town both ways in the next race at Sandown and two bob to win on Dark Lady in the four thirty at Towcester,' he said, sliding his last bit of silver through the small space under the metal grille.

She took his money and passed him the betting slip.

'Ta, luv.' He grinned. 'I'll pick up me winnings later, after I've wet me whistle.'

Swinging around the wooden post at the bottom of the stairs, Connie stowed her nurse's bag alongside the dozen or so already in the hallway. Judging by the chatter coming from the room at the end of the passageway, a number of her fellow nurses were already enjoying the first meal of the day.

As she started for the refectory, the letter box rattled and a wodge of letters landed on the coconut mat. Connie walked over and picked them up. Sifting through them, she found two addressed to her. One was her cousin Murial's bi-weekly letter; the other was written in Bobby's distinctive scrawl. Putting the Association's post in a neat pile and standing the letters for the other nurses in the rack, Connie slipped her own mail into her pocket and continued on to breakfast.

Once she'd collected her toast, scrambled egg and tea, she took them to a free seat in the bay window. The pale winter sun wouldn't be up for another half an hour, so there wasn't much light coming in through the windows, but it was a nice quiet spot where she could read her correspondence in peace.

Having stirred her allotted spoonful of sugar into her tea, she took her brother's letter from her pocket. She was just about to open it when, through the window, she saw a car pull up a little way down the road. The driver, wearing a wide-shouldered camel-coloured overcoat and a fedora, jumped out. He ground a cigarette butt under his heel, then swaggered around to the passenger side and opened the door. Gladys, muffled to the ears in a long coat, poured herself on to the street. She made a fuss of straightening her clothes and then, much to the surprise of the milkman and his old horse, threw her arms around her date in a lavish embrace. Releasing him, she tottered halfway across the road before dashing back to hug him again. When she finally crossed the road and let herself into the back yard of Munroe House, the man lit another cigarette and got back in his car.

Putting Gladys and her flashy young man from her mind, Connie opened Bobby's letter.

Beattie strolled over with her breakfast tray. 'No Millie?'

'The night phone rang just before my alarm and I heard her go out,' said Connie.

'I thought she was second on call,' said Beattie.

Connie nodded. 'She was, but I caught a glimpse of Sally cycling out as I was getting ready for bed last night, so goodness knows what time she got in.'

Beattie smiled and blew across the top of her cup. 'From your secret admirer?' she asked, indicating the sheet of paper Connie was holding.

'My brother Bobby.'

'Looks more like a shopping list than a letter,' said Beattie, sprinkling salt on her porridge.

'This is a novel compared to what Bobby usually sends,' Connie replied.

'How's he getting on in the army?'

'Well, he hates the food, reveille, kit inspections, bulling his boots and the sergeant major, but if the truth were told, he's loving every minute. He's in the Transport Corps, so he's able to muck around with cars all day and get paid for it. He's talking about signing on for an extra three years after his National Service to complete his City and Guilds as a motor mechanic. And if spending his day stripping engines down wasn't enough to tempt him to become a regular, he seems to have a different girlfriend each time he writes.' Connie's eyes flitted over the page. 'This month it's a young lady called Catherine.'

'Are there wedding bells in the offing?'

'I doubt it,' Connie replied. 'He'll have a Barbara or an Anne on his arm the next time I hear from him, or perhaps it'll be a Heidi or an Inga, as he's off to Germany at the end of February.'

'Well I hope for his sake that none of his wild oats take root, or he'll find himself lumbered with some foreign wife . . .' Beattie's expression froze. 'I didn't mean . . .'

'It's all right,' said Connie, trying to keep her voice level.

'No, really,' persisted Beattie with a nervous laugh. 'You know what I'm like, always blathering on without thinking . . .' She lowered her eyes and stirred her porridge. Connie put her cutlery together neatly on her half-eaten breakfast.

The door opened and Sally walked in.

'We're over here,' called Beattie with relief, pointing to the free chair between her and Connie.

Sally nodded, and after selecting her breakfast from the buffet, she came over and sat between them.

'Connie said you were called out last night,' said Beattie.

'Yes, just after cocoa,' Sally replied.

Beattie put her hand on her chest and looked imploringly at the moulded Victorian cornices above. 'Please tell me it was Mrs Farrow in Sidney Street. The poor woman's already two weeks past her due date.'

'No, it wasn't,' Sally replied, shooting a pensive glance at Connie. 'Connie, I—'

The door opened again and Gladys strolled in. Unlike every other nurse in the refectory, she was wearing a yellow dance dress rather than a navy nurse's uniform. If that weren't enough, her ginger hair was loose around her shoulders and she was still wearing make-up. She wandered over to the buffet table.

'She looks like she slept in that,' said Connie, watching Gladys get her breakfast.

'Or it's been lying on someone else's floor while she did,' Beattie replied.

She and Connie giggled and Gladys shot them a venomous look

Sally frowned. 'Connie—'

'Given that we've got report in half an hour, you'd think Gladys would make herself presentable rather than stuff her face, wouldn't you?' Beattie interrupted.

'Why should she care?' Connie replied. 'The superintendent won't say anything to her spy.'

Having made her selection, Gladys looked around for a free table. Unfortunately, the only one available was next to where the three friends were sitting. Forming her expression into one of bored indifference, Gladys wended her way across the room towards them.

'Been out all night again, have we?' asked Beattie, as Gladys settled herself into the chair.

'Not that it's any of your business, Beattie Topping,' she replied, 'but if you must know, I've been looking after a relative.'

'Your sick mother again?' asked Beattie innocently.

'No, my uncle, actually,' Gladys replied airily. 'We're very close.'

Connie laughed. 'I could see that by the way you were necking with him when you got out of his car a few moments ago.'

Above the frilly collar of her dress, Gladys's neck flushed, then her gaze shifted to Sally. 'Have you told her yet?'

'I was just about to,' Sally replied flatly.

Connie looked puzzled. 'Told me what?'

Gladys smirked. 'That your Charlie's Wop missus had her sprog last night.'

Something like a physical blow stopped Connie breathing and sent her head spinning.

Beattie glared at Gladys. 'You're such a cow.'

Gladys's smirk widened. 'I don't know why you're taking on so.'

Beattie and Sally sent her a hateful look.

Gladys shook herself theatrically. 'Brrr. It's a bit chilly over here. Perhaps I'll squeeze on the end of the table with Judy.' She stood up and, taking her tray with her, headed towards the far side of the room.

When she was out of earshot, Sally put her hand on Connie's arm. 'I'm sorry, Connie, I should have told you as soon as I came in.'

'Don't be silly, Sally. It doesn't matter. Really it doesn't.' Connie laughed. 'What did she have?'

'A boy. Six pounds three.'

'How lovely,' said Connie. 'And who does he look like?'

'You know it's difficult to see any real likeness in a newborn.' said Sally, not meeting her eye. 'But he's got a mop of hair like his mother and his father's eyes.'

Something dark pressed down on Connie.

'You've gone awfully pale, Connie,' said Beattie, from what seemed like a very long way away. 'Are you all right?'

Connie blinked to dispel the fog in her mind and gave her friend her brightest smile. 'I'm fine, honest.' She glanced at the clock over the door. 'Is that the time? We'd better get a move on or we'll have Miss Dutton docking our wages for lateness.'

Before her friends could reply, Connie jumped up and cleared away her crockery before heading for the treatment room.

Connie was the first one in for morning report, and although Beattie and Sally shot her worried looks throughout, she listened to Miss Dutton's droning monologue with a cheery expression on her face. She jotted down the patients to be seen and things to be done with exceptional diligence, even volunteering to help with the council's mobile TB screening programme once a month.

By the time she rose from her chair, Connie felt at peace and, if truth were told, somewhat relieved that Maria's baby had been born. After all, it was bound to happen sooner or later, and at least she hadn't been the one on call when it did. And why should it bother her? In fact it might help her finally come to terms with things.

Laughing and joking with the other nurses, Connie donned her outer clothing and wrapped her scarf tight before collecting her bag and heading for the back door. An icy blast cut across the back yard as soon as she stepped out. She crunched through the still-frozen puddles towards the bike rack, plonked her re-plenished case in the basket of her old bone-shaker, then heaved the front wheel from the metal rail. She waited until a handful of other nurses had cycled out, then hopped on her bike and bumped over the flagstones and through the back gate.

As she rang her bell and turned left into Commercial Road, the upbeat tune 'Accentuate the Positive' popped into her head, and she hummed it to herself as she sped along. The frosty air chilled her face and hands as she headed towards her first patient. Passing St Martha's and St Mungo's on her right, she stuck out her arm and was swinging left to cut through to Alyard Street when a pack of dogs dashed yelping and barking across the road in front of her. The horse pulling a milk float on the other side of the road whinnied as a large black dog dodged between its legs, and the Sainsbury's delivery van beside her swerved into her path to avoid crushing a group of raggedy terriers under its front wheels. Connie grabbed the brakes and put her feet on the ground.

The van driver pulled down his window. 'You flea-ridden buggers,' he yelled, waving his fist at the pack, which had now scampered into Arbour Square. He spotted Connie. 'Sorry, luv,' he said, giving her a toothy grin.

'It wasn't your fault,' Connie replied, hearing the wobble in her voice.

The driver pushed up his window and drove away. Connie gripped the handlebars and put her foot back on the pedal. Pushing off, she tried to get her balance, but her head swam and black spots popped into the corners of her vision. The bicycle veered into the railings and she jumped off. Feeling as though her legs were about to give way, she leant the bike on the wall and stumbled into a shop doorway. She braced herself against the Victorian tiles and closed her eyes.

An image of Charlie with his fair hair lifted by the breeze and the sun lighting his cornflower-blue eyes jumped into her head. In her mind, she saw his smile, heard his low laugh and felt his arms around her. An unbearable weight pressed down on her chest, and from nowhere a sob burst out, sending tears streaming down her cheeks. She tried to catch her breath, but she was weeping uncontrollably. Hugging herself, she bent forward, gasping and spluttering.

An arm slipped gently around her shoulder. 'Whatever is the matter, Sister Byrne?' a woman's voice asked.

Connie glanced up and through her tears found herself looking into Mrs Tatum's concerned face. She stood upright and tried to pull herself together. 'I'm fine, really . . .' Another flood of tears stopped her words.

'You're nothing of the sort,' said Mrs Tatum firmly, handing Connie a delicate lawn handkerchief. 'Why don't you come home with me and I'll make us both a nice cup of tea.'

Connie opened her mouth to say that she had patients to see, but instead she took hold of her bicycle's handlebars and let Mrs Tatum lead the way.

'Feeling any better?' asked Mrs Tatum as she came in carrying a tray loaded with a teapot and crockery.

Connie blew her nose and nodded. 'Yes, thank you.' She'd been sitting on Mrs Tatum's stylish sofa for fifteen minutes while her hostess busied herself in the kitchen. She was thankful that Mrs Tatum had taken so long over the tea, because she'd only just stopped sobbing and it was an occupation best done alone.

Mrs Tatum, dressed in a shimmering ivory evening dress and high heels, perched on the armchair opposite.

'This is very kind of you,' said Connie, tucking her handkerchief up her sleeve, 'especially as it looks like you've only just finished work.'

Mrs Tatum leant forward to pour the tea. 'Well I could hardly leave you sobbing in the doorway, could I? It's one sugar, isn't it?'

'Please, Mrs Tatum. If you can spare it.'

'Phyllis, please.' She stirred in a heaped spoonful and handed Connie the cup. 'After all, you're not here in an official capacity.'

'No,' Connie replied, forcing a smile. 'I'm here as a waif and stray you found blubbing in the street. And call me Connie.'

'I suppose it's a man?' Phyllis said softly.

'How did you guess?'

'It usually is. You're not in trouble, are you?' she asked, in a matter-of-fact tone.

'No, no . . . nothing like that,' said Connie, trying not to look offended.

Something like amusement flitted across Phyllis's face. 'Well then, it could be worse, and I can tell you this, Connie, whoever he is, he's not worth it.'

'That's what everyone says, and I know they're right, but . . .'

Between the odd tear and mouthfuls of tea, Connie told her all about Charlie.

'It was a shock hearing about it over breakfast, of course,' she finished, 'but I thought I was all right.'

'Numb, more like,' said Phyllis.

'It's stupid really,' continued Connie. 'With Maria lumbering in to the clinic every week, it's not as if I didn't know the baby was due, for goodness' sake.'

Phyllis frowned. 'And he didn't even write to tell you?'

Connie shook her head.

'Men! They're such bloody cowards,' Phyllis said. 'I wouldn't give you tuppence for the lot of them. And selfish, too. I tell you, I haven't met one yet who wouldn't lie through his back teeth at the drop of a hat.'

Connie's mouth dropped open in astonishment.

'Except my dear Gerald, of course,' Phyllis added hastily, her eyes flickering briefly to the portrait on the mantelshelf. 'But in my experience I wouldn't trust the rest of them as far as I could throw them. And if you've got any sense, neither will you in future.'

'But Charlie's not like that,' said Connie. 'And he's never lied to me.'

Mrs Tatum raised a finely plucked eyebrow.

Connie felt her cheeks glow. 'Well, there was that girl who lived off Cambridge Heath Road, but that was more of a misunderstanding than a lie, and we'd only just started walking out. And all this isn't Charlie's fault.'

'Isn't it?'

'No, it's the war and being away from home and that blooming woman,' Connie replied. 'What man wouldn't take what was offered to him on a plate? Then when she was in the family way, Charlie had to do the right thing, didn't he? I wouldn't be at all surprised if her family didn't turn up on the army base carrying shotguns, and for the sake of keeping peace with the locals the commandant ordered Charlie to marry her.'

Phyllis smiled politely and didn't comment.

Connie sighed. 'Still, what's done is done, I suppose. I just feel so stupid.'

'You're nothing of the sort, and not the first woman to be betrayed by the man she loves.' Phyllis's Summer Pink lips pulled into a harsh line. 'We've all had our hopes and dreams crushed under a man's feet as he walked over them to be with someone else, but if you've got the sense you were born with, you'll never be a doormat again.' Her face wore a contemptuous expression for a second, then it was gone. Her cool, unruffled exterior returned and she held up the teapot and smiled sweetly. 'Can I top you up?'

Chapter Nine

The icy wind tugged at Connie's coat as she made her way up Jubilee Street towards Mile End Road. She had the evening off and was going to have supper with her brother Jim. It had already been dark when she'd left her last patient of the day at 5.30, three quarters of an hour ago. In the time it had taken her to have a strip wash, change out of her uniform and leave Munroe House, the temperature had plummeted and ice was already forming in the inky gutter puddles. Tucking her scarf a little closer around her neck and wishing she had worn trousers, she picked up her pace, but as she reached the corner of Clark Street, she found a barrier and two policemen dressed in long capes barring her way.

'Sorry, miss,' said the older of the pair, holding his hand up as she approached. 'There's an unexploded bomb found in Sydney Street, so you'll have to go around.'

Suppressing her annoyance at the ten minutes added to her journey, Connie turned and headed down Aylward Street, intending to cut through to White Horse Lane. Just before she reached St Dunstan's church, her way was blocked again, but this time by a crowd of people milling around outside the Duke of Brunswick pub. Danny Dance was at its centre, dressed in a brown and burnt-orange checked suit and two-tone brogues, a heavy gold chain stretched across his middle.

'Wotcha, Sister,' he called as he spotted her.

'What's going on?' asked Connie as she joined him.

'The Duke's Christmas beano to Southend,' Danny replied. 'We're just waiting for the coach.' He burped and punched his chest.

'Are you all right?' asked Connie, noting his paler-than-usual colour.

He nodded. 'It's just a touch of heartburn. It's me own fault, but we had to celebrate our good news.'

'Good news?'

'Yes,' said Minnie, popping up at her husband's side.

If asked, Connie would have said that the long musquash fur coat with matching hat and high-heeled pixie boots was a little too dressy for a stroll along Southend promenade, but clearly Minnie had a different view.

She beamed at Connie. 'Our Angelica's been signed by Mr Box into his Company of Youth.'

'Who?' asked Connie.

'He's a film producer who's just set up an acting school for young talent in Hammersmith, and our baby's one of his first signings.' She clasped her hands together and looked skyward. 'It's what we've dreamed of since she took her first step, isn't it, Danny?'

'It is, gal,' Danny replied.

Connie smiled. 'Congratulations. Is she here?'

Minnie shook her head. 'She has to do extra acting lessons with one of Mr Box's assistants. He's a nice young man and says he's very keen on developing her talent. So much so that she's often at the studio well into the night.'

There was a blast from a horn, and a Grey-Green thirty-two-seater coach trundled around the corner. The crowd clapped and wolf-whistled as, with a screech of brakes, it shuddered to a stop alongside the pub. The door opened and the driver, a skinny chap in his mid-twenties, wearing the company's crest on his blazer pocket and a peaked cap, jumped out.

'Sorry I'm late, Danny, but I had to wait for my petrol ration,' he said

'Don't you worry none, Harry,' said Danny. He looked around. 'All right, you lot,' he called to those behind him. 'Let's get loaded.'

'Will there be enough room?' Connie asked the driver as the crowd surged forward.

'Should be,' said Harry, taking a roll-up from behind his ear. 'Mind you, they'll have to squash up. But don't worry, darling,' He winked. 'You can sit with me as long as you mind out for my gear stick.'

Connie smiled. 'Maybe next time.'

His eyes flickered over her, then he looked away. 'Oi, Danny, give us a bottle,' he shouted, indicating the last crate of beer being carried on to the coach. 'You know I drive better with a couple of pints in me.'

Danny grabbed a brown ale as it went past and flicked the top off with the bottle opener on his key ring. Harry took it and downed a couple of mouthfuls. 'Lovely stuff.' He wiped his mouth on his sleeve and climbed back on the coach.

'Have a nice time,' said Connie as Danny reached for the hand-rail beside the coach door.

'Thanks, Sister.' He burped again.

'You know, you really ought to have a dose of milk of magnesia to ease that,' said Connie.

'I already took some about an hour ago,' he replied. 'I'll get a brandy to settle it when we stop at the Orsett Cock.' He clambered on board and shut the door.

A puff of black smoke spurted out of the back of the vehicle as Harry revved up the engine. Connie stood back and waved at the pub regulars, who were already singing 'I Do Like to be Beside the Seaside'. There was a crank of gears and the old bus rolled away.

As she turned, Connie spotted Charlie walking around the corner, and her heart leapt into her mouth.

Strolling home and thinking about not very much, Charlie had to look twice to make sure his eyes weren't deceiving him as Connie stepped out from the pub doorway.

'Hello,' he said, thinking that blue always was her colour. 'What are you doing here?'

'I'm on my way to Jim's but got diverted by a bomb in Sydney Street,' she replied with a friendly smile. 'What about you?'

If the truth were told, Charlie was more than a little pleased to see Connie. Recently, usually when Maria was jabbering on about something or his ears were ringing because of the screaming baby, he had often found himself wondering what life would have been like if he were married to her instead.

'I'm just on my way home,' he replied, noting that, unlike

Maria's, Connie's hair curled around her cheeks and bounced as she moved.

'I thought you worked near Albert Dock,' she said.

'Me and the blooming slave-driver guv'nor didn't see eye to eye, so I left,' he replied. 'I'm working at Wrights' warehouse at the back of Stepney station. I'm my own boss there, in charge of all the electrical export orders.'

'Sounds like you've fallen on your feet,' she said, looking impressed, as she should.

Not only had his chance meeting with Tommy Timms put a nicker and a half in his back pocket when Dark Lady romped home, it had also secured him the job in the warehouse. Now, thanks to Tommy putting in a good word, Charlie got two quid more a week in his pay packet and, by tucking a packet of light bulbs under his overcoat now and then, a couple of bob on the side.

He nodded. 'Your Jim got home, then?'

'Yes, yes he did.' Connie smiled in that soft way of hers, stirring old memories. 'He came home a few weeks before you . . .' Her cheerful expression fell and she lowered her gaze for a second before looking up with a bright smile dancing in her blue eyes. 'I hear congratulations are in order. A boy, wasn't it?'

'Oh, yeah,' he said. 'He's got a right set of lungs on him, I can tell you.'

'You and Maria must be very happy.'

'Course,' he said automatically.

A look of hurt flitted across Connie's pretty face.

'I'm sure Maria will have your supper on the table by now, so I ought to let you go.' She tucked her collar up against the wind. 'Good to see you, Charlie.'

He toyed for a second with the thought of getting a Christmas kiss out of her, but then stepped aside. Her gaze ran over his face once again, waking latent emotions within him, and then she hurried past.

'You too, Connie,' he called, taking out a packet of Benson & Hedges and lighting one. Inhaling deeply, his gaze ran up Connie's shapely legs and over her bottom as she continued down the road. He watched her receding figure until she disappeared into Stepney Way, then turned and continued his journey home.

As he let himself into the house ten minutes later, he was greeted by the sound of his new son screaming upstairs.

'Is that you, Charlie?' his mother called from the parlour.

'Yes, Mum,' he called back, hanging up his coat.

'Put your feet up and I'll bring you a cuppa,' she replied.

The warm fug of a smouldering coal fire and drying laundry enveloped Charlie as he strolled into the front room. The stomach-rumbling smell of stew wafted from the scullery. Moving a pile of baby clothes off the fireside chair, he sat down just as his mother, wearing a pinny over her clothes, came in carrying his favourite mug.

'There you go, son.'

'Ta, Mum.' He took a sip.

'Good day?'

'Not bad, as it happens,' he replied. The guv'nor had been called to head office and so he'd won two shillings in the hastily convened card game in the back office.

'What's the matter with the nipper?' he asked, looking upwards.

'He's got a bit of colic, that's all, but she shouldn't pander to him,' his mother replied, perching on the chair opposite. 'Babies have to be left to cry, everyone knows that, or they'll grow up spoilt. But she won't listen to me and keeps picking him up. And I'm sorry about the mess.' Her eyes darted to the wooden clothes dryer in front of the fire, draped with steaming nappies.

'I'm getting used to it,' Charlie replied, noting the two used baby bottles on the mantelshelf.

'It's not right.' Ada's lips were tight with disapproval. 'I said to her, "My son's out grafting all day, the least you can do is finish the housework and have dinner on the table before he gets home."' Her expression soured further. 'She tries to make out she doesn't understand, but I know she—'

The door opened and Maria walked in, carrying their baby in her arms. She was wearing the red flowery winter dress she'd bought from the woman in Chapman Street who sold second-hand clothes, and the baby was wrapped in a white crocheted shawl.

'What you saying?' she demanded as she laid the infant in the pram wedged behind the sofa.

Ada crossed her arms tightly across her modest bosom. 'What I say to my son is between me and him.'

Charlie looked at his wife. 'She wasn't saying any—'

'You tell tales about me again?' interrupted Maria, without even glancing at him.

'I was just saying that a man's entitled to come home to a tidy house after a day's work, that's all,' said Ada, innocently moving over to Charlie's right side.

'What's for supper?' said Charlie, summoning up a jolly smile.

Maria faced her mother-in-law square on and copied her stance. 'House would be tidy if you and the church women weren't chatter, chatter, chatter in room all afternoon.'

Ada bristled. 'I don't see what the mission's bible study group has to do with—'

'You tell me not to hang out washing until they gone,' Maria cut in. 'Baby needs dry clothes, so—'

'You could have hung them in the kitchen.'

'Too cold.' Maria glared at her. 'You want I put Filippo in damp clothes?'

'Don't take that tone with me.'

'What's for supper?' repeated Charlie a little louder.

'It's your favourite, braised kidneys,' said his mother, patting him on the shoulder. 'It's in the oven.'

Maria's eyes opened wide with disbelief. 'I cook Carlos' meal. It's in the pan.'

Ada gave her an innocent look. 'I thought you were just boiling the baby's bottles.' She hurried out, and Maria spun around to face Charlie.

'Why you not say something?' she demanded, flinging her arms up. 'You never say something.'

'Like what?' asked Charlie.

'Tell her I,' – she slapped her chest – 'I, the wife, I should make supper.'

'I don't care who bloody makes it as long as I get some bloody grub,' he replied, and ignoring Maria's thunderous expression, he stood up and headed for the kitchen.

His mother was standing behind his chair at the table, where the cutlery had already been set out along with two thick slices of bread and butter on a plate.

'There you go, son,' she said, patting the seat as if encouraging a five-year-old to sit up nicely.

He slid on to the chair and, grabbing his knife and fork, waited expectantly.

Giving Maria a gloating look as she passed, Ada went to the oven and lifted out a steaming dish. Carrying it triumphantly before her, she set it in front of Charlie.

'That's more like it,' he said, spearing a chunk of kidney.

As he tucked into his supper, his wife clattered about with the saucepan on the hob. He was just about to scoop up a forkful of potato when she grabbed the dish and whipped it out from under his nose.

'What the . . . ?'

'You eat dinner I cook,' she announced, marching over to the pig-swill bin and dumping the contents of the dish in it.

Ada jumped up. 'That's two coupons' worth of meat you've just thrown away.'

Maria shrugged. Taking up a plate from the unlit hob, she swayed over to Charlie and placed it in front of him.

'What the fuck is this?' he asked, looking at what appeared to be a ball of string with squashed tomatoes on top.

'Spaghetti bolognese,' Maria replied.

'My Charlie wants proper food, not some foreign muck,' said Ada, staring down as if she were inspecting an unflushed privy.

Maria shrugged again. 'Then he'll have empty belly. And I want our coupon books.'

A flush spread up Ada's throat. 'Are you going to let her speak to your own mother like—'

'Now look here, Maria,' Charlie said, feeling indigestion threatening.

Maria glanced at him briefly then returned her attention to his mother. 'Mine and Carlos',' she said, holding out her hand.

Fizzing like a glass of Epsom salts, Ada went over to the windowsill and rummaged around in the earthenware jug, pulling out two ration books that she all but threw at her daughter-in-law.

Maria pocketed them. 'And I think perhaps me and Carlos, we look for our own place, so you can have your church women's meeting and I can dry baby's clothes.'

Ada's face drained of all colour. 'You'll leave, Charlie?'

He looked away and didn't reply.

Maria's lower lip jutted out. 'You say you get me nice house with garden for Filippo,' she moaned. 'Somewhere for Mama and Papa to stay too.'

Ada scowled. 'What the bloody hell have they got to do with anything?'

'They come see us in the spring, so you find house.' Maria fixed Charlie with a stiletto-like look. 'Or Papa no be pleased.'

An image of his bear-like father-in-law appeared in Charlie's mind. He shifted uncomfortably in his chair.

'All right. I ain't promising anything, but I'll ask around,' he muttered. Gripping his cutlery tighter, he gazed down at the plate in front of him. 'Now if you don't mind, I'd like to eat me bloody dinner.'

Ada stood staring at them both for a moment, then burst into tears and ran from the room. Smiling complacently at the sound of her mother-in-law thumping up the stairs to her bedroom above, Maria sat down next to Charlie.

'Eat up, Carlos,' she said, nudging his arm. 'Before spaghetti go cold.'

The band blared out the last note of 'Sentimental Journey' and the dancers in the Memorial Hall stopped on the beat. Connie's partner, the undermanager from the Co-op, a well-padded young man with moist hands, released her and clapped enthusiastically.

'Can I buy you a drink, luv?' he asked, pulling down the waist-coat of his brown striped suit.

'That's kind of you, but I already have one.' Connie pointed to the table at the corner of the dance floor where Millie was sitting.

'Then perhaps I can catch you for a waltz later,' he said, sliding his hand around her waist and down towards her bottom.

Connie stepped out of his embrace. 'Just one dance per ticket, I'm afraid.'

He winked and pulled two pieces of green paper from his pocket. 'That's why I swiped a couple from my mates.'

In order to raise funds, the St George's and St Dunstan's Nursing Association committee put on a dance just before Christmas each year. Unless they were on call or had a dose of bubonic plague, the Munroe House nurses were required to play their part in keeping the Association afloat. This was done by issuing each male guest with a complimentary ticket as he walked through the door that entitled him to a dance with one of the Association's nurses. The fact that the nurses referred to the event as the Gropers' Ball indicated how much they looked forward to the evening.

'That looked like hard work,' said Millie as Connie resumed her seat.

'It was like wrestling with a sweaty gorilla but less fun. And you can take that smug look off your face, Millie Sullivan, 'cos King Kong has got two more tickets.'

Millie laughed and Connie took a restorative mouthful of G and T.

'It's a pity Alex couldn't come.'

'Yes,' sighed Millie. 'I'm disappointed, but it was this weekend or Christmas, and as Mum's invited him for Christmas dinner, he's working tonight.'

Connie nudged her. 'This time next year you'll be celebrating Christmas as Mrs Nolan.'

'Yes, I will, won't I?' A dreamy expression crept across Millie's face for a moment, then she looked at Connie again. 'What about you? Are you going to see that chap, Ronald, from the council again?'

Since everyone from her mother and sisters to her friends and patients was constantly badgering her to get out and meet someone else, Connie had forced herself to do just that.

She nodded. 'We're going to the pictures in two weeks.'

Millie smiled brightly. 'Good. He seems very nice.'

'He is,' Connie replied. 'Very nice, but he's just not . . .' She bit her lower lip.

Millie closed her hand over Connie's and they exchanged a fond look.

The band struck up again, and as no one clutching a dance ticket was headed their way, Connie picked up her drink and relaxed.

The committee had done their best to give the old Edwardian hall a seasonal dressing, but with rationing still very much in place and many things unobtainable, the dozen or so coloured balloons looked lonely rather than festive. There was a tree with a couple of baubles, but some bright spark had stuck it in the corner by the roaring stove, and it was shedding needles on to the parquet flooring. However, the seven-piece band was excellent, the bar was fully stocked and everyone was in the party mood as they celebrated Christmas without the fear of death raining down on them in the middle of the ladies' excuse-me.

'Annie and the other Queenies seem very jolly,' said Connie, indicating across the room to where the four Munroe House students were laughing and joking.

'Don't you remember how happy we were when we passed our QI exam?' Millie replied.

'I certainly do, and how we got caught in an air raid on the way home from Oxford Street after our celebrations.' Connie laughed as she watched the couples swing around the dance floor. 'How many have we got in the next batch?'

'Four, and Miss Dutton's already told me I'm to organise them as well as everything else,' said Millie glumly. 'Talk of the devil.'

She nodded towards the dance floor and Connie turned her head.

Considering that Miss Dutton expressed disdain for popular music, the cinema, the dance hall and anything else that most people enjoyed, she'd made quite an effort for the Association bash. Dressed in a shimmering red dress that wouldn't have looked out of place on Ginger Rogers, Munroe House's superintendent was swirling round the dance floor in the arms of the London Hospital's consultant surgeon, Mr Shottington. Although, Connie thought, the surgeon had more in common with the Fat Controller from her nephew's storybook than Fred Astaire. Resplendent in an old-fashioned dress suit complete with white tie and tails, Mr Shottington guided Miss Dutton around the room a half-beat behind the music's tempo.

'Connie?'

Connie turned her attention back to her friend.

'Would you to do something for me?' asked Millie.

'If I can.'

'Will you supervise the next intake of Queenies?' said Millie with an imploring look.

'But I've never done it before.'

'I know, but you've helped me steer at least six lots through, and I'll help if you get stuck with the paperwork,' Millie pleaded. 'Miss Dutton's got me doing the rota, the daily allocations, the ordering and the monthly return to the Queen's Nurses' Institute, and someone has to take it on when I get married and leave, so better for our January batch that you volunteer to supervise them than Miss Dutton picking one of her cronies.'

Connie frowned. 'I see what you mean. God help us all if Gladys was in charge of them.'

'Exactly,' said Millie.

'Well,' Connie gave an exaggerated sigh, 'I suppose if you're flitting off to be Mrs Nolan, I'd better learn how to organise the Queenies.'

Connie gazed down at Danny Dance lying cold and motionless in his coffin while the clock on the mantelshelf ticked off the seconds. There was an expression of calm contentment on his rounded face, and his nicotine-stained hands rested together on his chest. In death, the flush caused by constant drinking had faded and the blue tinge to his lips had also disappeared. He wore his best suit, but the buttons of the jacket strained to remain within the opposing holes and the trousers were so tight, Connie wondered if the funeral director had had to slit them at the back to get them on.

She looked sympathetically at Minnie Dance and her daughter, who were standing on the other side of the coffin dressed in black from head to toe. 'I am so very sorry.'

Minnie sniffed. 'It's very good of you to come, Sister,' she said, peering up at Connie from under her enormous black hat.

'Not at all,' Connie replied. 'Although I can't say I've ever been to a viewing in a public bar.'

'It's what Danny would have wanted.' Minnie blew her nose. 'Ain't it, baby?'

'Yes,' spluttered her daughter, her mascara smudged around her puffy eyes. 'It's what he would have . . .' She dissolved in a blubbering mess.

'Poor Angelica's taken it very hard.' Minnie smiled fondly at the over-made-up young woman by her side. 'She was always Daddy's special little girl. Weren't you, sweetheart?'

'Yes,' squeaked Angelica. She looked forlornly down into the casket. 'And he was the best daddy in the world. I still can't believe he's . . .' Somehow she drew a handkerchief from the pocket of her skin-tight dress and buried her face in it. Minnie put her arm around her. Mother and daughter cried on each other for a few moments, then regained control of themselves.

'How did it happen?' Connie asked.

'He was in good spirits all the way there. Leading the singing and joking with everyone.'

'That was my dad for you,' sniffed Angelica.

'Like we always did, we took a stroll from the Kursaal right along the front to the pier to have fish and chips in the Lighthouse Café. It was our favourite fish and chip shop, and even when Angelica was a nipper we'd wrap her up and take her with us.' She nudged her daughter. 'Do you remember, luv?'

Angelica nodded. 'Daddy used to take me to Never Never Land so I could see the fairy castle and the elves.'

Minnie looked at Connie. 'Poor Danny had been waiting all through the war for the lights to go back on again, and what happens? He pegs it before they throw the switch.'

Connie looked surprised. 'But I thought he died on the coach on the way back?'

Minnie and her daughter exchanged a glance.

'I suppose it won't do no harm telling you, Sister,' said Minnie.

'Telling me what?' asked Connie, as her nursing registration flashed before her eyes.

'Well, Danny had a bit of indigestion when we set out that morning,' explained Minnie.

'He'd been a martyr to it for years,' chipped in Angelica.

'But I didn't think anything of it,' continued Minnie. 'After a couple of brown ales, he perked up and seemed his old jolly self.'

'It were 'im that got everyone on the knock-knock jokes, weren't it, Mum?'

Minnie nodded. 'Anyhow, once we got there, we all piled off the coach and started out along the front. We'd got as far as the pier and Danny said his legs were aching, so we decided to have our supper at one of the cafés under the arches. We found a table outside and I went to powder me nose. When I came back, he had his eyes shut and I thought he'd nodded off. I sat down and the waitress brought the menus,' continued Minnie. 'I thought

I'd better wake him up, but when I shook him, his hand flopped down.'

'Oh my goodness,' said Connie. 'What did you do?'

Minnie looked anxious. 'Well I didn't know want to do. Luckily Harry, the driver, happened to stroll by, so I called him over. He said we ought to call the rozzers, but I said I didn't want to make a scene, not in front of all those people, so Harry said to make him presentable and order our dinner while he went off to sort things out. I splashed out and had wing of skate. I know Danny wouldn't have minded, would he, Angelica?'

Her daughter shook her head emphatically. 'Course not, Mum.'

'Just as I'd finished the last chip, Harry returned with an ancient wheelchair and heaved Danny into it.' Minnie chuckled. 'We got a couple of funny looks, I can tell you. Anyway, he pushed Danny along the promenade towards Leigh for a bit and then said to wait while he brought the coach around. So I had an ice cream and waited. About twenty minutes later, Harry came back, and a couple of the blokes carried Danny on to the coach. When we got back here, I called the local coppers and told them he'd died on the way home.'

Connie looked at her aghast. 'Harry was right, you should have told the Southend police.'

Minnie looked contrite. 'I know, but I couldn't leave Danny so far from home by himself, could I?'

'Course you couldn't, Mum.' Angelica reached into the coffin and smoothed a stray lock of Brilliantined hair from her father's forehead. 'I mean, poor Daddy's dead whatever way you look at it.'

Connie gazed down at Danny. That he was dead was true enough, and once he was laid to rest no one would be any the wiser as to where and how, but even so . . .

'And I'll tell you this.' Minnie's voice cut through Connie's thoughts. 'When we get back from the crematorium, we're going to have a right good booze-up, just as Danny would have wanted.'

Mo's eldest son Arthur, named for his grandfather, shoved his empty dessert bowl away and, resting his chin on his hands, looked adoringly up at his father. 'Dad, tell us again how you captured a platoon of Germans single-handed.'

After months of worrying about what to buy everyone and whether they'd be able to get enough dried fruit for the pudding, the first peacetime Christmas Day had finally arrived. As it was a special day, the whole family was gathered in Mo's rarely used front parlour. Pinned to the picture rails and slung across the room were the coloured paper chains that the children had been making for the past three weeks. The pastel-coloured Chinese lanterns dangling from the ceiling fluttered a little in the rising heat from the roaring fire.

As there wasn't a real Christmas tree to be had for love nor money in London, Mo had resigned herself to just having the crib with plaster figurines on display. That was until three days ago, along the Waste, she'd come upon a spiv selling small artificial ones from a tea chest. By the sounds of it she'd arm-wrestled several other women for the last one, then borne it home triumphant. It sat in pride of place on the table in the window alcove, cluttered with glass balls and tinsel and surrounded by brightly coloured parcels.

Now, after the weeks of planning, cooking and saving meat and sugar coupons, everything had been consumed. The large meat platter had just bones and a few dribbles of fat left to show where the rib of beef had been. The two tureens at either end of the table were empty too, with just a limp band of cabbage draped over the handle of one and a few stray peas in the base of the other. There was a thin crust of Yorkshire pud that couldn't be prised off the blackened roasting pan; all the pickled cucumbers had been eaten and the gravy in the blue and white jug had been drained.

As they all knew they'd be subject to weeks of tight-lipped rebukes from Maud if they didn't have Christmas dinner together, the whole family was there. This wasn't easy, as the table which normally sat six had more than double that number squashed around it. Eddy presided over proceedings at the head, but not to be overlooked, Maud had taken the seat on his right, which Mo had reserved for herself. Arthur, who had changed out of his old allotment trousers and jacket in honour of the day, sat next to his wife, with Bernie's middle daughter and two of Mo's sons alongside. In order to save space, the three children were sitting on a decorator's plank resting across two chairs. Connie was jammed into the bay window at the bottom end of the table with Bernie and Cliff to her left and Sheila to her right. Sheila's two, Lawrence and Janice, were sharing one of the old-fashioned chairs from the scullery, with Bernie's eldest, Marlene, taking the place between them and her Aunt Mo.

Eddy, who after four months of home cooking could only just squeeze into his demob suit, chuckled. 'Well, it was only three of them, and I was with two mates.'

'Oh go on, Uncle Eddy,' piped up Marlene. 'Tell us.'

Eddy wiped his mouth with his napkin and laid it beside his bowl. 'Right, there was me and Chalky.' He grabbed the salt and pepper pots and placed them next to the scraped-out gravy jug. 'We were by this French barn when Taffy . . .'

As her brother-in-law retold the story of his finest hour to the gathered children, Connie leant towards her sister sitting next to her. Six years older than Connie, Bernie had the same dark blond hair as Mo, but Connie's fair skin, a combination that was completed with a sprinkle of freckles over the bridge of her nose.

'How's Betty getting on?'

Bernie glanced down at the five-month-old baby wrapped in a pink blanket on the armchair. 'She's a poppet. I've been putting half a rusk in her last bottle for a week and she slept through from ten to six. You should come around for supper sometime.'

'What about next Friday?'

'That's grand.' Bernie nudged her husband, who looked round. 'Connie's coming for fish and chips next Friday.'

Cliff, a lean, fair-haired chap with a quiff and thick spectacles, smiled. 'Good.'

A wide-eyed, innocent expression spread across Bernie's face. 'I know, what about if you ask Tim to come too?'

Cliff looked puzzled. 'Who?'

'You know,' said Bernie, glaring at her husband. 'The new fella who started at the depot a few weeks back whose wife—'

'Oh, Tim,' said Cliff.

'Yes,' said Bernie. 'Didn't you say he was the life and soul?'

Cliff nodded. 'Happy-go-lucky is how I'd describe him, which is to his credit considering what he's been through.'

'His wife skipped off to the States with a Yank and left him with the two boys,' Bernie informed Connie. A sad expression settled on her face. 'Three and five they are. The poor little mites.'

Betty started to grumble and Bernie turned to pick her up.

'So then Taffy said, "Handy hup, Fritz!" and they did and we marched them back to camp,' Eddy boomed down the table.

'You were so brave, Dad,' said Arthur.

Eddy puffed out his chest. 'Just doing my bit, son. That's all.'

'Why didn't you shoot them, Uncle Eddy?' asked Lawrence, firing at his aunt's collection of china dogs on the mantelshelf with an imaginary rifle.

A sad expression crept into Eddy's eye. ''Cos they were just ordinary blokes like us.'

'I would have, Dad.' Arthur aimed an invisible pistol at his cousin across the table. 'Toosh! toosh!'

'Missed me!' yelled Lawrence, mowing Arthur down with his rifle.

'Take that, you dirty German.' Arthur retaliated with a hand grenade. His brother Bert ducked to avoid the blast and sent the gravy jug spinning. Mo caught it.

'Right!' She swung her arm at the children. 'You boys, out in the garden for ten minutes while we clear the table.'

Chairs scraped back as the boys squeezed between their elders to escape.

Mo stood up. 'Now that we've got some space, you girls can take the crockery out.' Dutifully the three girls started collecting the bowls and plates.

Connie rose to her feet. 'I'll give them a hand,' she said, grabbing a stack of bowls and heading after her nieces. 'Put them on the drainer,' she said as she followed the girls in. The children did as they were told, then left to fetch more crockery.

Connie turned on the Ascot heater. While the sink was filling, she unbuttoned her cuffs and rolled up her sleeves. Taking the spare apron, she slipped it over her head and secured it at the back. She took the box of soap crystals from the windowsill and shook a handful into the steamy water.

Watching her nephews through the window re-enacting the D-Day landings in the back yard, she lowered the first plates into the water and unhooked the washing-up mop from the nail in the wall.

'The King's speech will be on soon,' said Mo as she came into the kitchen. 'But if you wash and I dry we won't miss it.' She slipped her wraparound overall on and joined Connie at the sink.

'It was a lovely dinner, Mo,' Connie said, slotting the first plate into the rack to drain.

Her sister accepted the compliment. 'I was just thankful there was enough meat to go around. Those boys of mine eat more and more each day.'

'Well, they're growing lads,' said Connie, shaking the suds from a second plate and stacking it alongside the first. 'I wonder if you'll have a girl this time.'

A fond smile lifted the corners of Mo's mouth. 'I hope so, but I don't want to set my heart on it, just in case.'

Connie smiled. 'I'll keep my fingers crossed.'

Maureen took the tea towel from the back of the chair and picked up a plate. 'Did I hear you tell Bernie you were half-day on Sunday?'

'Yes, I swapped with my friend Hannah,' Connie replied, swabbing out a pudding bowl.

'Eddy's cousin Keith and his wife Rita are coming for tea with their new baby. Why don't you come too?' said Mo jollily.

'All right, I'll make my way over to you as soon as I'm finished,' said Connie.

'Rita's bringing her cousin Nigel with them. His mother went into a home recently and he's been a bit down, so Rita thought a trip might cheer him up. You must remember him from our wedding,' continued Mo, rubbing the plate she was drying vigorously. 'You danced with him a couple of times. He's a tall chap with wavy blonde hair.'

Connie did. Rita's cousin was a shade taller than her and had a right eye that rolled upwards from time to time. She forced a smile. 'Thanks, Mo. It sounds as if I'm in for an unforgettable afternoon.'

Chapter Ten

As the icy January rain lashed at the treatment room window, Miss Dutton smiled and cast her cool blue eyes over the four young women sitting, awkwardly balancing teacups in their hands. 'After the Great War, the St George's and St Dunstan's Nursing Association joined forces with the Limehouse and . . .'

Connie stifled a yawn and glanced at the clock above the door. Twenty minutes! Flipping heck! And Miss Dutton wasn't up to Hitler marching into Poland yet. At this rate she'd still be wittering on at teatime. Connie had only asked the superintendent to pop in and say hello to the new crop of student nurses, not bore them rigid for an hour.

Waving goodbye to 1945 four weeks ago had caused a frenzy of excitement in Munroe House, mainly because, so far, seven of their number had set their wedding dates for the first half of the new year. Connie would put a pound to a penny that there'd be at least a handful more before they linked hands for 'Auld Lang Syne' again. Not that she'd been one of those singing it this year.

Sally and Beattie had organised a New Year's Eve knees-up in the Boatman pub off Gravel Lane, and, as Miss Dutton had taken the week off after Christmas, the nurses had drawn lots as to who would stay on duty. Connie gave a silent prayer of thanks when she pulled one of the three short straws. After her sisters' not-so-subtle attempts at fixing her up with odd men – and in the case of Nigel, very odd men – it saved her from having to see couples locked in passionate embraces as the last note of Big Ben sounded from the wireless. So while her friends were welcoming in 1946 in the saloon bar of the ancient waterside pub, at the stroke of midnight Connie had been easing Rose Milligan's new daughter into the world instead.

Turning her attention back to the matter in hand, she studied the new batch of students who for the next six months would be undertaking Queen's Nurse training. They were all dressed in their Sunday best, either suits or formal dresses and cardigans. All of them wore gloves and hats and had a small suitcase on the floor beside them.

'. . . and that is where we find ourselves now.' Miss Dutton gazed dreamily over their heads. 'I wonder what our illustrious founder, Miss Robina Munroe, would have made of it all.'

The young women dutifully turned and looked up at the full-length portrait of a young woman in a crinoline and a tartan shawl hanging above the fireplace.

'And now, as the district doesn't run itself' – there was a ripple of polite laughter – 'I'll hand over to Sister Byrne, who will fill in the details.' Miss Dutton gave Connie the file containing the training plan that Connie herself had compiled and left on the superintendent's desk the night before. 'Finally, nurses, I'd like you to remember that we are all just one big happy family here at Munroe House.'

The girls all nodded excitedly, and a fresh-faced young redhead with a sprinkling of freckles across her cheeks stood up. 'Nurse Robb, Superintendent, and thank you for your time.'

Another, with short brown hair, jumped to her feet. 'Nurse Boscombe,' she announced, nervously clutching her handbag to her. 'And especially as you must be so busy.'

The other nurses nodded their agreement.

Miss Dutton smiled benevolently at her subjects and then swept out of the room, the long strings of her lacy nurse's cap trailing majestically behind her.

The two young women sat down and all of them turned their attention to Connie. She stood up.

'Well, good afternoon, nurses, and welcome again to Munroe House,' she said, giving them a friendly smile.

There was a mumble of 'Good afternoon, Sister Byrne.'

'As Superintendent Dutton has already told you, I will be in overall charge of your training. If there are any problems, I'm the one you should talk to instead of bothering the superintendent. As I'm sure you're all hungry and Mrs Pierce will be serving lunch in fifteen minutes, I'll quickly run through what you need to know for this afternoon.' She opened the file. 'Nurses Boscombe and Robb' – they both stood up as their names were called – 'you will be on the top floor in rooms fourteen and seventeen and you will be supervised by Sister Patterson and Sister Miles.'

'Thank you, Sister,' they replied in unison.

'And Nurses Tucker and Baxter' – the two remaining girls rose to their feet – 'you will be in rooms seven and nine, and as midwives you will be supervised by Sister Scott and myself.'

Her eyes lingered a second on the nurse who was to be her student. With her abundant chestnut hair bouncing on her shoulders and the freckles over her nose, Nurse Baxter, looked to Connie no older than twenty-one. However, allowing for the fact that it took three years to train as a SRN and another two to become a midwife, she had to be at least twenty-three. She was curvy in build and somewhere around Connie's height.

'I've left a list of mealtimes and your bathroom rota, which I ask you to stick to, for everyone's convenience, on your dressing tables,' Connie continued. 'You will have a change of bed linen each week and your laundry must be left out for the maids on Monday morning or you'll have to wash it yourself,' she added, scowling in mock severity. The nurses laughed.

'We have allocation at eight a.m. in the treatment room, and from Monday onwards you will be expected to be there promptly. Tomorrow morning you will also be given a pedal cycle, so I hope you can all ride one.'

The four girls nodded.

'Good, it saves me having to fish you out of the London docks.' They all laughed again. 'You'll also be given a bag to carry your equipment. You will be responsible for your case and its contents and woe betide anyone who loses or damages it, but I'll be telling you more about that tomorrow afternoon.'

The nurses looked suitably warned.

'Are there any questions?'

Connie's other student stood up. 'Nurse Tucker. How soon will we be allowed to visit patients by ourselves, Sister?'

'You will be with your supervising nurse for the four weeks of your probation,' Connie replied. 'I know it seems a long time, especially as you are all very experienced nurses, but as you'll find out, we do things differently on the district.'

The young woman tucked her skirt under her and sat down.

Connie looked up at the clock above the door. 'And now, as

it's nearly five to one, you have just enough time to take your suitcases to your rooms before Cook sounds the lunch gong. I suggest you spend the afternoon unpacking and getting your bearings. Tea is served at three thirty in the nurses' lounge and supper in the refectory is at six thirty. This evening I'd suggest you spend a little time getting to know each other and the rest of the nurses who live in. Have a nice afternoon and I'll see you tomorrow at eight o'clock for morning report.'

The nurses picked up their cases and headed into the hall.

'Nurse Baxter,' called Connie.

The young nurse stopped and Connie walked over to her. 'Welcome to Munroe House. I'm going to be your supervising sister and I'll do my very best to help you through the six months of QN training.' She held out her hand.

Nurse Baxter moved her suitcase to the other hand and reached out to shake Connie's. Unfortunately, as she did so, her cuff caught the catch and the case pinged open, spilling the contents, including several pairs of knickers and a girdle, on to the floor between them.

'I'm so sorry, Sister,' she said as, with cheeks flaming, she tried to stop the rest of her belongings from falling out while gathering up those that already had with the other hand.

'It's all right,' said Connie, bending down to retrieve the young nurse's washbag and a pack of Dr White's from the floor.

Nurse Baxter put her case on a chair and threw her clothes back in.

'They'll get crumpled,' said Connie.

'I'll sort them out when I get upstairs.' Nurse Baxter snapped the lock shut firmly. 'Sorry, Sister. I've always been a bit fingers-and-thumbs when I get nervous.'

Connie smiled. 'Don't worry.' She extended her hand again.

'Thank you, Sister Byrne,' her student nurse said, taking it. Nurse Baxter's handbag, which had been sitting perfectly securely in the crook of her elbow, now lost its mooring and slid down her arm, over their joined hands and on to Connie's forearm.

Nurse Baxter reddened again. 'I'm so sorry, Sister—'

'What's your first name?' Connie asked.

'Josephine,' Nurse Baxter replied. 'But everyone calls me Josie.'

'Well I tell you what, Josie,' Connie said, handing back the young woman's handbag. 'I'm out on visits all afternoon, but why don't we meet up in the small lounge after supper tonight when you've settled in?'

The sun had been below the winter horizon for the best part of an hour by the time Connie pulled up outside Dr Carter's surgery at 5.45. As the doctor stopped seeing patients on the dot of six, for once she didn't have to compete with a line of prams to find a place to chain her cycle.

After leaving Josie and the other trainees to settle in, Connie had set out on her afternoon rounds. Having helped Mrs Flint to get her wheelchair-bound husband on and off the commode, packed Mrs Royal's underarm abscess with ribbon gauze and delivered a rubber waterproof sheet up six flights of stairs in Stebbins House, she was just turning into Hannibal Road on her way to the first of her evening insulins when Stan, the landlord of the Hayfield, dashed out and told her that Dr Carter needed her to call in before she went off duty.

Shoving her gloves in her pocket and taking her bag from the front basket, Connie strode into the relative warmth of the surgery, passing the empty waiting room and continuing on to the consulting room at the back of the house. Reaching the brown door with its brass plate announcing *Dr W. R. Carter, FRCPS, MRCP, DRCOG*, she paused for a second, then squared her shoulders and knocked.

'Come!'

Dr Carter was sitting at his desk with his jacket off and his sleeves rolled up. He looked up. 'Sister Byrne, I haven't seen you for weeks.'

'Really?' she replied innocently.

'I thought perhaps you were avoiding me,' he chuckled.

Connie laughed light-heartedly. 'Now why on earth would I do that, Doctor?'

His gaze ran slowly over her and Connie felt her cheeks glow.

'You asked me to call?' she said, putting on her most professional smile.

'Yes. Would you mind if I cleared away while we discussed things?' he asked, nodding towards the dressing trolley with its dirty instruments next to the examination couch.

'Of course not.'

He rose from the chair. 'You look warm. Why don't you take your coat off and make yourself comfortable?'

'I'm all right, thank you, Doctor,' Connie replied.

'You won't feel the benefit when you go back out,' he said.

Connie glanced over to the cast-iron burner in the corner, which was kicking out enough heat to fill a room three times the size of this one. With a cardigan underneath and a scarf around her neck, she was actually beginning to feel quite hot.

'Hang it up on the stand,' he added.

Connie shrugged off her coat and hooked it and her scarf on to the peg next to his Harris Tweed jacket, then moved a medical dictionary from the seat beside the desk and sat down. Tucking her bag under the chair, she took out her notebook and pen.

'Mrs Willis is out of hospital, so could you resume your weekly bed baths? Mr Farmer's legs are weeping again and will need daily dressings, and the Klineman children who live on the third floor in the Guinness Trust building have all got measles. See what you can do to help,' he called over his shoulder as he went into the old scullery that served as the sluice.

Connie wrote it all down.

'Could you do me a favour and fetch the rest of the equipment?' he asked, dropping the soiled instruments in the sink and turning on the Ascot heater.

Connie stood up and tucked her notebook and pen into the side of her bag, then went over to the trolley. Putting the dressing scissors and speculum in an enamel bowl, she crossed the room to the sluice. It had once been the house's scullery and was no more than six foot square. What with the deep butler sink under the small window, a workbench with a sterilising unit on it and cupboards full of dressings, there was barely enough room for one person, let alone two.

Connie went to slide the implements into the water.

'Could you put them over here?' Dr Carter asked, indicating the draining board on the other side of him.

Not wanting to reach across, Connie squeezed behind him and placed them on the sloping wooden surface.

'That's the ticket,' he said, smiling down at her.

She was now wedged against the wall. She toyed with trying

to squeeze out, but he stepped back, which meant she didn't have enough room to retrace her steps without pressing into him. She decided to stay put until he'd finished.

He swilled around in the bowl for a moment, then picked up the paraphernalia she'd just brought in and dropped it into the foaming water.

'I'll let them soak for a bit,' he said, taking the towel from the hook on the wall. He turned towards her. 'You know, I've been thinking quite a bit about you, Connie,' he said, drying his hands.

'Have you?' asked Connie, trying to keep the panic from her voice.

A lazy smile crept across Dr Carter's face. 'Yes, I have.' His gaze travelled down to her Queen's Nurse badge, hanging around her neck, and although they were only inches apart, he moved forward.

Connie took an involuntary step backwards and her shoulder blades made contact with the wall. Dr Carter placed his hand on the wall behind her head, and a combination of sweat and after-shave wafted over her.

'You know you really are a pretty little thing, my dear,' he said.

Connie didn't reply.

'You and me could have a lot of fun together,' he said, looming over her. 'Discreet fun, of course, but fun nonetheless.'

'I—'

'I thought perhaps a spin in the old Jag out to a little country hotel I know for a spot of dinner and bubbly, and then . . .' Reaching out with his other hand, he tucked his finger under her badge, his knuckles grazing her breasts as he did so. He regarded the badge for a moment, then looked up and raised an eyebrow. 'What do you say?'

Although her heart was pounding in her chest, Connie smiled sweetly.

'Sounds lovely,' she said. 'And I'm sure you'll have no trouble finding someone to join you.' She ducked under his arm, and without pausing, snatched her bag from the floor and her coat from the stand. 'But not me. Good day, Dr Carter.'

With the cold February rain dripping off the peak of her hat, Connie peered through the steamy half-glazed door. Spotting

Millie sitting at a table near the back, she pushed on the worn brass plate and stepped into Kate's Café. Immediately, the warm fug of fried bacon and eggs and brewed coffee enveloped her, while the upbeat sound of *Music While You Work* drifted out from the wooden radio on the shelf behind the counter and mingled with gruff male voices.

Kate's Café was one of the lucky shops along the Highway that had escaped the Luftwaffe. Judging by the low ceiling beams dating back to the previous century, it had been a working man's eating house for a very long time. It had remained open throughout the Blitz, despite having boards instead of windows for much of the time. Like the rest of the area, it was looking a little tired now, but it was still packed to the gunnels every day with dockers and stevedores from the nearby London Dock. This was in no small part due to the owner, Pearl Watson, who had a cheery smile for all and made mouth-watering bacon butties. There was always a fresh pot of tea brewing, and at noon each day Pearl's husband, Bill, and Wilf, the old boy who cleared the tables, delivered meals to the elderly residents who lived within walking distance.

As the café sat between their patches, Connie and Millie always met there for their mid-morning cuppa, and since the only way Miss Dutton would have crossed the threshold would have been bound and gagged, it was now the unofficial nurses' office for the residents of Munroe House.

Weaving her way between dock workers and delivery men, Connie headed over to her friend.

'Have you been waiting long?' she asked, putting her bag down and taking off her gloves.

'A couple of minutes, that's all,' Millie replied.

Connie shook the rain from her coat and hooked it over the back of the chair. 'You look a bit under the weather.'

'It's Alex,' said Millie. 'It's been almost two months since he had the interview with the Palestine Police Authority and he's still heard nothing so he's convinced he hasn't got the job.'

Connie sat down. 'It's bad them not letting him know.'

'Yes, it is.' Millie took a sip of tea. 'But I can't say I'm totally sorry we're not going. I hated the thought of leaving Mum all by herself.'

Connie gave her friend a sympathetic look. 'The first year is always the hardest.'

'I know, and she's held up pretty well, what with the move and everything. She keeps herself busy helping her neighbours but she's still not a hundred per cent . . .'

'It takes time but perhaps Alex being turned down has worked out for the best in the long run,' said Connie.

Millie sighed. 'I hope so. He's putting a brave face on it though and is applying for a police flat in Warren House.'

Connie pulled a face.

'I know they're worse than some of the places we visit, but there's nothing for it and at least we won't have to share,' said Millie.

'And we'll still be able to meet up for a gossip in Kate's.'

The two friends smiled at each other.

Pearl shuffled over. 'Morning, girls.' The roll-up sticking out of the corner of her mouth moved up and down as she spoke. 'Is it still brass monkeys out there?'

'It certainly is,' Connie replied, rubbing her hands together. 'Even the puddles are frozen.'

'Tea and a slice?' Pearl asked.

'Please.'

Pearl headed back to the counter.

'How's your morning been?' Connie asked.

'So-so. Stan Drabble's been taken into the London again with fluid on the lung, and I've picked up three more twice-weekly bed baths from Dr Gingold.'

They chatted on about their morning calls for a bit before Pearl returned. 'There you go, girls,' she said, unloading their tea and a plate with two slices of bread pudding on to the table.

'What about you?' asked Millie as Pearl left them.

'The usual crop,' Connie replied, picking up her cup. 'Except you'll never guess . . .' She told Millie about her encounter with Dr Carter the previous afternoon.

'Dirty old man,' chuckled Millie when she'd finished. She put her tea down and leant forward. 'Talking about your love life, what about the chap you met at the Palais last week?'

'There's nothing to tell.' Connie looked down and made a play of stirring her tea as the dark cloud of unhappiness descended and tears welled up in her eyes. 'It's almost six flipping months since he came home. You'd think the pain would be better, not worse.' She took a handkerchief from her pocket and blew her nose. 'I'm fine most of the time, but then I'll see a couple arm in arm, or a picture of a happy bride in a magazine, and all the pain and anger comes flooding back. I don't want to love him, especially after what he's done, but I do. I just do.'

Millie covered Connie's hand with her own. 'It *will* get better.'

Connie forced a smile. 'So everyone says.'

Millie squeezed Connie's hand then picked up her slice of bread pudding. Connie did the same and they finished their tea in companionable silence while Connie pulled herself together. As she swallowed the last mouthful of tea, the café doorbell tinkled and Annie burst in.

'Thank goodness I've found you two,' she said breathlessly as she closed the door behind her. 'Pauline's twisted her ankle, so you'll have to come and sort out this afternoon's clinic.'

'Trudy will have to manage the clinic by herself like the rest of us,' said Connie.

'Miss Dutton gave Trudy the day off and she and Gladys have gone up West,' said Annie.

'Well let Miss Dutton sort out the mess,' Millie replied.

'She's gone out too, and no one knows where,' Annie said. 'But there'll be patients banging on the clinic door at two o'clock and no one to see them.'

'All right,' said Connie, putting her crockery together and standing up. 'One of us will come back and sort it out.'

'Thanks,' said Annie, giving them a grateful look. 'See you at midday.'

'That blooming woman,' said Millie crossly, tucking her scarf in tightly. 'I suppose I'll have to miss lunch again to get it all set up.'

'I just have a quick pre-delivery home visit, so if you take my two remaining morning patients, I'll cover the clinic until four, when I'm showing the new Queenies how to care for their bags,' said Connie.

*

Leaving Millie to continue on her rounds, Connie left Kate's Café and made her way north to Commercial Road.

The rain that had been falling non-stop for almost three days showed no sign of letting up, and the lorries, buses and cars had churned up the rotting veg and horse manure on the roads into a pungent slurry. In order to give herself an even chance of arriving at her morning visits in a reasonable condition, Connie had decided to leave her cycle at Munroe House and walk to the half-dozen patients on her books for the day.

Sidestepping an oily puddle, she turned into Jamaica Street, keeping as close as she could to the houses to avoid getting splashed by passing vehicles. Despite the inclement weather, the bomb site opposite the police flats was a hive of activity as bulldozers criss-crossed back and forth across the land. She nipped across the road between a lorry and an empty milk float and made her way down Smithy Street, past the Victorian school. Smithy Street had once been lined on both sides with two-up two-down houses built a century earlier. However, a high-explosive bomb had scored a direct hit at the eastern end in 1941, leaving a gaping hole where numbers 16 to 20 used to be.

The street was quiet, but on the other side of the road a black man wearing a pair of checked trousers that gathered at his ankles, a donkey jacket and a battered fedora with a colourful band around its crown and rain dripping from the brim was talking to a woman huddled in her doorway.

There were a number of black families dotted around whose ancestors had lived in the area long before Connie's had arrived from Ireland a hundred years before. Like the Jews in Spitalfields and the Chinese in Limehouse, the Caribbeans tended to keep themselves to themselves around the Royal Dock, and you didn't often see black faces this far north of the river.

Having finished his business with the lady of the house, the man slipped a small notebook back in his pocket and crossed the road. As Connie reached number 8, the young West Indian knocked on the door two houses down, which opened to reveal a bear of a man with a broad, flat face, an overhanging brow and tight dark curls.

'Goooood morning, sir, on such a fine day as this,' said the black man, flashing a set of spectacularly white teeth and looking skywards at the thunderous clouds. 'I'm sorry to trouble, but I's wondering if you or your good lady wife have the odd job that might be in need of attention.'

'Bugger off!' the man replied, his bull neck flushed purple.

'Very reasonable rates,' chirped the jolly tradesman, smiling affably at the man glowering at him. 'Just two bob an h—'

The man grabbed the West Indian's lapels and his jaunty fedora fell to the floor.

'Now you listen to me, you bloody coon,' he said, grinding the hat under his hobnail boot as he dragged the young man into the road. 'I don't want you or any of your kind knocking on my front door for anything, do you hear?' He lifted him off his feet until their noses almost touched.

'Yes, sir,' croaked the West Indian.

'That's better. Now get back to the bloody jungle where you belong.' He threw the black man away from him, and he landed in the gutter.

Connie dropped her bag and, heedless of the puddles around her feet, bent down.

'Are you all right?' she asked, taking the arm of the young West Indian floundering in the mud.

'Thank you for your kindness, miss, I's fine,' he replied shakily with a grateful smile. Leaning on her arm, he scrambled to his feet and retrieved his sodden hat.

'What's going on here, then?' a gruff voice asked.

Connie turned to see a well-fed police officer, rain dripping from his long cape, strolling across the road.

'This young man,' she indicated the black man, who was brushing himself down, 'was just enquiring if there were any odd jobs he could do when this man,' she nodded towards the brute standing in the doorway, 'assaulted him.'

The policeman cast a jaundiced eye over the West Indian, then turned to the householder. 'This man bothering you, sir?'

'Not any more he's not,' the man replied.

The policeman snorted, then turned his attention to the West Indian. 'All right, Sambo. Make yourself scarce.'

'But—'

'It's all right, miss,' cut in the black man. He doffed his hat to

Connie, then hurried away as the policeman and the householder, both with smug expression on their faces, watched him.

'What was he after?' asked the policeman.

'Work,' said Connie, giving them both a furious look.

'Lonely housewives more like, sweetheart,' the policeman replied.

The man sneered. 'Yeah, just like them Yankee coons.'

Connie straightened her hat and picked up her bag. 'He was offering to do a few odd jobs. That's all. There was no reason to attack him like that. And you,' she glared at the police officer, 'should have done something about it.'

The policeman frowned. 'A man has a right to protect his home. As far as I can tell, this gentleman acted in self-defence. A chit of a girl like you, miss, wouldn't understand about such matters, but you have to keep these darkies in their place.'

'He's right, luv,' the other man chipped in. 'A fucking good hiding is all these wogs understand.'

The policeman raised his eyebrows and glanced pointedly from the householder to Connie.

'Pardon my French, luv,' the householder said, looking distinctly unapologetic.

Connie gave him her chilliest stare. 'If you'll excuse me, I've an appointment with Mrs Webb.'

The Neanderthal took the roll-up from his lips and flicked it in an arc into the gutter. 'I know, my Val said you were coming.'

Stepping over the threshold into the main room of the house, Connie found herself in a handkerchief-sized space filled with two easy chairs either side of the tiled fireplace and a two-seat sofa pushed back under the window. There was a plain utility sideboard on top of which sat a domed Bakelite Bush wireless. There was brown lino on the floor covered with a threadbare rug in front of the glowing hearth.

'What's all that bloody racket, Ron?' shouted a woman's voice from the scullery behind.

'Nuffink, Ma,' the man Connie presumed was Ron called back. 'The nurse is here to see Val.'

The rough panel door creaked back and an old woman with a face like a pickled walnut and the bearing of a maddened sparrow walked in.

'Good morning,' said Connie. 'I'm Sister Byrne and I'm looking after your daughter-in-law during her pregnancy.'

Mrs Webb senior crossed her arms over her non-existent bosom and looked Connie up and down. 'I thought she saw you lot at the clinic.'

'She does,' Connie replied, smiling professionally. 'But I have to do a home visit to check that the house is suitable.'

'You saying my house ain't fucking clean or somefink?'

'No,' said Connie calmly, ignoring the layer of dust on the mantelshelf and the ominous stains on the flooring. 'I just need to check that you have running water, a warm room for the delivery and sufficient baby linen, that's all. Is Valerie in?'

'She's upstairs resting,' said the old woman, casting a contemptuous look at the rafters.

Ron's bull-like features twisted into an adoring expression. 'Now, now, Ma, Val has to rest up while she's carrying.'

'Rest up?' sneered his mother. 'I put in a full shift down at the rubber works until the day before you were born.' She pulled a grubby handkerchief from her sleeve. 'I couldn't have a lie-down when I felt like it. I didn't have no one to fuss over me.' She shoved the hanky into the pocket of her overall and turned. 'Well, seeing how your precious wife can't do it, I suppose I'll have to make up your lunch tin for the morning.' She sniffed and headed back to the scullery, slamming the door behind her.

Ron grinned at Connie. 'Don't mind 'er. My dad died before I was born so she had it hard. Come on, I'll show you up.'

Squeezing herself up the narrow stairway after him, Connie followed Ron Webb into the south-facing front bedroom. The room was freshly decorated with a flowery paper and there were net curtains at the window and a photo on the dressing table showing Valerie in a suit and Ron in his uniform standing side by side in front of St Dunstan's church. Their families were fanned out behind them in the usual way, except for Ron's mother, who stood next to her son looking like she was chewing a wasp.

Ron sat down on the bed beside his wife.

'Good morning, Mrs Webb,' said Connie. 'How are you?'

Valerie smiled. 'A bit tired.'

Connie put her case on the bedside table. 'Well that's to be expected. After all, you are—'

'Five months,' Valerie cut in, her eyes boring into Connie. 'I'm five months, aren't I, Sister?'

Connie held her patient's gaze for a few seconds, then lowered her eyes.

'Well, give or take, Mrs Webb,' she replied, making a play of taking her notes from her bag. 'Give or take.'

As the grandfather clock in Munroe House's hall struck 4 p.m. precisely, Connie, her nurse's bag in hand, opened the treatment room door and walked in.

'Good afternoon, nurses.'

The four student Queen's Nurses sitting at the two tables in the middle of the room stood up sharply.

'Good afternoon, Sister Byrne.'

Felicity Robb, Veronica Boscombe, Rosemary Tucker and Josephine Baxter were dressed in their stiff new uniforms and sensible flat shoes. Nurses had to supply their own uniforms. Five outfits would have been the optimum number to allow for washing, airing and ironing, but because the standard Queen's Nurse austerity uniform took six ration coupons, like any other dress, most of the nurses in Munroe House made do with three.

The trainees also had to part with their precious clothing coupons for other equipment. A shower-proof coat needed ten coupons, plus four for the hat and another six for shoes. Even with the extra ten coupons nurses received for work clothing, kitting yourself out to start Queenie training soon ate into a recruit's yearly allowance of thirty-four coupons. On top of that they had to shell out for their surgical scissors, tweezers and the like, along with a case to carry their equipment in.

All four nurses had plumped for the new aluminium case that had a waterproof covering. The cases were roughly the same size as Connie's old Gladstone bag, but one side opened flat to form a small platform.

Connie indicated that they should sit down. Taking up her position behind the desk, she put her bag in front of her and surveyed the four young women.

'I trust you've all settled in and have started to get to know each other.'

'Yes, Sister,' they replied, exchanging shy smiles.

'Good,' said Connie. 'You've got a lot to squeeze into six months, including visits, monthly lectures and an observation by the regional education officer, before you take the Queen's Institute exam in June. But don't worry,' she added, in response to the looks of terror on their faces. 'If you all work together and help each other with studying and revision, there's no reason why you won't pass with flying colours – just like the last set of students did in December.' She took a sheet of paper from her breast pocket and unfolded it. 'Now, before I show you how to care for your bags, I'd like to read out the programme for the next few days.'

The nurses took out their new notepads and pens and Connie scanned the list.

'Tomorrow morning, Sister Ashton will take you through the clinic store cupboard in the basement and explain the procedure for loaning out equipment to patients. Then in the afternoon . . .' She ran through the schedule, finishing, 'And after the weekend, you will start in earnest at Monday's morning report. Are there any questions?'

'No, Sister,' they replied as one.

Connie placed her hand on her bag. 'Now, if you could all put your nurse's case on the table, we can start. I'm only dealing with the general district bag this afternoon, not the midwifery bags Nurse Tucker and Nurse Baxter will be issued with. Although the basic principles are the same, there are, as you will appreciate, some additional items, so we'll go through that next week. As you can see, my nurse's bag is old.' She ran her hand over the worn leather. 'But in terms of care, it is exactly the same as yours.' She flipped the catch and pulled the jaws of her bag wide. 'I'd like you to open your bags and take out all the equipment.'

The nurses followed her example and carefully stacked the half-dozen pristine corked bottles, enamel bowls and jug on the tables in front of them. Connie did the same.

'You'll notice there is a detachable lining with pockets for you to store bottles and pots,' she said, releasing the catch of her own and pulling it out. 'This must be taken out every week and, if it is contaminated in any way, boiled. The same goes for your bottles. Because your cases are metal, they can be soaked in Dettol if necessary, but a thorough wipe at the end of the day should suffice.

There are also fabric bags,' she held up the cotton drawstring bag containing her kidney bowl, 'to store your metal equipment. Should any instrument become soiled, it should be washed and cleaned with soap and water in the patient's house, swabbed with Dettol, then placed in one of these' – she ferreted in the side pocket and pulled out a folded red cloth bag – 'and brought back for proper sterilising.' She tucked it away again. 'The outer compartment is for patients' notes as well as your soap, nail brush and hand towel, and this.' She pulled out a large paper bag.

'Is that for rubbish?' ventured Rosemary Tucker, raising her hand.

Connie smiled. 'No, rubbish is wrapped in newspaper and put on the fire. This is for you to store your coat in while you are in the patient's house. I'm afraid some people we visit aren't as clean as we would like, and if you're not careful, you'll find yourself taking on unwelcome visitors.'

The nurses looked puzzled.

'Bedbugs and fleas,' Connie explained.

Felicity wrinkled her nose and Veronica reached down and scratched her ankle.

'Also, check your rubber goods regularly, especially your gloves and enema tubing, as they perish easily because of the constant boiling. Now, the last thing you need is sterile gauze, and you'll find tins like this' – she lifted a rectangular tin from the table in front of her – 'in the dressing cupboard. Although patients' families are supposed to bake them in the oven ready for your visit, sometimes when you open the tin the dressings aren't sterilised, so I'd advise you to carry two. There's nothing worse than having all your equipment set out and ready only to find you haven't got any dressings.' She gave a wry smile. 'Believe me, I've done it.'

The nurses laughed.

'Excuse me, Sister,' said Veronica. 'How do you know they aren't sterile?'

'Because they aren't singed around the edges,' Connie replied. 'If the patient's family doesn't put them high enough in the oven, they don't get hot enough. That's why you should never use a home-baked dressing that doesn't have scorched edges.'

The four nurses looked amazed.

Connie raised an eyebrow. 'See, I told you we do things

differently on the district. Now, take your bag apart so you're familiar with it, then put it back together. After that, using the list in your Queen's Nurse's handbook, I want you to pack it ready for use. You'll have to look around, but you'll find everything you need in the treatment room. And remember to help each other.'

As the four nurses got up and started unclipping the innards of their bags, Connie snapped hers back in and started returning the contents to their time-honoured places. She had just slipped the jar containing her clinical thermometer into the elastic pouch when there was a little cough. She looked up.

'I'm sorry, Sister,' said Josie Baxter, raising her hand. 'But I seem to be in a bit of a muddle.'

Leaving her bag half packed, Connie went over.

'It doesn't seem to fit,' said Josie, frowning as she lifted the stiff drill lining upwards.

Connie took it from her. 'That's because you've managed to pin it inside out and upside down,' she said brightly. 'Don't worry, we'll soon fix it.'

She slid her index finger between the case and the lining and tried to unpop the fastening, but it wouldn't budge.

'You've fixed this good and proper, Nurse Baxter,' said Connie, picking at the stud with her nail.

'I'm so sorry,' said Josie. 'It looked easy when you did it.'

Connie smiled reassuringly. 'That's because I've been putting the lining in and out of my bag for over two years. But don't worry, I'll soon have it— Ouch!'

The press stud snapped free, and unfortunately so did Connie's fingernail. She stuck her finger in her mouth and tasted the metallic flavour of blood.

'I'm so sorry,' repeated Josie, looking as if she was about to burst into tears.

'It's all right,' mumbled Connie, trying to ignore her throbbing finger. 'Just turn it the right way and line up the three studs along the top.'

Josie turned the fabric back the other way and married up the fastenings.

'Oh, it is easy, isn't it?' she said, tucking the lining into the corners of her bag. 'I don't know why I made such a muddle of it.'

'Now fill your bottles and get your equipment together as I've told you, and then pack them into your case,' said Connie.

Josie gathered up the bottles from her bag and headed over to the marble bench under the window where the other three nurses were busy decanting liquids from the clinic's stock bottles into their own.

'Is that surgical spirit you're pouring, Nurse Robb?' Connie called across.

Felicity tucked a wisp of hair behind her ear and looked around. 'Yes, Sister.'

'Then don't crowd over it or the fumes will make you dizzy,' Connie warned as she returned to her case.

Leaving the nurses to complete the task she'd set them, Connie inspected her finger. Thankfully the bleeding had stopped, but with the nail torn raggedly to the inner corner, it would be sore for a week. Trying to keep it clear of anything that might snag on it, Connie finished repacking her bag, then checked through the following morning's visits while she gave the students twenty minutes to complete their task.

'Right,' she said, closing her book firmly and slipping it back where it came from. 'Let's see how you've got on.'

The students stood back from the table as Connie walked over to them.

'Not bad,' she said, snapping shut a loose fastening in Veronica's bag.

She pulled the scissors from the strapping that held them flush against the front flap of Rosemary's case. 'You want to place them so the end you grasp is on the outside,' she said, turning them around and slotting them back.

'Thank you, Sister,' said the young nurse, copying her actions and turning the tweezers and surgical clamps.

Connie's gaze ran over Josie's case. 'You've forgotten your sinus probe.' She indicated the narrow seven-inch-long instrument still sitting on the table.

'Sorry, Sister.' Josie picked it up but it slipped through her fingers so she bent down to retrieve it.

'And lastly,' Connie reached across and picked up the small bottle filled with proflavin from Felicity's bag, 'make sure—'

Josie straightened up and head-butted Connie's outstretched

arm. The lid popped off the bottle of proflavin, splashing the bright yellow lotion across the bib of Connie's apron.

There was a gasp, and Connie looked down at the glutinous golden liquid seeping through the starched white linen on to her navy uniform underneath. The dress would wash, but no amount of bleaching would restore the pinafore. She looked up at Josie, who had her hands clamped over her mouth, her blue eyes wide with panic.

'I'm so sorry,' Josie said, for the third time in the space of an hour. 'Let me get something to clean it.' She dashed over to the paper roll on the examination bench and tore off a strip, then hurried back.

Pushing aside the thought of the three precious clothing coupons she'd have to sacrifice, Connie smiled and took the handful of tissue. 'It's all right, it was an accident.'

There was a knock on the door.

'Come!' shouted Connie, dabbing at the liquid on the bib of her apron.

The door opened and Joan came in. She was wrapped up in her coat and hat and was obviously just on her way out. 'Sorry, Connie, but Mrs Tubbs' neighbour just rang to say she's in labour. I know Gladys is supposed to be on call but she's gone off with Miss Dutton somewhere and everyone else is out.'

'All right, Joan,' said Connie with a sigh. 'Mark me down for it.'

Joan picked up a stub of chalk and wrote the patient's name in one column and Connie's name alongside it on the blackboard beside the door.

'Would you do me a favour, Nurse Tucker, and get Mrs Tubbs' notes from the file, please?' said Connie.

Rosemary stood up and went to the filing cabinet.

'And I can't go to a delivery like this, so you'll have to swap aprons with me,' Connie said to Josie, reaching around to untie the bow at the small of her back. Josie did as she was asked, and Connie flipped the clean apron over her head and secured it firmly. She handed Josie the soiled one. 'Could you put this in the laundry, please?'

Rosemary came back and handed her the patient's file, and Connie picked up her bag and smiled at the four nurses. 'Well done for this afternoon, we got there in the end. Now unpack and pack your bags again, and then I want you to start familiarising yourselves with the contents of the lotion cupboard.'

Suppressing a yawn, Connie swaddled the newborn infant in a towel and handed him to his mother. 'There we are, Mrs Tubbs, all wrapped and ready.'

June Tubbs, a bright-haired young woman in her early twenties, reached out to take her firstborn.

'Look, Mum, isn't he beautiful?' she said to her mother standing on the other side of the bed.

Ida Peters, a chubby, good-natured woman, stared down misty-eyed at her grandson. 'He's the most beautiful boy in the world.'

'What are you going to call him?' asked Connie as she took off her mask and rubber gloves.

'Herbert, after me dad,' June replied.

'God rest him.' Ida crossed herself. 'I only wish he'd lived to see his little namesake. Leave that, Sister,' she said as Connie went to gather up the soiled sheets. 'You've done enough and you ought to get home to bed.'

Connie was happy to do as she was told, as it was now after three o'clock in the morning. Leaving mother and daughter to themselves, she made her way down the narrow stone stairs to the street. She tucked her scarf tightly around her neck and pulled her gloves on, then put her case in the front basket of her bike and unfastened it from the railing.

The earlier downpour had passed, and now the puddles left on the pavements and in the gutters sparkled with ice. With the chilly air nipping at her nose and cheeks, Connie jumped on her bike and pedalled slowly towards Commercial Road. A green night bus carrying a handful of workers ambled past, followed by the occasional lorry. In the distance, the booming sound of the barges knocking into each other as they sat anchored in the docks echoed in the still air.

With the traffic lights by Cavell Street flashing blindly at the empty road, Connie turned into Sutton Street. As she headed for Munroe House's rear gates, she spotted a familiar figure crossing the road.

'You're out late!' she called.

Phyllis Tatum turned around just as Connie reached her. Although she had a fur wrapped around her shoulders and wore an elegant beaded evening dress, her usually perfectly set hair was dishevelled and her make-up was smudged. There was also what looked like a fresh bruise on her cheek.

'What on earth happened?' Connie asked.

'There was a bit of trouble at the club,' Phyllis replied. 'A flash type downed a bottle of Scotch then started cutting up rough.'

'Did you call the police?'

Phyllis shook her head. 'Our own security handled it. We have some very wealthy and well-known clients who pay good money for our discretion. If it got out that the police had been visiting, we'd lose their custom and the club would be out of business,' she said, smiling wearily. 'But don't worry, it's not the first time, and I'll be right as rain after a bath and a sleep.'

'Are you sure?' said Connie. 'I'll pop in tomorrow afternoon and ch—'

'Pop in tomorrow by all means.' Phyllis put her satin-gloved hand on Connie's arm. 'But as a friend, for coffee.'

Connie smiled. 'I'd like that, but I won't be able to get to you until four.'

'Perfect,' said Phyllis, patting her arm. 'Grace will be home from school and she'd love to see you, I'm sure.' She raised an eyebrow. 'Now get yourself home to bed, Sister Byrne. You almost look as bad as me.'

Chapter Eleven

'I'll have three pounds of King Edwards,' said Maud, jabbing her finger at the pile of potatoes at the end of the barrow. 'But make sure you knock some of that mud off before you weigh them, or I'll have the council after you.'

Paddy O'Rourke, the larger-than-life stallholder who'd been selling Maud her weekend veg for the past thirty years, grinned. 'Right you are, Mrs B.'

Connie and her mother were halfway along the Waste, on the opposite side of the road from the London Hospital. Maud got her Tuesday and Wednesday meat and green groceries around the corner from her house in Salmon Lane. Thursday she put on her hat and jumped on a bus to meet her sisters Peggy and Dolly in Roman Road. The three of them had a morning mooching around the stalls for bargains followed by an in-depth discussion about everything and everybody over pie and mash. But every Friday, come Luftwaffe or Doodlebug, Maud would trundle her rickety old pushchair up White Horse Lane and along Mile End Road to the age-old market for her main weekly shop. The unenviable job of accompanying her on these weekly pilgrimages usually fell to Mo, but as she had a doctor's appointment and Bernie's baby had a cold, Connie had reluctantly taken her place.

They'd already walked along the Waste once so her mother could have a look and pass comment on all the butchers' windows, which was pointless because as she was registered with Matthews she had to get her meat from them anyhow. In addition, they couldn't go more than a couple of feet without her mother running into an acquaintance. Feeling more like a five-year-old than a twenty-five-year-old, Connie was forced to stand beside her mother and listen to the same chat about the shocking price of things in the shops and the latest feud with the neighbours over and over again.

Taking the spike with the price chalked on it out of the mountain of potatoes, Paddy dug deep with the brass scoop and heaved it onto the claw of his scales. With a flick of the wrist worthy of any card-sharp, he put on and took off various weights until the beam rocked evenly on the central fulcrum. The second it hovered, he grabbed the scoop and deposited the contents into Maud's bag. Then, taking a stubby pencil from behind his ear, he scribbled the price on a paper bag.

'Can I add in half of long and round?' he asked, holding the scoop poised and ready.

Maud nodded. 'As long as the carrots aren't those blooming twigs you sold me last week.'

Paddy plunged into the carrot and onion mix and did his sleight of hand with the weights again. 'No Mo?' he asked as he shovelled the vegetables in on top of the potatoes.

Maud shook her head. 'Got to see the school quack about her eldest's flat feet.' She pointed at a cabbage on a hook overhead. 'Stick that in, will you?'

Paddy took it down and placed it in her bag. 'So she got the pleasure of your company instead,' he said, smiling at Connie.

Connie forced a smile. 'Yes.'

'It's so long since she did the Friday shop with me, I'm surprised you even remember her,' said Maud.

'Of course I do,' beamed Paddy. 'Everyone on the market knows Sister Byrne. And a credit she is to you, Mrs B.'

'How's your daughter and her little one?' asked Connie, before her mother could speak again.

A soft expression crept across Paddy's weather-beaten face. 'Just grand so she is, and expecting another.'

'So how many's that?' asked Maud.

'Seven,' Paddy replied, grandfatherly pride beaming out from him. 'And every one of them a joy to behold. Is that your lot, Mrs B?'

'As you haven't got any parsnips, I suppose it'll have to be.'

Paddy shook his head mournfully. 'I might be lucky and have some spring greens in a week or two, but what with the petrol shortages and the weather, everything's in short supply.'

Maud rolled her eyes and tutted. 'You wouldn't think we'd won the war, would you? All right, what's the damage?'

Paddy retrieved his pencil and, after dabbing the end on his tongue, totted up her bill. 'One and three.'

Maud fished into her bag for her purse and handed him a florin. Paddy counted out coppers from the scooped-out wooden block that served as a till and handed them to her. Maud put the change in her purse and Connie placed the bag of veg on the seat of the pushchair.

'Are we done?' she said, praying that they were.

Her mother gave her a sharp look. 'What's your rush?'

'I just thought after three hours of trudging up and down the same stretch of pavement in the freezing cold, you would have got everything,' Connie replied. 'And I am going to the pictures with Millie later.'

Her mother regarded her thoughtfully. 'Is she still knocking around with that copper from Arbour Square?'

'I should hope so,' Connie replied. 'She's marrying him in June. I did tell you. Don't you remember?'

'Of course I do, I'm not doolally,' said her mother, who had clearly remembered no such thing. 'But if you don't mind me saying, she's not much of a friend, is she?'

'I don't know how you've come to that conclusion,' snapped Connie.

'Well if you're such good chums, why hasn't she got her chap to introduce you to one of his mates?'

Connie looked heavenward. 'For goodness' sake, Mother! Give it a rest.'

Maud took hold of the pushchair. 'I'm sorry, Connie, I speak as I find.' She kicked off the brake. 'Now I just need to get my meat and we can head home.' Barging her way between a group of women by the second-hand clothes stall, she headed for the butcher's next to the bookie's.

There was a line of prams outside the shop containing infants either asleep or grizzling, all of them wrapped up like knitted parcels against the cold. The older ones, strapped in with harnesses, sat up with dummies stuck in their mouths or clutching bottles.

Shoving her battered pushchair to the end of the line, Maud indicated the shiny new coach-built pram with fashionable matching cover and bag. 'Someone's got money to burn,' she said.

'Probably the first grandchild in the family,' Connie replied, lifting out her mother's shopping bag.

Maud bent over and peered in. 'Awww, bless,' she said, a sentimental expression lighting her heavy features. 'Look, Con, this one can only be a month or two old.'

Connie, who spent most of her waking hours looking at babies, sighed and looked into the pram. The baby, swaddled in blankets, lay with its head turned to one side, its delicate eyelids flickering and its small mouth pulled into a tiny rosebud. Although most of its head was covered by a crocheted bonnet with pompoms on each side, a wispy fringe of dark hair fanned its face.

'I've never seen a hat like that,' she said.

'Looks like a Yid kid,' her mother sniffed.

'What, outside a gentile butcher's?' Connie replied. 'And look.' She pointed at a small silver pendant pinned to the baby's shawl. 'There's a St Christopher.'

'They're lucky no one's nicked that.' Her mother's simpering smile returned. 'I wonder if it's a boy or a girl.'

'Hissa boy,' said a woman's sharp voice.

Connie turned to find Maria standing behind them. Her features had none of the chubbiness of a new mother, and her hair, luxurious and black, was swept up under the wide-brimmed hat framing her face. Her figure, too, had returned to what must have been its original proportions, the mustard coat she was wearing hugging her curves.

Before she could stop herself, Connie's eyes fixed on the man standing beside Maria, the man whose handsome, angular face invaded her dreams almost nightly, leaving her empty and aching at dawn. Charlie was wearing a brown-striped suit that fitted him like a glove, with a Windsor knot at his throat and a hat sitting at a jaunty angle over one eye. Although she knew she should look away, she couldn't, and as her gaze locked with his, everything else around her faded. Charlie's clear blue eyes ran over her face, and the corners of his mouth lifted ever so slightly. Her heart did a little dance, then a backward flip in response to the familiar expression.

'His name is Filippo,' said Maria in a triumphal tone that sliced through Connie's chaotic emotions. She dragged her eyes from Charlie.

'Lovely name, and congratulations,' she said, the words clogging her throat. 'To both of you.'

Maud smiled pleasantly at Charlie. 'How's your mother? She must be loving having a screaming baby in the house and your wife's plaster saints on her mantelshelf. I bet that causes a bit of a stir in her bible study group.'

'As it happens, we—'

'Carlos' mama, she too religious,' interrupted Maria. 'Too, too, 'ow you say?' She waved her hands in circular motions. 'She quarrel. Too much disagreement between me,' she tapped her chest dramatically, 'and mother-in-law, so we go. Nice house in Shandy Street.' She gave Connie a smug look. 'We much happy, yes, Carlos?' she glanced at Charlie. He didn't reply, just gazed broodingly at Connie.

Maria looked back at Connie and her eyes narrowed. 'You know Charlie long time. You think my baby look like 'im?' she said, gazing adoringly down at the sleeping infant.

'I thought it was a Jew kid myself,' said Maud, giving the baby a contemptuous glance.

Maria's coal-black eyes sparked with fury. She grabbed the handle of her pram, then, shooting another hateful look at Connie and her mother, stormed off down the road.

Maud watched her for a moment, then turned to Charlie. 'Do give your mother my regards, Carlos.' She ambled past him and into the shop. Connie went to follow her, but as she came abreast of him, Charlie caught her hand and she looked up into the face she'd loved forever. The urge to reach up and kiss the familiar lips almost overwhelmed her, but mercifully, she held it back.

His eyes scrutinised her face. 'You're looking very pretty today, Connie.'

Connie's heart soared for a second, then she snatched her hand away and stumbled into the shop.

With a steaming mug of cocoa in each hand, Connie kicked Millie's door gently with her toe. It opened immediately. Millie was in her dressing gown with her hair wound up in a towel after her bath. Connie was in her night clothes too, minus the towel as she'd dried her hair while Millie had been soaking.

'Mind my shoes by the bed,' Millie said, as Connie padded into her friend's bedroom.

Millie's room was a mirror image of her own, with a dressing table, an easy chair with more springs than stuffing, which Millie had brightened up with a couple of colourful cushions, a sink with a rectangular mirror above, a small fireplace with an electric fire and a wrought-iron bedstead, which Millie had covered with her own quilted bedspread. There was also a standard single wardrobe on which was hanging the wedding dress that Connie had once dreamed of wearing as she walked down the aisle.

She could have sold it easily enough, but when Millie announced her engagement, Connie offered it to her best friend instead.

Turning away from the wedding gown, Connie put the drinks on the bedside table and settled herself on her friend's bed. 'So how goes the preparation for the big day?'

Millie unrolled the towel and sat on the stool in front of her dressing table. She picked up her hairbrush.

'Well, after a lot of trudging about, we managed to book the Hoop and Grapes for the reception,' she replied, brushing through her wet hair. 'Uncle Bill is giving me away, Uncle Tony's driving me to the church and Aunt Ruby is making the cake.'

'Well I bet you're glad you've got all that sorted at last,' said Connie.

'Yes, I am,' said Millie.

In the mirror, Connie saw concern flit across her friend's face. 'What's wrong, Millie?'

Millie put her brush beside her trinket tray then turned to face her. 'Alex has been accepted as an officer in the Palestine police force. A letter arrived in the early post, and he waylaid me in a police car to tell me.'

'Why didn't you tell me at lunch time?' asked Connie.

'I needed to get it straight in my mind before I told anyone,' Millie replied.

Connie gave her friend a sympathetic look. 'You're worried about your mum, aren't you?'

Millie stood up and came over to sit on the bed at the opposite end from Connie.

'She tries to hide it and is even talking about coming out to see us when we told her but . . .' tears welled in her friend's eyes.

Connie leant across and squeezed Millie's hand. 'It's only natural she should miss you, but I know she wouldn't want to stand in the way of your happiness,' said Connie.

'You're right.' Millie put on a brave smile. 'I'm sure it will be fine once everything is sorted out. Now,' She leaned over and took a dress pattern from her bedside locker. 'What do you think about this for your bridesmaid's dress?'

Connie took the Butterick envelope from her.

Millie picked up her cocoa. 'It takes three and a half yards, but my aunt has a friend who works in a clothing factory in Shoreditch, so we might be able to get a couple of remnants off rations.'

'What colour are you thinking of?' asked Connie, her eyes still fixed on the sketched image of two girls wearing stylish afternoon dresses.

'Well, that sort of depends on what's in stock, but I thought with your colouring perhaps a fern green.'

Connie handed the pattern back. 'Sounds perfect.'

Before she could stop herself, her gaze flickered over to the wedding dress hanging on the door of the wardrobe, and a lump formed in her throat.

'You are all right with me wearing your dress, aren't you, Connie?' asked Millie.

Connie lowered her eyes and blew across the froth on her drink. 'Don't be daft.'

Millie reached across and took her free hand. 'No, really, you would say, wouldn't you?'

Connie smiled brightly. 'Millie, you'll look beautiful, absolutely stunning, in fact, and I'm sure Alex will agree.' She gave a hollow laugh. 'And I wouldn't want to wear it to marry someone else the next time. That's if there *is* a next time.'

Millie rolled her eyes. 'Now who's being daft? I bet this time next year you'll be asking me if I like the matron-of-honour outfit you've chosen for me.'

Swallowing a couple of mouthfuls of cocoa, Connie looked up.

'I saw Charlie along Whitechapel market on Friday,' she said in a matter-of-fact tone. 'He was with Maria and their baby.'

Millie's brown eyes stretched wide with astonishment. 'What did he say?'

The lump in Connie's throat made its presence known again, but she shrugged. 'Nothing much.' Feeling tears start to gather, she buried her nose in her cocoa.

Millie put her drink on the bedside table. 'I tell you what,' she said. 'Why don't I pop down to the kitchen and see if there are any of those jam tarts left over from teatime.'

Connie smiled. 'Sounds just the ticket.'

Millie grinned. She shoved her feet into her slippers and left the room.

Connie's gaze drifted back to the wardrobe. She put her cocoa next to Millie's and got off the bed. Walking across the room, she studied the dress she'd made so lovingly for a few moments, then, taking one of the sleeves, she closed her eyes and pressed the fabric to her cheek.

'They here, Carlos!' screamed Maria, pointing towards the ticket barrier for platform 4.

They were on Waterloo station's main concourse on a brisk March afternoon. It was two o'clock, and although Charlie had tried to tell Maria it wouldn't take an hour and forty minutes to get from Stepney Green, to avoid yet another row they'd set out at 12.20 as she'd insisted. This meant they'd been waiting around for almost an hour for the train from Southampton, which had arrived just five minutes ago.

On the pretext that he'd run out of cigarettes, he'd left Maria feeding the baby in the station tea room while he had a swift half and a whisky chaser in a nearby pub. Now that he was about to come face to face with his in-laws again, he wondered if he should have had a double.

'Mama!' yelled Maria, waving frantically.

Rosa Fabrini, who had come through the barrier ahead of her husband, looked up. Catching sight of her daughter, she waved back as Maria, pushing the pram containing their sleeping son, dashed across the concourse, narrowly missing several passers-by. She hugged and kissed her mother before turning to her father. Rosa pulled out a handkerchief and dabbed her eyes, and even Bruno's heavy features softened a fraction. They all embraced again, and then, waving their arms around as if swatting flies, started an animated conversation around the pram.

Taking a pack of Bensons from his pocket and lighting one, Charlie strolled over to join them. They carried on their high-pitched babble and squawking for a good five minutes before Maria's mother drew breath and noticed him.

Although Rosa's hair retained its ebony sheen courtesy of a bottle and her dark eyes were framed by wrinkles rather than her daughter's thick lashes, she was in essence an older version of Maria. She had Maria's petite frame too, and despite having borne four children could have easily fitted into her daughter's clothes. Dressed in a stylish navy suit and matching hat, she looked a good deal younger than her forty-five years.

'Welcome to London, Mrs Fabrini,' Charlie said, smiling at her.

'*Grazie*,' Rosa replied, inclining her head.

Charlie turned his attention to the man beside her. Thickset and with paws rather than hands, Bruno Fabrini had been the head chef in the town's swanky hotel but had taken to the hills to lead the partisans when war broke out. Tough, pugnacious and uncompromising, he was reputed to have strangled a fleeing German he'd caught hiding in a shepherd's cottage. He'd probably have done the same to Charlie for ruining his daughter's honour had Charlie's commanding officer not intervened.

'Mr Fabrini,' Charlie said, offering his hand.

After just a moment's hesitation, Bruno took it, crushing Charlie's fingers in his vice-like grip.

'Good trip?' Charlie asked chirpily, extracting his hand.

Bruno grunted by way of a reply.

Maintaining his jolly expression, Charlie rubbed his palms together briskly. 'Right then, enough of the chit-chat. If you get your things, I'll find a taxi.'

Maria frowned. 'Mama and Papa had long train trip and need drink first.'

Charlie glanced at the clock hanging above his head. He was meeting Tommy in the Grave Maurice at five and had reckoned on having his in-laws bundled in a taxi and away by four.

'I just thought they'd like to get settled in their hotel,' he said.

Maria shook her head. 'You get luggage and we have coffee and talk.'

Before he could argue, they'd set off towards the tea room, flapping their hands and jabbering away again. Damping down his annoyance, he turned and made his way back to platform 4.

By the time Charlie had located their two suitcases from the baggage van and fetched them back to the tea room, his son was awake and cradled in his new grandmother's arms. She and Maria were clacking away ten to the dozen while Bruno sipped his drink and smiled benignly at his womenfolk.

'Oh Charlie,' Rosa exclaimed, pressing her crimson lips to his son's downy head. ''E's so . . . so . . .' She frowned and clicked her painted fingers. ''Ow say *bello*?'

'Handsome,' Maria replied, tickling her son under the chin.

'Takes after his old man then,' Charlie replied, dropping their surprisingly heavy suitcases on the floor.

'Or his *nonno*,' said Maria, looking lovingly across at her father. Bruno puffed out his chest and basked in the adoration of his only daughter. 'Tell Carlos about the fish shop, Papa,' she said.

'Fish?' asked Charlie, trying to look interested. 'I thought you ran a restaurant?'

'Not in Italia,' laughed Maria. 'Here. Papa's got a shop here.'

'But you've only just arrived,' said Charlie.

'I write to my mother's cousin's grandson who owns a restaurant in Is-lin-g-ton,' explained Bruno with a shrug. 'I tell him to find me food business and he found a fish shop called Murray's near you in Stepney Green.'

Charlie looked incredulously at his in-laws. 'You're buying a chip shop?'

'If it has good trade,' Bruno replied.

'*Si*, we going tomorrow and see,' added Rosa, then explained something to Maria in Italian.

Maria looked pleased. 'Mama says there is six rooms for family above, so room for everyone, Charlie.'

Rosa kissed the baby in her arms again. 'And *molti, molti bambini*.'

'But who's going to run it when you go back to Italy?' Charlie asked.

Rosa looked puzzled. 'No back. All family have new life in England.'

An image of Maria's three brothers, all of whom looked disturbingly like their father, rose up in his mind.

'Yes,' said Maria. 'Stephan and Gina coming in three months with children, and Victor and Tina coming after with Nico and Marcia later. Cousin Tito's coming too, soon.' She smiled pleasantly. 'It's a nice *sorpresa*. No?'

Charlie didn't reply.

Bruno threw back the last of his drink and pulled a face. 'The British no make coffee,' he said, getting out of his chair.

'Perhaps we should open coffee bar too, Papa,' said Maria.

He grinned. 'Maybe we will when cousin Tito arrives, but now we should go.'

Rosa rose to her feet and put her grandson back in his pram. 'I push *piccola mela*.'

Maria stood and slipped her arm through her father's. 'And I'll walk with my *big* apple.'

They laughed and Bruno patted his daughter's hand affectionately as they made their way towards the door, chatting away in Italian. Wearily, Charlie took out his packet of cigarettes again and lit one. Holding the cigarette firmly between his lips, he picked up his in-laws' suitcases and followed.

Securing her bicycle to the nearest lamp post, Connie made her way to the last house in Nelson Street. She grasped the lion's head knocker and rapped on the front door. There was a pause before it was opened by a fresh-faced young woman with a colourful scarf wrapped around her head, a curly blonde fringe skimming her pencilled brows.

'Good morning, Mrs Henstock,' said Connie pleasantly. 'I'm Sister Byrne. Dr Quinn asked me to call to dress your leg ulcer, but,' she cast her eyes over the women's slender lower legs, 'perhaps I've got the wrong address.'

'Right address, ducks, wrong pins,' the woman replied, opening the door for Connie to enter. 'You'll find 'erself and her bacon and eggs in the front room. I'm 'er char.'

Connie blinked with surprise. At nine in the morning on a weekday you would find every woman in the street on her knees scrubbing her step and a circular section of pavement immediately in front of it. An hour later those same women would be hanging out of windows polishing the glass with newspaper before dusting, polishing and sweeping the whole house from top to bottom. It was a matter of reputation and pride, not to mention fierce competition between the housewives. Not doing your own daily chores wasn't something you boasted about.

Leaving Connie standing on the coconut mat, Mrs Henstock's daily help ambled off towards the back of the house.

Connie knocked on the door to her left. 'District nurse.'

'Come,' called a feeble voice from within.

The room was decorated with a dark, Edwardian-style floral wallpaper, with brown-painted woodwork, and lace panels rather than net curtains at the window. There was a solid sideboard against the longest wall with a whitework embroidered runner along its length, a pair of Japanese-style vases at each end and a bowl full of wax fruit taking pride of place in the centre. A small drop-leaf mahogany table stood at the far end of the room; on top of it was an aspidistra and a pre-war Philco People's set, out of which drifted the strains of Anton and his Orchestra playing a selection from *The Merry Widow*.

There was a large pre-war leather sofa with bulbous arms and squat legs under the window and matching armchairs either side of the oval tiled fireplace. Mrs Henstock, a short, slightly built woman with a pale complexion, sat in the chair facing the window with a fringed tartan shawl over her legs and her feet up on a pouffe. Although a good ten years younger than Connie's mother, she was dressed in the lilac, lace and pearls of a much older woman. Her honey-coloured hair, which would have suited a modern bob, was scooped up into a large topknot and held in place by tortoiseshell combs.

Connie smiled. 'Mrs Henstock?'

'Yes, dear,' said the woman, waving a limp hand for Connie to come closer. 'Thank goodness you've come. It's so painful.'

'I'm sure it is,' Connie said soothingly. 'Dr Quinn asked me to dress your wound.'

Mrs Henstock smiled sweetly. 'So kind.'

Connie slipped off her coat and laid it over the arm of the chair opposite, then knelt down in front of Mrs Henstock and put her bag on the floor beside her.

The older woman's agreeable expression slipped a little.

'Would you mind not putting your bag on the rug, dear? It's Persian and I wouldn't want it to snag.' She pulled a copy of the *Star* from beside her chair and Connie slipped it under her bag. 'I'm afraid you'll think me a terrible fuss,' laughed Mrs Henstock lightly.

'Not at all. If you could just remove your stocking, I'll take a quick peek before I get started.'

Moving the shawl aside, Mrs Henstock lifted her skirt and, after taking off an elasticated garter, unrolled her left stocking to reveal a toe-to-knee bandage. Although there was no sign of blood or fluid leaking through, from the size of the all-encompassing dressing, Connie guessed the wound beneath would need a lot of gauze squares to cover it.

She rocked back on her heels and stood up. 'I'm going to get myself some boiled water and set out my equipment so I have everything to hand before I take a look. Is there a stool or table I could use?'

'That one there,' said Mrs Henstock, pointing at an occasional table next to the sofa.

Connie fetched it and covered it with newspaper, then went to the kitchen, returning within a few moments with freshly boiled water from the kettle in a chipped cream jug. Setting the jug on the edge of the table, she opened her case.

Mrs Henstock coughed. Connie looked up.

'You will be careful . . . with the water, I mean,' Mrs Henstock twittered. 'It's just that I've only recently had the floor buffed and polished, and water would so . . .' She gave a girly shrug.

'Of course,' said Connie, struggling to preserve her pleasant manner as she set out her equipment.

Having got everything ready and to hand, Connie knelt down again. After spreading out the centre page of the newspaper ready to catch the soiled bandages, she untied the reef knot next to Mrs Henstock's knee.

'This is very neat,' she said as she unwound the evenly spaced herringbone pattern around the older woman's leg.

'My son Malcolm did it,' Mrs Henstock replied, puffing out her modest chest. 'He was in the medical section of the Home Defence.'

'He wasn't called up, then?'

The older woman shook her head. 'He so wanted to go and fight like all his pals, but he has weak bronchials.' She tapped her chest. 'Inherited it from his father, God rest him, so we got a Harley Street chest specialist to certify him exempt. He did his bit, though, let me tell you. Out and about each night dragging people from bombed houses and patching them up.' Her eyes filled with motherly pride. 'That's him. My one and only,' she said, looking up at the photo on the mantelshelf.

Connie followed her gaze to a picture of a man wearing a box-shouldered suit and standing against a painted classical backdrop. He was proudly holding a roll of paper with ribbons dangling from it and grinning at the camera with a pipe clenched between his teeth. Judging by his features, Malcolm Henstock looked to be only a year or two older than Connie herself. He was wearing a tweed jacket and twill slacks, an outfit that might have made some men of his age look drab and out of date, but on Malcolm Henstock's strapping figure it gave him an air of solid competence and dependability.

'That was taken in '38, when he received his East London College surveying diploma in the People's Palace at Mile End,' Mrs Henstock explained. 'He's got one of the top jobs in the council highways department now.'

Connie dropped the unravelled bandage on the newspaper beside her and surveyed the half-dozen squares of gauze on Mrs Henstock's leg. She picked up a pair of tweezers and Mrs Henstock gripped the arms of the chair.

'You won't hurt me, will you?' she asked, her eyes full of terror.

'I'll try not to,' Connie replied. 'I'll try and ease it off, but if it's stuck, I'll wet it. Are you ready?'

Pressing her thin lips together determinedly, Mrs Henstock nodded, then turned her head.

Steeling herself for ten minutes of picking encrusted dressings off inch by inch, Connie tucked the ends of the tweezers under one of the squares. It fell off surprisingly quickly and plopped on to the paper below.

Mrs Henstock's knuckles cracked. 'I'm sorry,' she whispered. 'It's so painful.'

'I'm sorry too, but it has to come off,' Connie replied firmly. Tucking her instrument under the next gauze, she lifted it an eighth of an inch. It slid off, taking the rest of the dressing with it. Mrs Henstock gave a little yelp.

'Can you stop, Sister,' she said, taking a lacy handkerchief from her sleeve and mopping her brow. 'I'll have to have a moment or two to recover.'

While Mrs Henstock regained her composure, Connie studied the flat, pink, moist wound the size of a half crown on her patient's inner ankle.

'Well,' she said as Mrs Henstock's breathing returned to normal. 'I'm pleased to say I don't think this will take too long to heal.'

Mrs Henstock clasped her hands together and looked heavenward.

With an experienced hand Connie re-dressed the wound, using a very much smaller dressing. When she'd finished, she wrote out a set of new patient's notes and took her payment book out of the side pocket of her bag.

'That will be one and thruppence a visit,' she said. 'Payable weekly every Monday.'

'Thank you, my dear,' said Mrs Henstock, inclining her head imperially.

'Though to be honest,' Connie continued, 'you could just visit the daily dressing clinic at Munroe House. The walk would help your circulation and it would save you the cost of the daily nurse.'

Mrs Henstock smiled condescendingly. 'I'm afraid my son wouldn't hear of it. He spares no expense where his "dear mother" is concerned.'

'He's not married then?' asked Connie, almost certain of the answer.

Mrs Henstock shook her head. 'Of course, he's had many girl-friends; in fact he was walking out with one of the girls in the office a little while back.' She pulled a sour face. 'But it didn't last. Not that I interfered or anything, but I wasn't surprised. The first time I met her, I knew she wasn't right for him.' She laughed. 'I mean, she was a typist, for goodness' sake. And,' her gaze returned to the portrait on the mantelshelf, 'as he's so fond of telling me, I'm his best girl.'

*

Three days later, Josie closed Mrs Archer's back door firmly, dodged under a line of billowing washing strung across the small yard and joined Connie, who was standing by their bicycles.

'I really am sorry about the picture frame,' she said. 'Do you think I should pop back later and speak to her daughter?'

They had managed to visit six patients that morning without Josie knocking anything over, but it was only a matter of time, as Mrs Archer's Edwardian picture frame had found to its cost.

'It's all right, I'll do it later,' Connie replied. 'If you do have to pay for the damage, you can apply to the Association to recompense you, but with funds the way they are, I wouldn't hold my breath.' She took her notebook from her pocket and opened it. 'Now, standing around here won't get the work done. We've just got Mrs Dutch's insulin, and then after that we can head back for lunch. And never mind what the Dutton says, call me Connie when we're by ourselves.' She concluded as she heaved her bike off the outside wall of the toilet.

Side by side they wheeled their bikes out of the dank alleyway between the houses and into the warmth of the early spring sunshine, then joined the traffic on the Highway, giving a wide berth to the brewer's dray parked outside the Pole and Compass. They turned into Garnet Street, then over the swing bridge spanning the cut between East Dock and Shadwell Basin, before bouncing across the cobbles as they passed Wapping Wall.

They'd just come abreast of the Prospect of Whitby when a crowd of some fifty men, dressed in the rough clothes and cloth caps of dock workers, spilled out from Millard Street on their right and filled the road, walking four or five abreast. At the head of the procession two men held a long banner depicting a pair of solidly built individuals, one brandishing a docker's hook and the other shouldering a barrel, with the words *Riverside and Wharf Workers Union* embroidered between the images. Behind the leaders, other men carried home-made standards proclaiming *Jobs for Our Brave Boys* and *We Won the War Not Foreigners*.

As the mob advanced, chanting and waving their fists, a delivery lorry pulled over, as did a milk float with crateloads of empty bottles. Connie and Josie hopped off their bikes and, along with a handful of other pedestrians, moved to stand on the pavement.

'Morning, Sister!'

Connie looked around to see Ron Webb, dressed in his shirt-sleeves and rough cords, step out from the ranks and bowl over to them.

'Morning, Mr Webb,' she replied. 'What's going on?'

'We just got wind that the council's taken on a couple of bloody Cypriot families in Stebbins House, so as the shop steward I naturally called the boys out,' he replied, thumbing over his shoulder at the men trudging along behind him. 'We're marching to the town hall to register our protest at what we in the Riverside and Wharf Workers Union regard as a betrayal of everything our members fought for.'

'But hasn't Stebbins House been condemned?' asked Connie.

'It has,' replied Mr Webb.

'Well then, whoever the council put in there will have to move again anyway,' said Connie.

Mr Webb drew a long breath. 'That's not the point,' he said, as if explaining to a child. 'It's bad enough with the Four Per Cent building up in Thrawl Street crammed full of Yids, without having this end of the manor taken over by foreigners. Stebbins House was built for honest working-class families, not the Bubble and Squeaks.'

'I thought they were Cypriot?' said Josie innocently.

A mottled flush stained Mr Webb's unshaven cheeks. 'Same difference as far as I'm concerned and I wouldn't give you tuppence for the lot of 'em. You'd better watch out too. I 'eard as how some hospitals are thinking of shipping in darkie nurses from the colonies.'

'To be honest, Mr Webb, we're so short of nurses in Munroe House that if they found SRNs on the moon I wouldn't worry.' Connie smiled pleasantly. 'Now, I've got a list of patients as long as your arm and I want to be at the other end of Wapping before the dinner hooters sound. Give my regards to your wife,' she said, pressing on the pedal and inching forward.

Out of the corner of her eye she saw Josie do the same, and as the last of the protesters filed past, the two nurses set off again. Mr Webb stood aside but shouted after them. 'You might not be worried now, Sister, but you won't be so blooming jolly when some woman with a bone through her nose takes your job.'

'Who on earth was that?' asked Josie as they bumped westwards over the cobbles.

'Mr Webb,' Connie replied. 'I'm looking after his wife. Now let's get a move o—'

Her voice was drowned out by the sound of a dozen hooters. The factory and wharf doors that lined both sides of Wapping High Street burst open and men hurried out, eager to make the most of their forty-five-minute midday break. Almost to a man they were dressed in the uniform of baggy canvas trousers, shirt-sleeves and cloth caps, with roll-ups dangling from their mouths. They swarmed around as Connie and Josie rode on, many muttering suggestions about bed baths and black stockings as they passed.

They were almost through the surge of men when a younger group, with slicked-back hair and flamboyantly knotted ties, stepped out of a bonded warehouse just to their right. The leader, a tall chap with russet hair and his hands in his pockets, stepped out into the two nurses' path, causing them both to slam on their brakes and lurch to a stop.

'Oi, darling! Can you take my pulse?' he asked, flapping the front of his trousers. His mates jostled around hooting and whistling.

'Go on, Ginger,' shouted someone at the back.

Josie's cheeks flamed and she looked down.

'Just ignore them,' said Connie, cycling forward to put herself between her student and the crowd.

With an injured look, Ginger threw his arms wide. 'That ain't very friendly, is it?' he said as his friends elbowed each other. 'And just when I was going to offer myself for a bed bath.' He winked at Connie. 'If you know what I mean.'

Despite her pounding heart, Connie gave him her frostiest matron look.

'Excuse me,' she said, tonelessly, pushing her bike forward.

Ginger stood firm for a couple of seconds, then his assured gaze wavered and he stood aside.

'No need to take on, luv, I was just having a bit of fun,' he said as Connie swept past him, taking Josie in her wake.

'Goodness, I was scared to death back there,' said Josie as soon as the crowd of men were out of earshot. 'But you were so calm.'

'On the outside,' replied Connie. 'And that's why I wanted to get down Wapping High Street before midday. If you ever get caught like that, Josie, don't joke or argue with them. It only makes them worse. And as they said in the war, keep calm and . . .'

'. . . keep pedalling,' said Josie with a rueful smile.

Connie smiled back. As they slowed to let a dust cart pass, Josie's stomach rumbled.

'I'll tell you what,' said Connie. 'You cycle back and get your dinner, and I'll do Mrs Dutch's insulin.'

'Are you sure?' asked Josie.

Connie nodded. 'Just as long as you leave me some shepherd's pie.'

Connie held up her hand mirror and looked at her rear view in the larger mirror attached to her dressing table, then moved the hand mirror from side to side to try to get a better angle. She watched the fluted skirt of her green dress swish back and forth a couple of times, then took it off and threw it on the bed to join the red polka-dot frock and her smart maroon gown. Going back to the wardrobe, she pulled out her new royal-blue dress with the Peter Pan collar and slipped that over her head. Fastening the tiny daisy-shaped buttons at the front, she tied the sash and inspected the result in the dressing table glass.

There was a knock at the door.

'It's open,' she called, quickly brushing her bouncing curls into some sort of order to complete the effect.

The old brass handle rattled and Millie, wearing her dressing gown, walked in.

'I didn't know you were going out or I wouldn't have made you a drink,' she said, holding up two mugs.

'I'm not,' replied Connie. 'I'm trying to decide on an outfit for Martha and Pete's wedding next Saturday. Does this look OK?'

'Very nice,' said Millie, putting Connie's mug on a copy of *Woman's Weekly* on the bedside cabinet. 'The colour suits you. I'm sure you'll have a wonderful time.'

'I'm sure I would if Charlie wasn't Pete's best man,' Connie replied.

Millie kicked off her slippers and made herself comfortable on the bed. 'That could be a bit awkward.'

'Yes, won't it? Especially with Maria being there too,' Connie replied

She removed the dress, hanging it and her other clothes back in the wardrobe before shrugging on her dressing gown.

'Still, there's safety in numbers,' Millie added jollily as Connie sat on the bed next to her. 'So you'll be able to avoid talking to him.'

Connie smiled wanly. 'Speaking to him isn't the problem,' she replied. 'It's seeing him with Maria that worries me. I just pray I'm strong enough to hold up.'

'I'm sure you'll be fine,' said Millie. 'And anyway no one will think it strange if you have to wipe away a tear in the church. After all, doesn't everyone cry at a wedding?'

'True,' said Connie. 'But they don't blub all the way through the reception which is what I might do if I have to watch Charlie and Maria being all lovey-dovey together.'

Chapter Twelve

'So are you a friend of the bride or the groom, my dear,' asked the stout middle-aged woman in an emerald suit and matching hat on Connie's right.

She was sitting on a warm April afternoon in the upstairs room of the Cauliflower pub with forty other relatives and friends who had gathered to celebrate Martha Croft and Peter Lord's nuptials. The room, which had once been a Victorian supper room, had four long sash windows along one side with elaborate mock-Roman columns between them. The ceiling above still retained the heavy plasterwork depicting cherubs holding wine jugs and grapes, but the landlord had tried to brighten the classical interior by painting it white. Tucked in the far corner was a semicircular stage where the band would set up once the tables were cleared away.

The pub staff had done the couple proud with spotless tablecloths and matching crockery. They'd even provided a magnificent cardboard replica of a three-tier wedding cake complete with plaster flowers and swags to put over the plain fruit cake beneath. The wedding breakfast comprised toad-in-the-hole with carrots and peas followed by spotted dick and custard.

'The bride,' Connie replied. 'We were at school together.'

The woman smiled. 'Me too. Her mother and me have worked together in the rag trade for almost twenty years. I'm Winifred, but everyone calls me Win.'

'Pleased to meet you,' said Connie. 'I'm Connie.'

Win's eyes drifted past Connie towards the top table. 'Doesn't the bride look lovely?'

Dressed in a petrol-blue suit with wide-brimmed hat and matching veil, Martha did look every inch the bride, but it was the man sitting next to Martha's mother that Connie's attention fixed on. With a roguish smile playing across his lips and his blue eyes twinkling with merriment, Charlie certainly was the best man. It had been bad enough in the church, though at least there she was able to hide among others, but here there was nothing to hinder her view, and try as she might, Connie couldn't tear her eyes from him.

'Yes, breathtaking,' she replied, watching Charlie scrape the last morsel off his plate.

As if he sensed her eyes on him, he looked up. Their gazes locked and Connie's heart did a little dance.

'Who's that woman over there?' asked Win, her voice cutting through Connie's jumbled thoughts.

Connie turned her head and found herself looking into the implacable face of Maria, sitting on the opposite table.

'That's the best man's wife,' she said, lowering her eyes.

'Oh,' said Win, her fair eyebrows rising. 'The Italian woman. Someone was telling me outside the church that her family are buying Murray's fish bar opposite Stepney Green station.'

'Really?' said Connie.

'Yes, a bit of cheek I call it,' Win continued. 'I mean, they only arrived a month ago and now they're setting up in business.'

The sound of a knife hitting a glass rang out and Connie turned her attention back to the top table as the room fell silent.

Charlie stood up. 'Well, everybody, before the girls downstairs serve the afters, we get to the important part of the proceedings: the speeches. I therefore call upon the father of the bride, Mr Croft, to say a few words.'

Mr Croft, a portly man with a receding hairline and wearing a shiny navy suit, rose to his feet. Taking a slip of paper from his pocket, he cleared his throat. 'Unaccustomed as I am to public speaking . . .'

As Martha's father told everyone how it only seemed like yesterday he used to dandle his 'little flower' on his knee, Connie's eyes returned unbidden to Charlie. He smiled at something Mr Croft said, and her heart ached.

When Mr Croft finished, Charlie introduced the bridegroom. Peter, his hair slicked back, and freshly shaved to the point of soreness, stood up. In a shaky voice he told everyone he was the luckiest man in the world and promised his new father-in-law he'd take care of Martha. To appreciative applause he sat down and received a peck on the cheek from his new wife as his reward.

Charlie rose to his feet again and the clapping ceased.

'Thank you, Pete. Now it falls on me to round off the proceedings, and I've just written a few notes to keep me on track.'

He pulled a huge sheet of paper from his pocket and the room groaned.

Charlie looked puzzled for a second, then smiled at his audience. 'Next week's runners and rider at Goodwood,' he said, flicking it to the floor.

Everyone laughed as he retrieved a small note from his breast pocket and unfolded it.

'I'm going to keep this brief, as the bar's open downstairs. Firstly I want to say what a treat Martha's sister Mary looks as chief bridesmaid.' There was a ripple of applause and Martha's twelve-year-old sister went red. 'Now, for those of you who don't know me, I'm Charlie and I've known Pete since we were both nippers with our arses hanging out of our trousers,' he said, earning himself a reproving look from Martha's mum. 'And I've got to say there ain't no better mate to be had in a tight corner, as the Hanbury Street boys found to their cost.' A chorus of hoots and wolf whistles went up from Pete and Charlie's old classmates. 'But then the good times came to an end when Hitler came calling and me and Pete were summoned to fight for King and country.' He looked down the table at his life-long friend. 'Thank God we made it back, although it was touch and go at Tripoli, wasn't it, mate?'

Pete nodded, and a sober hush fell while people remembered those they'd lost.

'But we did make it back,' Charlie continued, lifting the mood with his tone. 'And now we can look forward to a happy future, just like Martha and Pete.' He raised his pint of beer. 'I give you Mr and Mrs Lord.'

There was a scrape of chairs as the guests rose to their feet. Connie took hold of her bitter lemon and stood up.

'Martha and Pete,' she repeated with everyone else. As she raised her glass, again her eyes caught Charlie's. They stared at each other for a moment, then Charlie held up his pint again.

'Another toast,' he called, his gaze still on Connie. 'A toast to love.'

While everyone around her raised their glasses for the second time, Connie stood stock still, her heart thumping painfully in her chest.

The other guests, having finished their meal, had started to mill around. Tearing her eyes from Charlie's, Connie put her drink down and gathered her handbag and gloves.

'Are you going?' asked Win.

Connie forced a smile. 'I've got a bit of a headache.' Before the older woman could speak again, she'd scooted around the back of the top table. Squeezing between Martha and Pete's father, she hugged her friend.

'Congratulations, it was a lovely wedding,' she said, kissing her on the cheek. 'But I'm afraid I'm on early call so I have to dash.'

'Oh, what a pity,' said Martha, her mouth turning down at the corners. She caught Connie's hand. 'I'll let you go if you promise to have tea when we get back from honeymoon so I can tell you all about Skegness.'

'Promise,' said Connie.

Waving to the odd friend as she passed, Connie hurried towards the door leading to the bar below.

Seeing Connie head for the door, Charlie threw back the last of his pint and went after her. He guessed that if he used the stairs into the main bar, he'd be able to catch her before she left. With her looking so trim and pretty, he had to.

Shoving open the door, he took the stairs two at a time. There were the usual Saturday-afternoon drinkers in the bar listening to the football commentary on the radio as they supped their beer. Hurrying through the smoky atmosphere, he crossed into the private bar at the side of the pub just as Connie reached the bottom of the staircase.

'You're not leaving, are you, Connie?' he asked, blocking her path to the door.

'I'm on call in the morning,' she replied.

'Oh, that's a shame.' His gaze ran slowly over her face, bringing a flush to her cheeks.

'Yes, but,' she smiled apologetically, 'duty calls.'

'I suppose it does,' he said, conversationally. 'It was a nice wedding, wasn't it?'

'Lovely.' She gave him a hesitant look. 'I really ought to be . . .'

'Shame you've got to rush off,' he said. ''Cos I was hoping to catch you for a dance.'

She smiled politely. 'Perhaps another time.'

'You look good in that,' he said, his eyes flickering over her blue outfit. 'That shade really suits you.'

She blushed deeper and lowered her gaze.

They were just a hand's width apart now in the dimly lit passageway, and alone. A rakish smile lifted the corners of his mouth. What would she do if he gave into temptation and kissed her?

He inched closer and caught a hint of her perfume.

'You had a hat that colour, didn't you?' he said softly.

She raised an eyebrow. 'I'm surprised you remember.'

'How could I forget?'

Pain flitted across her face. 'You forgot other things, though, didn't you?'

'I know, Connie luv, but—'

'I have to go.' She turned from him, but not before he saw tears gathering.

He caught her arm. 'I need to see you, Connie,' he said softly.

'I don't think so,' she replied, pulling away.

'Please.' He took her into his arms, enjoying the familiar feeling of her against him.

'Don't, Charlie,' she said, but she didn't break from his embrace.

'I can't stop thinking about you. Meet me in our old place next Friday and we can—'

'Carlos!'

He looked up and saw Maria glaring down at them from the top of the stairs.

Connie sprang back. 'Take care, Charlie,' she said, brushing past him and into the main bar.

As the door slammed, Maria clumped down the stairs. 'What you doing?'

'Nothing.'

'Not look like nothing to me,' his wife said, scrutinising him suspiciously.

'We were just chatting about the old days, that's all,' he replied, forcing a light laugh.

Maria's expression soured further. 'What, when she was your girl, I suppose?'

'Don't be silly,' he said. He tried to put his arms around her, but she shoved him away.

'You big liar, Charlie Ross, but no matter.' Her lips curled back in a malicious smile. 'If you start up with old ginger girlfriend, I'll tell my papa and he'll—'

'For the last time, Maria,' Charlie said, raking his hair with his fingers, 'we were just talking.'

'Good.' She smiled, then turned and headed back up the stairs.

As he watched his wife ascend to the function room above, despondency pressed down on Charlie. What sort of stupid bloody idiot had he been to let a sour-faced nag like Maria sink her claws into him when he had a darling little sweetheart like Connie waiting at home?

Connie's stomach rumbled as she chained her cycle to the railings outside the house on Clarke Street and trotted up the couple of stairs to the door.

Like many of the practices on Connie's patch, the premises where Dr Robinson worked was a terraced house that had been converted to make a surgery at street level with accommodation above. The front room, which had once served as a family parlour, was now the waiting room. The doctor's consulting room was at the back, and the adjacent scullery had been turned into a minute sluice where he undertook messy procedures such as lancing boils, examining sputum and testing urine.

Nodding hello to the dozen or so sniffing and coughing individuals sitting on mismatched chairs and awaiting their turn, Connie continued through to the back and knocked on the door. Dr Robinson barked something that she took to be her invitation to enter, so she turned the handle and went in.

Instead of being seated at his desk, the doctor was standing next to the examination couch peering down at a middle-aged man who, by the light layer of brick dust covering him, appeared to be in the building trade. He was lying face down with his shirt pulled halfway up his back and his trousers gathered around his ankles.

As usual, Leo Robinson, who was just the right side of fifty, was dressed as if going to view the Royal Academy's Summer Exhibition. Today he wore navy trousers, a red-striped shirt and a three-pocketed waistcoat with a chain slung across it. With a close-clipped moustache that hugged the contours of his top lip, and hair curling just over his collar, he was seen as a bit of an oddball by some of the older GPs. They dismissed his beliefs that apples should be eaten without removing the skin and that smoking was bad for your lungs as nothing short of bizarre, but the patients liked him. As they would never argue with their betters, they agreed with all his suggestions then went away and carried on as before.

He looked over his spectacles at Connie as she walked in.

'Sister Byrne, come and look at this,' he said, pointing at the huge expanse of white buttock. 'Have you ever seen one as big as that before?'

Connie strolled over and studied the inflamed area on the unfortunate chap's coccyx. 'Not for years I haven't.'

'See, I told you, Mr Kemp,' Dr Robinson said gleefully, indicating that his patient could get off the couch. 'Even Sister Byrne, with her years of experience, has never seen a pilonidal sinus the size of yours.'

Connie averted her gaze while Mr Kemp wriggled his pants over his nether regions and stood up.

'Well you could 'ave a bit of sympathy, Doc,' he said, slipping his braces back over his shoulders and buttoning his flies.

Dr Robinson pulled out his chair and sat at his roll-top desk. 'I'm afraid my sympathy is with Sister Byrne and her nurses,' he said, rummaging around among the leaflets, notes and prescription pads. 'They're the ones who'll have to dress your rear for a month.' Excavating a tortoiseshell pen from under the debris, he scribbled something across a sheet of headed notepaper and handed it to his patient. 'Now take this to Casualty and they'll sort you out, after which Sister Byrne or one of her nurses will visit to dress it each day.'

Mr Kemp took the note. 'Thanks, Doctor.' He plopped his cap back on and left the surgery.

Dr Robinson completed his records and filed the manila envelope in the box with the others, then looked at Connie.

'First, before I forget, I've just seen Mr Wiseman, and the

calamine lotion seems to have done the trick. His legs are much less inflamed,' she said, perching on the chair beside the desk.

'Good,' said Dr Robinson.

'And you left a message at the clinic about a new patient,' Connie said.

The doctor rummaged around in his papers again, then extracted his notebook and scanned it. 'Ah yes, here we are. Mrs Margaret Hogan, who lives in Pole Street. Nice woman, in her mid-thirties. Took on her sister's three children when her sister was killed in an air raid, and doing a fine job of it too, by all accounts. Her husband is a dustman with the council so they struggle financially, especially now she's had to give up work. She's three and a half months pregnant, you see, but has an unstable uterus. Sadly, she's already lost four babies, the last one at . . .' he glanced over the notes, 'twenty-three weeks. All very distressing, as you can imagine.'

'Poor woman,' said Connie.

'Indeed,' agreed Dr Robinson. 'Of course, one should never give up hope, and it has been almost five years since her last pregnancy, so her womb has had time to return to normal, but even so.'

'Would you like me to pop in and see what I can do?' asked Connie.

Dr Robinson gave her a grateful look. 'I appreciate your help, especially as I know how short staffed you are at Munroe House.' He heaved a sigh. 'If we can just keep her going until her sixth month, we might have a happy outcome this time around.'

Connie rolled her bike to a stop just after the decorator's yard and hopped off. Pole Street was like the other tightly packed streets running off the old village thoroughfare of Stepney Green. The houses had been built around the turn of the century, with bay windows in the front and handkerchief-sized gardens behind.

The late April sun was almost at its zenith and the morning fog from the river, which Connie's spokes had swirled up as she had left Munroe House that morning, had given way to a warm day with just a hint of summer around the corner. The women of the street were taking full advantage of the weather and almost every window had been thrown open to air the rooms within. Having completed their morning's housework, several of them were milling around in the street as they waited for their children to come home from school for their midday meal. They acknowledged Connie with a nod as she secured her bike on the spear-topped railing in front of number 12 and knocked on the door.

'Who is it?' a woman's voice called through the open window.

'District nurse!'

'Come in, it's open,' the woman called back.

Connie pushed the door open and walked into the uncluttered hallway. In the living room at the front of the house she found a woman with wavy blonde hair and a grey, careworn face sitting in a fireside chair with her feet up.

Although the sitting room was furnished with almost antique furniture and the wallpaper was so faded you could barely make out the design, the room was immaculately clean. You could have happily eaten your dinner off the small sideboard, and even the hearth had not a speck of coal dust.

The woman was the same. Her dress was of a pre-war design and the original midnight-blue colour had been washed to mute navy; the wraparound apron covering it had frayed edges but had been neatly darned.

'Mrs Hogan?' asked Connie.

'Yes.'

'I'm Sister Byrne. Dr Robinson asked me to call,' she continued, putting her bag on the carpet.

'That's kind of him,' said Mrs Hogan. 'Do you want a cuppa?'

'Thank you, but I've just had one.' Connie settled herself in the armchair opposite her patient and took a fresh set of notes and her fountain pen from her bag. 'Now I need to run through a few things, if you don't mind. I understand you're expecting your baby at the end of October.'

'Yes. Doctor said the twenty-third.'

'And this is your fifth pregnancy.'

'Yes, it is,' she replied, twisting her wedding ring back and forth.

'Have you had any morning sickness?' asked Connie.

Mrs Hogan shook her head but didn't look up.

Connie smiled. 'And how are you feeling in yourself, Mrs Hogan?'

'I'm tired,' she replied. 'But Alison, my sister's eldest, is a great help. Her and her two brothers came to live with us three years ago after Dora was killed in an air raid. She was widowed young, so me and Wilf have looked after the three of them off and on since they were born.'

'I can see they're well cared for,' said Connie, indicating the toy box tucked in the corner.

A soft expression stole over Mrs Hogan's face. 'It's not easy to make ends meet some weeks, but after all the trouble I've had trying to have one of my own, the three of them are a real joy.'

'They are very lucky to have you,' said Connie.

They were. There were hundreds of orphaned and abandoned youngsters in London alone, all in desperate need of loving parents.

'Now, I believe your husband works for the council?' Connie asked.

'Yes, as a dustman.'

'I'm sorry to ask, Mrs Hogan,' she moved on to the financial assessment sheet of her notes, 'but what does your husband bring home each week, and what are your family outgoings?'

'I'm not sure about his wages,' Mrs Hogan replied. 'But the rent's three bob, and we put a shilling in the gas every other day and a tanner in the electric when it goes out. He gives me ten and six every Thursday for housekeeping and doesn't have much change in his pocket after that.'

Connie quickly totted up the amount and looked up. 'I think for now we should visit you weekly for three or four weeks just to keep an eye on you and make sure everything's as it should be.'

Mrs Hogan frowned. 'How much will it cost?'

'It would usually be sixpence a visit, but under the circumstances I'm sure no one will query it if we did them all for that price.'

'Thank you, Sister, you're very—' Mrs Hogan buried her face in her hands and sobbed. 'I know it's going to be just like all the others. I can't go through it again. I just can't.'

Connie placed a comforting hand on the woman's knee. 'I'm not promising anything, Mrs Hogan, but we will do all we can to make sure you deliver a healthy baby.'

Mrs Hogan raised her tear-stained face and gave a brave little smile. 'I know you will, Sister, and God bless and keep you.'

And God bless and keep Baby Hogan, thought Connie.

Having left the telephone number and clear instructions to call Munroe House day or night if there was a problem, Connie closed the door on Mrs Hogan and unchained her bike. She had one final morning call, Mrs Cohen in Greenbank, who needed help with her lunchtime toileting. But as she approached the end of Nelson Street, Connie veered right. The last time she'd seen Mrs Henstock's wound, three days ago, it was all but healed, so if she popped in quickly to check, she might be able to take her off the books. With four nurses short and two on holiday, even one patient not needing a visit helped.

Swerving around the decorator's bicycle and sidecar complete with ladders and dangling buckets, she came to a halt outside Mrs Henstock's. Leaving her cycle secure, she knocked on the door. It was opened a few moments later by Mrs Henstock herself, wearing a flowery dress, with several loops of pearls dangling around her neck and a finely woven shawl draped across her shoulders. She was also leaning heavily on an ornate walking stick, which as far as Connie knew she had no need of.

'Oh,' she said when she saw Connie standing there. 'I thought you might be the vicar.'

'Sorry,' said Connie with a friendly smile. 'I know I said I'd pop by this afternoon, but as I was passing, I thought I'd visit a little earlier. But if you're expecting the vicar, I'll come back later.'

'I've been expecting him for three weeks,' said Mrs Henstock testily. 'Still, now you're here, you might as well come in.' She turned, thrusting the stick back in the umbrella stand, and led Connie into the lounge.

Sitting herself in her usual chair, Mrs Henstock put her foot up on the pouffe and unrolled her stocking. Connie took a copy of the *Daily Sketch* from the discarded pile of newspapers beside the coal scuttle and set her bag on it. Her knees cracked as she knelt down.

'Do you go to St Philip's?' she asked as she unravelled Mrs Henstock's ankle bandage.

'I used to until they replaced the old complete edition of *Hymns Ancient and Modern* with the new revised edition,' Mrs Henstock replied, wincing dramatically as Connie took the single gauze dressing off. 'So now I go to St George's, and despite the fact that I'm chairwoman of the Mothers' Union and I organise the monthly tea rota, it seems the vicar can't find the time to visit me, even though I've been poorly for weeks.'

Connie didn't comment and turned her attention to the wound, or at least to where the wound had been, because now there was nothing but a little patch of newly formed skin.

'Well, Mrs Henstock, I'm pleased to tell you that as from today, you're officially completely well,' she said, discarding the old dressing on to the newspaper.

Mrs Henstock twisted her leg so she could see, and frowned. 'I'm not trying to tell you your job, Sister, but I don't see how it can be healed if it's still so sore—'

The front door clicked. 'Only me, Mother,' a deep male voice called.

Mrs Henstock's expression went from sullen to ecstatic in a blink of an eye.

'In here, Malcolm,' she warbled.

The door opened and her son walked in.

Dressed in twill trousers, tweed jacket, an Argyle V-necked jumper and with a pipe jutting out of the side of his mouth, Malcolm Henstock appeared to have just stepped out of a Sirdar knitting pattern. With his broad shoulders and chest, he looked a great deal better in colour than in the black-and-white photograph on the mantelshelf.

'What a lovely surprise,' his mother continued. 'But why are you home so early? Not your old problem playing up again?'

'No,' he replied with a pleasant smile. 'The workmen demolishing bombed-out houses behind the office ruptured the gas pipes, so we had to evacuate the building.' His gaze shifted to Connie. 'Hello.'

'Hello,' she replied. 'I'm Sister Byrne, your mother's district nurse. Well, that was until today, because I'm pleased to say her leg has completely healed.'

Malcolm stepped forward so he was opposite Connie and peered at his mother's white leg.

'So I see.' He looked up and his hazel eyes ran admiringly over her. 'All due to your gentle care, no doubt.'

Connie blushed. 'Well, that's very kind . . .'

She went to get up, and Malcolm offered his hand. Connie grasped it and felt the smooth warmth of his palm slide against hers.

'Thank you,' she said as she stood and faced him.

The corners of his mouth turned up and they exchanged a look.

'It's still very painful,' bleated Mrs Henstock.

Impatience flitted briefly across Malcolm's square features. 'I'm sure it is, Mother,' he said with a heavy sigh. 'But I don't think there's anything Sister Byrne can do for that.'

Mrs Henstock grabbed his arm. 'Could you pop around to the surgery later and ask Dr Quinn to call?'

'But Mother, the surgery doesn't open until four thirty, and with Wilfred still laid up with his hernia, I'll have to be at the model railway club at five to set out the tables.'

Mrs Henstock let her hand drop limply. 'Well, if the people at your toy club are more important than your own mother . . .' She turned her face away.

'Look, I'll pop in first thing tomorrow,' Malcolm said to the back of her head. 'How about that? I'm sure Mr Chivers won't mind if I work my dinner break to make up the time.'

Mrs Henstock took a handkerchief from her sleeve and blew her nose. 'Well, I suppose I'll just have to suffer the pain until—'

'I'll drop in to the surgery if you like, Mrs Henstock,' said Connie.

Mrs Henstock turned. 'Would you, dear?' she said feebly.

Connie nodded. 'Of course. It's no trouble.'

Malcolm gave her a grateful smile and Connie smiled back.

The old woman's eyes darted from one to the other and then narrowed. 'Well, we mustn't keep you from your other patients, Sister,' she said sweetly.

'No.' Connie snapped the catch of her case shut and picked it up. 'Goodbye, Mrs Henstock.'

'I'll see you out, Sister,' said Malcolm.

Gripping her case firmly, Connie walked passed him into the hall, and he followed.

He opened the front door and smiled down at her. 'Thank you for all your help, Sis—'

'Malcolm!' Mrs Henstock called from the lounge.

He sighed. 'Yes, Mother?'

'I need you to close the curtain. The sun's in my eyes.'

Chapter Thirteen

It was nearly twenty to nine by the time Connie pushed open the door of the small corner public house on the west side of Stepney Green. Despite telling herself since Martha and Pete's wedding six days ago that she wouldn't come, with Charlie waiting for her how could she stay away? He hadn't said a time, but she knew he'd be there whenever she arrived.

As she stepped inside, her head was swimming, not just because of the thick cigarette smoke clogging the atmosphere but with the memories the place brought back. The Ship was a working man's watering hole, but it was far enough away from both sets of parents that she and Charlie had spent many hours tucked in the corner planning their future.

As many of the local factories and sweatshops paid their weekly wages on a Friday, the place was jam-packed with drinkers. On the far side, a lively game of darts was in progress, while the landlord, a lean-faced man, and his wife, who had tangerine-coloured hair and blood-red nails, were pulling pints for all they were worth.

Ignoring the leers from a couple of young brewery workers lounging by the bar, Connie looked across the room to where she knew Charlie would be sitting. She spotted him behind a crowd of labourers in dusty clothing and hobnailed boots, staring into his glass. Freshly shaven and dressed in a casual tweed jacket with a tie knotted at his throat, he had obviously taken care over his appearance.

As if sensing her presence, he looked up. A flash of delight sparked in his blue eyes, and Connie's heart dissolved. He stood up. Although she tried to stop herself, Connie's gaze flickered to his freshly shaven cheek that she'd kissed a thousand times or more.

'You look nice,' he said, his eyes running slowly over her.

Connie's heart did a little quickstep. 'Thank you.'

'The usual?' he asked, placing his hand lightly on her arm.

'Please,' she replied as her pulse broke into a tango.

Pulling a handful of change from his pocket, Charlie went to the bar. Connie gazed after him, studying his pronounced cheekbones and square jaw as he gave their order to the barmaid. After a few minutes, during which she felt as if every pair of eyes in the house were on her, he returned.

'I'm glad you came.' He placed her drink in front of her and resumed his seat. 'I was afraid you wouldn't.'

She lowered her eyes and took a sip of her G and T. 'I nearly didn't. After all, what's the point? You're married to Maria.'

Charlie gave a harsh laugh. 'I am married to her, aren't I? God help me.' He took her hand and wove his fingers in hers. 'But I'm in love with you.'

Connie snatched her hand away. 'Don't say that.'

'Why not? It's true.' His eyes captured hers and excitement shot through her. 'And after the way you looked at me across the room in the Cauliflower, I'm guessing you feel the same.'

'Even if I do, what does it matter? It's too late,' she said, looking away as tears stung her eyes. 'Much too late.'

He shifted forward in his chair and his knees pressed into hers. 'But it doesn't have to be. I could get a divorce.'

For a moment her emotions galloped away, but she reined them in. 'Don't be ridiculous, Charlie. It would cost hundreds.'

'Who says I haven't got the money?'

'Have you?'

'Not all of it.' He gave a wry smile. 'But I can lay my hands on it. I know this chap from the snooker club who's a clerk for some posh law firm in the City. He says he's arranged lots of divorces, and for ordinary people like you and me, too.'

'But even if Maria agreed, you've got a child,' Connie replied. 'I couldn't be a home-wrecker.'

'I've got no home to wreck, Connie,' said Charlie earnestly. 'To tell the truth, most days me and Maria don't speak to each other. I doubt she'd even notice if I wasn't there.'

'Even so, imagine what my family would say, not to mention Father Gregory.'

'I know I'm asking a lot, but is it right for us to live miserable lives just because of one stupid mistake?' He pressed her hand to his lips and the hue of his blue eyes darkened. 'I know that after all the hurt and unhappiness I caused you I don't deserve anything. I'm just asking – no, begging – that you give me a chance to make you happy.'

Although every part of her screamed 'yes', she shook her head. 'It's too late. And you're not being fair to me or to Maria. She's your wife whether you like it or not, and you have to let me go.'

'But I can't live without you,' he whispered.

'I'm sorry.' She gathered her handbag and stood up. 'You'll have to learn to, just as I have learned to live without you. Goodbye, Charlie.'

Ignoring the look of utter devastation on his face, she stepped out from behind the table, and with tears distorting her vision, stumbled towards the door.

With her right ear pressed against the smaller end of the foetal stethoscope, Connie counted to the steady beat of the unborn baby's heart.

It was mid-afternoon Thursday, and as usual the antenatal clinic was packed to the gunnels with pregnant women, many with their previous offspring. Outside, the prams used to transport them all to Munroe House were lined up along the railings at the front of the old house.

Josie was at the desk booking in new mums, of whom there were at least half a dozen, while Connie examined them. Sally should have been manning the other cubicle, but she'd been called out to a lunchtime delivery and hadn't yet returned.

It was now a full year since the cessation of hostilities, and Connie and her fellow nurses were delivering daily the results of the celebration. Not that Connie minded one little bit, but she couldn't help but ponder, as she eased another new life into the world, how this time last year she'd thought she'd be one of those new mothers.

The second hand of her watch moved past the number twelve and Connie straightened up.

'That's all as it should be,' she said, putting down her equipment. 'You can sit up now, Mrs Webb.'

'Thank you, Sister,' said Valerie Webb as she repositioned her underslip over her swollen stomach and swung her legs off the examination couch.

Connie picked up Mrs Webb's file. Sitting on the chair next to the stainless-steel trolley, she took her pen from her top pocket and started writing up her notes.

'I suppose you've examined lots of women in my condition,' said Mrs Webb.

'Hundreds.'

'And I suppose all women are different, aren't they? I mean, some are big and others you can hardly tell are in the family way at all.'

Connie smiled absent-mindedly. 'Women carry differently, but babies grow at a steady rate and that's how I can tell if there's a problem.'

'Someone in the market said that she'd 'eard that some babies, like Chinese, come out quicker,' said Mrs Webb, fiddling with the buttons on her blouse.

Connie laughed. 'Well I can't say I've delivered many Chinese babies, so I wouldn't like to say. As far as I know, be they yellow, black, sky-blue or pink, all babies take the same nine months to cook.' She looked down at the notes again and dotted the line on the chart for the baby's heart rate.

'I suppose by the same token some babies, like say Arabs or Negroes, might take longer,' continued Mrs Webb in a matter-of-fact tone.

Connie looked up. 'Are you worried about something, Mrs Webb?'

A scarlet flush splashed up Valerie Webb's neck and she lowered her eyes. 'Whatever gave you that idea?' she said, picking at the hem of her skirt.

Connie put her hand over the other woman's. 'If it's something to do with the baby, I need to know.'

On the other side of the flimsy screen the chatter of the women waiting their turn abated a little.

Mrs Webb glanced over her shoulder and beckoned Connie closer.

'I'll tell you if you promise not to tell my Ron,' she said, her voice dropping to a whisper.

'I promise,' Connie whispered back.

Although they were alone, Mrs Webb looked over her shoulder again. 'Remember I told you that Ron came back two days after VJ day?' she said in a hushed tone.

Connie nodded.

'Well I'm afraid,' continued Mrs Webb, 'I celebrated a little too much on VJ night. With an American soldier.' She smiled sheepishly. 'A coloured one.'

'Oh!'

'I don't know what came over me, I really don't,' continued Mrs Webb. 'One moment I was dancing the conga in Trafalgar Square, the next I was lying beneath a bush in St James's Park with my knickers around my ankles. When I had my monthly visitor two weeks later I thought I'd got away with it, but when you said I was a month further on . . .' She pulled a handkerchief from her sleeve and blew her nose. 'It was just a moment of madness, honest. I wouldn't hurt my Ron for the world. We'd hoped to start a family years ago, but nothing happened. Ron was stationed at Sheerness all through forty-four, and even then I used to meet him every weekend in Southend for . . . you know, but not so much as a missed period, and now after one tumble in the bushes I'm up the duff.' She dabbed her eyes. 'And I know that when the little chap pops out, he'll have a brown face and black frizzy hair.'

Connie tucked the notes back in the box file. 'Well, Mrs Webb, there's nothing you can do except wait.'

Mrs Webb nodded and dried her eyes. 'You're right, Sister. And me and Ron were at it like rabbits when he got back, so that stacks the odds in his favour.'

Connie smiled professionally but didn't comment. 'We'll just have to wait and see,' she repeated, moving the screen aside. 'See you next week, Mrs Webb.'

Valerie Webb picked up her handbag and waddled towards the door.

Sally, who had just returned, gave the pregnant woman a questioning look as she passed her, then came over to Connie.

'What's the problem?'

'I can't say,' Connie replied. 'But I hope to God I'm not the midwife on call when Mrs Webb goes into labour.'

*

As Charlie mentally marked off two likely-looking horses in to-morrow's 3.15 at York, his mother walked back into the room carrying a tray of tea. As always, she'd put on the full works, including a white lawn tablecloth, half a fruit cake, sugar and milk in a bowl and jug respectively, and flowery side plates that wouldn't cover the palm of his hand.

Since he'd been forced to leave the comfort of Ada's house, he'd fallen into the habit of popping by for a cuppa every Tues-day after work, but now that he and Maria had moved in with her parents, he found himself dropping by two, three, sometimes even four times a week.

As his mother set the ensemble on the coffee table in front of him, Charlie took a last drag on his cigarette, then stubbed it out in the ashtray balanced on the arm of the fireside chair. It nestled alongside the other two he'd smoked since arriving twenty min-utes ago. He folded the paper and tucked it beside him.

'You're not gambling, are you, Charlie?' His mother gave him a severe look.

'Course not, Mum.'

'I hope not, because the Bible tells us that the devil tempts the gambler to foolishness,' she continued, scrutinising his face closely.

Charlie gave her an artless smile. 'Well that's all right then, as I was just having a gander at last week's report on the Hammers game against Spurs.'

'Oh Charlie,' she laughed. 'You always were a wag.' She picked up the cake slice. 'Can I cut you a piece?'

'Need you ask?' He grinned.

An indulgent look softened his mother's expression as she cut him a wedge. She handed him a plate, and then stirred three heaped spoonfuls of sugar into his tea.

'I'm sorry, but that's the last of it until next week,' she said, passing him the steaming mug.

'Thanks, Mum,' he said, cradling it in his hand and sinking back into the chair. 'If you want a bag or two of sugar, I can get you some.'

She looked uncertain. 'I don't know, Charlie. I know every-one gets the odd thing under the counter, but I couldn't condone stealing.'

He looked affronted. 'Honestly, Mum, do you think I'd have anything to do with the black market?'

'Of course not.' She reached over and patted his arm. 'I know you've always been a good boy. Not like some I could mention.'

'It's stuff the Ministry of Food can't pass on for sale 'cos it's been in the light too long,' he said.

'I've never heard of that,' she replied, looking impressed at his knowledge of such things.

'No, me neither. It don't affect the taste and it's as safe as houses, but the government can't let the shops sell it. So do you want some?'

She nodded. 'It would help a great deal with the cake stall for the mission's supper fete, but only if it's all above board.'

Charlie yawned.

'You look done in,' she said, settling herself in the chair opposite.

'I'm all right,' he said.

'You work too hard,' she continued.

'I'd hardly call dispatching orders all day hard work,' he replied.

'Well, are you getting a full night's sleep?'

'Mostly.'

In truth, he didn't get to bed much before one most nights, as the Cohens' snooker hall didn't close until twelve, after which he and Tommy always found an obliging pub landlord offering afters.

Ada tutted disapprovingly. 'Filippo's six months now. He should be in his own room, not disturbing your sleep. How is he?' she added.

'Right enough,' Charlie replied, biting into his cake.

'Has he got any teeth yet?' asked Ada.

He shrugged. 'If I ever prise him off Maria's mother, I'll tell you.'

Ada's lips pulled tight with disapproval. 'And I suppose they're still jabbering on at him in their own lingo.'

He nodded.

'How is that poor little darling ever going to learn to talk proper English? It's not right, you know,' she continued, warming to the subject. 'You're his father and the head of the house. You should say something.'

'Don't you think I've tried?'

'I know you have, son,' said Ada in a softer tone. 'But it breaks my heart, I can tell you, to see you, a man who fought for his country, having to kowtow to a bunch of Nazi-lovers.' She watched him for a few moments, then spoke again. 'I suppose you realise now that she only married you for an easy life.'

Charlie took another mouthful of cake.

'She's caught you, my lad, good and proper,' his mother continued, her voice rising a tone. 'With the oldest trick in the book. You just have to wonder how many others she tried it on before she got her hooks into you.'

She extracted a handkerchief from her sleeve. 'If only you'd married Connie. Such a lovely girl.'

Charlie raised an eyebrow. 'You've changed your tune.'

'No I haven't,' his mother replied. 'Even though she's Irish and a Roman Catholic, I've always regarded Connie as a sweet girl. Pretty, too.'

An image of Connie's laughing eyes, curvy figure and shapely legs flitted through Charlie's mind. She wasn't pretty; she was a proper eyeful.

'No, it wasn't dear Connie I objected to,' Ada said, cutting through his thoughts. 'It was her family. Common as muck, the lot of them. And that mother of hers.' She looked heavenward. 'Mouth like a foghorn and language that would make a sailor blush. But I'll tell you this for nothing. Not once did I hear Connie had been playing fast and loose behind your back, not even with a Yank, not like some around here. I doubt that so-called wife of yours would have been so loyal. First flash of a pair of stockings and *she'd* have been off like a shot with one of those GIs. I bet you wished you were married to dear Connie now, don't you?'

'For fuck's sake, Mother.'

Ada bristled. 'There's no need to use that sort of language, Charlie.'

'I don't need you to keep telling me what Maria's like. I live with the bloody woman!' he yelled, raking his fingers through his hair. 'And I don't need to be told what an idiot I am for not marrying Connie, because seeing her at Pete's wedding made me realise that myself.'

He looked up at the bowl lampshade suspended from the

ceiling. As he studied its gold filigree pattern, a feeling of utter despair pressed down on him. His nose felt tight and the corners of his eyes pinched, so he closed them. Images of Connie swirled in his head as he listened to the slow tick of the mantelshelf clock. Ada broke the silence.

'I'm sorry, Charlie,' she said in a quiet voice.

Reluctant to leave the blissful world filled with Connie, he opened his eyes slowly.

'It just breaks my heart to see you so miserable all the time, it really does,' his mother said, looking mournfully at him. 'I just wish you were happy.'

Charlie gave her a wan smile. 'So do I, Mum. So do I.'

Chapter Fourteen

Connie turned on the hot tap and threw a handful of carbolic soap flakes into the treatment room's deep butler sink. Leaving the water to run, she went back to her bag, which she'd left sitting on a chair. She took out her dirty instruments and returned to the sink, dropping them into the frothy water to soak, then went to the cupboard and collected a large bottle of Dettol. She poured some into the long tray that looked like a fish steamer, ready to soak the equipment overnight.

Resting her hands on the sink, she gazed at the leaden sky. Not that you'd know it from the rain lashing at the windows, but it was the start of June next week. She let her head hang as the now familiar weight of dejection settled on her shoulders. It was all very well people telling her there were plenty more fish in the sea and that she'd get over Charlie, but it didn't ease the pain lodged in her chest. She was beginning to seriously question whether she would ever be happy again.

The door opened and Sally walked in. Pulling herself together, Connie lifted her equipment out of the sink and placed it in the disinfecting tray.

'You still here?' asked Sally, plonking her bag on the table. 'I thought you were a half-day.'

'I was, but I picked up another toe-to-knee ulcer dressing at the surgery, and as Anne was called to a delivery at eight, I added her two newborn visits to my three. But now I'm done,' she said, wiping off her hands. 'I'm going to get changed and head off for an evening listening to the wireless with my feet up in front of my sister's fire. If I don't see you later, I'll see you at breakfast.'

Handing her friend the towel, she left the treatment room. As she closed the door behind her, the hall telephone rang. She picked it up.

'Munroe House, Sister Byrne speaking. How can I help you?'

'Is that the clinic?' a woman asked in a feeble voice.

'Yes, it is. Who's calling?'

'Mrs Henstock,' she replied. 'Oh dear, I don't feel well at all.'

'I'm sorry to hear that,' said Connie, taking out her pen and pulling the message pad towards her.

'Byrne?' said Mrs Henstock. 'You're the pretty little nurse with the strawberry-blonde hair, aren't you?'

'That's right,' said Connie. 'What seems to be the problem?'

'Well you know I'm not one to complain,' Mrs Henstock continued in a faltering voice. 'But it's my heart. It's weak, you see, very weak.'

Connie frowned. 'Dr Quinn didn't mention you had a problem with your heart.'

'Well I have,' snapped the woman at the other end of the phone. 'And if he was any kind of doctor, he'd recognise it.'

'I'll get the late nurse to pop in, Mrs Henstock,' Connie replied.

'Oh, I thought as I'm your patient you'd come yourself, Sister,' said Mrs Henstock.

'Well you're not technically my patient as your leg healed several weeks ago,' Connie explained. 'And I am just going off duty—'

'It's all right, I wouldn't want to put you out,' Mrs Henstock cut in tersely. 'I'll telephone my dear boy. He'll no doubt have to cancel an important meeting or something, but I'm sure he'll come without a second thought.'

An image of poor Malcolm Henstock being dragged out of work by his peevish mother flashed through Connie's mind. She glanced at the clock.

'All right, Mrs Henstock,' she said with a sigh. 'I'll be with you in fifteen minutes.'

Connie arrived at Mrs Henstock's door some fifteen minutes later. By the time she'd gathered her bag from the treatment room, donned her raincoat and overshoes and stepped out of Munroe House, it had stopped raining. As she didn't want to have her legs covered with mud from her cycle wheels, she'd walked the quarter of a mile to Nelson Street.

She found the door open and Mrs Henstock reclining, eyes closed and arm across her forehead, on a chaise longue. A lacy shawl was draped across her recumbent form and a bottle of smelling salts sat on the table at her elbow.

She opened one eye as she heard Connie come in, then closed it again. 'Thank goodness you've arrived, Sister,' she whispered.

Connie walked over and put her bag on the table, then looked down at her patient. 'How are you feeling now, Mrs Henstock?' she asked, noting the woman's pink cheeks and lips and even, unlaboured breathing.

'I can't describe it.' Mrs Henstock clutched at her chest. 'I have pain all over.'

'All over?'

Mrs Henstock nodded. 'And palpitations so bad I'm afraid my heart will stop.'

Taking her patient's wrist, Connie felt her pulse.

'It's so feeble you might not be able to find it,' said Mrs Henstock, her hand limp in Connie's.

Glancing down at her watch, Connie counted Mrs Henstock's textbook seventy-two beats per minute. She placed her patient's hand back on her chest and wrapped the sphygmomanometer cuff around her arm. Like her pulse, her blood pressure was completely normal.

'That's all fine,' said Connie, unwinding the fabric cuff.

Mrs Henstock didn't look convinced.

The handle rattled and Malcolm walked into the front room.

He must have been out in the rain earlier and the damp had put a curl in his hair, and as it was the end of the working day he had a visible five o'clock shadow. He was dressed in a charcoal-grey suit, with a buff trench coat over it and a blue tie knotted at his throat. Although a little old-fashioned, the double-breasted jacket fitted his tall frame well.

'I'm home!' He spotted Connie. 'Oh, hello.'

'Hello,' Connie replied.

They smiled at each other.

'Malcolm,' Mrs Henstock croaked, holding out a limp hand.

He stepped forward and took it. 'It's all right, Mother.'

'Oh Malcolm,' she said. 'I thought I was about to breathe my last.'

'I'm sure you did,' he replied patiently. 'You've just had one of your turns, haven't you?'

She gave him a wide-eyed look and nodded.

'Have you taken one of the tablets the doctor gave you?'

She shook her head.

Letting go of her hand, Malcolm walked to the dresser and pulled open the top drawer, taking out a small bottle of pills.

'I'll fetch some water,' said Connie. Leaving Malcolm to deal with his mother, she hurried to the spotless kitchen at the back of the house and filled a glass from the tap. She was just about to re-enter the front room when Mrs Henstock spoke.

'I said I'd wait for the night nurse, but when I told Sister Whatshername my symptoms, she said it sounded serious and she'd come straight round,' she warbled. 'Mind you, it still took her half an hour to get here.'

'Her name is Sister Byrne, Mother,' Malcolm replied. 'I expect she got here as quickly as she could.'

'Well she was lucky she didn't find me dead in the chair,' Mrs Henstock snapped back. 'She said herself my blood pressure was sky high.'

Smiling broadly, Connie walked back into the room. 'Here we go,' she said chirpily. 'I hope I wasn't too long.'

Mrs Henstock smiled sweetly. 'Thank you, dear. I was just telling my son what an angel you are.'

Malcolm shook a pill into his mother's hand, then took the glass from Connie. His fingers touched hers briefly, and they were firm and cool.

Mrs Henstock popped the tablet in her mouth and took a gulp of water, pulling a face as she swallowed. She rested back and closed her eyes.

Connie reached for her unravelled blood pressure machine but Malcolm beat her to it. 'I'll put that away while you write up your notes.'

Connie gave him a grateful smile. 'That would be a help. I'm already late.'

'Lucky chap.'

'No, I'm having tea with my sister.'

'Then I'll give you a lift,' he said, stowing her sphygmomanometer in the side pocket of her bag.

'That's kind of you,' Connie replied. 'But I've got to change first.'

'No problem. I've got a few notes of my own from a site visit. I'll polish them off while I wait in the car.' He smiled boyishly. 'Well, it's the council van actually, but the front seat's clean.'

'What about . . . ?' She looked at Mrs Henstock, who was now lying with her mouth open, snoring.

'She'll be out for hours.'

Connie regarded the sleeping woman for a few moments, then looked back at Malcolm. 'Your mother's blood pressure and pulse were perfectly normal, you know.'

'I'm certain they were,' he said in a matter-of-fact tone. 'I'm going away this weekend with the Stratford Train Club, so I was expecting one of her funny turns sometime this week.'

He grinned, and Connie grinned back. He picked up her nurse's bag.

'Now, madam, if you're ready,' he swept his free hand towards the front door, 'your carriage awaits.'

Hearing a little murmur, Connie rested her knife and fork on her empty plate and stood up from the table.

'If she's awake, can I pick her up?' she asked Mo, who was sitting opposite her at the kitchen table.

Thanks to Malcolm's kind offer of a lift, rather than being late to her sister's Connie had actually arrived about fifteen minutes early. Mindful of him sitting in the van outside, she had dashed upstairs and changed out of her uniform in record-quick time. Even with the homebound traffic heading east on the Mile End Road, she'd arrived at Mo's just as the boys returned from school. Looking as if they were back from fighting a battle rather than a day of lessons, Arthur, Bert and Mike had greeted her with the day's playground news but soon wriggled out of her embrace, considering themselves too grown-up to be hugged in public.

The boys had bolted down their supper and were now out in the evening sunshine playing football with the lads from the next street. As Eddy wouldn't be in from work for another hour, his dinner was resting over a saucepan of simmering water, a lid over the plate to keep in the heat. Connie and Mo were enjoying a quiet cuppa before tackling the washing-up. Mo's home, with the steady tick-tick of the mantel clock and the music drifting from the wireless, was a welcome change from the clattering feet, ringing telephone and constant comings and goings of Munroe House.

'You'll spoil her if you keep picking her up,' Mo replied, the contented smile belying her words.

Connie grinned and went over to the pram wedged between the kitchen dresser and the mangle. Leaning over it, she pulled a happy face at baby Audrey, the newest member of the Byrne family. She lifted her out, then returned to the table and sat down.

'Have you time for another cup?' asked Mo, rising to her feet.

Connie nodded. 'Yes, I've got a bit of time before I have to get back I'm not on duty until eight this evening, and I'm only covering Eva for a couple of hours. She's second on call so Mary will be the first out if there's a delivery.'

Mo crossed to the stove and relit the gas under the kettle. Rinsing out the teapot, she set it ready on the dresser.

'She's putting on weight already,' said Connie, enjoying the feel of her newborn niece in her arms.

'I know. They grow up so fast, don't they?' Mo replied with a sigh, reaching for the tea caddy. 'It doesn't seem that long ago that Arthur was that size, and now look at him, with his shirts halfway up his arms and trousers around his bum. And the other two are just the same. Cost me a fortune in clothes, those three do.'

Mo made the tea while Connie blew raspberries on Audrey's soft cheeks and tickled her.

'She is such a sweetheart,' Connie said as her sister handed her a fresh cuppa.

A soft expression spread across Mo's face. 'Yes, she is. And the apple of her dad's eye.' Resting her elbows on the table, she picked up her own drink. 'It suits you, Connie.'

Connie looked up.

'A baby,' her sister explained. 'You look just right holding her.'

'I'm used to them, that's all,' said Connie, running Audrey's fine hair through her fingers.

Mo regarded her thoughtfully. 'So who did you say gave you a lift?'

'Malcolm Henstock; he's the son of one of my patients,' Connie replied.

'That was kind. How old is he?'

Connie laughed. 'For goodness' sake, Mo.'

Mo folded her arms. 'I just want to see you happy with someone, and with kids of your own,' she said, adjusting her bosom and looking remarkably like their mother. 'You know, I was only thinking the other day it's a pity it didn't work out with Eddy's friend Bernard. He really liked you, you know.'

Bernard worked with her sister's husband and she'd foolishly agreed to meet up with him. The memory of his body odour and his conversation about the best way to breed and show budgerigars loomed in Connie's mind.

'Oh, he was nice enough,' she said. 'But . . .'

'But he's just not Charlie.'

The baby caught sight of the buttons on Connie's blouse and reached out to explore. Connie caught the little hand and pressed her lips to it, and didn't answer.

Mo reached across and closed her hand over Connie's. 'In time you'll meet someone a hundred times better.'

Connie smiled sadly at her sister. 'I know I will.'

They exchanged a fond look, then Mo picked up her tea. 'And anyway, from what I hear about Charlie, in a few years you'll count yourself lucky you're not shackled to him.'

Connie looked up sharply. 'What do you mean?'

'I've heard he's friendly with Tommy Timms, who heads up the Cable Street Gang.'

'Who told you that?' asked Connie.

'Doris Roberts. Tall girl, thick glasses, her mother runs the second-hand clothes stall under the railway arch in Chapman Street. She was in my year at school, you must remember her,' Mo explained.

'I can't say I do.'

'Well, anyways,' Mo continued with a wave, 'she's married to Bill Unwin, whose uncle knew Tommy's old man, and he said that since Charlie came home, him and Tommy have been as thick as thieves. From what I hear, the honeymoon's well and truly over in the Ross household.'

Connie's heart thumped uncomfortably in her chest as Mo swallowed a mouthful of tea.

'After confession last week I ran into Marge Moore. She lives next door to the chip shop and says the screaming and shouting has to be heard to be believed. And they even had the police turn up last week 'cos Maria was out in the street going bonkers at Charlie.' A smug expression spread across Mo's face. 'I bet Charlie Ross is beginning to rue the day she got her claws into him.'

'He is,' said Connie without thinking.

Mo's eyes narrowed. 'And tell me now, how would you know such a thing, Constance Mary Byrne?'

Connie felt her cheeks glow but she forced herself to hold her sister's accusing stare. 'Well if you must know . . .'

Mo's jaw slowly dropped as Connie told her about meeting Charlie.

'Are you mad?'

'There was nothing in it.'

'Nothing!' Mo gasped. 'You're supposed to be the brainy one of the family and you think meeting a married man in a pub is nothing?'

'Perhaps it wasn't the most sensible thing to do, but I wanted to clear the air,' said Connie, annoyed at the defensive tone in her own voice. 'That's all, and it's not as if I'm going to make a habit of it.'

'I should blooming well think not.'

'Mo, you won't tell Mum, will you?' asked Connie.

Mo's expression lost some of its ferocity. 'I suppose there's no harm done, and you've had a rough time of it in the past few months.'

Connie let out a long breath. 'Thanks, Mo. And you're right, I've got to forget Charlie and find someone else.'

'You have,' Mo agreed. 'So why don't you give Bernard another chance?'

Although Connie's heart sank at the prospect of breathing through her mouth for three hours while listening to another monologue about egg hatching, she smiled. 'All right, perhaps we can go and listen to the band in Victoria Park in the fresh air.'

Fixing her eyes on the poster behind the examination couch advertising rosehip syrup, Connie inched her fingers over Mary Taplin's eight-and-a-half-month stomach.

It was a week after her visit to Mo's, and, as always these days, the Thursday afternoon antenatal clinic was heaving. However efficiently Beattie weighed the mothers and tested their urine for sugar, and Annie worked through the examination checks, the place was still jam-packed. Connie had brought an extra half-dozen chairs from the nurses' refectory into the treatment room to relieve the crowd in the hallway, which meant that they'd been forced to shift the examination couches back, and she'd already caught her hip twice on the lotion cupboard behind her.

Having satisfied herself that the baby was head down, facing backwards and engaged, she retracted her hand and straightened up.

'Absolutely fine,' she said to the young woman lying on the examination couch.

Mary Taplin ran her hand over her bump and smiled. 'I can't wait.'

'Well perhaps you won't have to for much longer. I think young Master or Miss Taplin might be with us any day now. Have you got everything ready?'

Mary nodded. 'Yes, just as you asked.'

'And you know what to do if you think baby's on its way?' Connie asked, helping Mary to sit up.

'Fred has it all written down,' laughed Mary.

Connie smiled. 'Good. You can get dressed now.'

As her patient dressed, Connie quickly wrote up her notes. Throwing away the ruffled length of paper on the couch, she covered it with a fresh one ready for her next patient, then pulled the screen aside.

'And if you don't call on us before, I'll see you here next week, Mrs Taplin.'

She followed Mary out and went over to the desk, where she handed the completed notes to Doreen and got another set in return.

'Mrs Conner,' Doreen informed her. 'She sitting outside and she's got all four children with her.'

Connie's heart sank. May Conner's brood would have made a chimpanzees' tea party look like a Quakers' meeting. Steeling herself, she headed for the hall.

Glancing around, she spotted May Conner surrounded by her squabbling offspring at the far end, but before she could call her name, the front door burst open.

'Where isss she?' screeched a woman's voice.

All eyes turned towards Munroe House's main entrance as Maria stepped into the hallway with her son on her hip. With her dark hair loose around her shoulders and her black eyes spitting fury, she looked wildly around for a moment until she spotted Connie.

'There she isss,' she snarled, jabbing her finger at Connie. 'The 'usband stealer.'

The chatter stopped instantly as women threatened their children into silence and all eyes turned back to Connie. Filippo let out an ear-piercing scream and clung to his mother, sobbing.

Somehow Connie forced a smile. 'Mrs . . . Mrs Ross,' she said pleasantly, as the blood pounded in her ears.

Maria's eyes narrowed and her full mouth pulled into a hard line. Shoving her way between the rows of expectant women, she stopped just in front of Connie.

'Yes, I am Mrs Ross,' she snarled. 'Carlos's lawful wife.'

Connie felt her cheeks glow. 'Perhaps we could go into the office and chat abou—'

'We no chat! I talk. You listen. My friend, she tell me, "I see your Carlos drinking and laughing in pub with red-blonde-haired girl." And I know it you.' Ignoring the distraught infant in her arms, she thrust her left hand up at Connie's face. 'See this?' She wriggled her third finger with the thin band of gold on it. 'This is the ring Carlos give me when he marry me. But more greater than him saying "yes" and signing papers' – she yanked on the chain around her neck and pulled out a crucifix, which she held up between them – 'Priest made us man and wife for ever.'

The superintendent's office door opened and Gladys stepped out. She opened her mouth to speak, but then, seeing the confrontation, just leant on the frame and smirked.

Connie looked back at Maria's furious face. 'I really think we should—'

'So you, Sister Connie Byrne, 'usband stealer,' she jabbed Connie in the chest, 'you find your own man and stop after mine. *Capisce?*'

She marched out. The dozen or so women sitting on either side of the hallway watched open-mouthed as she passed between them. When the front door banged shut behind her, they swivelled back to stare at Connie.

Connie, her cheeks ablaze, looked down at her notes and, ignoring Gladys's giggles, forced a professional smile. 'Mrs Conner, we're ready for you now.'

Concentrating on the way the ivy wound itself in and out of the lattice pattern on the wallpaper, Connie popped another chunk of braised kidney in her mouth. Usually she would have eaten her evening meal with one of her friends, but as Millie was at home with her mother, Sally had just been called out and Connie's other friend, Eva, was visiting her young man's parents, she was forced to have her supper alone.

Well, not really alone, because although she'd left coming down for supper as late as she could, there was still a handful of nurses in the refectory. Unfortunately it was Gladys and three of her chums. They were sitting two tables over and had spent the last twenty minutes casting her sly glances.

As Connie cut through the crust of her pie and speared it with her fork, the phone rang in the hall outside. She wished heartily that she was the on-call midwife. There was a pause, then the refectory door opened and Veronica's head appeared.

'It's a call for you,' she said, looking across at Connie. 'He didn't say who he was.'

'He doesn't need to,' Gladys muttered. There was an outbreak of communal nudging and giggling on Gladys's table. Someone whispered "usband stealer' in an exaggerated Italian accent, while another muttered 'Capisce'.

'Thank you,' said Connie, putting her cutlery together and standing up. Trying her best to look unconcerned, she went out to the hall table and picked up the receiver lying beside the telephone.

'Hello,' she said.

'Thanks goodness I've got hold of you, Connie,' said Charlie. 'Maria's found out about us meeting.'

'I know,' hissed Connie. 'She—'

The refectory door opened and Trudy, Gladys's best mate, walked out. Her eyes flickered over Connie as she made her way to the coat stand. Connie regarded her coolly as Trudy searched in her coat pocket for something and then went back into the dining room.

'She turned up at the clinic today,' continued Connie, her hand around the mouthpiece to muffle her voice.

'I'm sorry, sweetheart, I—'

'Don't sweetheart me, Charlie,' Connie snapped.

The door opened again. This time it was Marge, Gladys's other sidekick, who strolled out and pretended to search through the afternoon post on the dresser.

Connie turned her back on her and hunched over the phone. 'I can't talk now.'

'Then meet me in the Hayfield at eight and—'

'No, Charlie.'

'But I love you, Connie, you know I do, and I know you feel the same,' murmured Charlie, his voice warm as honey.

'It doesn't matter,' Connie replied.

The pips went.

'I'm sorry, but don't call me again,' she snapped, slamming the receiver down.

Chapter Fifteen

'Do you think Miss Knott will be here soon?' asked Josie.

Connie, who was sitting on the other side of the desk in the nurses' office checking through Josie's workbook, looked up. Her student sat with her knees pressed together, her anxious gaze riveted to the door.

'Any moment now, I'd say, but if you don't calm down you'll faint at her feet when she does,' Connie replied, turning the book and pressing it on to the blotting paper. 'And don't worry. Miss Knott won't eat you.'

'I'm not so sure about that,' said Josie, looking unconvinced. 'Did you see the state Felicity was in last week after she'd been out with her?' She glanced at the door again. 'Perhaps I should spend another penny before she gets here.'

'You've already been twice since breakfast.' Connie handed Josie her workbook. 'Just relax and you'll be fine.'

The doorbell rang.

'She's here!' Josie cried, and forgetting that her bag was perched on her knees, she jumped up. The case crashed to the floor, the catch sprang open and the contents spilled out over the brown lino.

'Don't dawdle, girl, show me through,' boomed a voice in the hall as Josie dived to the floor to retrieve her equipment.

The brass handle rattled and Daisy, Munroe House's newest maid, stepped into the room. 'There's a Miss—'

'Thank you,' bellowed Miss Knott, barging the young girl out of the way and striding in. 'You can get back to your chores.'

The Queen's Nursing Institute official in charge of trainee nurses throughout London was a bone-thin woman somewhere in her late sixties with a downy shadow on her upper lip. Her steel-grey hair was cut in a bob that stopped halfway down her ears and her mud-grey eyes sat a little too close together beneath her unplucked eyebrows.

She'd been one of the last nurses to have her St Thomas's hospital medal presented to her by the redoubtable Miss Nightingale, just after the end of the Boer War. Coming from a military family who could boast a major or colonel in every conflict since the Restoration, it was only natural that she should join the Queen Alexander Imperial Military Service. She'd served in India, Sudan and Kenya before settling on district nursing.

But old habits died hard, and although the Queen's Institute of District Nursing had introduced a coupon-saving utility uniform at the onset of the war, Miss Knott had clung to the military style of dress she was used to, complete with hip-length cape and cloche hat. She wore her St Thomas's hospital cross and the oval Queen's badge pinned to her chest like campaign medals instead of hanging around her neck like other QNs.

Now, she planted her black size nine lace-up shoes in front of Connie and Josie, put her battered Gladstone bag on the desk and clasped her hands behind her back.

'Good morning, Sister Byrne,' she barked. 'I was given to understand that you were expecting me.'

'I am,' Connie replied, feeling like a novice Queenie herself under the education officer's gimlet eye. 'This is Nurse Baxter, who will be accompanying you this morning.'

Miss Knott's critical gaze shifted to Josie as she gathered up unravelled bandages. 'Indeed.'

Hugging a bottle of surgical spirit, a kidney bowl and a two-foot length of enema hose, Josie stood up.

'Very nice to meet you, Miss Knott.' She stepped forward and offered the education officer her hand. Miss Knott shook it. Unfortunately, the movement released the rebellious rubber tubing, which sprang up and slapped Miss Knott across the right cheek.

Josie's eyes stretched wide with horror. 'I'm so sorry.'

Miss Knott repositioned her glasses and glared at the student nurse.

'I have Nurse Baxter's workbook for you,' Connie said hurriedly. 'It's all up to date, and as you can see, she has completed many of the competences already.' She flipped it open to show the senior nurse the neat line of signatures next to the skills listed.

Miss Knott glanced over the page, then tucked the book under her arm and loomed over Josie.

'When you're ready, Nurse Baxter,' she barked, looking pointedly at the upended kidney bowl and artery forceps at her feet.

Connie gathered up the last few bits of equipment and packed them in Josie's case while Josie secured a bottle of iodine in the inside pocket. Then Miss Knott picked up her Gladstone bag and, snapping her heels together in true army fashion, marched out of the office.

'Off you go,' said Connie.

Josie gave her a forlorn look. 'Wish me luck.'

'Don't worry, you'll be fine,' said Connie encouragingly.

Josie forced a smile. Dragging her feet like a condemned man on his way to the scaffold, she followed Miss Knott out of the room.

Connie eased herself back into Phyllis Tatum's comfy chair and idly watched the particles of dust dancing in the sunlight streaming through the lounge window. After seeing Josie off, she'd helped Annie with the last two dressing clinic patients before setting out on her afternoon calls. Doing nothing for half an hour was just what she needed. Well, that and a cup of real coffee from Phyllis's American percolator, which was why she'd decided to take a break before heading back to the clinic to greet Josie and Miss Knott when they returned.

Since bumping into Phyllis in the wee small hours, Connie had fallen into the habit of dropping by for a relaxing chat every now and then. She was surprised to discover that despite her glamorous job, Phyllis was actually quite lonely. The fact that she didn't know either Connie's family or the girls at Munroe House meant that Connie soon found herself taking the older woman into her confidence.

The door opened and Phyllis walked in carrying a tray with two cups and a plate of biscuits.

'You look deep in thought,' she said, setting it in the middle of the coffee table. 'Are you worried about your student?'

Connie shook her head. 'A little. She's a bit fingers-and-thumbs with someone standing over her. What I was really thinking, Phyllis, was whether I should just give up men altogether and become a nun.'

'That's a bit drastic,' laughed Phyllis, handing Connie her drink and taking the seat opposite.

'To be honest, the thought of spending another afternoon with Bernard the bird man and his damp armpits makes a lifetime of celibacy seem very appealing,' Connie told her.

Phyllis pulled a face. 'I take it you're not looking forward to this date.'

Connie shook her head. 'No, but I'd never have heard the end of it from Mo if I hadn't agreed to it.'

Phyllis took a sip of coffee. 'You know, marriage isn't everything, Connie.'

Connie raised an eyebrow. 'Try telling that to my mother and sisters.'

'Things are changing for women,' continued Phyllis. 'And you're in one of the few professions where women can make their own way in the world. With your experience you could get a superintendent's post easily. I'm sure you'd be a blooming sight better than that Miss Dutton of yours.'

'I couldn't be much worse,' Connie replied.

'All right,' said Phyllis, shifting forward to the edge of her seat. 'But you're not limited to London, are you? With your qualifications you could work abroad in the colonies – Kenya or Rhodesia or even Australia. I'm sure they have need of district nurses and midwives.'

'Australia! I'd like to see my mum's face when I tell her that one,' laughed Connie. 'All hell broke loose when Bernie moved to West Ham. She'd have a heart attack if I told her I was going to the other side of the world.'

Phyllis looked at her intently. 'I'm just saying don't limit yourself, and use your qualifications to decide what *you* want to do, not what other people want. That's why I'm so keen on Grace going on to college, or even university.'

Connie's eyebrows rose. 'Goodness, other than doctors, I don't know anyone who's been to university.' She took a custard cream from the plate and bit it. 'It's not that I'm against taking a job somewhere else and moving away, but we're already nurses short at Munroe House, with three leaving by the summer, so I couldn't let the girls down and just leave.'

'You've seen him, haven't you?' said Phyllis flatly.

Connie's shoulders slumped. She had, almost weekly, but this was the first time she'd mentioned it to Phyllis since she'd stupidly met him at the Ship.

She looked at her hands. 'Yes.'

Phyllis glanced at her sharply. 'He didn't ask you to meet him again?'

'No. And I wouldn't go even if he asked me.' Connie forced herself to hold the other woman's gaze.

Phyllis scrutinised her closely. 'Yes, you would.'

Unhappiness pressed down on Connie. 'It's been months since he came back. You'd think I'd be over it by now.'

'He shouldn't have asked you in the first place, and if he asks you again, say no.' Phyllis continued to study Connie's face carefully. 'You know in your heart of hearts that you shouldn't get involved with him.'

'I know, I know,' sighed Connie. 'I'll be the other woman and it's a mortal s—'

'I'm not talking about the rights and wrongs of it,' interrupted Phyllis, with a dismissive wave of her hand. 'I'm talking about you getting hurt all over again. No matter what any married man promises, for your own sake, Connie, don't believe him.'

As Connie coasted along Chapman Street, a new display of toys in Feldman's shop window caught her eye. It was young Arthur's birthday in a couple of weeks, and she was in no hurry to return to Munroe House, so she pulled on her brakes and rolled to a stop. As she gazed in the window, a familiar figure stepped out of the stationer's opposite.

Connie had seen Charlie's mother a number of times, but after everything that had gone on, not least Maud's very public row with her just before Christmas, she'd always given her a wide berth. She was therefore surprised to see an expression of pure joy light up Mrs Ross's face.

'Oh, hello, Connie dear, how are you?' she exclaimed, positively beaming at her.

'I'm very well,' Connie replied. 'I'm just trying to decide whether to buy my nephew the Spitfire or the train with the Great Western livery for his birthday.' She indicated the display next to her.

Mrs Ross followed her gaze. 'I bought Charlie a Great Western train set for his tenth birthday,' she said. 'It had the tender and three carriages, a signal box and ten foot of track. It even had little passengers and a stationmaster and porter.'

'I remember, he told me about it,' said Connie feeling the inevitable pang of longing that thinking about Charlie engendered.

'He used to play with it for hours in front of the fire.' A sad smile lifted the corner of Mrs Ross's mouth. 'I can see him now, with his shirt adrift from his short trousers and his long socks gathered around his ankles, pushing his train around the track while making choo-choo sounds.' She looked mournfully at Connie. 'I always thought that when the time came, I'd see his son doing the same, but . . .' She forced a bright smile. 'And your family?'

'They're all fine,' Connie replied. 'My sister Mo had a little girl in—'

Mrs Ross's chin started to wobble. 'Oh Connie,' she burst out, tears welling in her eyes. 'Why couldn't my Charlie have married you instead of *her*?' She grabbed Connie's arm. 'I tried to make her welcome,' she sobbed. 'I really did.'

'I'm sure you—'

'But it seemed the more I tried to tell her the right way to look after my son, the worse she got. And you should see the state she made of my kitchen,' Mrs Ross continued. 'She tried to tell me her family had owned a restaurant, but I can't believe that after some of the foreign muck she put on the table.'

'I suppose she's finding things here a bit different from where she comes from,' said Connie.

'Well she should learn our ways,' countered Mrs Ross. 'I've told her she can use my new washing machine as long as she doesn't break it, but what does she do? Puts all Charlie's shirts in a tub in the yard then stomps up and down on them barefoot so all the neighbours can see. And her temper!' Mrs Ross continued without taking a breath. 'Don't ask me about her temper. Yelling and screaming fit to burst your eardrums. My poor Charlie didn't get a moment's peace with her nagging and rowing and weeping about getting their own place. In the end he was so worn down he found somewhere. He didn't want to go, you know.'

'I'm sure.'

'I know it's torn his heart out being forced to leave his own mother.' She shook Connie's arm. 'You wouldn't have made him do that, would you, Connie? You know, leave me, a poor widow, all alone.'

'Well, I—'

'I know you're a Catholic and do all the Mass stuff I don't agree with, but at least you're a local one, not like *her* and her Pope-loving Latin mumbling. You wouldn't have stuck a foot-high plaster statue of the Virgin Mary on my mantelshelf where everyone could see it, would you, dear?' Mrs Ross's face crumpled. 'And my poor little grandson, being cursed with such a mother. It's the devil who's done this, just to test my faith. Everyone at the mission says so.' She clasped her hands together and looked heavenward through the overhead tramlines. 'But I'm praying for God to lead little Filippo to true salvation.'

Connie smiled politely. 'I'm sure once he's old enough Filippo will appreciate—'

'She doesn't love him, you know, Connie,' Mrs Ross said, fixing her with a piercing stare. 'I told him, she only married him for an easy life. She wouldn't have stayed faithful to him for all those years like you did. "I bet you're sorry now, aren't you, Charlie?" I said. "Sorry you didn't come back and marry Connie." And he agreed. He said he'd been a stupid fool ever to let you go.'

Tears pinched the corners of Connie's eyes. 'I'm sorry,' she said and turned away. 'I have to get on.'

'Of course you have.' Mrs Ross caught her arm again. 'And I'm sorry too, Connie, that my Charlie chose *her* for a wife instead of you.'

Throwing a handful of grated carbolic soap into the treatment room's butler sink, Connie turned on the Ascot heater. The steaming water splashed on the pink shavings, sending up an acidic smell that tingled in her nose. At least if anyone saw her red eyes they'd assume it was due to the fumes from the carbolic rather than her unsettling encounter with Mrs Ross. It was blooming annoying and increasingly embarrassing that these days the slightest thing – a display of wedding stationery in the printer's window or a dance tune on the radio – could set off the waterworks.

Leaving the water to run, she went over to the draining board and gathered the dirty instruments from the tray.

It was nearly 6.30, and the afternoon visits had only just finished. Of course there should have been two of them clearing up, but Beattie and her fiancé, Collin, had a meeting with the vicar to go through their wedding arrangements, so Connie had sent her packing as soon as the last mum-to-be had waddled out. There was another reason why she was happy to stay behind, and that was to make sure that Josie's day with the superintendent had gone without any further upset.

Turning off the hot water, she threw the collection of foetal stethoscopes, kidney bowls and urine collection cups into the sink. Leaving them to soak, she turned her attention to the examination couches, and had just picked up the bottle of surgical spirit to clean them when the door burst open and Miss Knott marched in. Her eyes narrowed as she saw Connie.

Connie put down the bottle and cloth.

'You made it back in one piece then, Miss Knott,' she said pleasantly.

'I did, but no thanks to your trainee.'

Connie looked past the educational officer to the open door. 'Where's Nurse Baxter?'

'She was a little fraught, so I sent her to her room,' Miss Knott replied.

'That was kind of you,' said Connie. 'So how did you get on?'

'Get on!' bellowed the education officer. 'This is how *I* got on, Sister Byrne.' She held up her freshly bandaged right index finger. 'Not content with almost blinding me with an enema tube this morning, Nurse Baxter decided to douse me with Dettol before somehow managing to wedge the lid on the tin of paraffin gauze, which caused me to slice my finger trying to open it. And if that wasn't enough for one day, having confused her left from her right on several junctions, she finally managed to entangle the spokes of her bicycle in mine, which resulted in this.' She thrust her muscular left leg forward to reveal a gash in her woollen stocking running from ankle to knee.

'Oh dear,' said Connie.

'In almost thirty years of nursing I can't recall a clumsier nurse than the one I've had oversight of today,' snapped Miss Knott. 'The girl falls over her own feet, and thank God she doesn't field for England's first eleven, that's all I can say, or we'd never retain the Ashes.'

'But she's very caring with the patients and has a gentle touch,' said Connie.

'She has a pleasing way about her, I'll grant you,' conceded Miss Knott. 'And her bandaging, when she can get to grips with it, is neat enough, but she's forever knocking and dropping things.'

'She was nervous, that's all. After all, we all have our off days,' replied Connie lightly.

Miss Knott's severe expression didn't flicker. 'I hope, Sister Byrne, you are not suggesting that the care our patients receive should be dictated by the whims and fancies of a nurse's mood.'

'Of course I'm not,' Connie replied.

'Or that we at the Queen's Institute for District Nursing should lower the rigorous standards set down for us by Miss Nightingale, our most illustrious and esteemed founder?'

'No, but—'

'Then you will understand why I have had to fail Nurse Baxter,' Miss Knott concluded.

'Surely you can't fail a caring, compassionate nurse just because she's a bit clumsy when someone's watching her every move,' said Connie, feeling her cheeks grow hot.

A smug smile spread across Miss Knott's ruddy face. 'Oh, but I can, Sister Byrne.' She took Josie's workbook from under her arm and handed it to Connie. 'There will be a letter in the post confirming my assessment and giving Nurse Baxter a week's notice. In the meantime, I suggest you help her look for another job. Good day.'

She turned, and with a satisfied expression on her face marched out of the treatment room.

Connie stood there for a moment with her mouth open, then dashed into the hall and, taking the stairs two at a time, hurried towards Josie's bedroom. She knocked lightly, but there was no reply. She knocked again and opened the door a couple of inches.

'Josie, it's me,' she said softly, creeping in.

Predictably, Josie was lying face down on her bed, sobbing.

Connie closed the door quietly before crossing the small room and perching on the corner of the bed. Josie rolled over and looked at her with red-rimmed eyes for a second or two, then scrambled upright.

'I knew she was going to fail me as soon as that blooming rubber tubing hit her in the face,' she hiccuped, wiping her tear-stained face with the palms of her hands.

Connie took her unused handkerchief from her uniform pocket. 'But that was an accident.'

'I know I can be a bit clumsy, and I'll admit I dropped a bandage in Mr Lammings' house and got tangled in Mrs Dean's knitting when I moved it, but . . .' Tears streamed down Josie's cheeks again.

'Just tell me what happened,' said Connie calmly.

Josie blew her nose. 'We went to Mr Isaac first, and despite Miss Knott looming over me I laid out the equipment and drew up the insulin without a hitch. It was the same when I got to Mrs Wainscott. I set out the boiled water, baked gauze, forceps and all the rest, but then she started on at me about what I would do for a wet wound. So I explained that I'd use dry gauze if there wasn't an infection present and iodine if there was. Then I explained how I'd use Jelonet for burns and how wood wool was better than cotton under Gamgee if the wound was very oozy. Then she fired a load of other questions at me like what was the correct temperature to sterilise milk, how would I make up a charcoal poultice and when would I use a starch one instead, and I told her.'

'What did she do then?' asked Connie.

'Stood chewing her lip until I'd finished,' Josie replied. 'I tried to keep calm like you told me to and ignore her, but it's very difficult with her breathing down my neck. Then just as I was finishing up, she picked up her bag and knocked the table. The bottle of Dettol was uncorked and a couple of drops hit her coat. She was furious and accused me of throwing it over her. Poor Mrs Wainscott tried to help and told Miss Knott I was one of the nicest nurses at Munroe House, to which Miss Knott replied that she didn't care if I was agreeable if I wasn't efficient. She stood there like thunder until I'd finished, then stormed out. I'd just about got myself back on an even keel, but when we got to Mrs Peters' in Bigland Street, Miss Knott started quizzing me about Latin abbreviations on prescriptions before I'd even spread everything out on the table. I was shaking so much from trying to remember the difference between *omn. bid.* and *omn. bih.* that by the time I got to that old toffee tin Mrs Peters bakes her dressings in, I could barely hold it and Miss Knott snatched it out of my hand. I tried to warn her about the sharp edge but she'd already caught her finger, and it all sort of went downhill rapidly after that.'

'What about the accident with the bicycles?' asked Connie.

'She tore off in a huff from Mrs Peters', and by the time I caught up with her she was by the town hall in Cable Street,' Josie explained, blowing her nose again. 'We were just about to turn into Cannon Street Road when her front wheels got caught in the tram lines. I turned right but she couldn't so we ended up in a tangle on the cobbles. Thankfully, one of the Charrington's brewery wagons was passing and the driver helped us back on our feet.' Tears welled up in Josie's blue eyes and she covered her face with her hand. 'Even before I started my nurse training I knew I wanted to be a district nurse. I worked hard and got to the top of my set so I would be considered for Queenie training, and now . . .' She looked mournfully up at Connie and her chin wobbled. 'What am I going to do?'

Connie's lips pulled into a tight line. 'What are *we* going to do, you mean.'

Josie managed a brave smile. 'Thank you.'

Connie stood up. 'First of all, you're going to get yourself changed for supper and I'm going to see Millie.'

Leaving Josie to tidy herself up, Connie went down to the first floor and knocked on Millie's door. Millie was standing by the sink and had just taken her uniform off. She looked around as Connie walked in.

'Can you do me a favour? I—'

Connie stopped. Millie looked exhausted.

'How's your mum?' she asked quietly, sitting on the dressing table stool.

'Oh, you know,' Millie replied, forcing a smile. 'I managed to coax a bowl of porridge down her this morning, but she just picked at her shepherd's pie tonight. I'll have to try and make stew out of it tomorrow as I can't afford to throw away half our meat rations.'

'Is she sleeping any better?' asked Connie.

Millie shook her head. 'A few hours at most, usually from midnight until the sun comes up at four, but that's it.'

'You can't go on like this,' said Connie.

'Don't worry, I know the rules about staying out all night but I only do it if I'm not on call and I'm always back before everyone's awake so Miss Dutton will be none the wiser,' Millie replied.

'I'm not talking about being caught AWOL. I'm talking about you doing a full day's work and then being up half the night. You'll make yourself ill.'

'Don't worry, I'll be fine.' Millie suppressed a yawn. 'So what's the favour?'

'Can you finish clearing up the treatment room for me? I've got to get an urgent letter to QN headquarters in the post before supper.'

It was just before 5.30 when Connie was finally satisfied she'd put Josie's case clearly but respectfully in writing. As it was still an hour until supper, she decided that if she hurried, she'd be able to get to the main sorting office opposite Whitechapel station so the letter would catch the evening post.

As it was a fine afternoon, the street's younger children were in the middle of a spirited game of tag in the road outside Munroe House while their older brothers and sisters milled around at the corner. Connie turned into Arbour Square to cut through to Whitechapel Road, but as she entered the small ornamental garden in the middle, someone called her name. She looked round to see Malcolm Henstock with a fishing rod in one hand and a basket over his shoulder. He was accompanied by a boy wearing short grey trousers and a navy blazer with a ship's wheel badge on the breast pocket.

'Mr Henstock, how nice to see you,' she said, smiling at him as he reached her.

Dressed in olive slacks, a Tattersall shirt with a tweed tie and leather elbow patches on his brown corduroy jacket, he looked as if he should be striding across a farm rather than down an East End street. It was the sort of get-up Charlie wouldn't have been seen dead in, but with the summer breeze ruffling his rich brown hair and putting a sparkle in his hazel eyes, Malcolm Henstock looked quite appealing.

'Malcolm, please,' he said, smiling at her.

Connie laughed. 'All right, and as I'm off duty, I'm Connie. How's your mother?'

'Bearing up, as she likes to put it,' Malcolm replied. 'But thanks to your ministrations, she hasn't had any more problems with her leg.'

'I'm pleased to hear it.' Connie turned her attention to the boy. 'And who's this?'

'I'm Pete,' the boy replied.

'And you go to Redcoat school, I see.'

The boy nodded. 'I'm going into the second year soon.' He looked up at the man beside him. 'Uncle Malcolm, can I go and look for dragonflies in the square?'

'If you like,' Malcolm replied good-naturedly. 'But don't scuff your shoes or your mum with be after me.'

Pete grinned and ran off across the grass.

'And don't tread on the flowers,' Malcolm called after him.

'I thought you were an only child,' said Connie, noticing the clean line of his jaw as he looked away.

Malcolm turned back. 'Pete calls me uncle but he's my cousin really.' The corners of his mouth lifted in a boyish smile. 'A late surprise for my Aunt Ida, and since my Uncle Harold died on fire watch three years ago, I've taken him under my wing.'

'That's good of you,' Connie said, feeling oddly touched by his care.

He gave an embarrassed shrug. 'I'm not one for going drinking or hanging around in dance halls, so I'm happy to give Pete a bit of my time. My father passed away when I was eight, so I know what it's like to grow up without one. And it gets me in practice for when I have my own children.'

'Are you getting married?'

His eyes twinkled. 'Not yet.'

They stared at each other.

'Guess what, Uncle Malcolm,' Pete shouted as he tore across the soft turf towards them. 'I saw something with at least a hundred legs!'

'Cor,' said Malcolm, looking suitably impressed. He ruffled the lad's hair. 'We ought to let Sister Byrne get about her business, and *we* ought to get to the canal before it's time to come back.'

Connie suppressed a smile. 'Well, it's nice to see you, Malcolm.'

'You too.'

'And I hope you catch something,' she said, indicating the fishing rod with a nod of her head.

He laughed. 'Probably just old boots and pram wheels as usual, but,' his eyes sparkled again, 'you never know, one day I might just get lucky.'

Pulling on the brass handle, worn smooth with age, Connie stepped into the cool of the nurses' home just as the supper gong sounded. Hanging up her jacket, she turned to follow the nurses heading for the refectory, but before she'd taken a couple of steps, Hannah's blonde head popped out of the treatment room.

'Oh Connie, thank goodness you're back,' she said, looking visibly relieved. 'Your mother's waiting for you in the quiet lounge.'

'My mum?'

'And she looks none too happy about something.'

Puzzled, Connie made her way back along the hall and into the lounge at the back of the house. Maud was sitting on the two-seat sofa by the window. She was dressed as if going to a mothers' meeting at the church in a flowery day dress, a navy jacket with the marcasite brooch Mo had bought her for Christmas, and her best hat. There was an empty teacup at her elbow and a look of smouldering displeasure on her face.

Connie gave her a bright smile. 'This is a nice surprise, Mum.'

'Don't you "nice surprise" me, Connie,' her mother barked. 'What's all this about you carrying on with Charlie?'

'It's nice to see you too, Mum,' Connie snapped. 'And just to put you right, I'm not carrying on with Charlie or anyone else for that matter.'

'That's not what I've heard.' Maud adjusted her bosom with her crossed arms. 'It was the talk of the Sainsbury's queue, it was. I didn't know where to put my face.'

'I suppose you're talking about Maria turning up at the clinic,' Connie replied.

'Me and everyone else,' her mother said. 'I hope you know we've always been a respectable family. Neither Mo nor Bernie had to hold their bouquet high when they walked down the aisle, not like some I could mention around here.'

'I know that,' Connie replied. 'But I'm not doing anything I shouldn't.'

'What about meeting Charlie in the Ship?'

Connie felt her cheeks glow. 'I suppose you wheedled that out of Mo.'

'Too right I did.' Maud snorted. 'I'm not surprised you asked her to keep shtum.' She tutted and shook her head. 'My own daughter a floozy.'

'For goodness' sake, Mum,' said Connie, struggling to keep hold of her temper. 'I met him for a drink, that's all. Tell the truth, he realises now that he made a big mistake.'

'Does he indeed?'

'Yes,' retorted Connie, remembering Charlie's miserable expression. 'He's very unhappy, and after the way Maria carried on the other day, I can understand why.'

'Serves him right,' said her mother smugly. 'That'll teach him not to let his blooming willy do all the thinking.'

'Look, Mum,' said Connie, slumping wearily into the closest chair. 'We were in the Ship for an hour at the most. Charlie told me what a fool he'd been and how he wished he'd never set eyes on Maria. He said he wasn't thinking straight when he married her.'

'And what did you say?'

Connie swallowed the lump in her throat. 'I said what's done is done, and I was sorry it hadn't worked out with Maria but he was married to her and that was an end to it.'

'And did he ask you to take up with him again, Connie?'

With some difficulty Connie held her mother's gaze. 'Of course not,' she laughed lightly as tears gathered.

Sympathy replaced anger in her mother's eyes. 'I know it's hard, luv. But you'll get over it.'

'I know,' Connie replied, wondering if she ever would.

Maud placed her hand over Connie's and squeezed. 'I just don't want to see Charlie hurt you again, that's all.'

Connie forced a smile. 'Don't worry, Mum. I've got no intention of wasting myself on a married man, and especially not Charlie Ross.'

Chapter Sixteen

Connie sat up and for the third time plumped her pillows, then lay down again. She resumed her study of the ceiling and found it exactly the same as it had been for the past three hours. With Miss Dutton marking nurses' files for being three minutes late and a full day cycling around East London, another sleepless night was really not what she needed. Blooming men! Well, more particularly, blooming Charlie. Perhaps the convent wasn't such a bad idea after.

She closed her eyes and tried to think about anything but her ex-fiancé.

The phone in the hall rang and Connie heard Eva, who was on night call, open her door, pad along the landing and down the stairs. She forced her mind on to other things, concentrating instead on the trip to see *A Matter of Life and Death* at the ABC that she and Millie had planned for Friday. Eva's steps sounded on the landing again, and then there was a knock and the door opened.

'Con,' Eva whispered.

She sat up. 'It's all right, Eva. I'm not asleep.'

Eva came into the room. 'I'm sorry, and I wouldn't wake you, but it's West End Central police station and they're asking for you.'

'What do they want?' Connie said, throwing off the blankets and swinging her legs out of bed.

Eva shrugged. 'They wouldn't say. Just asked for you.'

Shoving her feet in her slippers and grabbing her dressing gown from the back of the door, Connie left her room and hurried down the stairs. She picked up the receiver lying beside the phone and held it to her ear. 'Hello, Sister Byrne speaking.'

'It's Desk Sergeant Woolmer here, at West End Central,' said the gruff male voice at the other end. 'Do you know a Phyllis Tatum?'

'Yes, I do.'

'Well we've got her in custody here and she's given you as a person who might stand her bail.'

'She's been arrested?'

'Along with the rest of the Imperial Gentlemen's Club,' the sergeant replied. 'She's in the cells now, but as there are two dozen women and only two female lock-ups, the matron is getting a bit unhappy. Can you come?'

'Yes, of course,' Connie replied, trying to make sense of what she was hearing. 'But it'll take me about an hour.'

'That's all right, luv, she ain't going nowhere,' the sergeant replied. 'Just come to the front desk and ask for me.' The phone went dead.

Connie replaced the receiver, then made her way upstairs. Eva's door opened.

'Not bad news, I hope,' she said, sticking her head out.

'No,' Connie replied. 'At least I don't think so, but could you let me have a couple of bob for a taxi?'

After standing on Commercial Road for almost ten minutes, Connie finally flagged down a cab. Thirty minutes later, she was staring up at the solid white building planted among the delicate Regency town houses on Savile Row. She paused for a moment, then made her way up the dozen steps leading to West End Central police station.

Before she reached the door, it opened and two police officers walked out, then held it open for her. Stepping into the main entrance hall, Connie looked around, noting the block marble and gilt fixtures that revealed the building's 1930s origins. She took the stairs on her right, which led to another set of doors. Pushing them open, she walked in. Whereas the main entrance hall was chilly and smelt of floor polish and carbolic, here Connie was overwhelmed by the cloying atmosphere and the aroma of bodies and fried food.

Behind the public counter was a screen with alternate stripes of frosted and clear glass, which allowed the radio operators sitting on the other side to view the front desk and give assistance if needed.

Connie could hear the low hum of male voices somewhere out

of sight, and the occasional crackle followed by the tinny sound of the police radio. At the far end of the room were a couple of young constables chatting to an older colleague, who was pointing at a map of the area, while a policewoman over by a filing cabinet was bashing on an antiquated typewriter. The front counter was just six feet or so long and had been rubbed smooth by countless individuals who had either leaned on it or been pulled over it.

'Can I help you, miss?'

Connie turned and found a young constable with a smattering of shaving rash and a prominent Adam's apple looking enquiringly at her.

'Good evening,' she said, shifting her handbag from one hand to the other. 'I had a phone call from a Sergeant Woolmer regarding a Mrs Tatum who's been arrested.'

The officer glanced at the open log book on the desk in front of him and his index finger moved down the columns of names.

'No Tatum listed as far as I can see,' he said, looking up again. 'Are you sure it was here and not down the road at Vine Street?'

'Yes, I'm sure,' Connie replied. 'It's Mrs Phyllis Tatum. Are you sure she isn't—'

'She'll be down as Philomena De Bohun, it's her working name,' said the station sergeant as he appeared around the partition. Standing an inch or two over the regulation five foot ten, the officer was somewhere in his late thirties and had made a good start at acquiring middle-age spread. He had the letters C712 on his upright collar.

The young constable scanned the names again, then jabbed the page with a bony finger.

'Cell two.' He looked curiously at Connie. 'You know this wo—'

'Thank you, Hanson,' cut in the sergeant. 'I'll take it from here.'

Constable Hanson gave Connie another look then went back to whatever he'd been doing.

'Her working name?' Connie asked when he was out of earshot.

'All the girls have 'em,' the sergeant explained in a matter-of-fact tone. 'Well, I suppose it saves some loony bugger trying to—'

'I'm sorry, Sergeant,' said Connie, feeling a headache starting at the back of her eyes. 'It's three thirty in the morning, I'm standing in a police station and I haven't the faintest idea what's going on. Could you just tell me what Mrs Tatum has been arrested for?'

He looked startled. 'Prostitution. She's one of the regular toms in one of those top-class knocking shops at the back of Shepherd Market. Didn't you know?'

Connie stared blankly at him.

He looked concerned. 'You're still going to stand her bail, aren't you?'

Connie nodded.

'Good,' he said, visibly relieved. 'Old Phyllis is always as good as gold, and we know she's got a kid so we're happy to kick her out.' He pulled out a black bound ledger and opened it. 'If you could just fill in your name and address and sign here.' He indicated a dotted line at the bottom of the page and handed Connie a pen. She completed the bail form, then handed it back. The sergeant glanced over the page. 'That's fine. If you'd like to take a seat, I'll go and fetch her.'

He disappeared behind the partition again and Connie sat down on one of the wooden benches fixed to the wall. She didn't have long to wait. Within a few moments, the door at the far end opened and Sergeant Woolmer stepped out.

'Off you go then, luv,' he said, standing aside.

Phyllis hobbled out, her gold satin evening dress torn, her immaculate hair dishevelled, an earring missing and mascara caked on her lashes. As her gaze fell on Connie, there was desolation in her eyes.

Connie stood up and went over to her.

'Connie, I'm so, so sorry,' Phyllis sobbed. 'I didn't know who—'

'It's all right,' said Connie, taking Phyllis's coat from the officer behind her and slipping it around her shoulders. 'Let's go home.'

Phyllis had sat silently on the back seat of the taxi for the entire journey home. After trundling though an empty City, they reached Albert Square just as the first traces of light were streaking the sky.

Connie helped her out, paid the taxi and then followed her to the front door. Phyllis retrieved her key from the bottom of her handbag, but her hand shook so much, Connie took it from her and let them both in.

'Come on,' she whispered, taking Phyllis's elbow. 'I'll make you a cuppa.'

Without protest from Phyllis, Connie guided her towards the kitchen at the back of the house. Phyllis took her shoes off and slumped on a chair as Connie went to the modern cooker, which her sisters would give their eye teeth for, and lit the gas under the kettle. After searching out cups and milk, she whisked the kettle off the hob before its whistling woke Grace and Rebecca upstairs.

When she'd made the tea, she placed a cup in front of the other woman and took a seat opposite. Phyllis wrapped her hands around the hot mug, then looked up.

'I'm really sorry, but I didn't have anyone else to call. I'm usually home by six and couldn't bear to think of Grace getting up and wondering where I was, or worse, having the police call and tell her.'

'Well, I'm late on-call midwife tomorrow, so at least I can get some sleep before I start at midday.'

Phyllis regarded her thoughtfully for moment before she spoke again. 'Are you shocked?'

Connie glanced at the Prestcold fridge, the coffee percolator, the full biscuit tin and the new clothes washer with built-in mangle, then back at the woman in front of her. 'No, but I feel a bit stupid not to have realised for myself.'

'It's all that ruddy new copper in charge of Vice's fault, trying to up his cut. Old Lockhart was much more accommodating, even dropped by for a drink now and then,' said Phyllis, as if she was talking about her maiden aunt rather than the head of the Metropolitan Police's vice squad.

She stirred her tea and took a sip. 'It's always the same. New broom comes in and shakes everyone down. Usually they just nick a couple of girls who work the street to give us all notice. The owners pay up and everything settles down. But this bugger wanted to up the levy to twenty pounds a week. The owner baulked and so we were raided.'

'What will happen now?' asked Connie.

Phyllis sighed. 'We'll all be up before Marlborough Street magistrates' court in the morning and we'll have to cough up a fine, but then it'll be back to normal by the weekend.'

'But surely the court will close the bro— club?' asked Connie.

A cynical smile crept across Phyllis's lips and she shook her head. 'The girls will be charged with soliciting but the coppers won't mention the club as they don't want to kill the golden goose.'

Connie looked puzzled. 'How did you . . . you know, end up a . . .'

Phyllis raised her eyebrows. 'A prostitute? For the same reason most girls I know are on the game. A man. In my case a low-life bastard called Edward Faraday.' She ferreted around in her handbag and pulled out a packet of twenty Kensitas and her Dunhill lighter. 'I'm from Romford originally, but my mother died when I was about Grace's age,' she said, lighting the cigarette between her smudged scarlet lips. 'No one would ever call my father warm or loving even before my mother died, but after her death the house was like a mausoleum. He did his best, I suppose, to keep a roof over our heads, but as the eldest of three girls I bore the brunt of the household chores. Despite that, I did well at school and there was talk of college, but my father vetoed that, saying he needed my money. He tried to find me work on the bottling line at the brewery, but I got a job in the town hall instead. That's where I met Grace's father, Eddy Faraday.' A bitter expression twisted her lips. 'He viewed the typing pool as his personal harem, and he must have been rubbing his hands with glee the day I walked in.' She drew on her cigarette. 'His father was in banking and his mother's family were rolling in it.' She gave a mirthless laugh. 'And when he said he loved me and promised we'd be married, I, like the brainless idiot I was, actually believed him. Of course, he changed his tune when I told him I was in the family way. He denied flat out that the baby was his and said he'd have me locked up in an institution for moral weakness if I tried to cause trouble. I was heartbroken that the man I'd built my life and future around had deceived me.'

Connie looked grim. 'I know what that feels like.'

'But at least you weren't seven months gone,' continued Phyllis drily. 'I hid my condition for as long as I could, but when one of the supervisors found out, I was sacked. I went home and told my father.' Her cool blue eyes clouded. 'I can see him now, sitting in that old armchair by the fire in his shirtsleeves, with a roll-up dangling from his lips. Just sat there he did, silent as the grave, while I sobbed out the story. When I'd finished, he got up, went upstairs and came down with a suitcase. He told me to pack my things and leave. Twenty minutes later I was outside on the pavement with a handful of clothes and five shillings in my pocket.

'One of the girls in the typing pool told me about a mothers' hospital in Plaistow, so I caught a bus from the marketplace straight there. It was market day, and the smell of cow dung made me retch as I waited.' She smiled at Connie. 'It's funny how you remember silly things. Anyhow, the home took me in and Grace was born nine weeks later. The rules were that they would care for you until the child was eight weeks old but then you had to give it up for adoption. It seemed like a fair exchange to me. I had it all planned out, I'd even skimmed the papers to see what jobs were on offer, and then . . .' All hostility left Phyllis's expression, and she smiled. 'And then, after twelve hours of labour, I held Grace for the first time, and I knew I'd kill rather than ever give her up. I left the home after eight weeks with her in my arms, determined to keep her.

'After six months, I found myself in a basement in Hackney with fungus on the walls, a hungry baby and no food in the cupboard, so I left Grace with the woman downstairs, got myself into my best clothes and caught a bus to Marble Arch. I went into the Dorchester and bought a drink at the bar. I kept glancing at my watch as if I was waiting for someone, and it wasn't long before a man came up and asked to buy me another. I had a double brandy and found out he was down from Birmingham on business and was staying in a smaller hotel around the corner. When he asked how much, I hadn't got a clue, so I said a guinea and he handed it over. We went back to his hotel and I left forty-five minutes later with enough money to keep me and Grace for a month.'

'So who's the chap on the mantelshelf?'

'Some bloke who needed a glamorous woman on his arm for a swanky do,' she replied, flicking ash into the ashtray in the middle of the table. 'He sent me the photo, so I just pretend he's my dead husband.'

'But how do you . . . you know.'

'Every time I was with a man, I just thought of the reason I was letting some stranger sweat and grunt on me – Grace.' She took another puff on her cigarette. 'Even with the ones who want you to do things you . . .' She cast a furtive look at Connie. 'Well, to cut a long story short, I built up a trade and moved me and Grace out of the damp basement to a snug two rooms in Hackney and then to a nice little flat in Bethnal Green. I staked out a territory in Mayfair and slipped a few bob to the doormen in the big hotels, and would work the bars most nights. Then war broke out and the demand for private company went through the roof. I met Mrs Kilpatrick, the owner of the Imperial Gentlemen's Club, and joined her girls. Safety in numbers and all that. Then the Yanks arrived, God bless them' – she looked heavenward – 'and the money came rolling in. That's when I bought this place.'

'You own this house?' said Connie in astonishment.

No one she knew owned a shed, let alone a three-bedroom house with a garden.

'Yes,' Phyllis replied, stubbing out her half-smoked cigarette. 'I got it at a knock-down price of two hundred and thirty pounds because it was so near the docks and could have been flattened by a stray bomb. It's ideal. Far enough away so no one knows me but just a short ride from Mayfair.'

'But you're an intelligent woman, Phyllis, with a good education. Couldn't you stop and find an ordinary job?' asked Connie.

A cynical smile lifted the corner of the other woman's mouth. 'I could, Connie, some do, but I can earn more money in a night than you earn in a week, and that's too good to turn my back on. I wouldn't be able to give Grace her piano lessons or the private tuition that will get her into the grammar school if I worked in a shop or an office. Don't judge me, Connie. I do it for Grace.'

'I don't judge you,' Connie replied. 'Who knows? There but for the grace of God . . .' She drained the last of her tea and stood up. 'I ought to get back. I'll pop in on Tuesday and—'

'No, don't,' Phyllis cut in. 'If word got out that you were pally with a pros—' moisture glistened in her eyes, 'with me, it would damage your reputation and you'd probably lose your job as well.'

Sadness welled up in Connie.

Phyllis blinked and put on a too-bright smile. 'I'll be moving soon anyway, just in case one of the cops from West End Central gets transferred to Arbour Square,' she continued. 'I'll probably try to get a place around Devons Road, nearer to Grace's school, so . . .'

'I understand,' said Connie softly. 'Give my regards to Grace and tell her I wish her well.'

She turned to leave, but Phyllis caught her arm. 'I'm sorry you had to find out like this, Connie.'

Connie patted her hand. 'So am I, Phyllis. So am I.'

The old chestnut horse between the shafts of the milk float was plodding slowly up the street while the milkman collected empty bottles and deposited full pints on each doorstep as Connie turned into Sutton Street.

The early morning chill had vanished and now sunlight was peeping over the houses on the other side of the street, warming her face.

Turning over the revelations surrounding Phyllis in her mind, Connie turned down the small alley at the rear of Munroe House heading for the back door but as she did she saw Millie and Alex coming towards her from the opposite direction.

They looked worried and bone-weary and oddly, they were both dressed in their uniforms.

Relief flooded across Alex's haggard face when he spotted Connie hurrying towards them.

'My goodness, what's happened?' asked Connie, stopping just in front of them.

'It's Mum,' said Millie, looking at her through red-rimmed eyes. 'She's in the London Hospital . . .' She turned her face into her fiancé's chest and sobbed.

'It must have all been too much for Doris,' Alex explained, hugging Millie to him. 'Millie popped in to see her this afternoon and found her with her head in the oven.'

'Oh my goodness! Is she all right?' asked Connie.

'Thankfully, Millie arrived just in time,' continued Alex, as

Millie continued to sob. 'And the doctor doesn't think there is any permanent damage but he is running some tests and we'll know more later once the results are back.'

Millie pulled herself together and, taking a large handkerchief from her sleeve, blew her nose. 'We've been there all night. I couldn't leave.'

'Of course, you couldn't,' said Connie. 'I'd have been the same.'

Alex hugged Millie and kissed her head. 'I'm sorry, sweetheart, I don't want to go but I have to get back before the duty sergeant marks me up as absent—'

'It's all right, luv,' Millie replied, forcing a smile. 'I'll be fine. You'd better get some shut-eye before you have to go on duty.'

'But I'll see you later at the hospital,' said Alex. 'I'll get there as soon as I can after I've started late turn.'

'I know you will.'

'And ring me at the section house if you need me—'

'I will, now you get going before you fall asleep on the pavement,' she said, disentangling herself from his embrace.

Alex kissed her briefly. 'I don't like leaving you so upset—'

'Don't worry, Alex,' said Connie, putting an arm around her friend. 'I'll make sure she's all right.'

He hesitated for a second or two then kissed Millie again before striding off.

They watched him until he disappeared around the corner then tears welled up in Millie's eyes.

'It's my fault,' she said.

'Of course it's not,' said Connie, placing a comforting arm around her friend's shoulder.

'But I should have seen how unhappy she was instead of fretting and worrying about the wedding,' continued Millie.

'I'm sure she'll be fine,' said Connie, leading her friend across the yard. 'Once she's had a couple of weeks rest she'll be her old self again by the time you and Alex get married. And it's not as if the big day's next week, is it?'

'No, there's still six weeks and three days until we wed.'

'Not that you're counting,' Connie winked.

Millie tried to smile but her expression remained bleak. 'If only we didn't have to leave so soon after the wedding.'

'I'm sure everything will be fine,' said Connie, praying it would be so. 'Now, it's been a long night for both of us, why don't we have a nice cuppa before we turn in?'

Millie gave her a puzzled look. 'Why? Where have you been then?'

'It's a long story,' Connie replied, yawning and opening the back door.

Chapter Seventeen

Connie tied the elaborate head bandage just above Brian Hamersley's ear. 'There we go,' she said, tucking in the ends.

It was almost 10.30, and she and Sally were battling to get through the dozens of patients still sitting in the hallway waiting to be attended to at the Thursday morning dressing clinic. With the summer sunshine streaming thought the treatment room windows, Connie had already done two ear syringes, dressed the hand of a child who'd touched the bars on an electric fire and now had a festering wound, poulticed an oozing carbuncle and sluiced industrial-strength starch out of a laundry woman's eyes. At this rate they'd probably have to work through lunchtime to be out of the treatment room in time to start the afternoon antenatal session.

'And don't let me hear of you and your chum over there,' she glanced across the treatment room to where Sally was dabbing iodine on a gash across Michael Connor's forearm, 'playing Captain Kidd with your dockers' hooks again.'

Connie vaguely knew both Brian and Michael, as they'd boxed with her brother Jim before the war. After being demobbed, they had returned to their previous occupation in the Royal Docks. It had clearly been a slow day on the quayside, as they'd idled away their time fencing with their foot-long curved hooks, resulting in injuries on both sides.

'No, Sister,' Brian replied, looking suitably chastised.

'I should think not,' Connie continued in her best unamused matron voice. 'Now, I want you to leave the dressing alone until next Tuesday morning's clinic, when the nurse on duty will take another look at it.'

'Righty-ho, Sister,' said Brian, standing up and shrugging on his donkey jacket.

Connie wrapped up her dirty instruments, then headed over to the nurses' desk.

'That'll be one and six for today and another shilling for when you come back next Tuesday,' she said, taking the pen from her top pocket and writing his name on the next empty line in the ledger.

Brian brought a handful of change out of his pocket and counted out the fee.

Handing him the receipt, Connie said, 'If you feel feverish or pus starts to leak through the bandage, then come back to the clinic if we're open or drop a message in the out-of-hours box next to the front door and a nurse will call. Now, take a seat outside until Sister Scott has patched up Captain Blood.'

'Right you are, Sister,' he said, grinning at her and stuffing his battered cap in his pocket.

Connie returned to her dressing station and gathered up the dirty equipment, taking it through to the sluice room. After dropping the instruments into the soapy water to soak, she went to the smaller hand sink and turned on the tap. She'd just lathered her hands when Gladys's flushed face appeared around the edge of the open door.

'Oh, you're here then,' she said, casting her piggy eyes over Connie.

'Where else did you think I would be when my name's chalked up for clinic and the place is heaving with patients? Timbuktu?' Connie replied. 'More to the point,' she continued, picking up the nail brush, 'with Ruth and Linda off sick, why aren't you out on your rounds?'

'There's no need to take that tone with me,' Gladys replied. 'And not that it's any business of yours, Connie Byrne, but if you must know, I've been helping Miss Dutton.'

The corner of Connie's mouth lifted in a wry smile. 'There's a surprise.'

Gladys's cheeks started to colour. 'Well she has to have someone she can rely on, especially as you and Millie seem to go out of your way to annoy her.'

Connie elbowed the taps off. 'What do you want, Gladys?'

'Miss Dutton wants to see you in her office, now.'

Connie's stomach flipped over in an uncomfortable way.

'But I'm in the middle of clinic,' she said, unhooking the towel.

'Aren't you going to ask me what it's about?' asked Gladys with a syrupy smile.

'No,' Connie replied coolly.

'Well you'd better get your skates on or you'll be in even more trouble,' said Gladys, her face disappearing back around the door.

Connie laid the towel over the rail to dry, then walked back into the treatment room, where Sally was fastening a sling around a young woman's neck.

'I'm sorry, Sister Scott, but I have to—'

'I heard,' interrupted Sally with a sympathetic smile. 'Don't worry. I'll carry on here.'

Connie headed out into the corridor and turned towards Miss Dutton's office. Josie was hovering outside.

'I heard the superintendent was looking for you,' she said as Connie reached her. 'It's about the letter, isn't it?'

'I expect so,' she replied. 'Although I wasn't expecting them to reply so soon.'

Josie twisted the edge of her apron. 'It's all my fault. I should have just put my letter of resignation in there and then.'

'Nonsense. You were unfairly treated by Miss Knott, and as the supervising sister for the Association, it's my responsibility to draw the Institute's attention to that fact,' said Connie with a lot more bravado than she felt. 'Now off you go, make yourself scarce.'

Josie hurried away and Connie knocked smartly on the door.

'Come!'

Smoothing her apron straight, she walked in.

Miss Dutton was sitting behind her desk, writing in the clinic order book, her shoulders rigid and the lace on her cap shaking a little with the movement of her pen. After what seemed like an eternity, she rolled the teak blotter over the page and set her pen down. She looked up, and a sour expression tightened her narrow face.

Ignoring her pounding heart, Connie forced a pleasant smile. 'You wanted to see me, Superintendent?'

A glint of fury sparked in Miss Dutton's ice-blue eyes.

'Did you write to the Queen's Nursing Institute's education committee complaining about Miss Knott?' she snapped.

Connie held the superintendent's gaze. 'I wouldn't call it a letter of complaint exactly; more a request for Nurse Baxter to have a second chance to pass her home visit assessment.'

Miss Dutton picked up a headed letter from the pile next to her. 'I believe you state that in your opinion Miss Knott was, and I quote, "intimidating" and "overbearing".'

'She was,' Connie replied. 'The home visits are nerve-racking enough for the student Queenies without having someone like Miss Knott barking orders and finding fault at every turn.'

'The other three passed,' countered Miss Dutton.

'They did, but Nurse Robb spent an hour sobbing after she returned and Boscombe had a migraine for two days,' said Connie. 'Even Tucker, who is as stoic as they come, had nightmares for a week after her encounter with Miss Knott.'

The superintendent scanned down the page. 'You also state that a number of the questions she asked Baxter were outside the course requirements.'

'They were,' Connie replied. 'She quizzed her about stuff that went out with the Ark.'

A flush splashed up Miss Dutton's neck and she looked back at the letter.

'You also had the bald-faced impertinence to request that Baxter be given a second chance to pass her external assessment,' she spat out.

Connie squared her shoulders. 'I did.'

'And may I ask you why you didn't feel the need to request my permission before you scribbled off these accusations against one of the Institute's most senior officers?'

'You made it quite clear when they arrived that you didn't want the trainee Queenies under your feet, so I decided to take on the responsibility myself,' Connie replied, her gaze steady.

Miss Dutton glared at her for a moment, then her eyes returned to the letter. 'Well, although I'm sure any dedicated nurse such as myself would regard it as a deplorable lowering of standards, it seems the committee has acceded to your request.'

'You mean Nurse Baxter will be able to retake her home visit assessment?' said Connie, almost afraid she'd misheard.

'Yes, they will be writing to us in due course once they've arranged a date.' Miss Dutton set the letter aside, placed her hands on the open book in front of her and fixed Connie with a vindictive stare. 'But if you ever go behind my back again, I'll have you out in the blink of an eye, and I doubt you'll find it easy to get another district nurse position without a reference. Do you understand?'

'Yes, Superintendent,' said Connie.

'Good, now get out.'

Leaning on the closed door, Connie looked up at the ornate cornice plaster above and let out a long breath.

Just then, the phone on the message table at the other end of the hall rang, and Hannah came out of the nurses' office.

'Munroe House, Sister Green speaking. How can I help you?' she said, taking the pen out of her top pocket in readiness.

There was a pause, and then she looked at Connie. 'Thank you, Doctor, I'll tell her.'

She covered the mouthpiece with her hand. 'It's Dr Robinson. He wants you to meet him right away at Mrs Hogan's. She's in labour.'

With her legs aching from the quarter-of-a-mile dash, Connie screeched to a halt outside Mrs Hogan's and jumped off her bike. There was a huddle of anxious-looking women, all dressed in faded wraparound overalls and headscarves, hovering outside the Hogans' front door.

'Don't worry, luv,' said one of them as Connie reached for her cycle chain. 'I'll get my Bob to lock yer bike. We'll take the kids too, when they get home from school.'

'That's very good of you,' said Connie, lifting her bag from the front basket.

'Least we can do,' said a second woman, holding a chubby-faced infant on her hip. 'Mags 'as helped us lot out often enough.'

There were nods of agreement and murmurs of 'poor woman' and 'a crying shame'.

'You just get yourself in the 'ouse, Sister, and tell her not to worry,' continued the young mother. 'And tell her we're all finking of her.'

Connie went in and made her way up the stairs to the main bedroom. Dr Robinson, dressed in a navy blazer and tawny slacks and sporting a red bow tie, was already there, sitting on the bed taking Mrs Hogan's blood pressure while she stared blankly at the ceiling. He acknowledged Connie with a nod as she walked in but continued with his task.

Mrs Hogan looked every day of her thirty-six years. Her hair was plastered to the pillow beneath her head. Her face was ashen with fear and her eyes swam with unshed tears. Other than her swollen stomach, the pregnant woman hardly disturbed the blankets covering her.

Connie put her bag under the table that had been set out for her, and prayed to God that she wouldn't need it yet. She took off her coat and hooked it over the two dressing gowns on the back of the door.

Dr Robinson removed the stethoscope from his ears and took Mrs Hogan's blood pressure.

'Well that seems fine enough,' he said, packing the sphygmomanometer back in its case.

'But what about my baby?' Mrs Hogan's hands lay protectively on her stomach. 'Am I going to lose it?'

'Not if we can help it,' Dr Robinson replied, smiling professionally. 'That's why I've called Sister Byrne.' He patted Mrs Hogan's hand. 'And now that she's arrived, I need to have a quick word with her outside.'

Mrs Hogan forced a heart-wrenching smile. 'Yes, Doctor.'

Dr Robinson stood up and ushered Connie out of the room and towards a small window overlooking the back yard.

'What's happened?' asked Connie in a low voice as they huddled in the alcove.

'Mrs White next door called me about an hour ago saying Mrs Hogan was having pains. I told her to tell Mrs Hogan to go straight to bed with a pillow under her rear. When I arrived thirty minutes later, the pains were no worse. Her vitals are stable and the baby's heartbeat is thumping along at a steady hundred and eighty, and the little chap is wriggling around.'

Connie let out a long breath. 'Thank God.'

Dr Robinson's grim expression didn't change. 'Unfortunately, the mucus plug has dislodged, but as far as I can tell, the fore and hind waters are still intact. In view of her history, I thought it wiser not to examine her internally, so I have no idea if she is dilating. However, judging by the irregular nature of the contractions, and given that they haven't progressed, it's my considered opinion that Mrs Hogan is in the very early stages of labour.'

'But she's only twenty-five weeks,' gasped Connie.

'Which is why I'm going to try to stop her labour by giving her morphine.'

'But might that—'

'Have the opposite effect and speed it up?'

Connie nodded.

'It's a chance I'll have to take. You know as well as I do that if labour progresses . . .'

Connie felt a lump form in her throat. 'I know.'

'That's why I called you. I'm going to give her twenty grams, but I need you to monitor her.' His gaze locked with hers. 'I'm sorry, Connie. I know if it doesn't work you'll be the one to deliver a stillborn baby, but . . .'

'If it works, at least Baby Hogan has a fighting chance,' Connie said softly.

Dr Robinson gave her an approving nod.

Mrs Hogan was lying with her hands still clasped over her stomach and her eyes shut, but she opened them as they walked back into the room.

'Now, Mrs Hogan, are the pains any worse?'

She shook her head. 'About the same.'

'Good,' Dr Robinson said, picking up his bag and plonking it on the end of the bed. 'What football team does your husband support?'

Mrs Hogan looked confused. 'West Ham, of course.'

Dr Robinson nodded. 'Well then, you've got one of their future strikers tucked away at the moment, but he's not ready for the whistle yet, so I,' he took a tin from his bag, 'am going to give you an injection that will hopefully keep him in the dressing room a little bit longer.'

'Thank you, Doctor,' said Mrs Hogan with tears glistening in her eyes.

Dr Robinson rose and took his bag to the dressing table. As he stood with his back to them drawing up the injection, Mrs Hogan turned to Connie.

'My baby will be all right, won't it, Sister?'

'Let's hope so, Mrs Hogan,' she said, giving the terrified woman a reassuring smile.

Dr Robinson returned holding a syringe in his hand. 'If you please, Sister.'

Turning down the bedclothes and lifting Mrs Hogan's night-dress, Connie uncorked the doctor's bottle of surgical spirit and swabbed an area at the top of the woman's thigh, then went around to the other side of the bed and took her patient's hand. Mrs Hogan flinched as the needle went in, but as the opioid spread through her system, her eyelids fluttered down.

The front door banged and she jolted awake. 'Wilf!'

'It's all right,' said Connie, gently placing her hand on the other woman's shoulder.

Mrs Hogan's eyes closed again and she sighed.

'I'll talk to Mr Hogan on my way out,' said Dr Robinson, rising to his feet. 'I'll be back after surgery to see how things are, but if you need me in the meantime, send someone to fetch me.'

Grasping the handles of his case firmly, the doctor left the room and his footsteps thumped down the stairs.

Connie sat back in the chair and watched as Mrs Hogan's chest rose and fell slowly. After a few moments, the door opened and Wilf, still dressed in his work clothes, appeared in the doorway. He looked bleakly at his wife, then pulled out a three-legged stool from under the bed and took up his position opposite Connie.

The clock in the room below chimed the hour and Connie stood up.

Mr Hogan, who had sat next to his wife without moving for the past three hours, watched with anxious eyes as Connie turned down the bedcovers. Rubbing her hands together to warm them, she lifted Mrs Hogan's nightdress and gently laid her palms on her bump. Although she could feel the full womb under her fingertips, there was no hint of tightening.

Mrs Hogan had slipped into unconsciousness within minutes of the morphine entering her system, but her uterus had continued to contract for a worryingly long time, so much so that when Connie had examined her an hour after Dr Robinson's departure, she'd considered laying out her instruments. Mercifully, when she'd checked the next time, the contractions had started to ebb. Now that Mrs Hogan seemed to be stable, Connie needed to ensure that her other patient had come through the ordeal.

Taking the foetal stethoscope from the side table next to her, she placed one end on the woman's stomach and pressed her ear against the other. Although she could hear Mrs Hogan's blood and bowel sounds, she couldn't hear the baby's heartbeat. Praying that the morphine hadn't proved too much for its immature systems, she shifted the stethoscope to another position.

With her pulse thundering in her ears, she closed her eyes and felt a lump form in her throat, but just when she was about to give up, she heard a regular, if slow, pitter-patter sound echo through the instrument.

Hail Mary, Mother of God, she thought as she straightened up.

'Is everything all right, Sister?' Mr Hogan asked.

'As far as I can tell, everything is just as it should be,' she replied, letting go of a long breath. 'Baby Hogan's fast asleep like your wife, but he seems fine and dandy.'

Mr Hogan's expression crumpled and he covered his face with his hands. 'Thank God.' He grabbed his wife's hand. 'Did you hear that, luv?' he asked her, and pressed his lips to her limp fingers.

The front door downstairs banged shut, and after a clumping of heavy footsteps on the stairs, the bedroom door opened and Dr Robinson strode into the room. His eyes flickered over Connie and then, with relief, on to the woman in the bed.

'So,' he said, plonking his bag on the chair Connie had just vacated. 'How's the patient?'

Connie gave him a quick summary of events. 'I've just checked Mrs Hogan again, Doctor, and as far as I can tell, the contractions have completely subsided.'

'And West Ham's newest player?'

'Understandably, baby isn't moving much at the moment,' Connie said. 'But the heartbeat is a regular one hundred and sixty.'

'Excellent.'

Connie stepped back and the doctor pressed his fingers against the sleeping woman's wrist. 'Has she woken up at all?'

Connie shook her head. 'Not yet.'

He let go of Mrs Hogan's wrist and eased her eyelid up with his thumb, studying her fixed and dilated pupils. Then he turned to Mr Hogan, sitting on the other side of the bed holding his wife's hand.

'It was a close-run thing, but I think things have settled down. Your wife is just over twenty-five weeks pregnant, which is a lot further along than she's ever been before, thanks to Sister Byrne and her nurses.'

'I know, they're all angels,' said Mr Hogan, giving Connie a grateful smile.

'Angels they may be, Mr Hogan, but they can't work miracles,' the doctor replied. 'For your little chap to have a fighting chance, he has to weigh at least three pounds, which he won't do for another four weeks, at the very least. Even then his chances aren't good, so we have to keep him where he is for as long as possible. The only hope we have of doing that is by your wife staying in bed. Sister Byrne will arrange for the loan of a slipper bedpan, but I can't emphasise strongly enough that Mrs Hogan must remain horizontal at all times or the pressure of the baby will trigger labour again, and next time I might not be able to stop it. Do you understand, Mr Hogan?'

'Yes, Doctor,' Mr Hogan replied. 'But I have to go to work.'

'I know,' said Connie. 'I'll organise for one of our nurses to call in twice a day to make sure everything is as it should be and check that your wife is comfortable.'

'But I can't afford a shilling a day for a nurse.'

'Don't worry about the Association's fees, Mr Hogan. I'll apply to the council's welfare officer on your behalf,' Connie replied.

Mr Hogan relaxed. 'Thank you, Sister.'

'I'm afraid Mrs Hogan won't be much company this evening, Mr Hogan, as I expect she'll sleep through to the morning. I'll call in again at the end of the week.' Dr Robinson closed his bag. 'Until then, I'm leaving your wife in Sister Byrne's care.'

'Thank you, Doctor,' said Mr Hogan, offering his hand. 'I'm very grateful for what you've done.'

When the doctor had left, Mr Hogan resumed his seat and took up his wife's hand again. Connie collected her coat from the back of the door and slipped it on.

'I have to be off now, but I'll get the on-call midwife to pop in on you later.'

'Thank you, Sister.'

'And if there's any problem, just call Munroe House.'

'I will, don't you worry,' Mr Hogan replied.

'You've been here for almost four hours, Mr Hogan. Since your wife's going to be asleep for hours yet, why don't you get yourself a bite to eat before the children come back from the neighbours?'

'I will in a while,' said Mr Hogan without taking his eyes from his wife. 'I'll keep Maggie company for a bit longer.'

As she picked up her bag, Connie's professional gaze ran slowly over the woman in the bed. No, Baby Hogan certainly wasn't out of the woods, not by a long chalk.

By the time Connie turned into the back yard of Munroe House, she was just about ready to fall off her bike with exhaustion. The treatment room lights were still on but there were no prams parked against the wall, so the afternoon clinic must have finished, for which she was thankful.

Coasting to a stop, she wedged her front wheels into a spare space in the bike rack and threaded the chain through the spokes, securing it for the night. Taking her bag from the basket. Connie tried to open the back door, but realising someone must have accidentally dropped the catch, she wearily trudged around the house to the front entrance. She had just put her foot on the bottom step when the solid front door flew open and Millie's fiancé, Alex Nolan, burst out, his jacket flying behind him and a look of thunder on his face.

He went to hurry past her but Connie caught his arm. 'Alex, what's wrong?'

He stared blankly at her for a moment then recognition flashed in his troubled eyes. 'Oh, Connie, I didn't—'

'Is Millie all right?'

A look of anguish cut across his face. 'I'm sorry, Connie, I have to . . .' he pulled away and tore off down the road.

Connie hurried into the house and was greeted by Sally and her student Rosemary who were standing in the hallway looking dumbfounded.

'Did you see Alex?' Sally asked.

'Yes, but—?'

'I think him and Millie have had a falling out,' Sally replied. 'She's in the quiet lounge.'

Connie stowed her bag under the sideboard and headed for the room at the far end of the hall.

Millie was standing staring out of the window that overlooked Munroe House's small garden. She spun round as Connie walked in and for a brief moment her face lit up, then she burst into tears. Connie crossed the space and cradled Millie in her arms as she guided her to the two-seater sofa.

After several moments of uncontrollable sobbing Millie looked up. 'Did you see Alex?'

'Yes,' Connie replied. 'He almost knocked me off my feet. What's happened?'

'I've told him I can't marry him.'

Connie took her clean handkerchief from her pocket. 'But why?'

'Because I can't leave Mum as she is, can I?' Millie said simply.

'No, of course you can't,' Connie replied. 'But can't he postpone his appointment date or arrange for your mum to go with you?'

Millie shook her head. 'He's been trying to change the date for his posting but the Ministry of Defence won't have it. He has to take up his commission on the appointed day or it will be withdrawn.'

Connie looked aghast. 'I'm surprised he didn't tell them what to do with their blasted commission.'

A sad smile lifted Millie's lips. 'He wanted to, but I told him I still wouldn't marry him.'

Connie stood up and dragged Millie to her feet. 'For goodness' sake! Go after him.'

'I nearly did, and when I heard the door open, I thought he'd come back.' Tears welled up in Millie's eyes. 'But really I knew deep down . . .' She blew her nose. 'Alex has been fighting for years to get a promotion, and if I make him pass up this chance, I know it'll just drive us apart in the end.'

Sympathy swelled up in Connie. 'Oh Millie, I'm so sorry.' She hugged her friend. 'I know it's a bit early for a G and T, but what about a nice cuppa?'

Millie shook her head again. 'Thanks, Connie, but I'm just

going to freshen up, then go back to the hospital to fetch Mum.'

'You didn't tell me they were discharging her today.'

'They're not,' her friend replied. 'I'm taking her home and looking after her myself so I can make sure she's properly cared for.' Connie couldn't blame her.

Although, thankfully, Doris was going to make a full physical recovery, her mind remained unsettled and because of this the consultant had transferred her to St Mungo's. It was now called a facility for the mentally ill, but the old workhouse on Mile End Road wasn't a place any loving daughter would want their mother to be.

Connie released her. 'If there's anything I can do, you only have to ask.'

'I know, and don't worry, Con,' Millie forced a bright smile. 'I'll get over losing the love of my life. After all, you did.'

Connie put on her sunniest smile. 'Yes, I did, didn't I?' she lied, as the image of Charlie's rascally grin danced in her head.

Tucking the paper bag containing his work clothes under his arm, Charlie trotted down the steps of the municipal bath house next to Stepney station just as the clock above hit seven o'clock.

It was Friday, the best day of the week. No more bloody slog until Monday, and two nights of booze, darts and larks to look forward to, which was why he'd just coughed up a tanner for a close trim and shave at the barber's, and a hot bath.

With his hands in his pockets, he joined the dozens of other men returning from their day's work along Mile End Road. As he strolled, he caught sight of himself in the London Gas showroom window and smiled. He ran his thumbs down his sharply cut lapels. Not bad, Charlie boy, not bad at all.

There was already a queue outside his in-laws' fish bar, so he had to squeeze through the crowd before entering the steamy atmosphere of the shop. Even though Murray's was under new management, as the banner pinned to the back wall announced, the interior looked very much as it always had, with black-and-white tiles halfway up the walls and a long marble serving counter with the frying vat beneath. However, in an effort to mark out their territory, as it were, Rosa and Bruno had placed a black-and-gold gondola complete with red-fringed canopy on the back shelf next to a plaster cast of some old tower leaning over at an odd angle. There was also a photo of Bruno wearing a sheepskin coat with a rifle slung over his shoulder, his free arm draped around an American general's shoulders.

Behind the counter, the hero of the Italian resistance himself was wrapping sizzling fish and chips in newspaper as fast as he could, while Maria's younger brother Giovanni, who'd arrived three weeks before, took the money. The youngest of the Fabrini offspring was a slender-hipped, brooding youth with a mop of pitch-black hair; his arrival had doubled the chippy's female customers almost overnight.

As Charlie walked in, Bruno looked up and murmured something to his son. Giovanni, his dark eyes fixed on Charlie, sneered. Charlie gave them a casual nod and strolled to the back of the shop, where Rosa, dressed in a wraparound apron, with her hair tied up in a scarf, was dunking fillets of fish into an oblong container filled with batter. Raising his hand by way of greeting, he hurried past and took the stairs two at a time as he made his way to the floor above.

The chippy's living quarters consisted of a kitchen, lounge and bedroom on the first level, with two further bedrooms and an old cracked toilet above. Rosa and Bruno had taken the bedroom next to the living room, while Charlie and Maria had the larger room upstairs. Despite having a squeaky bed and his in-laws in the room below, it wasn't too bad. He'd planned to shift the baby into the other room as soon as he could in order to get a bit of peace at night, but Giovanni's arrival had put paid to that, and with another sprog on the way, it was only going to get worse.

Maria was in the kitchen, hand-washing baby clothes. There was a festering bucket of nappies on the floor to her right and a basket of other garments to her left. Filippo was in the highchair, propped up with cushions and munching on a grubby Bickiepeg fastened to his jumper with a ribbon and safety pin. He regarded Charlie curiously for a moment, then stuck the teething biscuit back in his mouth.

Throwing his dirty work clothes on top of the linen basket, Charlie delved into his jacket pocket and pulled out two banknotes and a handful of change.

'There you go,' he said, tossing them on the kitchen table.

Wiping a strand of hair from her forehead with the back of her hand, Maria glanced at the money, then turned back to her task.

Charlie glared at her averted face. 'A bloody thank you wouldn't go amiss.'

Resting her hands on the side of the sink, she gestured with her head towards the table. 'I need more.'

'What on earth for?' he asked. 'My mother brought me up on half that amount.'

She shrugged. 'That before war. Everything expensive now.' She plonked the wet items on the draining board. 'I need more for baby.'

'All I've got is me beer money,' he said innocently.

Maria's eyes flickered over him. 'New suit cost more than drink money.'

Charlie pressed his lips together and held his wife's implacable stare for as long as he could before shoving his hand in his pocket again and pulling out another ten shilling note and half a crown.

He slammed them on the table. 'Happy?'

Drying her hands on the tea towel, Maria took the money, slipped it in her apron pocket and returned to her task.

Charlie glared at his wife's back for a few moments, then spoke again. 'So when's supper?'

'When shop shut,' Maria replied, without looking around.

'But I'm going out.'

Maria shrugged. 'You always go out. Mama and Papa busy, so we eat after.'

'Well what about a pigging cup of tea, then?'

'Water in the tap and kettle on the stove,' Maria replied, wringing out a small blue romper suit.

'It's a fine bloody thing, ain't it, when a man comes home from a hard day's work and he ain't even got a cuppa waiting!' Charlie shouted.

Filippo's bottom lip started to wobble and he whimpered.

'Stop shouting,' snapped Maria. 'You scaring *bambino*.'

'Never mind the sprog, what about me?' Charlie bellowed.

Rosa's shrill voice shouted something up the stairs in Italian. Maria left her washing and went to the top of the stairs to answer.

'What was she going on about?' Charlie asked when Maria returned.

'Nothing,' replied Maria. 'Sit. I'll make tea.'

Charlie threw himself on a kitchen chair while Maria filled the kettle and put it on to boil. Flicking a speck of dirt from his trousers, he pulled out a packet of Bensons and his lighter and lit a cigarette. As the flame sparked, Filippo looked up. Charlie grinned and flicked it on and off again. His son reached out his chubby hand and took the lighter, cramming it in his mouth.

Maria dashed over and snatched it from her son's hands.

'*Stupido*,' she muttered, giving Charlie a scalding look and the baby his wooden rattle.

Jamming his cigarette in his mouth, Charlie stood up and grabbed the front of Maria's apron.

'Yeah, I must be bloody stupid to fall for your little game,' he shouted.

Her face contorted with rage. 'And I stupid too, because I thought you were nice British soldier, not lazy man.'

He dragged her towards him. She stumbled and knocked a chair over. Filippo's little face screwed up and he let out an ear-piercing scream. Maria kicked out at Charlie as he balled his fist.

'Lazy, am I?' he bellowed. 'Well I'm not too lazy to teach you a fucking—'

Something hit the side of his head, shaking his focus and rattling his teeth. He wheeled around ready to strike, only to find his arm twisted up behind his back and his father-in-law's burly forearm across his windpipe. He tried to pull it away, but the pressure only tightened.

'Let go,' he croaked.

He caught a fleeting glimpse of Maria and heard her repeatedly screaming, 'No, Papa!' Black spots popped at the corner of his vision, and his eyelids started to flutter. Noise crashed in his ears as his muscles relaxed, then suddenly the pressure was gone and he fell to the floor.

He gasped as air rushed back into his lungs. His mind cleared, but as he struggled to his knees, he was lifted up and found himself dangling in his father-in-law's colossal grip.

His eyes wild with rage, Bruno shoved his face into Charlie's. 'You touch my daughter again, I kill you. *Capisce*?'

Charlie tried to speak, but no sound came out.

'*Capisce?*' Bruno growled again, flecks of spit landing on Charlie's cheeks and chin.

'Yes,' whispered Charlie.

Bruno shook him like a rag doll and then threw him against the table. Catching the side to stop himself falling, Charlie hawked spit back into his mouth and coughed. With the grey mist still clogging his thoughts, he stumbled towards the door.

Thirty minutes later, with his throat still aching from his father-in-law's murderous grip, Charlie stumbled into West Arbour Street. His first thought had been to go to his mother, but she would have wanted to know what had happened, and even if he told her, what could she do to help him? Which was why he was heading for the stout brick-built communal hall next to the 1930s council flats.

Straightening his tie and fixing a happy-go-lucky grin on his face, Charlie pushed open the half-glazed door and went in. The tiled hallway and concrete stairs leading up to the rooms above echoed with shouts from the various clubs who used the hall for their weekly activities. Continuing along the corridor towards the large room at the back of the building, he heard the familiar dull thud of punchbags being pummelled, indicating that the Arbour Amateur Boxing Club was in full swing.

Pulling down the front of his jacket, Charlie shoved the door open and bowled in. The smell of sweat, leather and liniment oil engulfed him instantly. The walls were the colour of tidal mud, but it wouldn't have mattered if they'd been sky blue and pink, as you could barely see the dingy decor for the faded posters advertising ancient boxing contests. At the far side, and in pride of place opposite the long windows, was a glass-fronted cabinet displaying the various cups and title belts won by the Arbour Boys.

The club was already full of sweaty men improving their footwork by skipping in front of long mirrors or grunting as they jabbed at punchbags. Charlie cast his eyes over the scene until he saw Tommy, dressed in a loose white singlet and baggy navy shorts, walloping the speed bag hanging on a spring for all he was worth.

'You come for a bit of a pop?' he called as he caught sight of Charlie.

'What, in these togs?' Charlie called back, indicating his suit. Shoving his hands in his pockets, he swaggered over, walking past a couple of lads sparring in the central ring just as one of them hit the canvas in a cloud of chalk and dust.

Tommy punched the ball, setting it swinging wildly. 'All right then, Charlie?'

'Yeah, I'm good, Tommy,' he replied chirpily. 'Thought you might want that drink I owe you.'

Tommy grinned, picking up a towel from the bench behind him and throwing it over his shoulder. 'Keep me company while I get myself spruced up.' He headed for the changing room and Charlie followed.

With its white tiles crazed with age and a strip light overhead, calling the building's old boiler room a changing room was pushing it a bit, but there were metal lockers on either side for the boxers to store their belongings, and a double-sided bench in the middle.

Discarding his towel on the bench, Tommy strolled into the shower at the far end, which had once been the coal storage area. The wall dividing it from the rest of the boiler room stopped at chest height. He thumped the antiquated plumbing to get a jet of water from the mouldy shower head, while Charlie lounged against the wall and took out his cigarettes.

'So, how's tricks?' said Tommy, lathering up with a craggy block of yellow Sunlight soap.

'Good.'

'Job working out all right?' asked Tommy, scrubbing his left armpit vigorously.

'Couldn't be better,' Charlie replied. 'I owe you one for that.'

Tommy waved the notion away, splattering suds across the floor. 'You're me mate, ain't you? And you've paid your dues.'

That was true. If a driver turned up with a docket from Imperial Export Co., Charlie knew to load whatever was on the chit and not record it in the sales book.

'Well, we're mates, ain't we?' Charlie replied, repeating his friend's words and blowing a stream of cigarette smoke upwards.

As Tommy soaped and scrubbed himself, Charlie leant back against the cold tiles and closed his eyes. The scene in the chip shop flashed into his mind and the grey weight that constantly hovered above him descended.

Tommy turned off the tap. 'Chuck us a towel.'

Shaking off his despondency, Charlie opened his eyes. He grabbed a clean towel from the pile on the shelf and threw it over. Tommy caught it and wrapped it around his waist, then stepped out and sidled over to the battered metal locker with 'TT' painted in gold on the front. Pulling out a wooden hanger with an Italian-style suit draped over it, he hooked the suit on one of the wall pegs and grabbed another towel before sitting on the central bench.

'You all right, mate?' he asked, regarding Charlie thoughtfully as he dried himself off.

Charlie flicked his cigarette butt into the central drain and idly watched the soapy water carry it away. 'It's her at home.'

'Ain't it always?' chuckled Tommy.

'Not for you, you lucky bugger.'

'That's 'cos I'm too smart to get caught,' his friend replied. 'Love 'em and leave 'em, that's my motto.'

'Mine too.' Charlie's face dropped. 'Well it was until her pigging father complained to the company commander about me ruining his daughter.'

Amusement flitted across Tommy's fleshy face. 'Well you did, didn't you?'

'True,' Charlie conceded. 'But now they've all come to live over here, so I'm stuck with the bugger and the rest of Maria's poxy family.'

Tommy let out a low whistle. 'You poor old sod.'

'I tell you straight, Tommy, I came that close' – he pinched his right thumb and forefinger together – 'to landing her old man one tonight. If I don't get out of there, I'll end up swinging for them, truly I will.'

'So you skipping off then?' asked Tommy, stepping into his trousers and pulling them up.

'I'd like to, and get myself a little place out of the way somewhere,' Charlie replied.

His friend smirked. 'Somewhere to entertain a bit of company, I suppose.'

Charlie gave an arrogant shrug. 'Well I ain't a monk, but what with her and her grasping relatives screwing me for every penny, I'm a bit short of the old readies . . .' He looked expectantly at his friend, who was buttoning his shirt.

'As it happens, I do have a bit of action in the offing,' said Tommy, flicking his braces over his shoulders. 'If you want in.'

Charlie paused. Whatever Tommy was offering, it was bound to be on the wrong side of the law, but what choice did he have?

'What do I have to do?'

Taking his camel-coloured Crombie with a velvet collar from the locker, Tommy shrugged it on. 'Can you drive a ten-ton Bedford?'

Charlie nodded. 'Drove 'em all the time in the desert.'

'You'll do. Now' – he put a muscular arm around Charlie's shoulder – 'how about we take a stroll along to the Blind Beggar, and after you buy me that drink you mentioned, I'll introduce you to the crew.'

Chapter Eighteen

'And as Sister Potter is on half-day today, Green and Hooper will take half each,' said Miss Dutton, her piercing voice cutting though Connie's thoughts.

Miss Dutton was holding court at the far end of the table, with the thirty or so nurses squashed around her. Until she'd taken over as superintendent, they'd just sat in any free space, but now they rushed their breakfast to ensure they sat as far away from her as possible. Except, of course, Gladys, who made sure she was very much in Miss Dutton's eyeline.

'How come Dutton's letting her have a half-day each week but it's too busy for us to take ours?' whispered Sally, who was behind Connie.

'Need you ask?' said Eva over Connie's other shoulder.

'It's so unfair,' murmured Annie on her right.

'Byrne!' barked Miss Dutton.

Connie rose to her feet. 'Yes, Superintendent.'

'You and your friends have something to say?'

'We were just wondering, Superintendent, if we could all have an afternoon off with the same regularity as Sister Potter.'

The superintendent's mouth pulled together and her eyes bulged. 'As you are well aware, Byrne, it states quite clearly in the Association regulations that patient care comes before all other considerations and therefore half-days can be waived if the workload necessitates.'

'And I have a sick mother,' Gladys butted in, giving Connie a smug look.

'Yes indeed,' said Miss Dutton sympathetically. She turned her attention back to Connie. 'Nurses will be allowed time off when I see fit. Do you understand?'

'Yes, Superintendent.' Connie resumed her seat. 'It's as clear as day.'

Miss Dutton gave Connie another acerbic look, then lowered her eyes to the book in front of her again.

'And lastly, I received a letter from the educational officer at the Queen's Institute for District Nursing informing me that Miss Knott will be revisiting us in two days' time for Nurse Baxter's second supervisory visit.' She cast a menacing glance at Connie's student on the other side of the table. 'I trust there will be no problems.'

'No, Superintendent,' Josie replied.

'Good.' Miss Dutton closed the book. 'That's all for this morning, but make sure you check the message book before you go out after lunch.' She clapped her hands briskly. 'Now there are patients waiting, so don't dawdle.'

There was a scrape of chairs as the nurses stood up and made their way out of the room. Reaching beneath her chair, Connie picked up her bag and followed them.

Josie met her as she reached the door. 'I hope I won't let you down when the educational officer comes.'

'You won't,' Connie replied, patting her arm. 'I have every confidence in you.'

'Byrne!' Miss Dutton's shrill voice called after her.

Connie turned. 'Yes, Superintendent?'

Miss Dutton gathered up her books and smiled pleasantly. 'Can I have a word before you go out?' She swept past, the showy tails of her frilly hat fluttering behind her.

Connie shrugged her shoulders and followed the superintendent down the corridor to her office. Miss Dutton was already in her chair by the time Connie shut the door.

'Firstly,' said Miss Dutton, weaving her fingers together and laying her hands on the desk, 'it is not your place to question my decisions about nurse rotas or time off.'

'It won't happen again,' said Connie, trying to look contrite.

Miss Dutton sniffed. 'See that it doesn't.'

'Is that all you wanted to say to me, Superintendent?'

'No, it isn't,' said Miss Dutton as she picked up a sheet of paper from her desk. 'Just so you know, the relieving officer telephoned yesterday to tell me he has turned down your request to the council's welfare department requesting reimbursement for Mrs Hogan's care.'

Connie looked incredulous. 'But why?'

'Because, as he pointed out, the council already contribute towards Munroe House's maternity services in the form of our yearly grant. His view, and I have to say I agree with him, is that we run a weekly antenatal clinic here, at St Jude's in Limehouse and at the Memorial Hall in Ben Jonson Road, so he doesn't see why the rate-payers should stump up for extra visits.'

'But didn't you explain she's got an unstable uterus?' asked Connie, still not quite believing what she'd heard.

Miss Dutton looked at her blankly.

'Of course,' said Connie. 'I keep forgetting you're not a midwife.'

'Well explain it to me then,' said the superintendent, twiddling her thumbs.

'Mrs Hogan's cervix is incompetent, and as the weight of the baby increases, there's a real risk it will open and the baby will be born prematurely. She's already lost several pregnancies in a similar way. It almost happened this time, but thankfully a shot of morphine stopped the contractions. However, unless she is closely monitored and remains in bed, she'll lose this baby too.'

'Well I'm sorry, but the Association isn't a charity. Nursing services are provided only to people who can pay. Women threaten to miscarry babies every day, and the Association would be bankrupt in a week if I allowed nurses to visit them all. I'm very sorry about this woman, but such is life, so you are to cross her off your list and tell her to visit the clinic like everyone else.' Miss Dutton picked up her pen and looked down at the pile of papers in front of her. 'That will be all, Byrne,' she said without glancing up.

Connie stared incredulously at the profusion of lace crowning Miss Dutton's matron's hat, then turned and left the room, shutting the door behind her.

Josie was sitting waiting for her on one of the chairs set out for the morning clinic. She stood up when Connie emerged.

'What did she say?'

'That the council won't pay for Mrs Hogan's visits,' Connie replied.

Josie's eyes widened in shock. 'No.'

'Yes,' said Connie. 'And we're to take her off our books.'

'What are you going to do?'

Connie's mouth pulled into a hard line. 'Carry on visiting her.'

Sidestepping to avoid a puddle left behind by an earlier shower, Connie pushed open the snug door to the Boatman pub, which sat between New Gravel Lane and Wapping Wall.

Although the Prospect of Whitby and the Town of Ramsgate might claim to be the oldest pubs in the area, judging by the centuries of black soot on the ceiling, Connie reckoned that the Boatman would call them newcomers. Bert Fallow, the publican, was fond of telling any who would listen that the pub had once been the den of an infamous gang of river pirates, and as it was no more than a hop, skip and a jump from the Thames, he might have been right.

A hundred years ago, the alleyway the old pub stood in must have been a pretty hostile location, but now, with every other building in the area little more than rubble thanks to the Luftwaffe, the Boatman stood alone. In fact, considering its decrepit state, it was a surprise the old timber structure stood at all without its neighbours to support it. But stand it did, and although there were at least a dozen pubs closer to Munroe House, the Boatman was the one Connie and her friends frequented most.

A warm fug of cigarette smoke and beer enveloped her as she walked into the little side bar. No bigger than the size of her bedroom, the secluded bar had hard wooden benches fixed to the wall with just a few chairs dotted around. In addition, there were three small circular tables, and at one sat Sally, Beattie, Annie and Hannah. Connie acknowledged them with a smile as she headed for the corner of the main bar that jutted into the snug.

'You're being a bit cheeky,' said Vi, the landlady, glancing at Connie's uniform and the QN medallion around her neck.

'I know, but I've told my student to ring me here if there's a call-out,' Connie replied. 'Is that all right?'

Vi took the cigarette from her Tangerine Blossom lips and rested it in a chunky glass ashtray. 'Course it is, luv. What you having?'

'Just a bitter lemon, thanks.'

Taking down a glass hanging just above her head, Vi reached

for a small bottle of Schweppes in the display behind, snapped off the lid and poured the fizzy drink.

Connie pulled out a shilling and held it out.

'On the 'ouse,' the landlady said, handing her the glass.

Connie thanked her and joined her friends.

'OK, Mata Hari,' said Sally as Connie pulled up a seat. 'What's all the cloak-and-dagger stuff about?'

'Well . . .' Connie filled her friends in on Mrs Hogan's history and situation.

'So the welfare officer will sanction daily visits to this poor woman and Miss Dutton agrees?' Annie asked when she'd finished

'Correct,' replied Connie.

'But you did explain to the old dragon that if we didn't at least try to help, Mrs Hogan would certainly lose her baby?' said Hannah incredulously.

'Such is life, apparently,' Connie said, mimicking Miss Dutton's shrill tones.

'It's a blooming disgrace,' Sally snapped. 'What's the point of being a midwife if you can't care for women like your Mrs Hogan?'

'My thoughts exactly,' said Connie. 'And that's why I wanted to talk to you here, away from flapping ears.'

'Away from Gladys and her gang, you mean?' said Hannah.

Connie nodded. 'I've decided that I can't stand by and just let Mrs Hogan's baby die without a fight. I can squeeze in the visits when I'm out and about or on my days off, but if I'm called out on a delivery or rostered for a clinic—'

'So you'd like us to help?' cut in Annie.

Connie gave her friends a beseeching smile. 'I wouldn't ask if there was any other way, and if Miss Dutton finds out . . .'

'Don't be daft, of course we'll help,' said Beattie, and the others murmured their agreement. 'But we'll get a proper list going, not just for when you can't get there.'

'Yes, it'll be easy enough,' said Hannah. 'One of us can add her to our morning list and another to their afternoon visits.'

'That's kind, but if Miss Dutton finds out, you'll all be hauled up in front of the Association management committee, and you could even get the chop.'

Annie looked sceptical. 'They can't sack all of us or who would run the service? And if they do, then I know most of the other nursing associations in the area are desperate for experienced nurses and are paying thruppence an hour more.'

'I'll ask Joan and Pat to help too,' said Beattie. 'And Madge. Her sister has the same problem so I'm sure she'll be happy to lend a hand.'

'What about Millie?' asked Hannah.

Connie shook her head. 'I'll tell her, but I think she's got enough on her plate trying to look after her mum without us adding to it.'

'And the students?' said Sally.

'It's not fair to involve them,' Connie replied. 'If we get caught we can go somewhere else, but they'll be out on their ear.'

'And if Gladys gets wind of something she'll try and bully it out of them,' added Annie.

'Yes. The fewer people who know, the better,' agreed Beattie.

Connie looked around at her four friends. 'Thanks, all of you. If we can just get Mrs Hogan up to six months . . .'

Hannah raised her glass. 'Let's drink to Baby Hogan.'

'Baby Hogan,' the friends said in unison.

They all took a sip, and then Sally lifted her G and T again. 'And to Miss Dutton's knicker elastic. May it snap and her drawers plummet to the ground when she stands up and gives her monthly report to the Association's esteemed president and all-round pompous arse Mr Algernon Shottington.'

The telephone behind the bar rang a couple of times and someone picked it up.

'To Miss Dutton's knicker elastic,' giggled Connie, throwing back another mouthful.

'Sorry to disturb, girls,' called Vi above the laughter. 'But someone needs a midwife.'

Connie turned to see the landlady holding out the receiver. She finished her bitter lemon, then disentangled herself from the fun and went to the bar.

'Sorry, but we've just had a call,' said Josie at the other end of the phone.

'It's all right, who is it?' said Connie, tucking the mouthpiece between her ear and shoulder and taking her notebook and pen from her pocket.

'It's a Mrs Webb,' Josie replied. 'In—'

'Smithy Street?'

'Yes,' said Josie chirpily. 'Do you know her?'

'Yes,' said Connie with a sinking heart. 'I'm afraid I do.'

Twenty minutes later, Connie knocked on the Webbs' front door. It was opened by Valerie's mother-in-law, who was wearing curlers in her grey hair and had cigarette ash sprinkled down her candlewick dressing gown.

'Took your time, didn't you?' she snapped as Connie squeezed past her. 'My Ron phoned your lot thirty bloody minutes ago.'

An ear-vibrating scream came from the room above them.

The old woman rolled her eyes and tutted. 'Listen to that. You'd think someone was cutting her bleeding throat.'

Ron Webb, dressed in a grey vest and scruffy trousers held up by braces, appeared at the top of the stairs. 'Thank God you've arrived,' he said, tearing at his hair with a beefy hand. 'She's in agony.'

'She's playing you up,' his mother said.

'Perhaps I'll just pop up and take a look,' Connie said.

She opened her bag and handed the old woman her pack of instruments. 'Would you mind boiling these for five minutes and then bring them up in the saucepan without touching them, please?'

Mrs Webb senior sniffed and took the delivery pack with her finger and thumb.

'If I'd known I was going to be expected to fetch and carry for Lady Muck upstairs, I would have stayed down the bleeding King's Head,' she muttered as she headed towards the scullery at the rear of the house.

Another scream cut through the air and Connie hurried up the stairs to where Ron was waiting.

'In here, Sister,' he said, ushering Connie into the bedroom.

Valerie Webb, dressed in a sweat-soaked nightgown, was lying in the middle of the bed staring blankly up at the ceiling. When she saw Connie, relief flashed across her face.

'Thank God it's you,' she sobbed, fat tears streaming down her face.

Ron was at his wife's side in an instant. 'There, there, I know it hurts, sweetheart,' he said, cradling her tenderly in his arms. 'But it'll all be worth it when you're holding our baby.'

Valerie's water-filled eyes stared fearfully at her husband. 'Our baby,' she mouthed.

Ron smiled tenderly at her. 'Yes, luv, the one we've been waiting for all these years.'

For a long moment, Valerie held his gaze, then she threw her head back and let out an almighty scream.

Connie put her bag firmly on the table.

'Now, Mrs Webb,' she said, slipping her arms into her gown. 'When did your pains start?'

Without opening her eyes, Valerie thrashed her head from side to side. 'I don't know, I don't know.' She grabbed her stomach and hunched over, screwing her face into a red ball.

Connie placed her hand gently on Valerie's bump as the contraction tightened, noting the time on her watch and counting until it subsided. With sweat glistening on her forehead, Valerie slumped back on the pillow, her knuckles showing white as she gripped the blankets covering her.

'How long, Mrs Webb?' asked Connie again.

'This morning,' said Valerie feebly, her eyes still closed.

'And they've got worse all day?'

'Yes.'

'They were every five minutes when I got home at eight,' added Ron, looking fearfully at his wife curling forward as another contraction began.

Connie counted it again, noting that it was just two minutes since the last one had faded. 'Why didn't you call me sooner?' she asked, smoothing out a sterile sheet of paper on the top of the bedside table and unpacking her equipment.

'I wanted to,' said Ron, looking anxiously at his red-faced wife. 'But—'

'I told him to get his evening meal down him before running errands,' cut in old Mrs Webb, standing in the doorway holding a battered zinc saucepan. 'I was in labour for three days wiv 'im. Agony it was, hours of it, only to be ripped apart like a gutted chicken when he came out. I've never been the same down there since.'

Valerie grunted and rolled forward. Ron rubbed his wife's back as she groaned.

A heartless glint sparked in the old woman's eye. 'I didn't have any bloody midwife helping me, just the old woman from the next street. Bled like a stuck pig for a week after. So much so that I could hardly sta—'

'If I could just have my sterilised equipment and a bit of space, Mrs Webb,' said Connie with her most professional smile.

The old woman's thin lips pulled into a tight bud and she plonked the saucepan in the middle of the table.

'I'll leave you to get on with it then, Sister, but do us a favour. Tell 'er,' old Mrs Webb shot her panting daughter-in-law a testy look, 'to put a sock in it. *Mystery Playhouse* is on in half an hour.' She clumped out of the room.

Valerie drew in a deep breath, screwed up her face and bellowed as another contraction swept over her.

Ron stood up, but Valerie grabbed his arm. 'You know I love you, Ron, don't you?'

A bashful expression lifted Ron Webb's heavy features. 'Now, Val, no need to embarrass the sister,' he said, glancing at Connie.

'Ron!' screeched his mother from below.

He disentangled himself from his wife and, with a sympathetic smile, trudged downstairs after his mother.

Tears gathered in Valerie's eyes as she watched her husband leave, then another contraction gripped her and she curled forward. Connie timed it to almost two minutes before Mrs Webb's shoulders slumped.

Connie turned down the bedclothes. 'Now if you could open your legs and lift your bottom, Mrs Webb, I'll see just how far on you are,' she said, fastening her mask in place.

With sweat glistening on her brow, Mrs Webb did as she was asked, but just as Connie tucked a towel under her, another contraction started. Valerie screamed, and a spurt of water dampened the towel.

'Try to stay on top of the pain,' said Connie, taking the rubber gloves from the boiling water and squeezing them on.

The pain subsided and Valerie sank back into the pillows. Using her elbows, Connie nudged the woman's knees apart and, reaching down, slipped two fingers into her. She didn't have far to go before she met the baby's head squeezing its way through the thinning uterus neck. After stretching her fingers apart to gauge the diameter, Connie skimmed over the baby's fontanelles and sent up a small prayer of thanks as she felt them in the correct position for a normal delivery.

She withdrew her hand and Valerie let out a long sigh. 'Well, Mrs Webb, you're almost fully dilated and the fore waters have ruptured, so despite what your mother-in-law said, I think you'll probably be ready to push in a few minutes.'

Valerie groaned and closed her eyes again.

Connie quickly set out basins of sterile water, swabs soaked in surgical spirit, her blunt and pointed scissors and the silk ligature to secure the cord.

Valerie opened her eyes and looked at her. 'I can't have this baby,' she whimpered. 'I just can't.'

'I'm afraid you haven't got much choice at this stage,' Connie replied, setting the two locking forceps within easy reach.

'But what if it comes out brown?' Valerie grabbed her arm. 'It'll break Ron's 'eart, I know it will, and then what will—'

She grunted and pitched forward.

'Look up, and try not to push for a bit,' said Connie, positioning herself ready to ease the baby's head through.

Valerie did as she was told, her cheeks puffing out as she fought the urge to bear down. Her paper-thin perineum bulged for an instant, then a circle of damp black curls appeared.

'Well done, Mrs Webb. You're doing fine,' said Connie. 'I can feel the head, so with the next contraction, grab the outside of your thighs and bear down.'

Mrs Webb yelled and, taking firm hold of either leg, strained with all her might. She went red in the face. 'I can't do it!'

'We're almost there, now push!' yelled Connie, running her fingers around the stretched skin.

There was a pop, and the baby's head was free. Valerie let out a sob and flopped back.

Connie wiped a strand of her hair from her forehead with the back of her hand. 'Well done. Now, I'm just—'

But before she could check for the cord, the baby's head turned and its shoulders slipped out. Connie grabbed the towel and only just got it under the infant in time. He had a liberal coating of waxy vernix all over, and judging by the square shoulders and plump limbs he weighed nearer to eight pounds than seven. As she clamped the cord with the forceps, the baby jerked, then let out an angry cry.

Relief swept over her. No matter how straightforward things were during a delivery, until she heard that first cry Connie was never totally convinced that the child was well.

'It's a boy,' she laughed as she tied the silk thread around the cord and snipped the baby free of his mother.

Mrs Webb struggled up on to her elbows. 'What colour is he?'

Connie's happy mood vanished instantly. Gingerly she peeled away the edges of the towel and stared at the baby's fuzzy black hair, broad facial features and cocoa-coloured skin. Cradling the new arrival in her arms, she held him aloft so his mother could see him.

Valerie Webb gazed at her new son for a second, then she threw back her head. 'No!' she screamed, making Connie's eardrums vibrate.

The door burst open and Ron stumbled into the room. His eyes shifted from his hysterical wife to the child Connie was holding and back again.

'Val?' he said softly.

She stopped crying abruptly, stared at her husband for a moment, then balled her fists and shrieked again. Ron stood with his shoulders slumped, a stupefied expression on his fleshy features.

'Oh Ron!' Val sobbed, covering her face.

The door swung open again and Mrs Webb senior stomped into the room. Her flint-like eyes darted from her son to his wife and back again. 'What's all the bloody racket about? And you, you big nancy,' she cuffed her son across his upper arm, 'stop fucking crying.'

Ron wiped his nose on his sleeve. 'But Mum, look . . .' He pointed at the baby in Connie's arms.

His mother's gaze shifted to the child. She squinted at it for a second, then lumbered over.

'It's a boy,' said Connie, shielding the newborn baby from the old woman.

'It's a bloody nigger,' bellowed Ron. 'And it don't take no genius to know how it got there,' he added, glaring at his wife.

Old Mrs Webb stared at the infant for a moment, then to Connie's amazement her chin started to tremble.

'It's my fault,' she wailed, bursting into tears.

Connie gave the new mother a questioning look, but Valerie shrugged. Ron turned on his mother.

'What in God's name are you talking about?'

Mrs Webb's hard-bitten face wore a repentant expression. 'I was 'oping never to have to tell you, but your dad wasn't really your dad after all; it was a chap off the banana boat.'

Ron stared goggle-eyed at his mother.

'I met him at a pub in Bermondsey,' she added, fleshing out the details a bit. 'When you were born I thought I'd got away with it, but it seems it just jumped a generation.'

'But you hate coons,' he bellowed.

'I know, but . . .' She gave a little shrug. 'Things . . . well, just sort of happen.'

Ron stared at his wife and baby for a moment, then spun around to face the blank wall behind him.

The baby started snuffling and rooting around. Connie looked at Valerie and she held out her arms.

'There you are, Mrs Webb,' said Connie cheerfully, handing her her son. 'Just put him to the breast and I'm sure he'll know what to do.'

'I think something's coming down below,' Valerie whispered as Connie helped her get the baby in position.

Connie quickly lifted the sheet to see the afterbirth sliding out. Scooping it up in the dirty towel, she deposited it in the kidney dish and set it aside to check later.

After staring at her son's unyielding back for five minutes, Mrs Webb senior went over to him. She laid her hand on his arm.

'I'm so—'

Ron spun around. 'You know what people will say when they see my boy, don't you?' he shouted.

His mother shook her head. 'No they won't, 'cos I'll tell them.'

'Too bloody right you will.' Ron went over to his wife and put a protective arm around her. 'I'm not having Val slagged off on every street corner because you couldn't keep your knickers on. And she's right. The sooner we move into our own place, the better. I'll go and chivvy that bloody council first thing tomorrow.'

The infant in his wife's arms hiccuped, and Ron smiled tenderly. He stretched out a thick finger and stroked the dark down on the child's head.

'Can I call him after me dad?' asked Valerie, smiling up at her husband.

'Course you can, sweetheart.' He turned and glared at his mother. 'After all, we can't call him after mine, can we?'

Connie picked up the kidney bowel and smiled. 'I'm sorry to be a nuisance, but I have to get on.'

Ron slapped his thigh. 'Of course you do, Sister, and thank you for what you've done for my Val.' He kissed his wife's forehead, then stood up and, shooting another hateful look at his mother, stomped out of the room and down the stairs.

Mrs Webb senior hurried after him. 'I know it's a bit of a shock, but . . .'

Connie let out a long breath as the old woman's voice faded. She reached out and took the infant, who'd stopped feeding, from his mother.

'I'll weigh him first, then wash him and you,' she explained.

She popped the baby in a net sling and hooked up the corners, then raised him on the fisherman's scale. After the needle had settled, she lowered him again.

'Eight pounds two.'

Valerie smiled fondly at her son. 'Isn't he beautiful?'

'Yes, he is.'

The new mother looked up at her. 'Who do *you* think his father is?'

As Connie gazed down at the infant, an image of Ron's flat, broad nose, pale lips and black curly hair sprang into her mind.

She tickled the child under the chin. 'Mrs Webb, I think your guess is as good as mine.'

The familiar smell of coal-dust-laden fog tingled Connie's nose when she stepped out of the Webbs' house thirty minutes later. That didn't surprise her, as it had been gathering when she'd arrived just after nine, but it took her a minute to realise that the darkness in the street wasn't just due to the fog having come up from the river.

Another blooming power cut, she thought, dumping her bag in the basket and unchaining her front wheel from the boot scrap inset in the wall. Rolling her bike into the road, she turned on the lamp at the front and hopped on.

She'd just turned into Jamaica Street when she jolted through a pothole and the pale beam of light flickered out. On the main road that ran between Commercial Road and Stepney Green, not only were the street lamps unlit but the houses too were shrouded in darkness. This, along with the swirling fog, meant she could barely see the mudguards covering her wheels

Holding fast to her handlebars with her right hand, she hit the old lamp with her left, but with no effect. She sighed, and having cycled home many a time in a blackout, she pedalled on. A car whizzed past, its headlights cutting through the gloom for a few seconds before disappearing and plunging her back into darkness. Within a few moments she'd reached Commercial Road, which, despite the lateness of the hour, was still busy with lorries and vans streaming to and from the docks, their ghostly yellow headlights looming out of the choking fog.

The fault at the power station must have been something serious, because here too the street was without light. Waiting until there was a lull in the traffic, she stood up on her pedals and darted across the road. A car whooshed past her so close that the draught lifted her skirt. Bumping into the kerb, she stepped off her bike.

Her nerves had been shredded enough by the events in the Webb household without fraying them further, so she decided to push her cycle the rest of the way. Turning into Sutton Street, she was immediately plunged into darkness again, but out of the corner of her eye she caught a movement in the shadows. A shiver prickled up her spine as her footsteps were joined by the sound of heavier ones keeping pace.

Although there was a police presence on some streets in the area, most were not patrolled. Despite this, by and large nurses were held in high regard and so travelled safely at all hours of the day and night, and Connie couldn't remember the last time one of them had been attacked during the course of their duty.

However, that didn't mean they couldn't fall prey to some maniac wandering abroad.

Trying to ignore her thundering heart, she fixed her eyes on Munroe House's back gate and hurried on, wishing she hadn't been talking to Josie about Jack the Ripper the day before. Her pursuer broke into a run to catch up. She was just a few yards from the safety of the clinic but she knew he would catch her before she could reach it. Feeling him just a step behind, she drew a deep breath.

A hand grabbed her arm. Connie threw her bike aside and balled her fists, lashing out in the direction she judged her attacker's head to be. He ducked and grabbed her upper arms, pulling her towards him.

'Connie, I—'

She heard the familiar voice say her name just as her knee connected with his groin.

Charlie grunted and doubled over. The single street lamp on the other side of the road popped back on, throwing dim light on them both.

'Oh Charlie, I'm so sorry,' Connie said. 'I thought you were going to attack me.'

Putting her arm around him to help him up, Connie was suddenly acutely aware of the hard muscles of his shoulders. He straightened, and she caught the faint smell of his aftershave.

He coughed. 'So you thought you'd strike first and ask questions later?'

'Well, the best form of defence is attack, isn't it?'

'I doubt my family jewels would agree,' he replied, looking up at her with a crooked smile.

'You've only got yourself to blame,' she snapped, shoving him away. 'Creeping up on me in the dark like that.'

'Perhaps it wasn't the wisest thing to do, but I had to see you. I phoned two hours ago and was told you were out on a call. I've been waiting around for you to come back.'

'I thought I told you not to ring.' said Connie.

Charlie shook his head. 'Don't worry, I just said I was a chap you met at a dance.'

Her shoulders relaxed a little. 'You shouldn't have rung at all and it wouldn't take much for some people to put two and two together and make five,' she said, thinking of Gladys and her gang. 'Anyhow, why are you hanging around anyway?'

'I told you. I had to see you,' he replied. 'I tried to stay away, but I love you and I can't go on like this.'

'Like what?'

'Living without you.' He took hold of her upper arms lightly. A fizz of excitement ran through her.

'You shouldn't say that,' she whispered, enjoying the pressure of his hands.

'But I do love you, Connie.'

He drew her closer, but Connie resisted the almost overwhelming urge to step into his embrace. 'You mustn't, Charlie. It's not right.'

'I know, but . . . I have to see you again, Connie.'

'I can't,' Connie replied.

His arms slipped around her. 'Please.'

The emotions she'd spent months trying to suppress started to rise up.

'I have to go,' she said, forcing herself to break from his embrace.

Charlie's arms dropped to his sides and he hung his head. 'I've been such a fool.' A grief-stricken expression distorted his handsome face.

Connie placed her hand on his arm. 'Oh Charlie,' she said, taking a step towards him.

His arms encircled her, and this time she didn't resist.

'I forgot just how well we fitted together,' he said, as his broad hands held her to him. Their eyes locked for a second, then he pressed his lips to hers. The months of pain, despair and longing vanished as she threw her arms around his neck and kissed him back.

The distinctive click of Munroe House's back door opening brought her back to reality with a jolt. She tried to tear herself from Charlie's embrace, but he held her firm. 'Someone's coming,' she whispered.

'I know, but meet me tomorrow,' he replied softly, his warm breath brushing her cheek.

'I can't, you know I can't.'

'Please,' Charlie begged, the lock of hair that defied all attempts to tame it flopping forward.

Connie could hear the rattle of a chain being dragged through wheel spokes as whichever nurse had taken the call unlocked her bike.

Charlie captured her lips again, and as his tongue filled her mouth, Connie's head swam.

The back gate squeaked open and she tore herself away. 'No, Charlie,' she murmured breathlessly. 'You mustn't.' He tried to kiss her again, but she pushed him away and grabbed her bike from the floor, shoving it between them.

That assured, devil-may-care smile of his lifted the corners of his mouth. 'I won't give up, Connie,' he said, stepping back into the shadow of the wall. 'You know I won't.'

The gate swung open, and with her heart all but bursting from her chest Connie pushed her cycle towards it just as Eva rolled hers out.

'I got called out to Mrs Webb,' she blurted out.

'I saw it chalked up,' Eva replied. 'Are you all right?'

'Yes, of course I am,' laughed Connie, feeling anything but. 'Why?'

Eva studied her for a moment longer, then shrugged. 'Oh, nothing. You just looked a bit odd for a minute, that's all. See you later.' She hopped on to her bike and cycled away into the gloom.

Connie watched her for a moment, then collapsed against the wall. Breathing in the smell of Charlie's cologne that still clung to her, she closed her eyes and ran her fingers lightly over her lips.

Chapter Nineteen

'There you go, Mrs Sullivan,' Connie said as she set a cup of cocoa in front of Millie's mum.

Doris Sullivan, a round, motherly person with fluffy light grey hair and pale blue eyes, looked up and smiled. 'Thank you, dear, that's very kind.'

As Millie was second midwife on call until midnight, Connie had volunteered to sit with Doris until she got home. She didn't mind: she'd known Doris for as long as she'd known Millie, and it was the least she could do to help her poor overworked and exhausted friend. She wasn't the only one helping out. Sally, Beattie, Eva and Annie had also stepped into the breach and popped round as much as they could to keep Doris company when Millie was on call.

As the opening bar of the Home Service's *Saturday Night Music Hall* theme sounded from the old Bush wireless on the sideboard, Connie resumed her seat in the chair opposite Doris.

'I like this one,' said Doris, as she'd done to every piece of music since Connie had arrived. So far they'd listened to *Those Were the Days*, which were old sentimental tunes that Connie had never heard of but which Doris hummed along to happily. This was followed by *In Town Tonight*, which was much more up Connie's street as it was a collection of show songs from current West End productions.

Although it was only eight o'clock, Doris had insisted on getting ready for bed an hour ago. According to Millie, her mother had been up and roaming since first light, so Connie guessed she probably thought it was much later than it actually was.

'How's your mother keeping?' Doris asked, smiling across at Connie.

'She's well, thank you, Mrs Sullivan,' Connie replied as she had done the last three times Doris had enquired.

'And your sisters and their families?'

'They're all fine,' Connie replied, smiling at her. 'Bernie had a bit of a scare that her Betty had German measles, so she had to keep her away from any friends who were expecting for a few days, but it turned out to be heat rash, and Mo's as pleased as punch that her eldest has got a place at Raine's.'

'Lovely,' said Doris. 'Your mother is so lucky to have so many grandchildren.' A happy twinkle glinted in her eyes. 'But I expect it won't be long once Millie and Alex are married before I'll be hearing the patter of tiny feet.'

Connie smiled sadly. 'Millie's not marrying Alex now, Mrs Sullivan.'

Doris looked puzzled. 'Isn't she?'

'No,' Connie replied, with a deep pang of sympathy for Millie. 'Don't you remember? Alex had to go to Palestine, so she decided to stay behind to take care of you.'

'Am I ill?'

'You have been, but Millie stayed to help you get better.'

Doris stared blankly for a moment, then her face crumpled. 'I'm so muddled these days,' she mumbled.

Connie stood up and went over to her, putting her arm around Doris's shaking shoulders. 'There, there,' she soothed. 'It's all right, Mrs Sullivan.'

Doris looked up. 'But what about Millie? I don't want to be a burden to her.'

'You're not,' Connie assured her. 'She wants to look after you as I'm sure you looked after her when she was small.'

Doris gave a tearful smile. 'She was such a pretty little girl.' She looked past Connie to the photo on the mantelshelf of her late husband. 'Apple of her father's eye. Of course, we hoped to have more, but as my dear husband always said, if God decided we should only have one, then at least he was good enough to give us Millie.' She took a handkerchief from her dressing gown pocket and dabbed her eyes. 'I wish he was still alive to walk her down the aisle.'

Connie smiled and handed Doris her hot drink. 'Why don't you drink your cocoa, Mrs Sullivan, before it gets cold?'

Cradling it in her hands, Doris took a sip. 'Lovely.'

As Millie's mother joined in with 'All the Nice Girls Love a

Sailor', Connie settled back in her chair with the Georgette Heyer novel she'd got from Cable Street library the day before. Doris sang on happily through 'Oh! Mr Porter', 'I'm Shy, Mary Ellen', the sentimental 'If You Were the Only Girl in the World' and a dozen others until the programme's compère wished them a good night.

Doris stood up. 'I think I'll wash these up then go to bed,' she said, taking Connie's empty cup from the coffee table.

'It's all right, Mrs Sullivan,' said Connie, putting her book aside. 'I'll do it.'

Recognition sparked in Doris's eyes. 'You're Millie's friend Connie, aren't you?'

'Yes, I am,' Connie replied gently.

Doris chucked. 'Silly me. Fancy me forgetting your name like that. How's your Charlie?'

Pain cut through Connie. 'Fine. Just fine.'

'I bet you can't wait until he gets back,' Doris continued. 'Well, not long now.' She opened the door leading to the narrow set of stairs. 'Good night, Connie, and give my regards to your mother.'

'Good night, Mrs Sullivan,' Connie replied through the lump in her throat.

As Doris made her way upstairs, Connie rested her head back and closed her eyes. In the darkness, her mind conjured up images of Charlie before moving on to the feel of his hand holding hers and his words of love.

Perhaps he could get a divorce. After all, he'd been under terrible strain and not thinking right when he meet Maria, that much was sure, and if neither of them was happy, then why not? It wasn't common or something to be proud of, but people did.

Connie opened her eyes and cast her gaze around the small sitting room, the very sitting room, in fact, in which she'd imagined her and Charlie spending their first years of married life. She stared bleakly ahead for a few seconds, then blinked and picked up her book again. She tried to get back into the story, but, having read the same paragraph three times, abandoned the attempt and picked up an old copy of the *Nursing Mirror* that was sitting on the kindle pile in the hearth.

Flipping past the sketched adverts for Probex beef liver tablets with iron, and Evernew nurses' wipe-clean collars and cuffs, she reached the News from the Nursing World section. After skimming through the report of Princess Elizabeth's visit to a West Country hospital and the installation of an X-ray machine in Charterhouse rheumatism clinic, she moved on to the vacancy section. There were the usual pages and pages of hospital boards advertising for every kind of nurse – night sisters for fever wards, tutors for training school, male nurses for a men's surgical ward – as well as overseas posts in places as far away as Zanzibar, Rhodesia and the Gold Coast. But as she turned to the community page, a bordered advertisement taking up the two central columns caught her eye.

The Board of Governors for the
Spitalfields and Shoreditch Nursing Association

seeks to appoint an experienced district nurse/midwife
as deputy superintendent to:

– *supervise and allocate nursing services;*
– *oversee and develop activities in Dorset Street clinic;*
– *teach and train the Association's twice-yearly intake*
of trainee Queen's Nurses.

Commencing salary of £400 per annum, plus accommodation in
the recently refurbished Fry House, which includes a modern
inbuilt electric fire and hot and cold water in all nurses' rooms.

Apply in writing before 28 July to:
Miss O'Dwyer, c/o Fry House, Dorset Street, Spitalfields, London E1.

Connie stared at it for a while, thinking that as the Spitalfields and Shoreditch were paying twenty pounds a year more than any of the other associations hereabouts, they would probably be inundated with applicants. Mind you, they needed to, because if anyone thought the St George's and St Dunstan's area was rough, they should take a stroll around Spitalfields.

She turned the page and looked at the adverts for clasp belt buckles, pension funds and holiday cottages offering special rates for nurses, but after starting to read a piece about afflictions of the heel, she turned back. Millie's words on VJ night about promotion returned to her, and she reread the advertisement.

Of course she could do the job, but why would she want to move? Well, it would save her bumping into Charlie at every turn, and what if she was the midwife on call if Maria had another baby?

She tore the page out, folded it twice and then slipped it into her pocket.

'I can't thank you enough for sitting with Mum,' Millie said, as Connie secured her hat and collected her handbag an hour later.

Her friend had returned just after ten from an uneventful on-call shift. Connie was glad. Millie had dark circles under her eyes, so the sooner she got her head on the pillow the better.

'Don't be daft. You'd do the same for me.'

Millie gave her a wan smile. 'I hope I never have to.'

Amen to that, thought Connie.

She hugged her friend. 'I'll see you in the morning, but make sure you wait under the lamp post so I can let you back in without Miss Dutton seeing you.'

Millie nodded. 'Mind how you go,' she yawned.

The moon was up and the heat from the day still hovered in the air, so Connie didn't really need the cardigan she wearing over her summer dress. Hooking her handbag over her arm, she headed up the street and was soon in Commercial Road. Of course, it would have been quicker to cut through Watney Street, but it would be chucking-out time soon, and as she'd have to pass at least half a dozen pubs, she decided it would be safer to go along the main road, where there were more people. She'd still have to pass the Prince of Denmark, but that was a bit more upmarket, catering for councillors and local businessmen.

Running through the little pep talk she was going to give Josie before Miss Knott's impending visit the day after next, Connie walked on. She'd just reached the small parade of shops past the four-storey Victorian public house on the corner of Sydney Street when someone shouted her name. She turned and saw Dr Carter lumbering towards her. He obviously hadn't been ministering to a sick patient, as he was dressed in a navy single-breasted suit and polished black shoes, his red silk bow tie hanging loosely around his unbuttoned collar.

Since their last encounter, Connie had managed to keep out of his way, but as he was just a few steps from her, she couldn't very well walk on. He stopped immediately in front of her.

'Good evening, Sister Byrne,' he said, swaying slightly.

Connie took half a step back. 'Good evening, Dr Carter.'

'Jusht what a chap needs after a good dinner: a pretty little nursey,' he slurred, looming over her.

'I'm glad you've had a nice evening, Doctor,' said Connie pleasantly. 'Have a safe journey home.' She went to walk past, but he stepped in front of her.

'What's your hurry?' he asked, breathing brandy fumes over her.

'I have to be back at Munroe House before the superintendent locks the door at—'

'Rubbish.' He winked. 'I know what you little nurses are like. Always sneaking back in when Matron's not looking or slipping your boyfriends up to your rooms.'

Connie looked away. 'Good night, Doctor.' She pushed past him, but he grabbed her.

'That's not very friendly, is it?'

Connie dropped her handbag as she tried to break free, but he was too strong and he backed her into the nearest shop doorway. She glared at him, but he just grinned. Grabbing her with one arm, his free hand closed around her breast.

'Fancy slipping me in tonight, Sister Byrne?'

Connie slapped his face and shoved him away. She twisted out of his grasp, but he caught her arm.

'Let go of me,' she snapped, trying to wrench free.

'You're a bit of a prick-teaser, aren't you, Sister Byrne?' he snarled, gripping her wrist painfully tight.

Connie tried to knee him in the groin, but he blocked her. He laughed and pushed her into the corner. Connie's heart thumped uncomfortably as he made to kiss her. She turned her head and his wet lips slid along her cheek. Nausea rose in the back of her throat.

'Please stop,' she sobbed.

Dr Carter ignored her. There was a ripping sound and she felt his hand on her bare flesh. As he pinned her to the half-glazed shop door, Connie pressed her eyes tight shut.

Suddenly he howled and released her as something jerked him back.

'I think Sister Byrne told you to let go,' said a familiar voice.

Connie staggered out of the doorway and was astonished to see Malcolm Henstock gripping Dr Carter in a headlock.

'Let go of me, you . . .' spluttered the GP, struggling to free himself.

Malcolm held him firm. 'Are you all right, Sister?' he asked calmly.

Unable to speak, Connie nodded.

Malcolm let the doctor go. Carter staggered sideways and crashed on to the pavement, his right hand landing in a whirl of dog dirt as he sought to break his fall.

Stepping over him and picking up Connie's handbag, Malcolm took her elbow.

'I . . . I . . .' Connie started, but then her knees gave way.

Malcolm tucked her arm in his. 'It's all right, Connie,' he said softly. 'I'll see you safely home now.'

Leaving Dr Carter floundering in the dirt, Malcolm walked her the short distance to the nurses' home.

'Here we are,' he said, as they came to a halt at the front door. 'All safe and sound.'

Connie turned to him. 'I'm so sorry, Mr Henstock, I haven't even thanked you properly for—'

'Malcolm, please, and there's really no need to thank me,' he replied, smiling down at her. 'I'm just glad I came by.'

Connie smiled back. 'So am I.'

Malcolm frowned. 'Did you know him?'

Connie nodded. 'He's one of the doctors I have to work with.'

'Blooming brute,' Malcolm fumed. 'A man in his position ought to know better. He should be reported to the General Medical Council.'

Fat lot of good that would do, thought Connie. In her experience, doctors just stuck together.

'Well thank you, anyway, for being my knight in shining armour tonight,' she said.

'You wouldn't say that if you'd seen me on a horse,' Malcolm chuckled.

They smiled awkwardly at each other, then she glanced at the front door. 'I'm on early call, so I ought to go in.'

'I've got to get up early too,' he replied. 'I'm inspecting drains in Limehouse.'

'And I'm dressing leg ulcers in Wapping,' Connie laughed.

'Such glamorous lives we live.' He smiled again. 'Good night, Connie.'

'Good night, Malcolm.'

He turned, and as she watched him stroll back up the street, Connie wondered if perhaps she should have been more polite and asked him in for a coffee.

With just a sliver of bright June sunlight creeping beneath the bottom edge of the blindfold, Connie stretched her hands in front of her and took a step forward.

'Over here, Auntie Connie,' squealed her niece.

Connie swung around.

'No, this way,' shouted Bert, Mo's middle boy.

She turned in the direction of his voice and lunged forward, catching a small body before it could escape. Holding the wriggling child in one arm, she lifted the covering from her eyes.

'Got you, Janice,' she laughed, swinging her brother Jim's daughter in the air.

'OK, kids, that's enough,' shouted Mo from the back door. 'You're making poor Auntie Connie dizzy. There's some squash and cakes for you in the front room.'

A cheer went up as the children raced each other back into the house, Betty, who had just started crawling the week before, bringing up the rear.

Connie sat down on the bench against the wall in the shade and surveyed her parents' back yard, which, except for a narrow border filled with bright dahlias, was covered with an assortment of broken paving slabs harvested from bombed streets. At the far end, hooked on the wall, were extending ladders, buckets and long-handled brushes – the tools of her father's decorating trade. Above her head, stretching diagonally across the space, was her mother's washing line, which tomorrow, Monday, would be laden with her father's shirts and her mother's baggy unmentionables.

As it was a sweltering afternoon, the family had decided to take their tea outside. Maud, wearing her Sunday outfit, minus the hat, was sitting like a queen bee on a kitchen chair next to the back door. She was flanked by Bernie and Sheila, who were chatting about the extortionate price of children's shoes. Under a line of swaying pink hollyhocks at the far end of the yard, Arthur, dressed in a suit and tie with a knotted handkerchief covering his bald spot, snoozed in a deckchair while Mo and Eddy chatted to Jim and Bernie's husband, Cliff.

The special guest of the afternoon's gathering stepped out of the back door holding two cups of tea.

Since he had thrown his kitbag over his shoulder and waved them goodbye six months ago, Bobby had changed from a fresh-faced boy into a confident young man. Despite Maud's insistence that he was looking thin, he had probably put on at least a stone, and all of that was muscle. His dress uniform now strained to contain his broad shoulders and chest. He still had the same cheeky grin, but it now had an assured confidence that would make any woman look twice.

'You managed to escape then, sis,' he called.

'Just about,' Connie laughed. 'And only because Mo put out the cakes.'

Sauntering over, Bobby handed her a cup.

'After being away for so long, everything must seem very different,' she said as he sat on the bench beside her.

He grinned. 'Not really. I mean, Mum's still nagging Dad, Dad's still turning a deaf 'un, Mo's still ruling the roost while Bernie tries to keep the peace, old Jim's still West Ham's number one supporter and you're still Stepney's answer to Florence Nightingale.'

'I suppose we do seem a bit dull to you after all the fun you've been having in Germany,' said Connie.

'I have had some larks right enough, and some I couldn't repeat.' He winked. 'But I'm glad to be home, even with Mum fussing.'

'It's just her way of showing she missed you,' said Connie.

'I know,' Bobby replied, 'although I caught her rummaging

through my kitbag yesterday. She said she was looking for dirty washing, but I think she was after evidence.'

'Of what?'

'She's convinced I've got some *Fräulein*.'

'And have you?'

He shook his head and grinned. 'It's a sergeant's daughter.'

Connie laughed. 'Oh Bobby, I have missed you.'

'And I've missed you too, sis. Are you walking out with anyone?' he asked.

'Not at the moment,' Connie replied.

'I suppose it's because of Charlie Ross.'

'These things take time,' said Connie. 'And I'm just not ready to get serious with anyone again yet.'

Bobby's face darkened. 'It makes my blood boil when I think of how that bastard treated you.'

Connie covered her brother's hand with her own. 'It doesn't matter. I'm over it.'

Bobby gave a grim smile. 'I'm glad. I never did like him much, and neither did the others.' He indicated Jim, Cliff and Eddy chatting by the coal shed. 'Too bloody cocky by half.'

'People change, Bobby,' Connie said softly.

He snorted. 'Not from what I've heard. Talk is he plays his missus up good and proper. I've heard he's in the thick of it with the Timms gang too.'

'I'm sure that's just a bit of gossip,' Connie replied.

Bobby frowned. 'You're not making excuses for him, are you, Connie?'

'Of course not,' she replied, swallowing a mouthful of tea. 'I'm just saying there are two sides to every story, that's all. And yes, the way Charlie acted was terrible, but it's water under the bridge now and I've put it behind me.'

'I'm pleased to hear it, sis,' said Bobby. 'You deserve better.'

'Oi, Bobby, fancy joining us for a game of cribbage?' Jim called. 'Ha'penny a point.'

'You're on.' Bobby threw back the last of his tea. 'See you later, sis.'

Resting back in the shade, Connie watched her brother stroll over to join the men of the family, knowing that even in her wildest dreams Charlie would never be counted as one of them.

Drumming her fingers silently on the top of her case, Josie looked up at the clock for the third time in as many minutes. She was wearing a freshly laundered uniform with her dry-cleaned jacket over it, and if she'd polished her shoes for much longer she'd have worn right through them. Her felt hat, which she'd spent hours the night before holding over a steaming kettle to restore its shape, sat firmly on her head.

'I'm sure she'll be here any moment,' said Connie with a reassuring smile.

It was 8.15 on a bright sunny morning and they were sitting beside the desk in the nurses' office waiting for Miss Knott to arrive. The clatter of chairs being set out ready for the Monday-morning dressing clinic sounded from the next room, while through the half-open window Connie could see the nurses in the back yard unchaining their bikes and getting ready to cycle off on their rounds.

Josie heaved a sigh. 'I'm going to fail again, I know I am.'

'No, you're not,' said Connie, reaching across and patting her hand. 'Especially after all the preparation we've done.'

'I know, I know,' replied Josie. 'But I'm bound to drop or spill something, and then what?'

'No you won't,' replied Connie firmly. 'But you'll have to calm down, Josie.'

'You're right, you're right,' said Josie, slowly breathing out.

'That's better. Now, let's just go through a couple of things to occupy your mind while we're waiting, shall we?' she said, sounding very like her old headmistress.

'All right,' said Josie, bobbing her case up and down on her knee.

'And for goodness' sake, Josie,' chuckled Connie, 'put your bag down, before the corks pop on the lotion bottles.'

Josie placed the bag on the mud-coloured lino floor and then clasped her hands together on her lap.

'Right,' said Connie. 'Tell me what advice you'd give if you discovered fleas in a house.'

'I'd advise them to get a five per cent DDT solution from the chemist and spray it in all the crevices around door frames and skirting boards to destroy the adult fleas and the eggs, then scrub the floorboards and furniture with twenty per cent soft soap,' Josie replied, all but quoting the standard Merry and Irven textbook. 'All linen needs to be boiled and exposed to the air. If the infestation is very bad, then the local council needs to be informed and they may have to come to fumigate.'

Connie nodded. 'And what about the individual?'

'A citronella or camphor solution applied to clothing can repel the insects, and the chemist will supply these too. You can use the same measures against cockroaches and steam flies, which can also be destroyed with Flit.'

'What about mice?' asked Connie, as the minute hand of the clock shifted down to 8.25.

Josie took another deep breath. 'Firstly, I would tell them to stop up any mouse holes they find, then clean the house thoroughly with Jeyes fluid. Then buy some traps and ratbane, but if there are children in the house to use syrup of squills, which is harmless, to prevent accidental poisoning. I'd then suggest they use sealed tins and jars when storing grocery items and that they dispose of all food waste in an outside dustbin.'

Connie smiled. 'See, you do know it.'

Josie smiled and her shoulders relaxed. 'Yes, I do. In fact I think I'll be dreaming of the correct mix for boracic lotion for months.'

Connie raised an eyebrow. 'I thought your dreams were filled with Jack Wallace.'

Josie blushed and lowered her eyes.

The doorbell rang.

'She's here!' Josie jumped up and knocked into the side of the desk. The flowery pot full of pens toppled over, spilling its contents across the writing pad.

'Oh my goodness,' she said, scrambling to gather the writing implements but just scattering them further.

'Calm down, Josie!' said Connie sharply as she gripped her student's arm.

'I will, I will,' said Josie, shaking out her hands and taking a number of deep breaths.

Connie reached down, picked up Josie's bag and handed it to her. 'Now, let's go and greet Miss Knott.'

Waiting in the hall was a rosy-faced elderly woman with white candy-floss hair. She was dressed in the older-style Queen's Nurse uniform, which stopped mid-calf. She wore flesh-coloured knitted stockings and a voluminous navy cap. When she saw Connie and Josie, she smiled.

'What ho! You must be Sister Byrne.'

'Yes,' said Connie.

'I'm Miss Pretty, from the education department at headquarters.'

'Nice to meet you, Miss Pretty,' said Connie. 'We were expecting Miss Knott.'

Miss Pretty chortled. 'I'm afraid Miss Knott was bitten on the leg by a costermonger's dog last week in Bethnal Green.'

'Oh dear,' said Connie, wondering if the dog had survived.

'The quack told her to keep off it for a week.' Miss Pretty grinned, revealing a set of teeth that a Grand National winner would have been proud of. 'So headquarters sent me.'

She shoved her umbrella in the stand but missed, and it clattered on to the black-and-white tiles.

'Blast!'

She stooped to pick it up and her hat fell off on to the floor.

Connie hurried forward and retrieved it. Miss Pretty plonked it on her head and looked at Josie. 'And is this the young Queenie I'm going to be joining today?'

'Yes,' said Connie, stepping aside. 'This is Nurse Baxter.'

Miss Pretty looked her over.

'Nice to meet you, me dear, and do smile,' said the education officer, her heavy features lifting in a friendly expression.

The corners of Josie's lips curled upwards slightly.

'That's better,' said Miss Pretty. 'I'm not going to eat you, you know.' She rubbed her hands together. 'Now, tell me what you have in store for me today.'

Josie glanced at Connie, who nodded. She took her notebook from her pocket. 'Well first we're going to visit Mr Philips to give him his morning insulin.'

'Splendid,' said Miss Pretty.

'Next we're visiting Mrs Dyson to get her up and give her breakfast.' Josie looked worried. 'I hope you're not sensitive to feathers, as she's got a parrot.'

'A parrot! My goodness. How jolly!' exclaimed the elderly education officer. 'After that I should think it'll be time for a cuppa, wouldn't you say?' She chuckled. 'When I was a young thing like you in Hastings, me and my chums used to go to this little tea shop on the front.'

Connie laughed. 'Out of the way of the super?'

Miss Pretty's eyes twinkled. 'Just so.'

Josie looked from her supervising sister to her examining education officer in astonishment:

'Why don't you take Miss Pretty to Kate's Café, Nurse Baxter?' suggested Connie.

'Sounds just the place. Shall we be off?' said Miss Pretty.

As she headed for the door, her cape swept the morning's post from the sideboard, while Josie, just a few steps behind, narrowly missed knocking the aspidistra off the hall table with her bag.

The door clicked shut behind them, and Connie smiled.

Suppressing a yawn, Connie pulled a jagged splinter out of Henry Irvine's grubby schoolboy knee and dropped the tweezers in the bowl of Dettol on the dressing trolley.

'I think that's the last of them,' she said, smiling at the lad.

'Ta, miss,' said Henry, a wiry ten-year-old with russet hair and freckles.

Connie and Eva had been working at their dressing stations behind the threadbare fabric screens since 8.30, and as it was standing room only in the waiting area, they'd be lucky if they had time for lunch before setting out on their afternoon visits.

As usual, the Monday morning clinic was full of weekend casualties, and Connie had already treated a lacerated brow, a split lip and scuffed knuckles – the results of too many pints on Saturday night – as well as a woman who'd caught her finger in a mangle and a baby who'd fallen against the fire grate and burnt the palms of both hands. She'd dressed the screaming child's wounds as best she could, then sent him and his sobbing mother half a mile down the street to the East London Children's Hospital for further treatment. She'd put him on Millie's book for a follow-up visit on Wednesday.

She picked up the bottle of iodine and a gauze swab. 'Now this is going to sting, Henry, but it'll stop any germs.'

The lad gave a nonchalant shrug, but gripped the side of the chair nonetheless. Uncorking the bottle, Connie dabbed iodine on the raw wound as quickly as she could, then covered it with a square of medicated lint, which she bandaged in place.

'All done,' she said, tying off the strip and tucking the ends underneath. 'Now, you wait there while I get your mother.' Dropping the dirty swab in the paper bag on the lower shelf of the dressing trolley, she slid the screen aside, then turned back. 'And don't touch anything while I'm gone,' she added, giving him a hard look.

'No, miss.'

Mrs Irvine, a short, plump woman in her late twenties, was waiting in the corridor between a docker with a bloody handkerchief tied around his thumb and a child with fly paper stuck across its face. Connie beckoned to her and Mrs Irvine came forward.

'Is he all right, Sister?' she asked anxiously as Connie led her back into the treatment room.

'Just about.' Connie moved the screen aside and gave the lad perched on the chair a fierce look. 'But no more playing cowboys and Indians on bomb sites.'

Mrs Irvine slapped her son across the side of his head. 'You do what Sister says, or I'll get yer dad to take his belt off to you, d'you 'ear?'

'Yes, Mum,' said the boy, cradling his ear.

'Good. Now wait outside while I pay Sister for all the trouble you've caused her,' Mrs Irvine said, nodding her scarf-swathed head towards the door.

The boy trotted out, and Connie led Mrs Irvine over to the desk and sat down behind it.

'You'll have to bring him back on Wednesday so we can check it, but as long as there's no pus, it can be left to the air after that.'

Mrs Irvine pulled her purse out of the handbag on her arm. 'What's the damage?'

Connie reached for the receipt book and slipped a carbon sheet under a fresh page. 'Sixpence,' she replied, quoting the minimum fee for treating a child.

Mrs Irving handed the money over. Connie unlocked the top drawer and deposited it in the cash box. Then she scribbled out a receipt and handed it to the woman on the other side of the desk.

'You know, I read somewhere that hitting a child around the head can damage them.'

Mrs Irvine looked puzzled. 'Who says?'

'A number of neurosurgeons. Doctors who look into how the brain works,' Connie explained.

'Doctors.' Mrs Irvine tutted and rolled her eyes. 'What the bleeding hell do they know? Whacking my five lads is the only way of keeping order sometimes. You wait until you've got a houseful of nippers, Sister, and then you tell me about fetching them one around the bonce.' She took a roll-up from behind her ear and stuck it in her mouth before ambling out of the room.

Connie sighed and got up to call the next patient. Just as she poked her head around the door, however, the telephone rang.

'Good morning, Munroe House, Sister Byrne speaking. How can I help you?' she asked, taking the pen from her top pocket.

'It's Desk Sergeant Mills here, from Arbour Square police station,' a deep voice replied. 'Is the matron around?'

'She's out at a meeting at the moment. Can I help?'

'It's in regard to one of your nurses, Sister Amelia Sullivan. I'm afraid there's been an accident.'

The low hum of voices and the steel-tipped heels of the nurses clicking on the lino as they walked back and forth about their business were such familiar sounds that they barely registered with Connie as she sat beside Millie's bed on the women's medical ward in the London Hospital.

Hanbury Ward, like the other wards in the main eighteenth-century block, was set out in the classic Nightingale formation. The beds were lined up along each wall, with the kitchen and sluice at one end and the patients' day room at the other. As it was 3.30 in the afternoon, a handful of nurses, in their lilac-striped uniforms with puffy sleeves, were huddled around the central desk completing their notes while the patients were occupied with their visitors. The rest were tidying away the linen or getting the trolleys ready for the toilet round after visiting.

When Connie and Millie had undertaken their third-year medical stint, the ward had been ruled by the fearsome Miss Puttock, but, thankfully, she'd retired some years before. The sister who was now in charge was a kindly fair-haired woman who obviously realised that bullying wasn't the way to get the best out of student nurses.

Connie's gaze returned to her friend. Swathed in a head bandage and with yellow iodine stains on her cheeks and chin, Millie lay with her eyes closed and a calm expression on her battered face. The right side had taken the brunt of the force when she'd hit the pavement. Not only was her eye black and blue, but it had puffed up so much that even if she'd been awake, Connie doubted she'd have been able to open it.

Her own eyes misted up and she took Millie's hand, which was resting on top of the covers.

According to the police, Millie had been turning right from Commercial Road into Cannon Street Road when a lorry jumped the lights. As she swerved to avoid it, she hit the kerb and flew over the handlebars. If she hadn't, she'd have been crushed under the front wheels. The Casualty doctor didn't think there were any broken bones, but they would keep her on morphine until she came round.

Tears welled up and Connie clutched the small cross under her uniform. She knew she could so easily have been looking down at her best friend on a mortician's slab rather than in a hospital bed.

'Begging your pardon, Miss Byrne, but can I get yer anuvver cuppa?'

Connie turned to find Bridget Kelly, who had been the ward orderly on Hanbury Ward for as long as she could remember, standing behind her.

The unfinished clinic records that had to be on the superintendent's desk by six o'clock, her bag full of dirty instruments that needed scrubbing and soaking, plus her untidy room that if Miss Dutton did one of her spot inspections would get two shillings docked from her wages all flashed through Connie's mind, but then she looked back at Millie.

'Thank you, Mrs Kelly,' she said, smiling up at the old woman. 'Another tea would go down a treat.'

Chapter Twenty

Millie drew a sharp breath and groaned. Connie said a small prayer of thanks and sat forward expectantly.

Annie, Sally and Josie had kindly divided half of Connie's afternoon patients between them, so after racing through her remaining list, Connie had arrived on the ward just as the door opened for afternoon visiting.

Squinting, Millie opened her left eye. 'Where am I?' she mumbled.

'Hanbury Ward,' Connie replied, feeling a lump in her throat. 'And thank goodness you're awake at last.'

'How long have I been here?' Millie asked, struggling to sit up.

Connie stood up to help her. 'Since yesterday,' she replied, buckling the backrest in place and repositioning the pillows.

Millie started to sink back, but then straightened again. 'My mum?'

'Don't worry. Your mum's fine,' Connie said, smiling reassuringly and patting the pillows. 'She's being well looked after.'

Millie grabbed her hand. 'She's not been taken back to St Mungo's, has she?'

'Of course not. Don't you worry, everything is under control.'

Millie sank back and closed her eyes again.

'That's better,' said Connie in her Sister-knows-best voice. 'Aunt Ruby came to see you yesterday, and she'll be down again tomorrow. Now don't worry.'

Millie let out a small groan. 'I don't think there's one inch of me that doesn't hurt.'

'I'm not surprised – you've taken half the skin off your arms and legs, not to mention knocking your head on the pavement,' said Connie, looking at her sympathetically. 'Thank God you weren't killed. Can you remember what happened?'

'Not really,' muttered Millie. 'One moment I was cycling down

Commercial Road and the next I was lying on the ground with people around me.'

'The policeman who came to see us said the lorry jumped the lights, so he'll be prosecuted,' Connie said. 'The doctor in Accident and Emergency thought you might have done more damage, but when the X-rays came back clear a couple of hours ago, they stopped the morphine.'

Millie shifted position and winced. 'I can tell.'

'Here.' Connie picked up a small china pot. 'The nurses left this for when you woke up.' She tipped two white tablets into Millie's outstretched hand. 'It's codeine. It'll take the edge off the pain,' she said, picking up the glass of water from the bedside locker and holding it to her friend's lips.

Millie swallowed the tablets and let her head fall back.

Connie took her hand gently. 'Oh Millie, you gave us all such a fright. When the police rang and said you'd been knocked off your bike by a lorry, well . . .' Tears pinched the corners of Connie's eyes. 'I can't tell you how relieved I was when I arrived and they told me you were alive and not too seriously injured.'

She felt a slight pressure on her hand as Millie squeezed it. Connie smiled, and Millie smiled back as best she could.

'The girls say they'll pop in when you're feeling a bit better. And we all clubbed together and bought you these.' Connie reached into the shopping bag at her feet and pulled out a bunch of bananas.

'Where on earth did you get those?'

'Don't ask,' she replied with an amused expression. 'Let's just say Annie has a patient who can "acquire" things, and leave it at that. Do you want one now?'

'Yes, please,' replied Millie, realising suddenly that she was hungry.

Connie peeled one and handed it to Millie, who bit the top off.

'Oh my goodness,' she said. 'I'd forgotten how sweet they are.' She broke the rest of the banana in half and offered it to Connie.

Connie hesitated for a split second, then took the fruit and bit into it. 'Mmm, so tasty,' she said, as the sweet ripeness filled her mouth. 'Perhaps I should tumble off my bike too.'

'I wouldn't recommend it,' Millie replied. 'I owe you and the girls for taking care of Mum, Connie.'

'Look, I was going to tell you when you'd recovered a bit more, but perhaps you ought to know now.'

'Tell me what?'

'Well, me and the girls are popping in once a day, but – and promise you won't get annoyed – Mrs Callaghan is the one who's taken charge. She's got a rota of neighbours caring for your mum.'

'I didn't think Mrs Callaghan even liked me,' said Millie. 'Why would she look after my mother?'

Connie could understand her friend's astonishment. Millie and Mrs Callaghan, the local busybody and folk-midwife, had crossed swords on more than one occasion and everyone knew there was no love lost between them.

'I have no idea, but if you want to find out, you'd better do as the doctors say and get out of here, and then you can ask her yourself. Would you like another drink?'

Millie gave a small nod and winced again. 'Please.'

'Good, because Mrs Pierce told me to bring you this.' Connie rifled in her bag again and brought out a bottle of lemonade. 'She made a new batch yesterday and says as you're poorly you can be the first to sample it.'

She poured out half a glass and held it to her friend's lips. Millie took a long drink, then closed her eyes and sank back in the pillows again.

'So what else is happening?'

'Well the good news is Josie has passed her home visit assessment,' said Connie.

'Thank goodness,' said Millie. 'I was so worried Miss Knott would find some excuse to fail her again.'

'Me too,' Connie replied. 'But Miss Knott was indisposed, so a Miss Pretty took her out instead, and apparently she and Josie got on like a house on fire. And to celebrate becoming a Queen's Nurse, Josie's announced her engagement.'

Millie's good eye blinked open. 'That's quick.'

'From what I can tell, her Jack isn't one to wait around,' Connie replied. 'They've even booked St Dunstan's for the seventh of September.'

'Well I wish her every happiness,' said Millie. 'It's nice to hear of someone who's lucky in love.'

'Yes it is, isn't it?' replied Connie. 'And I,' she continued, a satisfied smile spreading across her face, 'have got an interview at Spitalfields and Shoreditch on the sixteenth.'

'Oh, Connie, I'm so pleased for you,' said Millie, giving her a lopsided grin. 'I'm sure they'll grab you with both hands.' she sighed. 'And even though the old place won't seem the same without you I really hope you get the job.'

Connie smiled ruefully. 'Thanks, I wish I had your confidence. I'm sure they'll ask me something I don't know, and goodness only knows what sort of reference old Dutton will give me.'

Picking up the handbell, the staff nurse signalled the end of visiting time.

'Ah well.' Connie stood up. 'I'm taking over from Joan at six, so I'd better get back.'

'Thanks for coming, Connie.'

'Don't be silly. I'll be back tomorrow.' She patted Millie's bruised hand lightly. 'But you rest up and do as the doctor says.'

Millie nodded and shut her eyes.

Mrs Pierce was striking the supper gong as Connie walked back into Munroe House, and her stomach rumbled in response. Hooking up her coat, she ran upstairs and changed into her midwife's uniform. After quickly checking that she had the required delivery equipment in her bag, she hurried down to supper, but just as she set foot on the bottom step, the hall phone rang.

The treatment room door at the far end of the corridor opened and Joan, red-faced and carrying a pair of long tweezers, came out.

'Don't worry, I'll get it,' Connie called.

Joan gave her a grateful smile and returned to her task.

Connie picked up the phone. 'Good afternoon, Munroe House, Sister Byrne speaking. How can I help—'

'Thank God it's you,' said an audibly relieved Dr Robinson on the other end. 'It's Mrs Hogan. She's in labour.'

Connie screeched to a halt outside Mrs Hogan's house. Hastily securing her bike on the lamp post, she yanked her bag from the basket and shoved the door open. As she put her foot on the first step, Mr Hogan appeared from the scullery at the back of the house.

'Evening, Sister, you've just missed the Doc,' he said, in a too-jolly tone.

'Yes, I spoke to him on the phone.' Connie looked beyond him to the open scullery door. 'Where are the children?'

'Gloria next door's giving them tea,' he said. 'Said she'd bed them down too, if . . .' He broke off and sniffed. 'Doc said he couldn't do anything this time,' he continued, taking a red hanky from the pocket of his donkey jacket and wiping his nose.

'I know.' Balancing her bag on her knee, Connie took out her delivery pack. 'Can you boil these for five minutes, Mr Hogan, then, without touching them, fetch them up in the saucepan?'

'Right you are, Sister,' he said, taking the pack from her.

'I'll need a couple of newspapers and plenty of towels,' Connie continued. 'And could you heat two or three bricks by the range and then empty out a small cupboard drawer and bring it up as well,' she called behind her as she hurried up the stairs.

Mr Hogan caught her arm. 'Tell me the truth, Sister. Is there any hope?'

By her calculation, Mrs Hogan was just over the twenty-eight-week mark, and though infants delivered at that stage of pregnancy did survive, sadly it was rare. Much depended on the weight and vigour of the infant, but as Mrs Hogan's bump was only just about the right size for her dates, the chances of her baby tipping the scales at even four pounds were remote to say the least.

'There's always hope, Mr Hogan,' Connie said, smiling professionally. 'Now I ought to see how your wife is faring, so if you could bring up the instruments when they're ready, I'd be very grateful.'

With his shoulders slumped, Mr Hogan retraced his steps and Connie continued up the stairs. When she reached the bedroom, she found Mrs Hogan, wearing a washed-out old nightdress, standing at the foot of the bed and gripping on to the iron strut. As Connie walked in, she looked around.

'Thank goodness it's you, Sister Byrne,' she said in a shaky voice.

Connie smiled reassuringly and placed her bag on the floor before going over to her patient.

'When did the contractions start?' she asked, placing a light hand on Mrs Hogan's stomach and feeling a tight ball of hardness.

'I had a couple of twinges at about two, but I've been having a couple each day for the past week so I didn't think anything of it. Then about an hour ago I had to spend a penny.' She indicated the bedpan sitting on the commode in the corner. 'Suddenly, I got this almighty pain in my back, and by the time I got back in the bed I knew I'd started proper.'

'Have your waters gone?' Connie asked, feeling the contraction under her hand fade.

Mrs Hogan shook her head.

Relief flooded over Connie. A prem baby and a dry labour were not a good combination. The infant would be stressed enough from being forced into the world before it was fully formed, but if the waters stayed intact it would save the little chap some buffeting.

The muscles of Mrs Hogan's abdomen bunched again and tears filled her eyes. 'I've been praying so hard for just one more week, Sister.'

Connie put a comforting hand on her shoulder. 'I know you have, Mrs Hogan,' she said softly. 'We all have. Now, I have to get you on the bed so I can check baby and see what's happening.'

Quickly, she spread out two copies of the *Daily Mirror* and covered them with an old towel, then helped her patient back to bed. Mrs Hogan rested back and closed her eyes. Stretching her hand wide, Connie placed it just above Mrs Hogan's pubic bone.

'Good news,' she said cheerfully. 'Baby's still head down.'

Mrs Hogan gave a wan smile, then screwed up her face again as another wave of pain ran through her.

Connie opened her bag and set clean bowls and a tin of gauze on the table she'd already covered with a sterile sheet of paper. She added the silk ligature for tying off the cord and a freshly boiled pair of rubber gloves, then took a length of Gamgee Tissue and fashioned a small cap to cover the baby's head. As Mrs Hogan's contraction subsided, she took the foetal stethoscope from her bag and placed the wide end on her bump.

Connie closed her eyes and listened. There was nothing for a moment, then over the rhythmic sound of Mrs Hogan's blood whooshing through her veins she heard the faint but distinct beat of the baby's heart. Resisting the urge to laugh hysterically, she glanced down at her watch.

One hundred and ten. Within what the textbook defined as normal, but lower than Connie would have liked.

Mrs Hogan clenched her teeth and groaned.

'Another one?' Connie asked, placing her hand on the woman's solid stomach.

'Yessss,' hissed her patient.

'Try to take shallow breaths, Mrs Hogan,' Connie said, glancing down at her fob watch.

Mrs Hogan nodded and pressed her lips together, grabbing the eiderdown with both hands.

Connie replaced the stethoscope and studied her watch again. This time, however, before the second hand was even halfway round, a feeling of dread settled on her shoulders. The pressure from the contracting uterus had caused the foetal heart rate to drop dramatically. In its immature state, she was fearful as to how the baby would fare in a protracted labour. With her own heart thumping uncomfortably in her chest, she continued to listen as the contraction continued for a full minute. As it faded, the baby's heart rate picked up a little, but not enough.

She straightened up and dragged her gown from her nurse's case, shoving her arms into the sleeves.

'Mrs Hogan, I'm going to have to examine you inside,' she said. 'Could you lie back, draw your knees up and open your legs?'

Mrs Hogan did as she was asked.

Smiling reassuringly at her, and sending up a quick prayer to St Gerard, the patron saint of women in labour, Connie gently slipped two fingers into her patient.

Even though she was past the crucial twenty-eight-week mark, the chances of Mrs Hogan having a happy outcome were not high, but if she was only one or two fingers dilated, then those odds plummeted to almost zero. Not wanting to contemplate delivering a stillborn infant or struggling to extract a dead one, Connie focused on the wallpaper as she visualised her way forward. She felt the starting trembles of the next contraction, but as she skimmed her finger gently around the rim of the uterus, she all but sobbed with relief. Due no doubt to her underlying condition of an unstable uterus, Mrs Hogan was almost fully dilated.

Extracting her hand, Connie crossed the room in three paces. She knocked the handle with her elbow and kicked open the bedroom door.

'Mr Hogan!' she yelled. 'I need that equipment now!'

'Is my baby dead?' howled Mrs Hogan, tears streaming down her cheeks.

'No, he's not,' Connie replied firmly. 'And I'd say you have a right little fighter in there, but he needs to be born, so when the next contraction starts, I'm going to break your waters.'

A terrified Mr Hogan ran into the room carrying a cream enamel saucepan. 'What—'

'Drain the water into my bowls,' Connie told him. 'Then put the saucepan next to the dressing tin.'

He looked terrified but, with shaking hands, did as she asked.

'Now go and get the drawer, the towels and the hot bricks,' Connie added as she took her instruments from the saucepan and set them out ready.

He ran back down the stairs and returned just as she was tying her mask in place.

'Put the drawer on the dressing table,' Connie told him. 'Line it with the towels and then place the bricks against either side and at one end of it.'

Mr Hogan did as instructed and then made to leave the room.

'No, stay,' said Connie. 'I might need you.' He positioned himself at the other end of the bed and gripped his wife's hand.

Connie put another old towel between Mrs Hogan's legs, then took the slim amniohook from the boiled water and knelt on the bed.

'Now, tell me when you feel the next contraction starting.' She got into position between her patient's splayed legs.

Mrs Hogan curled forward. 'Now, and I want to push,' she grunted as the urge to bear down swept over her.

'That's good, but try to hold back until I tell you,' Connie replied.

Placing the hook end of her instrument parallel with the second finger of her right hand, she slipped it into Mrs Hogan. As she reached the soft bulge protruding down, she hooked the membrane and tugged. She felt a pop, and then a gush of warm liquid. She extracted her hand as the amniotic fluid gushed out, soaking the towel.

'Right, Mrs Hogan, the next time you feel a contraction, push.'

Mrs Hogan nodded and then grimaced again. She hunched her shoulders and, as the contraction built, pushed with all her might. Her vulva bulged and then a small patch of damp hair appeared.

'The head's crowned,' Connie cried. 'Another push like that and he'll be here.'

Leaning forward, Mrs Hogan grabbed Connie's arm in a vice-like grip. 'Baptise him.'

'But he'll be out with the next push,' Connie replied.

Tears welled up in Mrs Hogan's eyes. 'Please, Sister,' she whispered. 'You're a Catholic girl, so you know why I ask.'

Connie smiled sadly. 'That I do.' Although she, like many now, believed that a stillborn or miscarried child died in the mercy of Mary and was assured a place in heaven, some still clung to the belief that an unbaptised child would spend eternity in limbo.

She picked up the bowl. 'I baptise thee,' she dripped water on to the just-visible part of the child's head, 'in the name of the Father, the Son and the Holy Ghost.'

'Amen,' said Mr and Mrs Hogan, crossing themselves.

'Amen,' repeated Connie.

Mrs Hogan's jaw clenched again and she arched forward.

Connie put the bowl down. 'Right, Mrs Hogan,' she said, in her best matron's voice. 'Let's get back to the business at hand.'

A look of grim determination tightened Mrs Hogan's face and she took a breath.

Connie placed her outstretched hand against her patient's perineum, ready to ease the head out. Mrs Hogan bellowed as the pain swept through her, and the bones of her husband's hand cracked as she gripped on to him.

'Push!' shouted Connie as the small head bulged through the overextended aperture.

Mrs Hogan bore down until she was red in the face, and as the contraction ebbed, the head popped out. Holding it firmly with both hands, Connie got ready to draw the baby out, but there was a gush of fluid and the child, a little girl, slipped out without any further effort on her part.

Unfortunately, the birth residue also contained the sticky black first motion that indicated, as she'd suspected, that the baby had been in distress for some while. Also, as she balanced her in one hand, Connie thought that if the Hogans' daughter weighed anything close to three pounds it would be astonishing.

She placed the tiny infant on a fresh towel. 'You've got a little girl,' she said, rubbing her briskly and mentally imploring St Mary to give her breath.

Mrs Hogan tried to sit forward. 'Is she alive?'

'Yes,' Connie replied, praying again that it was so. 'But exhausted.'

Hooking her little finger in the baby's mouth, she cleared a quantity of mucosa. Then she turned the tiny body over and rubbed her back briskly, but to no avail. The child remained limp, her lips turning bluer as the seconds ticked by.

Connie laid the floppy infant on her back and gently pressed on her chest. Come on, sweetheart! she urged, as she massaged the baby's heart. The little girl remained unresponsive for what seemed like an eternity, then suddenly she twitched and gave a mewing cry.

Tears sprang into Connie's eyes as the child shuddered and drew a breath. Praise be to Mary!

'Did you hear that, Mags?' laughed Mr Hogan, his gaze fixed on his newborn daughter.

'Yes,' sobbed his wife. 'Yes, she's alive. Thank you, Sister. Thank you so much,' she said, gratitude spilling out of her eyes.

Quickly tying the cord in two places, Connie snipped cleanly between the knots, then covered the baby with Gamgee and popped the cap on her head before wrapping her in a towel and placing her on her mother's chest.

'Hold her against your skin to keep her warm,' she said.

Mrs Hogan did as she was told and kissed her daughter's damp forehead. 'Isn't she perfect?' she said to her husband.

'Yes, just perfect,' he replied, staring down at the minute human being in her mother's arms.

Mrs Hogan pressed her lips against the infant's forehead again, then a huge tear rolled down her left cheek. 'I can hardly believe it. After all our disappointments, we finally have our own little miracle.'

Studying the blissful new parents, Connie's mouth pulled into a dour line. Yes, Baby Hogan was alive, but at twenty-eight weeks and weighing no more than a bag of sugar, it would need another miracle to keep her so.

'There we are, Mrs Hogan,' Connie said, tucking the newborn baby into the crook of her mother's arm. 'All clean and tidy.'

'Thank you, Sister.' Mrs Hogan yawned.

Connie didn't blame her. It was twenty to six and the sun was only just over the horizon. She'd been so worried about Baby Hogan making it through the night that after she'd washed Mrs Hogan, and changed her nightdress and the sheets, she'd got Mr Hogan to phone through to Munroe House to let them know she'd be staying all night.

After showing Mrs Hogan how to use the breast pump to help bring her milk in, and satisfied that Baby Hogan, who had been named Joy, was stable, Connie had bedded herself down on the sofa with an alarm clock so that she could check on the baby every two hours. When she'd heard the milk float rattle past an hour ago, she'd got up. She'd decided that while Mrs Hogan slept, she would clean Joy of her birth residue. It wouldn't be as easy as it sounded. The usual practice would have been to bath the baby an hour or so after it was born, but unlike a full-term baby, Joy needed to be kept warm at all times, so Connie had washed each limb separately, then rubbed it in olive oil before tucking it back under the baby's improvised Gamgee coat. Now Joy was not only clean but wide awake, and so was her mother, which was what Connie needed for her next task.

Although Mrs Hogan had tried to feed her daughter during the night, like most newborns, Joy had been too tired to latch on properly, but today Connie was determined to get a feeding regime in place.

'Now try and put her to the breast,' she said.

Cradling her daughter to her, and with Connie's assistance, Mrs Hogan managed to get her in position. Joy rooted around for a bit, then latched on to the nipple, but after a couple of feeble sucks she dropped off again.

Mrs Hogan smiled. 'That's good, isn't it, Sister, that she knows what to do?'

Connie gave her a professional smile. 'Try her on the other side.'

Mrs Hogan shifted her daughter over. Again Joy rooted around and latched on, but after a few moments, as before, she nodded off to sleep.

Mrs Hogan looked anxiously at Connie. 'She's not taking enough, is she?'

Connie shook her head. 'She's not strong enough yet. You'll have to feed her another way while you're building up your milk supply. Now, where's the box of equipment I left with you last week?'

'In the pantry downstairs,' Mrs Hogan replied, mustering a brave smile.

'I won't be a moment. If she wakes up while I'm gone, put her back on the breast.' Connie found Mr Hogan and the three children, dressed in their school uniforms, sitting around the kitchen table eating porridge, which one of the neighbours had kindly dropped in. The new father listened with tired, anxious eyes as Connie explained to the excited youngsters that the new addition to the family was too small to cuddle and that no one other than her dad and the nurses could see her yet, to stop her getting dangerous germs.

Taking a half-pint of whey, which she'd asked the milkman to add to the Hogans' daily delivery, Connie measured out eight ounces, boiled it, then divided it between two of the sterile feeding bottles. She then placed the full bottles plus an empty one, a small tin of sweetened condensed milk and her other equipment on a tray and hurried back upstairs.

'How's she doing?' she asked, putting the tray on the bedside table and re-donning her face mask.

'She had another little go but fell asleep again,' Mrs Hogan replied.

Connie placed her hand in the improvised cot surrounded by the heated bricks. 'This is still warm; pop her in there and I'll show you what to do.'

Reluctantly, Mrs Hogan placed her baby in the improvised incubator.

'She's so tiny,' she murmured, gazing lovingly down at her daughter as she tucked her in.

'And that's why she has to be kept warm.' Connie fished out the breast pump from the saucepan and handed it to the new mum. 'Now, Mrs Hogan, I want you to express on both sides, as I showed you, and see what we can get.'

Mrs Hogan, turning away, did as instructed while Connie set out a measuring jug, a four-ounce feeding bottle, a glass pipette – the sort she usually used for giving eye drops – and a teacup of boiled water. After a few minutes, Mrs Hogan turned back.

'I'm afraid it's not very much,' she said, handing Connie the pump.

'It won't be at this stage, but it's very important for her to have the foremilk to help fight off infections, and for you to work up your supply,' replied Connie, carefully decanting the fluid into the sterilised feeding bottle.

Setting it down within easy reach, she went back to the cradle and picked Joy up. She settled herself on an upright chair and laid the featherweight infant on her lap.

'Joy weighs two pounds ten, so the aim for the next couple of days is to stop her losing any of her birth weight and get her to put on a couple of ounces by the end of the week,' Connie explained. 'Breastfeeding is the best way for all babies, especially babies like Joy, but since she can't do it herself just yet, we have to find a way of feeding her until she gets stronger.' She picked up the pipette and drew up some of Mrs Hogan's milk. 'Hold her like this.' She put her hand under Joy's head to bring it up a few inches. 'Then drop the milk in like this.'

Holding the baby's head firmly and watching her closely, Connie dribbled the milk into her mouth. Joy screwed up her face for a couple of seconds, but then swallowed. Connie's shoulders lost some of their tension. 'Carry on doing this until it's all gone.' She vacated the chair and handed the child to her mother. 'There you are, Mum, your turn.'

Mrs Hogan took her daughter, sat down and refilled the pipette. She trickled the milk into the baby's mouth. Again Joy swallowed it.

Connie smiled down at her. 'That's my girl.' Her attention returned to the baby's mother. 'Now I'll show you how to make up the rest of the feed.'

She picked up the feeding bottles containing the cooled whey.

'I'm going to make Joy's feed up today as one part condensed milk to sixteen, and I'll increase that each day until it's one to four before adding in cream. As Joy is just short of three pounds, she'll need eight ounces of milk each day to start with, which is an ounce every three hours, though I'd be happier if you fed her every two hours during the day. And remember,' Connie looked the new mother squarely in the eye, 'you put her to the breast first, then give her what you've expressed, before feeding her any of the made-up feed, and keep her warm at all times or . . .' She bit back the words.

Mrs Hogan's pale lips lifted into a sad smile. 'It's all right, Sister. I know the odds are already stacked against my Joy.' She pressed her lips to the baby's downy head. 'But don't worry. No matter what I have to do, I'm not going to let my daughter die.'

Chapter Twenty-One

Connie sat on the somewhat elaborate sofa, her handbag perched on her knees, as a midsummer thunderstorm gathered on the other side of the diamond-shaped panes of the tall windows in Toynbee Hall. She was waiting to be interviewed by the chairman, the secretary and the superintendent of the Spitalfields and Shoreditch.

Toynbee Hall, the late-Victorian mock-gothic building on the east side of Commercial Road, had been a centre for all sorts of philanthropic work for more than sixty years. Like the People's Palace three miles away, it was a place many ordinary people in the area flocked to for the help and guidance provided by fervent champions of the poor. Many well-educated members of the upper classes offered talks and lectures to the working man and woman, and many local residents had reason to be thankful for the educational classes and advice.

Connie glanced at the Edwardian clock on the wall at the end of the corridor as the hands ticked round to 2.25. Still not a hundred per cent sure she should be there, she straightened the bow at her throat. She was wearing her tailored suit with a pencil skirt and a white blouse beneath the jacket. Millie said it was just the ticket, but Connie was more worried about what she was going to say than how she looked.

The heavy door at the other end of the corridor opened and a middle-aged woman dressed in a Prince of Wales check suit accessorised with a perky hat and veil stepped out. She looked at Connie and trotted along the black-and-white-tiled floor towards her.

'Miss Byrne?' she said, her uncoloured lips lifting into a polite smile.

Connie stood up. 'Yes.'

The women offered her hand. 'Lovely to meet you. I'm Mrs

Broderick, the Association's secretary. If you would follow me.'

She led the way into the room she'd just come out of, and Connie found herself standing in the middle of what looked like a Jacobean baronial hall complete with a massive carved oak fireplace and matching panelled walls. The windows, like the ones in the corridor outside, reached almost to the ceiling and were framed by ruby-coloured velvet curtains with a matching brocaded pelmet above.

'Please take a seat,' said Mrs Broderick, indicating the lone chair set out in the middle of the room opposite a long table.

Putting her handbag on the floor next to the chair, Connie tucked her skirt under her and sat down.

As the secretary walked round to the other side of the table, Connie cast her gaze over her other two inquisitors.

In the centre of the group, and clearly in charge of proceedings, was a slightly built woman in her mid-thirties with honey-brown hair and clear eyes. She was stylishly dressed in a fawn woollen suit with brown velvet cuffs and collar and she wore pearls at her throat and clipped to her ears. Unlike Mrs Broderick, she had powdered cheeks, arched pencilled eyebrows and lightly coloured lips, which were turned up at the corners in a welcoming smile.

The third member of the panel was a woman with short curly brown hair, a scrubbed face and a pristine navy uniform topped by a starched white lacy cap. With her sturdy shoulders and strong hands, she looked as if she would be able to handle herself in a pub fight.

The woman in the centre spoke.

'Good afternoon, Miss Byrne. I'm Mrs Howard, the chairwoman of the Spitalfields and Shoreditch District Nursing Association. I hope you didn't have any problem finding us.'

'So do I,' chipped in the curly-haired woman. 'Isn't she after a job as a district nurse?'

'Quite so, Superintendent,' said Mrs Howard, her composure faltering a little.

The woman huffed and folded her arms across her substantial bosom.

Mrs Howard's attention returned to Connie. 'Mrs Broderick you've already met, and this,' she said, indicating the woman to her left, 'as you may have already guessed, is our esteemed super-intendent Miss O'Dwyer.'

Connie acknowledged her with a smile, which Miss O'Dwyer answered with a sharp nod of her head.

Mrs Howard scanned down Connie's letter. 'Now, Miss Byrne, we have all had a chance to read through your very detailed ap-plication and I must say we are very impressed by your wide experience as a district nurse and midwife. Aren't we, ladies?'

Mrs Broderick nodded enthusiastically while Miss O'Dwyer chewed her lip.

'I see you are a local girl,' said Mrs Broderick, putting on her metal-rimmed glasses.

'Yes, I was born in East London Lying-in Hospital and my family live in Gordon Street, just behind St Dunstan's Church.'

'And you went to Raine's Foundation School and then to the London in thirty-seven for your nurse training, which you com-pleted with honours, I see,' continued Mrs Howard.

'Yes,' replied Connie. 'I worked on Gloucester Ward, which was female surgical, and then Mary Ward, which was neuro-logical and orthopaedic, before going to Queen Charlotte's for my midwifery in nineteen forty-two.'

'And you applied to become a Queen's Nurse as soon as you came back a year later,' concluded Mrs Howard.

'Yes,' said Connie. 'Even when I was a student nurse, I knew I wanted to work on the district.'

'How lovely,' said Mrs Howard, in a sing-song voice. 'Now, Miss Byrne, you do understand that the post you have applied for is that of senior sister?'

'Yes.'

'But I see that at the moment you are a sister.'

'Yes, I am.'

Mrs Howard put her elbows on the table and steepled her fin-gers together. 'So tell me why we should consider you for this post.'

Connie took a deep breath. 'Firstly, because I am hard-working, conscientious and punctual. I have had only five days off sick in the last two years and am in general good health with no back problems,' she said, repeating the opening lines of the speech she had practised with Millie. 'I also have three and a half years' experience as a district nurse sister. I run my own patch and often deputise for the superintendent and senior nurse.'

'Can you give us a couple of examples of the sort of things you've done when acting in their stead?' asked Mrs Broderick.

As it was really Millie rather than Miss Dutton who ran Munroe House day to day, Connie ran through the various tasks she'd helped her friend with, such as monthly patient returns, deputising at meetings with the council's assistance officer, and the mountain of Queen's Institute paperwork that needed to be filled in in triplicate each month.

'I am also responsible for the clinic loans. I supervise the junior nurses' work return books and check that the fees they collect are correct each week,' she concluded after explaining the importance of good record-keeping as set out in the Merry and Irven district nurse textbook.

Mrs Howard and Mrs Broderick nodded their approval.

'And I see that you oversaw the recent batch of student QNs too,' said Mrs Howard, scrutinising Connie's letter again.

'Yes, and they all passed with flying colours,' Connie replied, feeling a little glow of pride.

'Golly, well done,' said the chairwoman, as if Connie had scored the winning goal in a school hockey match. 'Especially as you say you hadn't supervised trainees before?'

Connie smiled confidently. 'No. Sister Sullivan asked me to take over from her as she was getting married.'

Mrs Broderick looked alarmed. 'You've no similar plans yourself, Miss Byrne?'

'None at all.'

Miss O'Dwyer scoffed. 'Would you have us believe, Miss Byrne, that a pretty thing like yourself hasn't got a fella or two in tow?'

'Not at the present time,' Connie replied pleasantly.

'And that if Clark Gable turned up tomorrow you'd turn him down flat?' the superintendent said.

'Well, probably not,' laughed Connie. 'But according to *Picturegoer* he's quite tied up with Joan Crawford at the moment, so I doubt I'll meet him around here any time soon.'

Mrs Howard and Mrs Broderick smiled, but Miss O'Dwyer's stony expression didn't waver.

'And you say you've always wanted to work on the district?' the superintendent said.

'Yes, I have,' Connie replied, reassembling her calm professional expression. 'I find nursing people in their own homes very rewarding. I also enjoy working for general practitioners who know and understand their patients. Another reason why I would like to work as the senior nurse at Spitalfields and Shoreditch is that they, like my present association, also provide midwifery services, and I enjoy helping mothers to deliver healthy babies. I also like getting to know and chat to my patients without having to rush around answering bells and placating irate consultants.'

A perplexed look screwed up Miss O'Dwyer's round face. 'So if I hear you right, Miss Byrne, are you saying that compared to working in a hospital, the district is no more than a trip to the country fair?'

Mrs Howard frowned. 'I'm sure Miss Byrne doesn't—'

'Not when you have to wash and dress half a dozen patients and visit a batch of newborns before dinner,' said Connie, holding the older woman's steely gaze.

Although the superintendent's expression didn't alter, something sparked in her flint-like eyes before she lowered them to the papers on the desk in front of her.

'Now, references.' Mrs Howard shuffled her paperwork and frowned. 'I don't seem to have . . .'

'I'm afraid there was another walk-out at the post office, so they don't seem to have arrived,' Mrs Broderick replied.

'Well, now here's the thing.' Miss O'Dwyer chuckled, holding up a sheet of St George's and St Dunstan's headed paper. 'Didn't I pick up Miss Byrne's reference from the doormat meself this very morning?'

'What luck,' Mrs Howard said as she and Mrs Broderick exchanged a delighted look.

'Isn't it?' agreed Miss O'Dwyer. 'And, Miss Byrne, I'd like to ask you a couple of things about it.'

A prickle started between Connie's shoulder blades, but she smiled. 'Of course.'

Miss O'Dwyer took a pair of metal-rimmed glasses from the top pocket of her uniform and slipped them on.

'Miss Dutton confirms you have had only five sick days in the last two years and that you are punctual. But then she says that you have a habit of changing her meticulous clinic rotas to suit yourself.' Miss O'Dwyer looked at her expectantly.

'It is true I have changed rotas on a couple of occasions, but never to suit myself,' Connie replied in a level tone. 'The main reason I shift nurses around is to comply with the Association rules: for example, that the midwife in charge of the antenatal clinic must be a Queen's Nurse, not just a trainee.'

'I see.' The superintendent cast her eyes over Miss Dutton's letter again. 'And did you also go over her head and write to the Queen's Nursing Institute complaining about the regional education officer?'

Connie felt suddenly very hot. 'I did, because I didn't feel the education officer gave the student in question a fair chance.'

'Didn't you now?' chuckled Miss O'Dwyer.

'No, I didn't,' Connie snapped. 'Nurse Baxter is a good nurse and I wouldn't let her be bullied out of the district because some old . . .' She drew a long breath. 'Because the educational officer made her nervous.'

Miss O'Dwyer gave her a piercing stare, and Connie smiled diplomatically.

'And lastly, Miss Dutton, who must be a saint of a woman by the sound of it, says that she suspects you of visiting a patient every day whom she has specifically told you not to.' The superintendent leant forward and her eyes narrowed. 'Is that the truth of it?'

Connie's heart thumped uncomfortably in her chest. 'No,' she said, resisting the urge to cross herself at such a monstrous lie.

'Well, I'm very pleased to hear it,' said Mrs Howard, shuffling her papers. 'After all, someone has to pay for the upkeep of the clinic and the nurses' wages.'

'But if I ever did go behind my superior's back to visit a patient, it would be because they needed nursing care,' continued Connie, looking steadily at Miss O'Dwyer.

'And what sort of case might that be, Miss Byrne?' asked the superintendent.

'Perhaps a pregnant women with an unstable uterus who had already lost several babies late in pregnancy.' Connie gave the superintendent a cool smile. 'If you don't mind me saying, Miss

O'Dwyer, in my opinion sometimes compassion has to come before money.'

Again a flicker of something lit Miss O'Dwyer's gaze for a split second. 'Thank you, Sister Byrne, that's all I wanted to know.'

'Good,' said Mrs Howard, with a slightly perplexed expression. 'Have you any more questions?' she asked, looking at the Association's secretary.

'No, Madam Chairman,' replied Mrs Broderick.

'Miss O'Dwyer?'

'I'm grand, Mrs Howard.' The superintendent smiled sweetly. 'I think I have the measure of Sister Byrne.'

'Well then,' said Mrs Howard. 'I only have to thank you, Miss Byrne, for giving us all a very clear idea as to why you are applying to join us.' She tapped her paperwork in order. 'You'll appreciate, I'm sure, that we have a number of other nurses to interview for the post so it might take us a few weeks, but you will be hearing from us in due course.'

'Of course.' Connie retrieved her handbag from the floor and stood up. 'And thank you for your time.'

She exchanged a polite smile with the three women behind the table, then turned and made her way to the door. As she left, she consoled herself with the thought that at least she wouldn't have to tell her mother she was moving away.

Charlie regarded his reflection in the mirror for a moment, then turned sideways again.

'It's from our newest range,' said the elderly tailor, in a battered kippah and with a tape measure hanging around his neck. 'We've only made half a dozen so far and this is one of the first. Makes sir look a cut above.'

Charlie was standing in Maxie Cohen Bespoke Tailors next to the trolleybus station in Aldgate. The popular tailor's shop had a glass display cabinet running along one side of the room, on top of which were fat books of sample swatches. Handkerchiefs and neckties lay in regimented lines in the drawers beneath. The place smelt of pressed wool, tailor's chalk and beeswax. Conversations were muffled and muted by the bales of suit material stacked by shade, pattern and fabric on the shelves behind the counter.

'You're right,' Charlie replied, casting his eyes over the narrow lapels of the grey mohair suit. 'I'll take it.'

'Of course, sir. I'll write out your bill while you change,' replied the tailor, indicating the three fitting rooms to their right.

'No, I'll wear it. You can chuck that,' he said, indicating his old demob suit.

After taking a packet of Bensons, his lighter and his money from his discarded jacket and putting them in the pockets of his new suit, Charlie picked up his hat and glanced at himself in the mirror again before following the tailor to the back of the shop.

'There you go, sir,' said the elderly shopkeeper, placing the receipt book before him. 'If I could just have your clothing coupons?'

Taking the packet of cigarettes from his pocket, Charlie lit one. 'I'm a friend of Mr Timms.'

Fear flickered in the old man's eyes. 'Oh, I see.' He took the pen from behind his ear again and wrote 'second-hand' across the top of the bill.

Charlie grinned. 'That's more like it. Now we don't need to worry about no coupons, do we?'

The tailor forced a smile. 'No, sir.'

Delving into the inside of his jacket, Charlie pulled out a roll of banknotes. 'All right, what's the damage?'

'Two guineas,' the tailor replied.

Holding his cigarette between his lips, Charlie peeled off the notes and slapped them on the counter. The shopkeeper rang up the purchase and handed him his change, and Charlie strolled out of the shop.

The clock on St Botolph's church tower opposite was showing a few moments after 3.30 as he stepped on to the pavement. The sky above was black and thunderous and the heat that had been building all day was stifling. He had a couple of hours to kill until seven, when he was meeting Tommy and the lads in the Grave Maurice, so he decided to have a swift half in the Ten Bells before heading back to the bookie's.

The late-afternoon traffic heading east was already building up as the traders from nearby Spitalfields and Billingsgate headed home. Darting between the lorries, Charlie crossed the road. He was just about to turn left to cut through Middlesex Street when he stopped dead in his tracks.

There, not twenty yards away, at the bus stop outside Wool-worth's, was Connie. She looked cracking, too, in that snug-fitting jacket and skirt.

Throwing his cigarette butt in the gutter, Charlie strolled over. 'Hello, Connie,' he said, stopping just behind her.

She turned and blinked up at him. 'Hello, what are you doing here?'

'Getting myself some new gear.' He smoothed his hand over his lapels. 'Like it?'

She smiled politely. 'You must be doing well at the warehouse.'

Actually, since hooking up with Tommy and his crew, Charlie regarded the two pounds fifteen and six he got every Thursday from the warehouse as beer and fags money; his weekly cut was at least four times that much. Of course he was careful to keep that from Maria and her bloodsucking family.

'I am,' he said. 'But what are you doing all dressed up on a Wednesday afternoon?'

'Oh, nothing much, just a job interview at the Spitalfields and Shoreditch Association. I thought I had a decent chance, but . . .' She shrugged.

The wires above their heads hummed as a number 25 drew up. The people around them surged forward, giving Charlie the excuse to move closer.

'Warm, isn't it?' he said as the trolleybus trundled off.

Connie looked up at the clouds overhead. 'It's going to break any moment.'

'I suppose you're waiting for a fifteen,' said Charlie, catching a faint hint of Connie's favourite lavender perfume.

She nodded and looked past him for the next bus.

Charlie's eyes ran over the contours of her face, remembering what it was like to kiss her soft lips. He took her arm. 'Connie, I—'

She pulled away. 'How's Maria and the baby?'

'I love you,' he said softly.

She looked up, and something flashed between them. For one brief heart-stopping second they were the old Connie and Charlie again. Then she turned away.

'You can't,' she whispered.

'Please, Connie. And I know you still love me.' He reached for her but she stepped off the pavement.

'I'm going to walk.' She turned and hurried off.

There was a whip-crack overhead and lightning streaked across the sky, followed by a deafening crash of thunder.

Charlie strode after her. 'Wait!'

She ignored him.

Lightning forked through the clouds again, there was another crash of thunder and then the heavens opened. People screamed and ran for cover under shop awnings and in doorways. Pushing his way through the scattering crowds, Charlie dashed after her.

'Connie!' he shouted as fat raindrops splashed on his face.

She turned briefly, then hurried on, rain soaking her as she fled. Cursing the water and mud splashing his new trousers, Charlie tore after her. She darted across the pedestrian crossing and he lengthened his stride until he was within an arm's reach of her.

'Connie.'

He stretched forward, but before he could catch her, a trolley-bus flashed past. A car pulled out in its path, and as it slowed, Connie sprinted forward and jumped on. Grabbing the upright handrail at the edge of the platform, she swung inside as the bus picked up speed again.

Blindly, Charlie chased after it for a few yards, but as it raced on towards Mile End, he stopped running. Standing with his hands loosely at his sides and rainwater soaking through his new suit, he watched the bus bounce away.

He loved her! And it was as plain as the nose on his face that she loved him too. He had to make her see reason. He had to. His bloody sanity depended on it.

'Well I think it's despicable, even for Old Dutton,' shouted Sally over the sound of the band.

'The woman's got a heart of blooming stone,' Annie replied, her pretty face red with indignation.

It was now almost the beginning of September, and three weeks since Connie's unsettling encounter with Charlie on the day of her interview. It had taken a week of sleepless nights and numerous arguments with Charlie in her head, but finally she had mastery of her emotions again. At least for now.

She, Beattie and Annie were standing with drinks in their hands by a pillar in Poplar Town Hall, the venue for St Andrew's Hospital's annual fund-raising dance. Built less than ten years ago, the town hall embraced the art deco style both inside and out. The soft curls and heavy carving of the Victorian period of prosperity, evident in most public buildings in the area, were starkly absent; instead, chiselled square panels ruled supreme. The ceiling, with its clean-cut plasterwork, soared above them, reflecting the hopes of the jazz age.

However, tonight it was the sound of a big band that filled the room. The Swing Boys, playing on the stage at the far end, were doing a fair job of the popular dance numbers, and Connie was determined to enjoy herself.

After going through almost everything in her wardrobe, she'd settled on her lime-green and brown striped dress with the flared skirt. She'd tamed her wild curls, tanned her legs with permanganate and applied mascara and lipstick, and she was pleased to say that so far this was the only dance she'd sat out.

'And I bet Gladys was only too delighted to spill the beans about Millie's mum,' added Sally.

As Connie had feared, her friend's close shave with the lorry and her spell in hospital had brought to light how Millie had been struggling to look after her ailing mother alongside covering her patients.

'I thought Miss Dutton would give her a ticking-off, but I didn't expect her to take her to the Association committee for a formal disciplinary hearing,' added Eva. 'I mean, she only did what any of us would have done.'

The girls nodded in agreement as the final chords of 'Don't Sit Under the Apple Tree' blasted out.

'And Miss Dutton couldn't have done a thing if it hadn't been for the fact that Millie broke the Association rules by staying at her mother's some nights,' Connie said, clapping along with everyone else, 'which gave the old bat just the excuse she needed to try and get rid of her.'

'It's just not fair,' said Annie. 'What will we do if you and Millie both go?'

'What makes you think I'm going anywhere?' Connie replied.

'Well you're bound to get the job at the Spit and Ditch,' Annie replied.

Connie huffed. 'I wouldn't bank on it.' Not that she cared. With Millie still on sick leave, Connie had enough to worry about without gnawing over why she hadn't matched up to Miss O'Dwyer's expectations.

'I wish there was something we could do to help,' said Annie.

'Why don't we all write a letter to the committee telling them what a great nurse Millie is?' said Sally.

'That's a good idea,' said Eva.

'It is,' agreed Connie, consigning the episode with old O'Dwyer to the back of her mind. 'But wouldn't it carry more weight if we asked her patients to write too?'

Her friends' faces lit up.

'We'll start asking them tomorrow,' said Annie, linking arms with Sally and Eva. 'Won't we?' The other girls nodded. 'By the time we've finished, Mrs Harper and her crew won't dare sack Millie.'

'Will you please take your partners for a foxtrot,' the band leader announced over the tinny microphone.

A couple of smartly dressed men ambled over and guided Sally and Annie on to the floor. Connie spotted another such heading her way, but before he got to her, someone tapped her on the shoulder.

'Good evening, Connie.'

She turned and found Malcolm Henstock standing behind her.

'Hello,' she said, smiling up into his freshly shaven face.

'I wonder if you would let me have this dance?' he said, gazing admiringly at her.

A little thrill of anticipation she hadn't felt for a very long time shot though Connie. She smiled and offered him her hand. 'How could I refuse?'

'I'm glad the chaps in the office persuaded me to come tonight now,' he said as they stepped off.

'Didn't you want to?' she asked, enjoying the feel of his arm lightly around her.

'I'm not much of a dancer really,' he replied.

'Oh, I don't know,' laughed Connie. 'You haven't trodden on my toe yet.'

'Don't speak too soon. We've not even been around the dance floor once.' He smiled, and the fizz of excitement started again. 'No, seriously,' he continued, stepping her back to avoid another couple. 'I'm not one for modern music or drinking in pubs. Truth be told, I'm a bit of an old fuddy-duddy.'

'Don't be silly,' protested Connie.

He smiled and guided her through a sidestep.

'How's your mum?' she asked.

'Much the same,' he replied with a weary sigh. 'She was a bit put out that I was going out tonight, as we usually listen to *Have a Go* together.'

'My sister likes that too. She's a Wilfred Pickles fan. "What's on the table, Mabel?"' she mimicked, in a broad Yorkshire accent.

'Are you courting?' Malcolm replied.

'Er . . . I . . . not—'

'Isn't that one of the catchphrases too?' asked Malcolm seriously.

'Oh, yes, it is, isn't it?' Connie replied, feeling oddly foolish.

'It must be nice to be part of such a large family,' Malcolm continued.

'Sometimes,' Connie replied.

Malcolm paused for a beat while another couple glided by. 'Are either of your sisters nurses?'

'No, just me.'

'I couldn't do your job,' he said as they stepped off again.

Connie gave him a teasing look. 'I don't know, you might look quite fetching in the uniform.'

He shook his head. 'Haven't got the legs.' His eyes darkened. 'Not like you.'

Happiness bubbled up in Connie and she laughed, but as Malcolm swirled her around, she caught sight of a familiar figure. Twisting her head, she looked over Malcolm's shoulder to see Charlie leaning against the bar with a miserable expression on his face. Their eyes locked, and Connie's heart lurched.

'So have you?' asked Malcolm.

Connie tore her eyes from Charlie. 'I'm sorry, I . . .'

The music stopped and Malcolm released her.

They applauded the orchestra, then the band leader stepped forward again. 'Now, gentlemen, take your partners for a medley of much-loved waltzes.'

Malcolm looked at her. 'Shall we?'

Connie forced a bright smile as he led her back out on to the dance floor. The band struck up and they stepped off again.

'What I said before was, have you seen Fred Astaire's new film?' Malcolm said as they twirled around among the other couples.

'No, I haven't.'

'Everyone says it's worth seeing.'

'Do they?' Connie replied, wondering if Maria was also here.

'Yes, and I was wondering . . .'

The notes of 'The Anniversary Waltz' faded, then the saxophonist stepped forward and blasted out the opening bars of 'Moonlight Serenade'. Connie's head swam as memories of another band, another dance and another pair of arms around her filled her mind. She tried to push away the images of that night in 1942, the night Charlie had shipped out for the last time, but they crowded in and overwhelmed her. Tears clouded her vision.

'I'm sorry,' she whispered as she broke out of Malcolm's embrace.

Knocking into other dancers, she stumbled across the dance floor towards the exit and all but fell out into the cool quietness of the main corridor. There were a few couples smooching in secluded corners, so with tears streaming down her face, Connie turned and shoved aside the half-glazed door and staggered outside. Her legs felt unsteady, so she leant against the wall. Covering her face with her hands, she sobbed uncontrollably as the aching emptiness of life without Charlie overwhelmed her.

The door swung open and closed again, and she looked up to find Charlie standing a few feet away with an expression of grim determination on his face.

They stared at each other for a couple of heartbeats, then Charlie crossed the space between them. His arms encircled her, and Connie melted into him.

'Oh Charlie,' she sighed.

'I've been such a fool,' he said as his broad hands pressed her to him. His gaze locked with hers for a second, then he lowered his lips on hers in a hard, demanding kiss.

Throwing her arms around his neck, she returned his kiss, enjoying the roughness of his evening bristles. After a few moments his mouth opened on hers, sending Connie's senses reeling. Desire and need mingled together making her feel drowsy and bursting with life at the same time.

After a moment of heart-stopping excitement, Charlie released her lips. 'Oh Connie,' he said, his troubled blue eyes looking deeply into hers. 'I can't go on like this.'

Connie's gaze ran slowly over the face she felt she'd loved for ever, and she smiled. 'No, neither can I.'

Taking her shoes off on the cold back step, Connie slowly lifted the latch and let herself in to Munroe House. It had long been the practice of the night on-call nurse to leave the back door unbolted for any late returns. There had naturally been some concern that this convention might be stopped when Miss Dutton reintroduced the policy of lights-out at ten o'clock. However, as Gladys and her chums benefited from this arrangement too, it was one of the areas of Munroe House that she had chosen not to draw the superintendent's attention to.

Holding her shoes in one hand and without switching on the light, Connie tiptoed along the old servants' passageway into the main part of the house. Unsurprisingly, as it must have been somewhere close to 12.30 by now, the place was in silence. She hoped no one would wake up: she'd have a bit of trouble explaining why, after saying she was going home with a blinding headache four hours ago, she was now creeping in the back door.

Passing the sideboard with the phone and message pad on it, she grabbed the rounded end of the stair rail and hurried up to her room. She closed the door quietly behind her, flicked on the light switch and, skirting around her bed, went to the window. Drawing back the curtain, she looked out across the perimeter wall of Munroe House to the other side of the road, where Charlie was standing under the lamp post. Her heart burst with love and joy.

Illuminated under the yellow glow over his head, Charlie blew a slow kiss. With their gazes locked together, Connie pressed her fingers lightly to her lips and returned it. Charlie smiled and strolled back up the street.

Connie watched him disappear into the darkness, then turned and lay down on her bed. Breathing in the smell of Charlie's cologne that still clung to her, she closed her eyes and, ignoring the complications and obstacles looming around her, concentrated on the exquisite joy of the past four hours.

After a blissful five minutes or so, she peeled herself off the bed and took her dressing gown from its hook and her wash bag from the dressing table. She doused the light before quietly opening her bedroom door again and heading for the bathroom. There was a crack of light showing, so she waited outside for a few moments, then, deciding that someone had forgotten to switch it off, grasped the brass handle and pushed the door. It swung back about a foot, then jammed against something solid.

She pushed against the obstruction and there was a low moan. Squeezing herself through the gap, she found Gladys curled up on the floor fully clothed. Her face was the colour of window putty and sweat had plastered her wiry red hair to her forehead and cheeks.

'What's the matter?' Connie whispered, crouching down beside her.

'It hurts,' Gladys whimpered, clutching her stomach.

'What does?'

Gladys moaned by way of reply.

Connie looked up and caught sight of the blood splashed around the toilet seat. Her mouth pulled into a grim line. 'What have you done, Gladys?'

Gladys opened her eyes and, leaning heavily on the side of the bath, got to her knees. 'It's my monthlies, that's all.'

'Yes, and I'm the Queen of Sheba.'

Connie placed her hand on Gladys's forehead and found it hot and clammy. She placed two fingers on the inside of the other girl's wrist and took her pulse. It was thready and rapid, probably a hundred-plus at a guess.

'I'm calling an ambulance.'

Gladys grabbed her arm. 'No. Please, I don't want everyone to know.'

'But you're burning up,' Connie replied. 'I have to get you to the London or—'

'I've got a fiver in my purse, we can take a taxi,' pleaded Gladys.

'Don't be so bloody stupid,' snapped Connie. 'You're in no condition to be waiting on street corners. And what if we can't get one? The state you're in, you could go into shock at any moment.'

'Help me downstairs, then, so they don't have to knock and wake everyone up.' She squeezed Connie's arm painfully. 'Please, Connie. If the superintendent finds out I've . . .' Tears gathered in her eyes and her chin started to wobble.

'It's a bit late for that now, isn't it?' Connie replied flatly.

Gladys started crying and drew her knees up again, causing blood to seep through the skirt of her dress. Bending over, Connie grabbed her legs and rested them on the rim of the bath. 'You're bleeding, Gladys. Lie still while I get help.'

Leaving the door open, she ran down to the hall and telephoned the council ambulance department. After giving hurried instructions to the operator on how to find Munroe House, she dashed back upstairs. Gladys opened her eyes as she came back in.

'The ambulance will be here soon,' Connie said, kneeling next to her and taking her pulse again.

A half-smile lifted the corner of Gladys's pale lips. 'Is it all right?'

'Still too fast, but no worse,' Connie replied, placing Gladys's hand gently back on her chest.

Taking her flannel from her wash bag, Connie held it under the cold tap for a minute, then wrung it out and placed it on Gladys's fevered brow. As she replenished the flannel, the night doorbell rang.

'I won't be a moment,' Connie said, getting to her feet.

'Thank you,' whispered Gladys without opening her eyes.

Connie hurried down the stairs for the second time and let the two burly ambulance men in, leading them up to the first-floor bathroom. While they manoeuvred their patient on to the canvas stretcher, she popped into Gladys's room and quickly gathered her wash bag, towel, a fresh nightdress and dressing gown. As she stepped back into the hall, one of the adjoining bedroom doors opened and Joyce's curlered head appeared.

'What's going on?' she asked, tying the sash of her dressing gown.

'Gladys isn't very well,' Connie replied as the ambulance driver and his mate took the strain and lifted the stretcher. 'I think it might be her appendix.'

Joyce yawned. 'Do you want me to give Trudy a knock so she can go with her?'

Connie shook her head. 'She's chalked up for the morning clinic. It's all right, I'll go.'

Connie pushed open one of the double doors leading into Croft Ward in the London Hospital and walked in. The distinctive smell of detergent and surgical spirit wafted up. Although it was just a few moments past nine in the morning, most of the thirty women on the ward were already washed and sitting in freshly made beds awaiting the daily consultant's round.

The nurses busying themselves with patient observations looked across as Connie entered but after noting her navy district nurse uniform turned back to their task.

Walking past the sluice where the ward orderly was scrubbing the bedpans, Connie made her way over to the ward sister at the desk, who was checking a pile of student nurses' blue training books. The sister, an angular woman with sharp features and mousy hair scraped back from her face, looked up as she approached.

'Good morning, Sister Croft,' Connie said, using the time-honoured greeting. 'I know you're busy, but I wonder if I might just pop in on my friend Gladys Potter for a minute.'

The senior nurse's mouth pulled into a tight bud. 'I don't know about her being your friend, Sister, but Miss Potter is a very wicked girl.'

'I'd say more stupid than wicked,' Connie replied.

The sister gave Connie a scalding look. 'And a disgrace to nursing.'

'How is she?'

'Well enough,' the sister replied grudgingly. 'Especially now she's had two pints of blood and a shot of morphine.'

'I'm sure she appreciated that.'

'I doubt it. Girls like her never do.'

'I see she's in bed twelve,' said Connie, looking up at the large chalkboard on the wall behind the desk.

'She is, but I can only allow you five minutes,' the sister replied.

'Mr Appleton is doing his ward round in half an hour.'

'Thank you,' Connie replied. 'I wonder, has the doctor written her sick letter so I can take it back to the superintendent?'

The sister sniffed. 'Yes, it's here.' She unpinned a headed letter from the report book and handed it to Connie. 'He's given her diagnosis as excessive menorrhagia.' A heartless smile lifted the corners of her thin lips. 'But I felt, under the circumstances, that it was my duty to inform the police.'

Connie regarded her coolly. 'I'm sure you did.'

The sister bristled. 'Surely you don't expect me to condone immorality.'

'No, but I thought nursing was supposed to be about compassion.' Without waiting for the ward sister to answer, Connie swept past her and down the lines of beds to the one at the far end.

Despite her transfusion, Gladys's complexion was only a shade or two darker than the pillowslip she was lying on, making her russet hair all the more vivid. She was wearing a faded hospital nightdress, and stripped of all her eyeshadow, mascara and panstick she looked younger than her twenty-six years. A rubber tube snaking out of an upended glass bottle suspended from a drip stand was attached to her arm by means of a cannula. As Connie approached, she opened her eyes.

Connie sat down, putting her nurse's bag on the floor beside her. 'So, how are you?'

'Tired,' Gladys replied. 'And the bloody sister here is a class-one bitch.'

'Yes, isn't she?'

'Did she tell you she told the Old Bill?' asked Gladys indignantly.

Connie regarded her coolly. 'I'd have thought after seeing dozens of women with their insides ruined by botched abortions, you would have known better.'

'What sort of idiot do you take me for?' Gladys replied with a trace of her old bravado. 'I didn't go to some old woman with a crochet hook. I went to a proper clinic up West. The sort of place where snooty women sort out their little complications by booking themselves in for a D and C. Cost my friend a pretty penny, I can tell you.'

'Well your friend could have saved himself some money and found some old woman with a crochet hook, because smart place or not, getting out of your little complication nearly killed you.'

Gladys's expression soured. 'I suppose you and the rest of your mates have had a good old laugh at my expense.'

Connie gave her a chilly look. 'Don't judge me by your standards, Gladys Potter. You and your friends might enjoy gossiping about someone else's misfortune, but the rest of us have a bit more sympathy. Even for you. And just for your information, I haven't told anyone.'

'You expect me to believe that, do you?' sneered Gladys.

'I don't care if you believe it or not,' Connie replied. 'And to be honest, after the way you dropped Millie in it about her mum, I very nearly went straight to Miss Dutton.'

'So why didn't you?'

'Because, as you're always telling me, it's none of my business.' Connie smiled pleasantly. 'In the same way that what me and my friends do is none of yours. Do you understand?'

Gladys maintained her belligerent expression for a couple of seconds, then her pale face crumpled.

'Oh Connie,' she squeaked as her eyes welled up. 'The doctor said there was an infection in both tubes and because of that I might not be able to have children.' She covered her face with her hands.

Connie watched her shoulders shuddering for a second, then, chancing the ward sister's wrath, sat on the bed and put her arms around her.

'He said he loved me,' bleated Gladys, clinging on to her and sobbing. 'And he was going to leave his wife.'

Connie smoothed her fellow nurse's wiry red hair. 'I'm told that's what they all say.'

After bidding farewell to Gladys, Connie had unlocked her bicycle from the hospital bike shed and finished her last couple of visits. She'd collected her spare work shoes with their new soles and heels from Norman's repair shop and arrived at the back gate just fifteen minutes before Munroe House's lunch gong summoned the thirty or so hungry nurses to Mrs Pierce's Monday offering of faggots, peas and onion mash. But as she walked into the main hallway, she was surprised to see the usually unflappable Hannah scowling as she held the phone to her ear.

'As I said, I'll tell her you phoned as soon— No, I really don't know when she'll be— She's on her rounds but I'll inform her as soon as . . .' Hannah spotted Connie and visible relief swept over her. 'You're in luck. She's just walked in— Yes, I'll give her to you right away.' She cupped her hand over the mouthpiece. 'It's for you. And thank goodness, because I don't think my eardrums will take much more.'

'Who is it?'

Hannah shrugged. 'Some barmy Irishwoman. I didn't catch her name.' She offered her the phone. Connie took it and put it to her ear.

'Good afternoon, Sister Byrne speaking, how can I help you?'

'Is that yourself, Miss Byrne?' said the woman at the other end.

'Yes, it is.'

'Well that's a mercy, at least,' came the reply. 'It's Miss O'Dwyer.'

'Miss O'Dwyer!'

'Yes. The superintendent from the Spitalfields and Shoreditch Nursing Association,' Miss Dwyer continued. 'Don't break my heart and tell me you've forgotten us already.'

'No, I haven't,' Connie replied. 'I'm just a bit surprised to hear you on the other end of the telephone.'

'Well, I know these things are supposed to come through official channels and all that, but Mrs Broderick tumbled off a horse last week so the office is as muddled as a tinker's caravan. Although what a woman of her age is doing on a horse is the question I'd be asking,' the superintendent continued without pause. 'So, Miss Byrne, it falls upon me to offer you the position of senior nurse at the Spitalfields and Shoreditch Nursing Association and I'd like to know if you've a mind to take it.'

'I've got the job?'

'Isn't that what I've just been saying?' Miss O'Dwyer replied.

'Yes,' Connie replied, unsure that she was hearing right. 'Yes, I'll take the—'

'When can you start?'

'Er . . .' Connie tried to concentrate. 'I have to give a month's notice.'

'Shall we say Monday the thirtieth of September?' asked Miss O'Dwyer. 'I'm sure your superintendent will lament the going of you, but best we get the donkey on the road.'

'Well, yes, that should be—'

'Even if she has to type it with her toes, I'll have Mrs Broderick get a letter to you in the next few days, so—'

'I'm sorry, Miss O'Dwyer,' Connie cut in. 'I hope you'll forgive me for asking, but at the interview I got the impression you weren't very keen on me.'

'Did you?' asked the superintendent, sounding genuinely surprised.

'Yes,' Connie replied. 'I was sure I hadn't made a favourable impression when you said "I think I have the measure of Sister Byrne".'

'Well I have.' Miss O'Dwyer chuckled. 'I don't know what sort of regime your Miss Dutton runs down there, Miss Byrne, but up here in the Spitalfields and Shoreditch we are nurses, and any sister who puts her patients' care before pounds, shillings and pence is the sort of nurse we need. Now, I must be going, as old Mrs Drummond hasn't opened her bowels for a week and I'm determined to remedy that situation in the next hour or my name's not Bridget Mary O'Dwyer. Good day, Miss Byrne, and I'll see you on the thirtieth.'

Feeling excited and guilty in equal portions, Connie jumped off the number 253 before it stopped and hurried towards the pub on the corner. It had rained earlier and the puddles reflected the glowing pinks and yellows of the sunset.

She'd just emerged from the crowd of passengers gathered around the bus stop when Charlie stepped out from the shadows. She stopped and waited breathlessly as he strode towards her, his blue eyes fixed on her. He reached her in two heartbeats and swept her into his arms.

His mouth closed over hers and the world stopped as Connie melted into him. She wound her arms around his neck, and her stomach fluttered expectantly as his kiss moved from passionate to demanding.

After what seemed like forever, he released her.

'Connie,' he said, planting kisses over her cheeks and brow. 'How could I have ever let you go?'

Connie's gaze darted over his much-loved face. 'Oh Charlie.'

Someone wolf-whistled and she pushed him away.

'Not here, someone might see,' she said, looking around anxiously.

'I don't care,' laughed Charlie.

'Well I do,' Connie replied. 'I could lose my job for a start if the Association found out I was seeing a married man.'

'I'm only married in name.'

'That's not the poi—'

Charlie kissed her. 'All right, sweetheart, let's go in and find ourselves a quiet corner out of the way so we can talk.'

Charlie pushed the pub door open and Connie stepped into the dark interior.

'You tuck yourself in there,' he said, indicating the small table behind the door's draught screen. 'I'll get us a drink.'

The pub on the corner of Cambridge Heath Road and Roman Road was a typical Victorian gin palace, with lots of ornately carved mahogany, crystal-etched wall mirrors and row upon row of polished glasses. There was the usual crowd of early-evening drinkers, putting the world to rights as they downed an end-of-day pint or two while the blowsy barmaid pulled on the brass pumps to fill tankards. Thankfully, none of the customers looked familiar, so some of the tension Connie had been feeling since she'd slipped out of Munroe House forty minutes earlier ebbed away.

Her eyes returned to the man she loved. Wearing a well-fitted chocolate-brown suit and wide-brimmed buff fedora, he looked as if he'd just stepped out of a fashion catalogue rather than a electrical suppliers.

He paid the barmaid and ambled over carrying their drinks.

'There you go, brandy and orange,' he said, placing a tumbler in front of her and taking the seat beside her. 'And a double malt for me.'

Connie raised her eyebrows. 'You're pushing the boat out a bit, aren't you?' she said, taking a sip of her brandy.

'I am.' He downed a large mouthful of Scotch. 'To celebrate.'

'Celebrate what?'

His arm went round her waist. 'Us.' He squeezed her, and the fluttering in Connie's stomach started again. She took a gulp of her drink.

'We've got a long way to go before we can celebrate anything,' she replied, catching a hint of his aftershave.

'I know,' he said, pressing his thigh against hers. 'But I do love you, Connie.'

He smiled that old cheeky smile of his, and the dreams he'd destroyed on platform 5 at London Bridge burst back into life.

'And I love you too, Charlie.'

'I know you do. And that's why, no matter what people say, me and you being together can't be wrong, can it?' He took her hand. 'Not if we love each other.'

Connie stared down at his fingers joined with hers.

'I suppose not,' she replied, guiltily imagining their bodies similarly entwined.

'And I promise,' Charlie continued, stroking her fingers lightly, 'that as soon as I get the divorce rolling, I'll leave Maria.'

He smiled and then pressed his mouth on hers again briefly.

'Right, I'll get us another.' He stood up and headed back to the bar.

As she watched him wave a ten-shilling note to attract the barmaid's attention, Phyllis's words of wisdom about men and their promises flashed though Connie's mind. An undercurrent of unease started to bubble up, but then, as if sensing her eyes on him, Charlie turned and smiled.

A warm glow of love spread through her, scattering her qualms and doubts in an instant. Charlie loved her, and that was all that mattered.

Chapter Twenty-Two

There was a gathering of worried-looking women outside Mrs Hogan's house when Connie arrived.

'Fank Gawd you're here, Sister,' said a stout woman with thick glasses, as Connie chained her bike to the lamp post. 'Mags is in a poor way, I can tell you.'

'Yeah, fair breaks yer 'eart, after all she's been through,' agreed another, with a tight bubble perm and pencilled eyebrows.

Connie lifted her bag from the basket. 'Well she couldn't have done it without your help.'

It was true. In the weeks since Connie had delivered Joy, the street had rallied around, and not only brought supper over to the family most evenings but had taken it upon themselves to do their laundry and keep the house clean and tidy. It was just as well they had, as Mrs Hogan spent most of her waking hours feeding and tending to Joy, who thanks to her mother's unstinting care was now tipping the scales at just over four pounds. There was still a long way to go before any of them could breathe easy, however, as Mr Hogan's frantic phone call to Munroe House half an hour ago testified.

Leaving the women muttering about the perils of childbearing and the unfairness of life, Connie hurried upstairs to the front bedroom. She put on an assured smile as she grasped the door handle and walked in, but her usual cheery greeting died on her lips as she looked at her patient.

Mrs Hogan was staring down at her baby in the padded wooden drawer at the foot of the bed. Her hair hung lankly around her face and her eyes had dark smudges under them, telling of hours of lost sleep. Even at a distance Connie could hear Joy's croaky, laboured breathing. As she stood motionless in the doorway, Mrs Hogan looked up.

'She won't feed at all. What can I do?'

Dropping her bag on the chair, Connie walked over to the cot. Joy lay inert, with her eyes closed and her little chest rising and falling alarmingly fast as she struggled to breathe. Connie laid her hand on the baby's forehead and found it hot and clammy. Joy's almost transparent eyelids fluttered open in response to her touch, allowing Connie to see the child's unfocused stare.

Taking her thermometer jar from her bag, Connie unscrewed the lid. She shook the mercury down, placed the thermometer under the baby's arm and held it in place. After a few minutes she removed it and held it up to the light.

Ninety-nine point three! Allowing for the fact that the axilla reading was always a degree lower than the oral one, this meant that Joy's temperature was nudging a hundred. If it went any higher, there was a risk she could convulse, and if that happened . . .

'We have to cool her down,' Connie said, taking the baby out of the cot and laying her on the bed. 'Can you get me a bowl of tepid water and a sponge or flannel?'

Mrs Hogan nodded and hurried out of the room.

After pulling the top pane of the sash window down four inches, Connie returned to the bed and stripped off the baby's outer clothing, leaving her in her vest and nappy. Mrs Hogan returned with a bowl, and Connie tested the water, then picked up the flannel and wrung it out. She dabbed the cool cloth on Joy's thin legs, then moved on to her arms. She returned the flannel to the water, wrung it out again and then placed it on Joy's forehead. She continued the process for thirty minutes, then picked up her thermometer again.

Ninety-eight point eight. Praise be! The baby opened her eyes. 'It's working, Mrs Hogan,' Connie said, hearing the relief in her own voice. 'I'll get it down a bit more, then we'll try her with some milk.'

She looked up just as Mrs Hogan's gaze lost focus and she collapsed on the floorboards.

Connie dashed to the window and threw open the bottom pane. 'Someone run and fetch Dr Robinson, and tell him Sister Byrne says it's urgent.'

*

Dr Robinson, resplendent in a striped boating jacket, flannel slacks and a Panama hat, arrived twenty minutes later, by which time Connie had helped Mrs Hogan back to bed and found the root of the problem.

'I'm afraid Mrs Hogan has mastitis,' she informed him as he inspected Joy, who was now back in her cot. 'Her temperature is one hundred and two, with a thready pulse of a hundred and fifteen. I've given her two aspirin, but she's still burning up.'

'Oh dear.' He pulled up a chair next to the bed and took Mrs Hogan's wrist. After studying his watch for half a minute, he placed her hand back on the covers and smiled sympathetically at his patient. 'May I?'

A flush coloured Mrs Hogan's grey cheeks, but she opened her nightdress nonetheless.

He pulled a face. 'How long have they been like that?'

'A couple of days,' Mrs Hogan replied, rebuttoning the front of her nightgown. 'I thought if I kept drawing the milk off it would help.'

Dr Robinson looked at Connie. 'Is baby on the breast yet?'

'No, she still isn't strong enough to feed properly, and she has a temperature too.'

'How high?'

'Ninety-nine point three when I arrived, but I've managed to bring it down a degree since then. She seems more alert, but I struggled to get an ounce of milk down her.'

Dr Robinson took out his stethoscope and slipped it under Joy's clothing. His expression went from dour to bleak. He listened for a moment, then took the earpieces out and let the instrument dangle from his neck.

'I'm just going to have a little word with Sister,' he said, giving the woman in the bed a reassuring smile.

He caught Connie's arm and took her over to the window.

'The baby has a bilateral chest infection,' he said in a low voice. 'And Mrs Hogan is engorged on both sides and in danger of getting blood poisoning, so I'm afraid she'll have to stop feeding and put the baby on to formula.'

'But Joy's stomach is so immature she can still only just tolerate a one-in-eight dilution of whey and condensed milk, whereas she really needs to be on one-in-four by now,' Connie replied, in the same hushed tone. 'She's already dehydrated, and to be honest, Doctor, if she goes on to formula now, I think she'll just fade away.'

Dr Robinson chewed the inside of his lip. 'Do you think you could keep her stable for forty-eight hours, Sister?'

Connie frowned. 'I could try, but—'

'Good.' Dr Robinson turned back to face his patient. 'Now, Mrs Hogan, how do you fancy being a guinea pig?'

Connie and the woman in the bed stared at him as he flipped open his case and pulled out a small cardboard box with a red stripe across the top.

'I got this last week from a pharmaceutical salesman chap I met at a lunch in London,' he said, pulling a sterilised syringe from the elastic webbing in the lid. 'It's called penicillin and was used on the troops after D-Day with miraculous effect – if the medical journals are to be believed. I've been wondering who to use it on, Mrs Hogan, and you seem as worthy a case as any.'

He took out a vial and shook it, then upended it and filled the syringe. 'Roll over, Mrs Hogan.'

She shifted on to her side and raised her threadbare night-gown to reveal her washed-out knickers. Dr Robinson swabbed her thigh with a cotton wool ball loaded with surgical spirit, then plunged the needle into her leg. Mrs Hogan closed her eyes tightly as he injected the mixture, then let out a long sigh as he withdrew the syringe.

'I'm going to leave you in Sister Byrne's most capable hands now,' the GP said, dropping the used hypodermic into his open case. 'She will bind you up until the swelling settles down, and you'll have to stop expressing for a day or two, but after that you can return to feeding Joy as before.'

'Thank you, Doctor. I'll get my Wilf to pop by the surgery and settle up with you.'

Dr Robinson waved away the suggestion. 'It was a free sample, so don't worry. There should be enough for the three-day regime they recommend.'

'I hope you don't mind me asking, Doctor, but it won't hurt Joy, will it?' Mrs Hogan asked.

'I shouldn't think so,' Dr Robinson said. 'My best guess is that once it works its way through your system, it might even help her get over her snuffles.' He snapped his case shut and looked at Connie. 'If you drop by the surgery later, Sister, I'll have the letter of authorisation for you to administer the remaining doses.'

'Very good, Doctor,' said Connie.

He turned back to his patient. 'Now you rest up, Mrs Hogan, and try not to worry.' Adjusting his bow tie in the dressing table mirror, he left.

'I'll give Joy her next feed and then I'll pop back to Munroe House for the bindings,' said Connie.

'Thank you, Sister,' said Mrs Hogan, her eyes fluttering down as she spoke.

Connie placed her hand gently on Joy's forehead. Her temperature was no higher, but her chest rose and fell alarmingly fast and her pallor was waxy. Mercifully there was no blue tinge around her mouth and nose, but without her mother's milk, would she be able to cling to life?

Feeling a cloud of doom gathering around her, Connie picked up the bowl of water and made her way downstairs.

Mr Hogan had already boiled the feeding bottles before going to work and left them in the saucepan ready for her. As Connie took the whey from the stone milk kept in the pantry, there was a knock on the back door. With a sigh she looked round to see the stout woman who had been outside earlier standing in the doorway.

'Sorry to barge in, Sister, but me and the girls were wondering if there's anything else we can do,' she said.

'That's very kind of you all, but I think you've done as much as you can.' Connie laughed. 'Unless, of course, you've got some breast milk.'

The round-faced motherly looking woman chuckled. 'Not any more I ain't, ducks, but Ruby at number four still has one on the tit. So 'as Ulma on the corner. Shall I ask them to pop over?'

'Yes,' said Connie, almost giddy with relief. 'Yes please.' And please God – she glanced upwards – between us we can get Joy through the next forty-eight hours.

Recrossing her legs for the fourth time, Connie glanced up at the clock. Three thirty! Millie had been upstairs in front of the Association disciplinary panel for almost an hour.

337

Connie was sitting on a particularly uncomfortable bench in the main entrance of St George's Hospital, just off the Highway. Although the building was now a medical establishment, the functional half-tiled walls and unadorned iron stairway clearly revealed its workhouse origins. As with any hospital, there was a desk in the reception area, behind which a bored-looking woman talked on the phone while the lit cigarette in the ashtray beside her sent up a thin curl of white smoke. Behind her was a mahogany plaque with an armorial crest held in place by a unicorn and a bear, and the names of the great and good who had overseen the destitute of the parish since the early 1830s.

Of course, Millie might have been upstairs for such a long time because she'd been allowed to put forward her case and the committee were considering the mitigating circumstance. Or it could be that, as usual, Mr Shottington had arrived late and they'd only just started. Either way, Connie really felt for her friend. Despite the dozens of letters she and the other nurses had gathered from their patients, Millie was quite likely facing instant dismissal and a reference from Miss Dutton even worse than the one she'd given Connie.

To stop herself looking at the clock yet again, Connie picked up a dog-eared copy of last November's *Woman's Realm* and flicked through the first few pages until she came to the cookery section. She skimmed over recipes for beetroot and celery leaf salad and eggless mayonnaise before moving on to the homemaker pages. There was a photo of a man and a woman grappling with a paste board and a wayward roll of bright wallpaper. The decorating expert offered the suggestion that in order to economise on wallpaper, the modern couple should consider using it only on one wall and painting the other three to tone in, as the Americans were now doing.

Connie turned the page. Even though Charlie was certain he would be divorced from Maria within the year, it was far too soon to think about decorating their marital home.

She finally came to the knitting section, where a rugged-looking chap wearing a chunky Aran jumper, a faithful hound at his heels, sat in front of a painted mountain backdrop. Although it was close to seventy degrees outside, Connie read through the instructions for the winter woolly. The pattern was straightforward enough, and as it required big needles it wouldn't take her more than a month or so to make – just in time for Charlie's birthday in October.

She glanced over the illustration again and smiled as she tried to imagine Charlie wearing such a thing. He wore a sleeveless V-necked jumper only if there was frost on the puddles, and even then it had to be shop-bought from Burton's or Hepworth's, never home-made like every other man she knew. She was about to flip the page when something about the picture struck her. She studied it for a second, then laughed. Of course. The young man gazing off into the pretend horizon looked just like Malcolm Henstock.

A little jab of guilt darted through her as she remembered how rude she'd been running off in the middle of their dance. Perhaps she should have gone back and explained. But explain what? She was in love with her ex-fiancé, who was getting a divorce.

Tears spiked the corners of Connie's eyes.

It had been three weeks since the night of the dance, and she and Charlie had met as often as they could. She'd known that getting a divorce wouldn't be plain sailing, but she hadn't expected to feel more and more like a bit on the side with every day that passed.

She looked up at the plaster ceiling rose to try and disperse the grey cloud that seemed to be permanently hovering above her. It was just difficult, that was all; once she and Charlie could be together properly it would be all right again. They would be happy.

'Connie!'

She blinked away her tears and looked up to see Millie, grinning from ear to ear, trotting down the stairs. Throwing the magazine back on the table, Connie stood up and raced towards her.

'I take it you've still got a job!'

'I have.' Millie hugged her. 'Thanks to you and the girls rallying around.'

'I'm sure I don't know what you're talking about,' said Connie innocently.

Millie raised an eyebrow. 'All those patients' letters.'

Connie grinned. 'It worked, then?'

'It did.' Millie looked a little dewy-eyed. 'Thanks, Connie.'

'You'd have done the same.'

They smiled fondly at each other and hugged again.

'And it gets better.' Millie laughed. 'I've been promoted officially to deputy superintendent and,' she swung Connie round, 'I can live at home!'

Connie looked astounded. 'What?'

'I know!' Millie laughed again. 'I couldn't believe it either when Mr Braithwaite suggested it.'

'Mr who?'

'Some chap from the Ministry of Health.'

'Why was he there?'

'He said he was doing a fact-finding tour of the London district nursing associations.' If possible, Millie's smile widened. 'I wish you'd seen old Shottington's face when the man from the Ministry boxed him into a corner about promoting me and letting me live out.'

'So do I.' Taking the hem of her skirt, Connie curtsied. 'Well congratulations, Deputy Superintendent Sullivan,' she said in a plummy voice.

Millie giggled and did the same. 'And to you, Deputy Superintendent Byrne,' she replied in the same affected tone.

'This is a hospital, not a bloody dance hall,' the receptionist's shrill voice called across.

The two of them stopped bobbing and tried to look like senior Queen's Nurses rather than a couple of giggly schoolgirls.

'Come on,' said Connie, slipping her arm through her friend's. 'I'm covering Annie's late on-call tonight, so let's head back to Munroe House and have a celebratory cup of tea.'

Half an hour later, after treating themselves to two jam doughnuts from Anderson's in Watney Street, Connie and Millie trotted up the front steps of Munroe House and into the nurses' sitting room, where Millie was greeted like a returning hero by the dozen or so nurses just finishing their afternoon tea. While she was recounting the events of the afternoon to her rapturous audience, Connie slipped out to check the message book.

One of the new recruits, Nurse Parsons, had been called to a delivery just after lunch, so although she wasn't officially on call for another hour, Connie went back to her room and changed into her uniform before making her way back down.

'So that's why Miss Dutton had a face like thunder when she

'got back,' chuckled Hannah as Connie re-entered the room.

'Serves her right for being such a cow,' added someone else.

There were mutters of agreement.

'And of course it means that if Millie is allowed to live out, then others can too,' said Connie.

Sally glanced up at the heavy Victorian plasterwork above them and pulled a sad face. 'What with Connie going and you moving out, the old place won't feel the same.'

Millie laughed. 'Don't think you're getting rid of me that easily. I'll still be here to keep you all in order.'

Chapter Twenty-Three

Sheltering in the entrance of Mile End underground station, Connie peered anxiously along the street. A number 25 bus, its windscreen wipers barely clearing the torrential September downpour with each pass, trundled to a halt by the bus stop. A group of young women got off, giggling as they dashed through the puddles to join the queue lining up down the side of the Odeon cinema on the other side of the road.

Connie looked at her watch again.

The District Line train had just closed its doors as she'd stepped on to Stepney Green's eastbound platform and she'd had to wait five minutes for the next one, which meant she'd arrived five minutes late. But that was fifteen minutes ago, and she asked herself yet again what on earth she was doing.

Men unfurling umbrellas and women fastening see-through plastic rain hats under their chins surged up the steps behind her as another train brought people home from the City and beyond. The street vendor selling evening copies of the *News and Standard* as quickly as he could fold them gave her a sympathetic look.

Feeling a little knot of anxiety, Connie glanced at her watch again.

A car hooter blasted out. 'Connie!'

She looked up and saw Charlie, wearing a fawn suit with a club tie held in place with a gold pin, waving at her through the open passenger door of the car parked just a few feet away from her.

'Quick!'

She dashed across and jumped in next to him, closing the door behind her.

'I thought you weren't—' His mouth stopped her words in a demanding kiss.

Connie melted into him, enjoying the feeling of his body and his mouth on hers. After a pulse-racing few moments they parted.

'Sorry I'm late,' he said, retracting his arm and shifting the gear leaver on the steering column. 'There was an accident between two lorries in Limehouse and I had to wait until the coppers came along and shifted 'em.'

Pumping on the accelerator, Charlie roared away from the kerb, then yanked on the steering wheel and spun the car around, skimming past a couple of factory workers on the pedestrian crossing and heading off eastwards into the gathering gloom of Stratford High Street.

'Whose car is this?' Connie asked as they rumbled over the cast-iron Bow Bridge and then past the tiled image of a lavender gatherer with her two children displayed on the side of the Yardley works.

'Tommy Timms let me have it for the evening. It's an Austin Devon, just off the assembly line. Smart, ain't it?' Charlie ran a hand over the sleek dashboard. 'Don't look like that,' he added, seeing her disapproving expression. 'He ain't as bad as people say.'

'But wasn't he up in court for shoving a bottle in someone's face last week?' said Connie.

'It was self-defence.' Charlie took a cigarette packet from his pocket and drew out a cigarette with his lips. 'And it comes to something when a chap finds himself hauled up in front of the beak just for defending himself. It's not what we fought for, I can tell you.' He swerved to avoid a cyclist. 'There's a lighter in the glove compartment, sweetheart.'

Connie retrieved it. Flicking the roller to ignite the flame, she held it closer to Charlie. He drew on his cigarette a couple of times, then blew a stream of smoke out of the corner of his mouth.

'Where are we going?' she asked.

'I'd thought we'd motor out to a place I know in Woodford,' he said, overtaking a bus. 'A nice little trip into the country will perk you up.'

Connie forced a smile. 'Sounds lovely.'

As they drove around Maryland Point and up Leytonstone High Street, Charlie started chatting about the trouble he was having at work with the dispatch manager.

'. . . so I said to him, you carry on like that, mate, and the whole caper will go under,' he concluded, rolling down the window and flicking his spent cigarette butt out. 'I'm right, ain't I, Connie?'

'Sorry, Charlie, I didn't quite catch what . . .'

He grinned. 'You ain't heard one word I've said, have you, babe?'

'I've got a lot on my mind at the moment,' she said, guilt clawing at her.

Charlie smiled, then turned sharply left into Whipps Cross Road. Whizzing across the road in front of an ambulance, he pulled into the car park alongside the boating shed, coming to a halt behind the spreading branches of a willow tree.

'What are you doing?' Connie asked.

'Stopping the car so I can do something to take your mind off things.'

Sliding along the bench-like front seat, he took her in his arms. And as he pressed his lips on hers, all Connie's niggling worries vanished. With her senses filled with the man she loved, she wrapped her arms around him and kissed him back.

After a heart-pounding embrace, Charlie lifted his mouth from hers and smiled down at her. 'That's the ticket. It breaks my 'eart to see you unhappy,' he said, inching even closer to her, his eyes glowing bright in the fading light.

Connie frowned. 'I thought we were going for a meal.'

'We are,' he whispered, nibbling her ear. 'But I couldn't hold off kissing you any longer.'

Before she could reply, he pulled her against him in another passionate embrace. One hand moved up her back while the other made its way down to her hip. Connie closed her eyes and ran her fingers through his hair, then over his shoulders.

'Oh Connie,' he murmured, sending shivers up her spine. 'You feel so good.'

He planted feathery kisses along her cheek to her ear, sending Connie's pulse racing, then nuzzled down the sensitive line of her neck and under her collar. The top button of her blouse popped open. She reached up to refasten it, but Charlie's lips got there first.

'I love this perfume,' he murmured, as his hand slid up and cupped her breast.

Connie shoved him off. 'What do you think you're doing?'

'What?' he asked, trying to look innocent.

'You know.'

He grinned. 'I just got a bit carried away. You can't blame me, can you?' His arms tightened around her, and Connie's anger ebbed away. 'That's better,' he said in a soft voice, lowering her back on to the front seat. 'Oh sweetheart,' he murmured nibbling along her collarbone.

Connie relaxed again as the magic of his mouth on her skin stole all other thoughts from her mind. She felt another button of her blouse pop but it didn't seem to matter too much, neither did the fact that his hand had moved from her hip to her thigh beneath her skirt. His kiss deepened from adoring to ardent, and a floating feeling stole over Connie until she felt his fingers working their way over her suspender and under the edge of her knickers.

Pushing herself upright, she shoved his hand away. 'Stop it, Charlie.'

'Oh Connie, let me.'

'No, Charlie.'

'But Connie—'

'We agreed to wait.'

'But it ain't easy for a chap.' A suggestive look crept into his eyes. 'You know, getting all 'ot and bothered for nothing. If you love me you would,' he said in a low, persuasive voice.

Connie's mouth pulled into a tight line. 'If you weren't married, I might be tempted,' she replied, countering his charming expression with an implacable one.

Irritation flashed across Charlie's face for a second, then he sat up and snatched the pack of cigarettes from his pocket again. Connie straightened her skirt and refastened her blouse.

'I was going to tell you when we got to Woodford,' he said, tapping out a cigarette and jamming it in the side of his mouth. 'But I suppose now's as good a time as any. I had a pint with my chum at the solicitor's today.' He flicked the lighter and drew on his cigarette. 'He says we can get the divorce done, from start to finish, for about a hundred and fifty quid, and I've bunged him a pony to get the ball rolling.'

'But where on earth are we going to get all that?' asked Connie.

'I've got a bit stashed by at Mum's,' he replied. 'And I can get the rest.'

'From Tommy Timms, no doubt,' said Connie.

Charlie held her gaze for a moment, then blew a stream of smoke upwards. Connie studied his profile in the fading light.

'And have you spoken to Maria yet?'

'I'm just waiting for the right moment.'

'You know how I hate lying to my family and friends . . .'

He jabbed his half-smoked cigarette out in the dashboard ashtray.

'I hate it too, babe,' he said, sliding back over to take her hand again. 'And it'll be easier when you move to Spitalfields, but believe me, the longer I keep Maria in the dark, the better for everyone.'

Connie frowned. 'Wouldn't it be more honest to tell her outright?'

Charlie slipped his arm along the seat behind her. 'And where would we have been in the desert if we'd told Rommel where our guns were before we started firing?'

'But once your friend starts arranging things, she'll have to know,' said Connie.

'And she will,' Charlie assured her. 'But until then I have to carry on as normal.'

'Then there's the children,' continued Connie, guilt stabbing her under the ribs.

'I'll see them all right, don't you worry,' said Charlie earnestly. 'And remember,' he gave her a pulse-racing smile, 'I might soon have another family to support.' His blue eyes took on a darker hue, and Connie's mind started to wander on to all sorts of pleasant pathways.

Her heart melted. 'Oh Charlie, I do love you.'

'I know,' he replied softly, placing his hand on her thigh again. 'I know it's a lot of aggravation, but it'll be over by Christmas and then you can start planning for a wedding.'

Like the last time!

Charlie's lips pressed on to hers, and the disturbing thought vanished.

He lifted his head. 'I tell you what.' He kissed her again lightly. 'It's a bit uncomfortable in the front. Why don't we get in the back seat?'

Connie regarded him for a long moment, then smiled. 'I might just consider getting in the back seat with you once you've told Maria, but until then I'd rather have that meal you promised me.'

Dressed only in his Y-fronts, with his clothes over one arm and his shoes in the other hand, Charlie opened the bedroom door slowly and stepped through the narrow gap. He waited until his eyes adjusted to the dim light, then pushed the door shut quietly and tiptoed around the bed towards the dressing table. He draped his shirt, tie and suit over the back of the chair, then set his shoes on the lino beneath. Rummaging around in his trouser pocket, he pulled out a cigarette and lighter and edged over to the bed, carefully avoiding the loose floorboard.

Slipping under the covers, he waited a moment before lighting the cigarette. He took a deep inhalation. As the nicotine began to have its effect, he rested back against the headboard and peered at his watch.

Twelve thirty. Not bad. If he fancied going in, he'd even get to work on time in the morning.

Twisting his arm towards him, Charlie admired his latest purchase in the glow of the street light creeping under the curtains. It wasn't in the same league as Tommy's Rolex, but his new Omega, with the snakeskin strap and gold fitments, still marked him out as a main man. Stretching his other arm in a weary arc, he wedged his hand behind his head.

A contented smile spread across his face as he remembered the way blokes had looked at Connie when she'd walked into the restaurant on his arm. And who'd blame them? She was a real head-turner, with all those curls and curves. And she was brainy, too, for a girl. No wonder she'd got that new job of hers, whatever it was.

Stunning and smart, that was his Connie. That was what he loved about her, and always had. Right from the start. Even when he was still messing about with that willing blonde from Cambridge Heath Road, he knew Connie was the one for him. But then he wasn't short of brains either. After all, despite all those girls he could have had, he'd picked her out from the crowd as something special. And from the way his mother told it, she was the only girl between the Aldgate Pump and Bow Bridge not carrying on with a Yank.

His smile widened. You're a lucky sod, Charlie boy, he told himself as he remembered the feel of Connie in his arms. A right cracker and no mistake. Nice legs and a decent handful up top, too.

His penis swelled at the thought.

Of course, there could have been some cream on the cake if she'd gone along with his back-seat suggestion, but then Connie was always a good girl. Even when she'd had his ring on her finger she didn't allow any liberties.

In truth, it was what every proper fella wanted. A respectable girl; one who was entitled to wear white to the altar and needed a man to take the lead on the wedding night. A man felt safe with a girl like that, just as he always had with Connie. After all, if she wouldn't let you get your hands on her goods then she wouldn't let some other bugger either.

Maria stirred and rolled on to her back, her hair tangled on the pillow and her arm stretched out in casual abandon. Unlike most women, who buttoned themselves up for the night in a long-sleeved winceyette gown, Maria slept in an artificial silk nightie with ribbon straps. Her change of position had dislodged the lacy bodice, exposing her shoulder and nearly all of her breast.

Charlie's penis twitched again.

He took in another lungful of tobacco and then blew a series of smoke rings.

Perhaps he should have been a bit firmer with Connie, he thought, as his gaze travelled over his wife's bare flesh. Not forced her exactly, but been more persistent.

He took a last drag of his cigarette then stubbed it out in the ashtray on the bedside table. Shuffling down the bed, he rolled towards Maria, his arm encircling her waist.

She murmured something and stretched.

Charlie pushed her legs apart with his foot.

'What you doing?' she asked, rubbing sleep from her eyes.

Charlie didn't answer, just pulled up her nightdress and rolled on to and into her in one swift motion. As he'd said, until he got everything sorted with Connie, he had to carry on as normal.

*

348

Holding her hat on with one gloved hand and her handbag in the other, Connie hurried along Stepney Way as fast as she could in her new high heels towards the late-medieval church of St Dunstan's at the end of the road. She was dressed in her finery to witness the joining together of Miss Josephine Baxter, spinster of the parish, and Mr Jack Wallace, bachelor of the same, but she was running late. Little Joy Hogan had been snuffly that morning, so Connie had stayed a little longer than she intended to help Mrs Hogan feed her.

After waiting for a milk float full of empty bottles to rattle past, Connie dashed across Stepney High Street and up the church path. Blinking to adjust her eyes to the dark interior, she took a service book from the verger and walked in. Sally, Annie and Millie were sitting halfway down the left-hand side of the church. Millie, wearing a mulberry-coloured dress and jacket and matching hat, turned and waved frantically at her. Smiling at the congregation already assembled, Connie made her way to her friends.

'Thank goodness. I thought the bride was going to beat you to the church,' said Millie, shuffling along to make space on the wooden pew.

'Weren't you supposed to be a half-day?' asked Sally, dressed in a French navy ensemble and pillbox hat.

'Yes,' said Connie, tucking her skirt under her and sitting next to her friend. 'But I'd just got to the bottom of the stairs when the secretary of the Spitalfields and Shoreditch Nursing Association rang. Apparently they've found dry rot in the roof beams of the nurses' home, and as it's going to take a month to replace them, they've had to put off my start date until the twenty-eighth of October.'

'Did Dutton agree to you staying on an extra month?' asked Millie.

'With four nursing vacancies and Gladys in the convalescence home she couldn't do much else,' Connie replied.

'Oh well, I suppose we can put up with you until then, can't we, Annie?' laughed Sally.

'We'll just have to grin and bear it,' Sally replied with an exaggerated sigh.

The four friends exchanged affectionate smiles, then Sally and Annie turned round to chat to the people behind.

'I also popped in on the Hogans again,' Connie said softly to Millie.

Her friend gave her a sympathetic look. 'Is Joy still poorly?'

Connie nodded, as the image of the little girl lying limp in her improvised incubator flashed through her mind. 'Mercifully she's no worse, thanks to all the helpful neighbours.'

'And thanks to you too, Connie,' Millie replied. 'If it wasn't for all the effort you've put in since she was born, I'm pretty certain she wouldn't even be here now.'

'I know,' sighed Connie. 'But she's not out of the woods by a long chalk. If I can only get her up to five pounds I'd be a lot happier.'

'How much was she the last time you weighed her?'

'Four six.'

Millie looked impressed. 'That's not bad in five weeks from a birth weight of two pounds ten.'

'And she's taking a full two fluid ounces at each feed now, but there's been a few cases of whooping cough recently, and if she catches it, well . . .'

Swallowing her personal feelings, as a good nurse should, Connie looked ahead.

'I see Jack's here,' she said, watching the uncharacteristically nervous young man dressed in a tailored chocolate-coloured suit checking the rings with his best man. 'And so many people.' She glanced around at the friends and relatives filling the pews on both sides. 'But I don't see— Oh, Millie.'

'Don't take any notice of me,' said Millie, fumbling in her handbag for a handkerchief. 'I know I'm just being silly . . .'

'Alex?'

Millie nodded and blew her nose. 'I'm sorry.' She forced a laugh. 'Who'd have thought it, eh? You and me both with a ring on our finger and a wedding booked, and now sitting here un-married and with not the remotest prospect of being otherwise.'

Connie took a deep breath. 'Well actually, Millie, I've—'

'She's here,' squealed Annie.

Connie and Millie turned to see Josie, looking every inch the blushing bride, standing in the gothic archway between the church's age-blackened doors.

'Doesn't she look a picture?' said Connie wistfully.

Having somehow scraped together enough clothing coupons for five yards of fabric, Josie was dressed in an ivory full-length gown with a sweetheart neckline and leg-of-mutton sleeves. On her blonde curls sat a small veil held in place by artificial flowers on a comb.

The organist blasted out the opening bars of 'Here Comes the Bride', and the congregation stood up as one. Josie, clutching a small posy of blue and white flowers and hanging on to her father's arm, followed the rector, in full garb, down the aisle, beaming at everyone as she passed between the smiling faces of her friends and family, while her soon-to-be-husband stood open-mouthed in wonder watching her glide towards him.

Once the wedding party were in their designated places, the rector signalled for the congregation to be seated.

'Dearly beloved, we are gathered here today . . .'

As she listened to the familiar words, Connie's mind drifted off to the wedding she and Charlie were now planning. With a bit of luck, clothes rationing would have finished and she could wear something with a flared skirt. She could have her nieces as bridesmaids too. They'd love that.

'For so much as Josephine and Jack have consented together in holy wedlock,' said the priest, bringing Connie back to the here and now, 'and have witnessed the same before God and this company, and thereto have given and pledged their troth either to other, and have declared the same by giving and receiving of a ring, and by joining of hands, I pronounce that they be man and wife together, in the name of the Father, and of the Son, and of the Holy Ghost. Amen.'

As Connie chorused 'Amen' with the rest of the congregation, a pang of sadness rose in her. She gazed at the happy bride in her beautiful wedding dress and realised that, no matter what she wore, making her vows in a registry office would never be the same as being married in church.

'There you go, Bernie,' Connie said, handing her sister a strawberry Mivvi. 'I've given Marlene and Gloria a cornet each and said they could stay where they were if they didn't run about with them.'

'Thanks, Connie,' said her sister, adjusting Betty's sun hat.

It was a week after Josie's wedding, and the two sisters were sitting on the sunny side of the Valentine Park Lido. They weren't the only ones. The pool was packed with families taking advantage of the unseasonably warm September weather.

They'd arrived just after nine, and Connie had handed over a shilling for herself and Bernie and fourpence for the two older girls. After changing into their bathing suits in one of the minute cubicles surrounding the pool, they had staked their claim to an area at the shallow end, set out their towels and put Betty's pushchair loaded with their picnic lunch between them.

Being a respectable mother with three children, Bernie had plumped for a structured dark red bathing suit. Connie, however, was wearing her new two-piece polka-dot red one.

'They've over by the steps leading in,' Connie continued, pointing to where her nieces, in their rubber rings, were splashing about with a handful of other children. 'Watching them reminds me of when Mum used to take us to the lido when we were kids.'

'Yes, except we didn't have to take three trains to get wet,' Bernie replied, breaking off a corner of her lolly and popping it in Betty's mouth. 'It's good of you to give up your day off to help. I couldn't have managed the pushchair and the girls on the train on my own.'

'Don't be silly,' Connie replied, licking a rivulet of melted ice cream from her cone. 'I'm enjoying it, and what better way is there to spend a Saturday than basking in the sun eating ice cream?'

Two boys dashed by firing at each other with water pistols.

'You're not the only ones thinking that,' said Bernie, moving her feet aside.

Her sister's focus shifted past Connie and her eyes widened.

'Hello again,' said a familiar voice.

Connie turned to find Malcolm Henstock, wearing a snug pair of knitted bathing shorts, standing behind her. As her gaze ran over his broad shoulders and the dark curly hair on his chest, she was suddenly aware of the heat from the sun.

'I thought it was you,' he continued, smiling down at her.

'Did you?'

He nodded and looked up. 'Lovely day.'

'Yes.'

352

'I'm Connie's sister Bernie,' Bernie chipped in.

'Sorry,' said Connie, dragging her gaze from Malcolm's face. 'Bernie, this is Malcolm Henstock. His mother was one of my patients.'

'Nice to meet you,' her sister said, giving Malcolm an approving look.

'And you,' Malcolm replied politely. His gaze returned to Connie. 'You're a long way from home.'

'So are you.'

'Well, we usually take the boys to York Hall for their monthly swim, but as it was such a lovely day, we thought we'd venture further afield,' Malcolm replied.

'Oh, you're here with your family,' said Bernie, with more than a hint of disappointment.

Malcolm chuckled. '"The boys" are the Second Limehouse Scout troop, and "we" are the scout masters.'

Bernie's face lit up in an instant. 'So you're not married?'

'No, I haven't met the right girl yet,' Malcolm replied.

He smiled at Connie and she lowered her eyes.

'So what do you do for a living?' Bernie asked.

'I work for the council,' Malcolm replied. 'In the Highways department.'

'That sounds like a very important job,' Bernie murmured, as if he'd announced he was Lord Mayor of London.

'Not as important as the job your sister does,' he replied, his eyes returning again to Connie. 'Mother still talks about wonderful Sister Byrne.'

Complains about me scratching her woodwork more like, Connie thought, but it was kind of him to say.

'Are you all right now?' Malcolm asked. 'I mean after the dance?'

Connie felt a blush warm her cheeks. 'Yes, I'm fine. I'm sorry about dashing off like that.'

'Don't mention it,' he said, gazing down at her.

They smiled at each other.

'Mr Henstock!'

'Looks like someone needs your help,' said Connie, indicating a young man surrounded by a pack of excitable school-age boys at the far end of the pool.

'I should go,' Malcolm agreed, waving reassuringly back. 'Michael has only just got his leader's woggle and the boys can be a bit of a handful if you don't take a firm hand. Nice to meet you, Bernie.' He gave her a brief smile, then his attention returned to Connie. 'Perhaps I'll run into you a bit nearer to home next time.'

'Yes, perhaps,' Connie replied.

His gaze flickered over her again, then he walked away.

'For goodness' sake, Connie, why on earth haven't you grabbed him with both hands?' asked her sister when he was out of earshot.

'What?' said Connie, shading her eyes to see Malcolm better.

Bernie sighed. 'Good-looking fella with a solid job who fancies you and you're asking me "what"?'

'Don't be daft,' said Connie, watching Malcolm ruffle some lad's hair. 'He was just being polite, that's all.'

'And of course you're not interested at all?' Bernie replied, sounding uncannily like their mother.

'Not at all,' said Connie, smiling as Malcolm joined in a game of tag with the boys.

'Well,' her sister continued, with a wry smile, 'if that's the case, how come you've forgotten you're holding an ice cream?'

Connie frowned, then looked in astonishment at the melted mess running down her arm to her elbow.

Chapter Twenty-Four

The late-morning sunshine streamed through the window as Connie stood in Mrs Hogan's bedroom with her fingers crossed in the folds of her skirt. She held her breath as Dr Robinson repositioned his stethoscope on baby Joy's chest. She was sure she was almost as anxious as the baby's mother, who hovered by her daughter's cot.

Connie's eyes ran over Mrs Hogan as she watched the GP complete his examination. Despite having lost at least a stone to her recent illness, her patient now had a healthy colour in her cheeks, and thanks to a nourishing meal each night courtesy of her kind-hearted neighbours, she was putting on a bit of flesh.

'Well I'm pleased to tell you, Mrs Hogan,' said Dr Robinson, removing the chestpiece from the infant's ribcage, 'that both lungs are clear, which is remarkable.'

Putting her hand on the crucifix around her neck, Mrs Hogan let out a long breath. 'Thank goodness.'

'And what about you?'

'I'm on the mend too,' she replied. 'Thanks to those injections you gave me.'

The corners of his thin moustache turned upwards. 'Good.' He looked at Connie.

'Yes, Doctor,' she said. 'Mrs Hogan's fever disappeared after three administrations, and the inflammation has all but gone.'

Dr Robinson's eyebrows rose. 'That's very impressive.'

'As you said, Doctor, a miracle drug. And Mrs Hogan has started to feed Joy again this morning,' Connie added.

'Well done, Sister, for keeping her going.' The GP nodded approvingly.

'I think that should be well done to Mrs Hogan's neighbours, Doctor,' said Connie. 'Four of the women in the street who are still nursing their own infants came over each day to donate milk.'

Connie had ended up running a teaching session in Mrs Hogan's kitchen to show Ruby, Ulma, Janice and Christine the correct way to sterilise the equipment. She'd even got the corner shop to store some spare bottles of breast milk in their refrigerator in case it was needed and none of the women were around.

'Well, whoever the credit goes to, I'm happy to give Joy a clean bill of health.'

'Thank you, Doctor,' said Mrs Hogan.

Dr Robinson looked seriously at her. 'I have to tell you, Mrs Hogan, that when she was born, your daughter's chances of survival were not very good. Not good at all. In fact I can't recall the last time a baby weighing less than three pounds survived past four weeks.'

'She's a little fighter, Doctor,' said Connie, smiling at Joy, who was responding to the doctor's deep voice.

He gave a crooked smile. 'So it would seem. And also because you, Sister Byrne, and your splendid team have visited twice a day for the past umpteen weeks.'

'They've been marvellous,' said Mrs Hogan.

'Indeed. But you must still be vigilant,' Dr Robinson continued in a weighty tone. 'If she gets a temperature or the slightest hint of the snuffles, you need to bring her to the surgery straight away.'

'I will, Doctor,' replied Mrs Hogan.

'And I will still be popping in regularly,' added Connie.

'Very good.' He folded his stethoscope away and closed his Gladstone bag.

'Doctor, I was wondering if it would be all right for other people to see Joy now? Just the immediate family, I mean?'

Dr Robinson regarded the baby lying in her boxwood drawer thoughtfully. 'I think close family would be all right at this stage, but not if they have a cold or cough. However, the rest of the world will have to wait until Miss Hogan is eight weeks old and at least five pounds before she can make her first appearance.'

'Thank you so much for all you've done, Doctor,' said Mrs Hogan, gratitude and happiness brimming out of her eyes.

'My pleasure, Mrs Hogan.' He looked at Connie. 'Good day, Sister.'

'Good day, Doctor.'

Connie started tidying away her equipment. Mrs Hogan reached across and caught her arm.

'And thank you too,' she said. 'For all you've done.'

They exchanged a fond look, then the door burst open. Mr Hogan stood in the doorway with the three children crowded around him.

'Doctor said they could see Joy before they went to school,' he said, an infectious grin spread wide across his face.

'Of course they can, as long as they don't crowd around her.' Connie fixed the youngsters with her best matron glare. 'You don't want to give your Joy any nasty germs, do you?'

'No, Sister,' the children chorused.

They shuffled in and peered at her.

'She's so tiny,' said Alison, the eldest, pulling a sugary face at the baby.

'Cor, she looks like a doll,' said nine-year-old Keith.

Harry, a freckle-faced six-year-old, didn't look at all impressed. 'Don't she do nuffink?'

Connie smiled. 'Not yet she doesn't.' Gazing down at the baby, she placed Harry's finger in Joy's tiny hand and the baby's fingers curled around it. 'But I promise you, she'll soon be after your toys.'

Connie ran her pen down the page, checking that Student Queenie Angela Merriweather, one of the newest batch of trainees, had completed the required tasks, then signed at the bottom.

It was now just after six in the evening, and as she had a little time before supper, Connie had decided to go through the students' workbooks to make sure the Queenies were progressing as they should be. The small office was jam-packed with nurses furiously writing up their notes before going off for the weekend, so she'd tucked the workbooks under her arm and headed for the quiet lounge at the back of the house, where she could concentrate on her task without having to listen to the chatter about boyfriends and fiancés.

She was halfway through checking the industrial nursing page when the door opened and Josie came in. She'd changed out of her uniform and was wearing a pair of casual grey slacks and a bottle-green box-shouldered jacket, with her handbag in the crook of her arm.

'Oh, there you are,' she said, shutting the door behind her.

'Yes, I thought I'd just sign these off before supper,' Connie replied. 'Are you off?'

'In a while,' Josie replied. 'Jack's in a staff meeting until six thirty, so I'm going to stroll up to the school and meet him.'

'How's the new flat?'

'Very small, and the smell from the canal is a bit overpowering at times, but with so many families having to make do with just one room, we were lucky to get it,' Josie said. 'It's convenient, too, as we can both walk to work from Bow Common, but we're hoping to scrape a deposit together for a place in Plaistow by the end of the year. You must come over one night.'

Connie smiled. 'I'd love to, but it won't be until after I've moved.'

'That's all right,' laughed Josie. 'You've got an open invitation, and don't forget, if you need a hand with the packing, just shout.'

'Thanks, I will.'

Josie regarded her thoughtfully for a moment, then sat down in the chair alongside her.

'I hope you don't mind me asking,' she said, a troubled expression spreading across her pretty face, 'but is everything all right?'

'What an odd question,' said Connie, pulling a puzzled face.

'No, really,' persisted Josie. 'I mean, you're not worrying about moving to Spitalfields, are you? You shouldn't be; you'll be a terrific senior nurse, all the girls think so.'

'That's very kind of them,' said Connie in a jolly tone. 'To be honest, now that I've got a date, I'm actually quite excited to try something new, although I'll admit I'm a bit nervous about changing associations.'

'I suppose leaving Munroe House must feel strange,' said Josie.

'It is, but the old place isn't the same as when I first arrived.' Connie laughed. 'We have nurses like you, for a start. In my day, once you were married you had to leave, but now there are half a dozen of you who are married, and Winnie is even expecting a baby, which would never have happened before the war.'

'It wouldn't be happening now if the old bag had her way,' added Josie.

'I'm sure, though as we're six nurses short, even Miss Dutton has to move with the times,' said Connie. 'But other than suffering from broken nights and long days like the rest of you, I'm perfectly all right.'

Josie's shoulders relaxed. 'I'm glad, because I have to say I was a bit worried when Veronica said she found you crying in the linen cupboard last week.'

Somehow Connie maintained her cheerful smile. 'I wasn't crying,' she said with a light laugh. 'I'd just flicked myself in the eye with a pillowcase, that's all.'

'Well that's a relief,' said Josie. 'If it hadn't been for the fact that you've looked a bit sad recently, I wouldn't have said anything.'

The clock in the hall chimed the quarter-hour. Josie stood up and hooked her handbag over her arm. 'I'd better be off, or Jack will be standing outside waiting for me.'

'Have a nice weekend,' said Connie pleasantly.

'And you,' Josie called over her shoulder as she headed for the door.

The lock clicked shut and Connie looked back down at the workbook on the table in front of her, but her vision was blurred. For goodness' sake! What was wrong with her? And it wasn't even her time of the month. She had Charlie back, and after his divorce they could get married and start the life they'd planned before the war. So why then did she wake up with the weight of the world on her shoulders every morning and burst into tears at the drop of a hat when she was supposed to be happy?

Resting back in the chair, she closed her eyes and tried to get a grip on the wave of despondency that seemed to be engulfing her.

There was a knock at the door. She blinked away the last bit of moisture and looked down at her work.

'Come in,' she trilled.

The door opened and Gillian, another one of the new trainee Queenies, popped her head around it.

'Sorry to disturb you, Sister Byrne,' she said, looking respectfully through her spectacles at Connie. 'But there's a Dr Smallbone on the telephone. He urgently wants a nurse to visit a child with whooping cough to help the mother set up a vapour tent.'

'Thank you, Nurse March. How old is the patient?' asked Connie, screwing the top back on her pen.

'Nine months.'

Connie frowned. 'Oh dear.'

'I know,' said Gillian, her apple-like face full of compassion. 'It'll be touch and go. If you're in the middle of something, should I tell the next on call?'

Connie shook her head. 'Under the circumstances, I'd better go myself. What's the baby's name?'

Gillian glanced at a slip of paper in her hand. 'Filippo Ross. The family live above Murray's fish bar on the Mile End Road.'

Half an hour later, with her heart pounding in her chest and her stomach knotted with anxiety, Connie pulled up outside the fish and chip bar opposite Stepney Green station. As it was Friday night, there was a queue of people treating themselves to the traditional end-of-week supper, but they parted to allow Connie to secure her bicycle to the shop boot scrap.

Taking her bag from the basket, she squeezed past a mother with three fractious children and walked into the appetising aroma of fried fish blended with the sharp smell of vinegar.

Behind the counter, a burly dark-haired man and a youth with the first traces of a moustache on his top lip were wrapping fish and chips into sheets of newspaper at a remarkable turn of speed, while a woman in her early fifties with raven-black hair piled high took the money. Spotting Connie in the doorway, she wiped her hands on her greasy apron and hurried over.

'Good you come,' she said, taking Connie's free hand in both of hers and bowing. 'I'm Mrs Fabrini. My grandson, Filippo. Very sick.' She lifted the hinged part of the counter. 'Come.'

Connie followed Mrs Fabrini through a beaded curtain and up a flight of stairs to the rooms above. She could already hear the distinctive whoop, whoop sound of a child coughing.

'There.' The woman nodded towards the door at the far end of the corridor. 'When shop closed I come back.'

'Thank you,' said Connie. 'And is your daughter's husband around in case—'

''Im!' Mrs Fabrini's face contorted into an ugly expression. ''E's never here. Bad 'usband.' She gestured something with her thumb and forefinger that needed no translation, then walked away muttering to herself.

Praying silently that she wouldn't have to come face to face with Charlie just at this precise moment, Connie went in.

Although the room's wallpaper was so faded the pattern was nothing more than splodges of beige and brown, the bare boards were scrubbed clean and there were new curtains at the windows. Along with a double bed in the middle of the room, there was also a three-door wardrobe, and a cot bed on which Maria sat cradling her son in her arms. With her hair hanging around her face and dark smudges under her eyes, she looked tired and drawn. She was also wearing a navy dress with a white collar, the front pleat spread wide showing her to be five or possibly six months into her second pregnancy. Something that clearly had slipped Charlie's mind as he'd failed to mentioned it in any of their recent conversations.

The two women stared uncomfortably at each other for a couple of heartbeats, then Connie smiled.

'Good evening, Mrs Ross. Dr—'

'Why is it you come?' Maria cut in. 'I suppose you want to see if Carlos is here.'

'No, I'm here because—'

'Your fancy man, my 'usband, not at home,' spat Maria.

'In view of everything that has gone on between us, it's not easy for me to be here either, but I didn't come to see you or your husband,' said Connie, maintaining her professional persona. 'I came because your son is dangerously ill. You can throw me out if you like, but I am the only nurse on duty, so please allow me to care for your son through the next few crucial hours.'

Maria nodded, then ran her fingers through her son's hair and closed her eyes.

Connie's shoulders lost some of their tension. 'How is Filippo?'

The boy answered for himself as a fit of coughing gripped his little chest. His eyes bulged and his cheeks grew red as he gasped and spluttered, trying to draw air into his lungs.

Connie dropped her bag on the dressing table chair and rushed over. 'Put him over your shoulder.'

Maria did as she was told, and the sudden shift of position allowed Filippo's lungs the space they required to drag in desperately needed air. After a worryingly long few minutes, the bronchial spasm subsided.

'I'm just going downstairs for a moment, Mrs Ross,' said Connie reassuringly. 'If your son starts coughing again, just do as you did before.'

Leaving Maria comforting Filippo, Connie went down to the kitchen. She filled the kettle and set it on the stove to boil, then searched around until she found an old broom and mop. She hurried back upstairs with them.

'I'll have to use the sheets from your bed,' she said, stripping back the candlewick cover and blankets.

Ten minutes later, having wedged the upended broom and mop between the mattress and the bed frame, draped the sheets over the bristles, mop-head and headboard and then pinned them into place with a dozen nappy pins, she had completed the steam tent.

'Can you settle him in the middle of the bed while I fetch the water?' she said, holding open the front flap for Maria.

Taking her son's weight, Maria stood up and gently lowered him into the nest of pillows Connie had shaped for him. Then, without letting go of his hand, she fished out a cross from beneath her dress. Clutching it to her, she closed her eyes and her lips moved silently.

Connie studied her profile for a moment, then her gaze shifted to the child in the bed. His breathing was sturdier now, but as she studied the little boy's face, a band of pain tightened around her heart.

How could a child of such tender years resemble his father so much?

She pushed the unsettling thought aside, brushed a stray lock of hair from her forehead and left the room, returning a couple of minutes later with a bucket of boiling water, which she placed under the raised sheeting. The improvised inhalation cubicle soon began to fill with steam.

With the rasping sound of Filippo's laboured breathing echoing around the room, Connie quietly perched on the dressing table stool. Taking her nurse's notes and her pen from her bag, she started filling in her paperwork.

Maria's mother let out a low snore and shifted in the chair without waking. Mr and Mrs Fabrini, or Rosa and Bruno as they insisted she call them, had come up to help nurse their grandson as soon as they'd closed the door on the last customer four hours ago. After lugging buckets of boiling water up from below every half an hour, Bruno had been shooed off to bed just after eleven as he had to be at Billingsgate five hours later.

Maria, Rosa and Connie had nursed Filippo through three episodes of coughing, but finally the steamy atmosphere surrounding him had done the trick and the choking paroxysms had abated. His fever had broken just over an hour ago, and Maria had managed to get some milk down him. He now slept peacefully with his mother and grandmother on either side of him and a blue teddy tucked in his arms. Although it was close to midnight, Charlie had still not returned.

Standing up, Connie put her hands in the small of her back and stretched.

Maria, who was dozing, opened her eyes and rose to her feet. As she tiptoed over, the bedside lamp threw her shadow on to the far wall.

'Well, Mrs Ross, Filippo seems to have settled now,' Connie whispered. 'I think the crisis is over and I can safely leave him to your care, but I'll get a nurse to call in the morning to make sure he's truly on the mend.'

'Thank you, Sister, for what you've done for my son.' Maria took Connie's hand awkwardly. 'And I sorry, too. For shouting in your clinic and making trouble.'

Connie forced a smile. 'It was a misunderstanding, that's all,' she said, taking her hand back.

She turned to retrieve her jacket from the end of the bed, and as she ferreted around among the bedclothes, she felt something soft under her fingertips. She pulled the garment out to set it aside, but as she did so, the floor rose up to meet her and her heart thumped uncomfortably in her chest as she found herself holding a pair of neatly folded men's pyjamas.

'I didn't know, but Charlie 'e told me you Catholic like me.' Maria's voice echoed around her. 'So like me, you know that once a priest marry you, it done once for all time. Yes?'

A mixture of tobacco and Charlie's male aroma filled Connie's nose, sending her emotions reeling.

'Yes,' she repeated. 'Once for all time.'

Connie laid the letter dated August 1944 on the small pile on her right and took up another from her lap. It was close to one o'clock in the morning, and her alarm was set for 6.30, but it didn't matter. There wasn't a hope in hell of her getting to sleep anyway. Tilting the page into the soft glow of her bedside lamp, she scanned the messy handwriting. Another tear escaped, but she caught it with her handkerchief and read on.

The phone in the hall rang.

Connie gathered together the letters strewn around her and slipped them into her dressing gown pocket. Shoving her feet into her slippers, she tied her dressing gown sash and opened her bedroom door.

She met Valerie, the night on-call nurse, on the landing.

'I'm going down,' she said in a loud whisper. 'I'll give you a knock if you're needed.'

Valerie nodded and made her way back to her room, yawning.

Connie hurried down to the hall and picked up the telephone receiver. 'Munroe House. Sister Byrne speaking. How can I help you?'

'Thank God it's you, sweetheart,' said Charlie.

'I thought you'd phone, so I waited up.'

'Yeah, about tonight—'

'It doesn't matter.'

'I would have been there, you know I would have,' he asserted. 'But I had to do a bit of business.'

'Perhaps it was better you weren't at home when I arrived.'

He gave a short laugh. 'You're probably right. It must have been awkward, though.'

'Not really,' Connie replied. 'I was there to do a job. How is he?'

'Who?'

'Filippo?'

'Oh, he seems grand,' Charlie said. 'Although Maria's in a flaming temper.'

'Well, she's had a worrying time.'

'I suppose so.' There was a pause. 'You're all right then, Connie?'

'Yes.'

'Are you sure?' he asked. 'Because you sound a bit upset.'

'I'm tired, that's all.'

He let out a long breath. 'Well that's all right then. And we're still on for tomorrow night in the Hayfield?'

'I'll be there.'

The pips went.

'Night then, babe,' he called over the beeping.

The line went dead.

Connie replaced the receiver and wiped an escaped tear from her cheek. But instead of making her way back upstairs, she headed for the quiet lounge.

The heavy tapestry curtains were drawn back and the street light illuminated the room. Without turning on the central light, Connie walked over to the empty fireplace. Pulling the collection of letters from her pocket, she turned them over in her hand, then laid them on the bare grate. She took the box of matches from behind the mantel clock.

The hearthrug scratched her bare knees as she knelt and struck a match. The flame flared, and the image of the happy home she had dreamed of all those long years while he was away fighting flooded back into her mind. As the flame burnt up the phosphorus, she allowed herself to picture the house where Millie's mother now lived, but with the curtains she'd chosen at the windows and Charlie's dinner cooking in the oven.

She thought of how their first child would have been Charles if a boy or Jennifer if a girl. How they would have gone to Devon for their holidays, and in their own Morris Minor if they'd saved hard enough. In her mind's eye she saw the quiet nights by the fireside listening to the radio before going upstairs for pleasures she had yet to experience.

She let the happiness of the life she and Charlie would have had together dance around in her head for a few seconds more, then she held the match to the corner of the bottom letter.

Shaking off her rain hood and popping it in her mackintosh pocket, Connie stared at the brass plate on the snug door for a second, then she pushed the door open and walked in.

As it was a Saturday night, the Hayfield, which stood in the corner of Stepney Green, was relatively quiet, with just a few workers from Charrington's brewery standing at the bar. The barmaid, a motherly looking woman with curly auburn hair and spectacles, acknowledged Connie with a nod.

Charlie was hunched over a table in a dark corner, staring mournfully into his pint. He was freshly shaven and dressed in casual fawn slacks and a tweed jacket. Connie studied his profile for a moment before he sensed she was there. He stood up and hurried over.

'Hello, babe,' he said, giving her his most charming smile. 'Is it still rain—'

'Hello, Charlie.'

He caught her elbow and led her towards the corner table he'd just vacated.

'You look nice. I've always liked you in pink.' He leant forward as if to kiss her, but seeing Connie's expression, he pulled a chair out for her to sit on instead. Perching on the corner of the chair with her knees together, Connie put her handbag on the table.

He rubbed his hands together. 'The usual?'

Connie shook her head. 'I won't be staying.'

'Look, if it's about you visiting Maria the other day, then—'

'I was just doing my job, Charlie,' Connie cut in, the pounding of her heart almost deafening her. 'I've come to say goodbye.'

'Now, sweetheart, let's not be hasty,' said Charlie, raking his fingers through his hair. 'I know I said I'd tell her, and I would have if it had all gone as planned. But my mate has had a bit of trouble arranging things, you know how it is—'

'I don't know and I don't want to either,' said Connie sharply. 'What I do know is that you're married with a child, and Maria is never in a million years going to agree to a divorce. Even if she did, it wouldn't matter, because it's too late.'

Charlie took her hand. 'Look, I know you're upset, but never mind about Maria. We can move away and set up house together. Go up north or somewhere. Even abroad to Canada if you fancy. Make a fresh start, just you and me. No one would know and we'd be married in all but name.'

'And what about if we had children?'

He shrugged. 'It's not ideal, them being born you know but—'

'Illegitimate, Charlie. That's the word for children whose parents aren't married,' Connie cut in.

His gaze flickered for an instant, then his cajoling smile returned. 'But they'd be brought up in a happy home with loving parents. Surely that's more important.'

'And what about the child you've already got and the one Marie is now carrying?' asked Connie. 'Isn't it important that they're brought up in a happy home too?'

Exasperation flitted briefly across Charlie's face. 'I've already told you I'd see them all right.' He pressed her hand to his lips. 'Please, Connie. I know it's my fault we're stuck in this blooming mess, but me and you, we're made for each other.'

Connie's gaze ran over the face that had smiled out at her from a picture frame for four years, the face she'd thought she'd wake up to every morning for the rest of her life. She smiled sadly.

'I've loved you since I can't remember when, and when you asked me to marry you before you shipped out the last time, I thought my life was set,' she said. 'I spent four years dreaming about the day you'd slip a wedding ring on my finger, the happy home we would share and the children we would have. It kept me going through the bombs, the destruction and death, and on the day Churchill told us it was over, my first thoughts were for you. When you stepped down from that train with Maria, my whole world ended. I can't tell you how many nights I woke up crying, the torture of seeing you with her, knowing she was having your baby. Can you imagine the pain I went through?'

'I know, I kn—'

'I spent months trying to live without you, and then just as I'm getting my life back on track, you pitch up and tell me you've made a mistake and you still love me.'

'But I do,' pleaded Charlie. 'Surely that's what matters. How we feel about each other.'

'I thought so too,' said Connie. 'If I loved you and you loved me, then somehow we could be Connie and Charlie again. Just like before. But we can't. The truth is, Charlie, we can't turn back the clock. It's over. And that's what I came to say tonight.'

Charlie scowled. 'Well this is bloody rich, ain't it? You just swanning in here and telling me you've changed your blooming mind. And I've already bunged my mate a score for the hotel in Brighton.'

Connie stood up. 'I'm sorry.'

Charlie jumped to his feet, rattling the glass on the table. 'So that's it, is it? One minute it's all "I love you and can't live without you, Charlie", the next it's "I'm sorry, I've changed my mind and ta-ta"?' He loomed over her.

Connie didn't reply.

His face contorted into an ugly expression. 'Well that's all well and good for you, but what am I supposed to do?'

Connie held his angry gaze in her sad one for a couple of seconds. 'Go home and help your wife nurse your sick child,' she said.

Chapter Twenty-Five

Connie tucked her drawstring wash bag, the embroidered hand towel Bernie had bought her last Christmas and her beaded make-up case down the side of her suitcase and closed the lid.

'Is that it, then?' asked Millie, who was sitting with her back against the headboard and her legs stretched lengthways on the bare mattress of Connie's bed.

Connie snapped the lock closed. 'It is indeed. Just the last few bits.'

Millie gazed around the room that had been Connie's home for the past five years and sighed. 'It looks very bare.'

'Yes, it does,' Connie agreed, briefly noting the square of unfaded wallpaper where her picture of her family had hung. 'Though it's hard to imagine it took Jim two trips to shift all my stuff to Fry House.'

'Your poor brother,' Millie laughed. 'I'm surprised he didn't give himself a hernia carrying your two boxes of books and your clothes trunk down the stairs. Not to mention that old cast-iron sewing machine.'

Upending her case, Connie sat on the opposite end of the bed, with her legs up, in the comfortable and informal way she and Millie had sat together for eight years or more.

'It's difficult to believe the old place is still standing considering how many times we were blown out of bed by a bomb landing on the docks,' said Millie thoughtfully.

'Do you remember the night all the windows were blown in?' asked Connie.

'I blooming do.' Millie smiled. 'And when we scrambled into the superintendent's bedroom over the rubble, Miss Summers was still snoring in bed.'

'Clutching a bottle of gin.'

They both laughed.

'What about the time those villains pinched all the bicycles and we had to walk everywhere for three days?' said Millie.

'I've still got the blisters,' Connie replied. 'But I think the episode that sticks in my mind is the naked man.'

'Oh yes,' chuckled Millie. 'Although I'm still baffled as to why he was in the treatment room sluice in the first place.'

'Or what happened to his clothes,' added Connie.

'I can still see the look on the superintendent's face when he ran past us while we were having morning handover.' Millie sighed. 'We never did find out who he was.'

'Well, loose talk costs lives, remember, but I can tell you one thing about him.' Connie's eyes twinkled. 'He had nothing to be shy about.'

The two girls fell about laughing, then Millie got the giggles, which set Connie off too, and very soon they were holding their sides and taking deep breaths to control themselves.

'Oh Connie,' said Millie, wiping her eyes. 'You've been so out of sorts recently, it's good to see you laughing again.'

Connie straightened the flowery peach-coloured dress over her knees. 'It's been a tough year.'

Millie reached over and squeezed her hand. The two friends smiled affectionately at each other, and then Connie swung her legs off the bed.

'Right, I'd better get a move on before Dutton tries to charge me board and lodging for today,' she said, slipping her feet into high heels.

Millie stood up too, taking Connie's fern-green jacket from the back of the door. Connie shrugged it on and adjusted the collar of her blouse in the mirror fixed above the sink. Then she secured her beret and picked up her handbag.

'Ready?' asked Millie.

'Yes, I am,' Connie replied, grasping the handle of her suitcase.

The familiar sound of thirty-plus nurses eating their breakfast surrounded Connie as she entered the refectory.

Sally and Eva spotted her first and came rushing over, followed by Annie, Joan, Martha and Beattie. Josie was there too, having come in especially early to see Connie off on her last day.

They flocked around her thanking her for all manner of things, most of which she'd forgotten about, and wishing her well for the future. Even Gladys and her crew sidled over as Connie popped her head into the kitchen to say farewell to Mrs Pierce and her team.

Finally, after hugging and kissing everyone at least twice, Connie left the refectory for the last time.

The bright October sun cut across her eyes as she trotted down the front steps of Munroe House. Although it wasn't even 8.30, the working day had already started. Well-heeled office workers waited at bus stops, and freshly scrubbed boys and pigtailed girls with satchels slung across them trudged to school. In addition, a steady stream of vans and lorries chugged their way westwards into the City, while a policeman in the centre of the junction kept the traffic flowing with sharp toots from his whistle and frantic signalling. At the end of the road, the gas board were laying new pipes, and the ear-numbing sound of a pneumatic drill thudded through the chaos.

Spotting a number 15, Connie strolled up to the bus stop and hopped on to the backboard as it slowed. She stowed her case in the luggage compartment under the stairs for the twenty-minute journey to Aldgate, then paid her thrupenny fare and made her way to an empty seat at the front. Resting her handbag on her knee, she looked out of the window as the vehicle rolled westwards.

After a few moments the bus pulled to a halt next to a crowded request stop. Connie studied the display of flyers in the printer's window outside as people got on and off. The conductor pulled on the overhead cord and rang the bell. The driver revved the engine and the bus pulled away from the kerb.

'Hello, I thought it was you,' said a man's voice. 'Can I join you?'

Connie looked up and saw Malcolm Henstock holding on to the upright handrail behind her seat.

'Of course,' she replied, thinking that at almost six foot, he only just missed bashing his head on the roof of the bus.

He paid his fare to the conductor behind him, then swung into the seat, stowing his tan briefcase by his feet.

'You off to work?' she said as he tucked his ticket into his breast pocket. It was a daft question really. At 8.30 in the morning, dressed in a double-breasted grey suit, subdued tie and fedora, he couldn't very well be going anywhere else.

'Planning meeting at County Hall,' he said. 'The LCC want the boroughs to coordinate their road repair programmes.'

'Sounds important,' said Connie.

'It sounds like hours of arguing, stewed tea and stale biscuits to me,' he replied. 'However, you, Miss Byrne,' he said as his eyes ran admiringly over her, 'look as if you're off somewhere much nicer.'

'Yes and no, Mr Henstock,' Connie replied. 'I'm starting a new job today.'

'Not too far away, I hope?'

'No,' Connie replied, and she told him about the Spitalfields and Shoreditch Nursing Association.

'Congratulations on your promotion,' he said, sounding suitably impressed. 'Though I'm sad I won't be running into you as often as I have been doing.'

'I'm only going to Spitalfields, not Timbuktu,' said Connie.

Malcolm pulled an overly worried face. 'Perhaps, but from what I read in the local rag, Timbuktu might be safer.'

Connie laughed and Malcolm joined in.

'I wish you success in your new job,' he said, his deep tones sending a little ripple of warmth through her.

'Look, Mr Henstock, I—'

'Malcolm,' he corrected.

'Look, Malcolm, I know I said it at the lido that time, but I really am sorry for the way I dashed out on you at the St Andrew's dance. I—'

'It's all right, Connie, really,' he said softly. 'I guessed you were going through a miserable time.'

She nodded. 'I was, and that night it all just got a bit too much.'

A glint of something very pleasant sparked in Malcolm's eye. 'You're forgiven.'

The bus pulled up at a pedestrian crossing. Feeling her cheeks glowing, Connie looked ahead. As she tried to unravel the long-forgotten feelings of excited anticipation and emotional curiosity, she spotted a couple of familiar faces among the people on the crossing. A warm glow of satisfaction enveloped her as she watched Mr and Mrs Hogan, the three elder children beside them, pushing a pram across the road in front of the bus.

She smiled fondly, and then something akin to bright light flooded through her brain.

So Charlie had broken her heart. And she'd been a complete and utter fool. So what? It was nothing compared to what thousands of people endured every day. Joy Hogan and all the other babies she'd delivered over the years, as well as the countless men, women and children she'd seen pulled from blitzed buildings, or who'd cheated death by surviving deadly infections, should have taught her by now that there was always hope.

She turned to Malcolm. 'Am I really forgiven?'

He looked puzzled. 'Er . . .'

'Truly?' Connie persisted.

'Yes, of course you are,' he laughed.

Connie gave him a dazzling smile. 'Well then,' she said brightly, 'and as long as you don't think I'm being too forward, would you like to come to the pictures with me on Friday?'

Acknowledgements

I've had quite a challenge bringing Connie's story to the page. not least because I have written hers and Charlie's story along the same timeline and events of my first East London nurse series, *Call Nurse Millie*. This meant drawing up an Excel chart to plot the two stories against each other, plus spending a fortune on post-it notes to ensure I haven't got Connie delivering any 12 month pregnancies or enjoying time with her family on Easter Sunday just two weeks after they've sat down to Christmas dinner.

As with the previous books, I've tried to keep true to the strands of her and my profession as a District and Queen's Nurse before the NHS, and the tough austerity years immediately after World War 2.

As always, I would like to mention a few books, authors and people to whom I am particularly indebted.

Again, to ensure the treatments and care Connie gave her patients was authentic to the period, I returned to the nursing biographies I found so helpful for *Call Nurse Millie*, including Lucilla Andrews' *No Time for Romance,* Edith Cotterill's *Nurse on Call* and *Yes, Sister, No, Sister* by Jennifer Craig, which, although set in Leeds, gave much of the flavour of post-war nurse training and culture, as does *Of Sluices and Sister*, by Alison Collin. I garnered a couple of self-published gems in my travels, including *My Life and Nursing Memories (from 1914–2008)* by Nurse Corbishley, and *Nurse* and *Yes, Sister* by Dorothy Gill. I, of course, read Jennifer Worth's accounts of 1950s East London in her popular books, *Call the Midwife* and *In the Shadow of the Workhouse*, although the most detailed account of a pre-NHS Nursing Association came from Irene Sankey's biography, *Thank You Miss Hunter* (unpublished manuscript). Ms Sankey became the superintendent at the East London Nursing Society in 1946 and it's her detailed account of that time that most helped me bring the Munroe House nurses to life.

I also drew on *Learning to Care: A history of nursing and midwifery education at the Royal London Hospital, 1740–1993*, by Parker and Collins (1998) in association with the London Hospital Museum, and *The London Volume II 1840–1948*, Clark-Kennedy (1963).

For Connie's professional life I have used several text books of the period, including *Handbook of Queen's Nurses* (1943); a 1940 edition of Faber's *Nurse Pocket Encyclopaedia and Diary and Guide*; *Parenthood, Design or Accident*, Fielding 4th edition (1943); *Psychiatry and Mental Health* Rathbone-Oliver (1950); *Nursing and Disease of Sick Children* Moncrieff 4th edition (1943); and *A Short Text Book of Midwifery* Gibberd (1951), which has a number of medical illustrations that are not for the faint hearted.

For general background of the period I used *Our Hidden Lives*, Simon Garfield (2005); *Nella Last's Peace*, ed. P & R Malcomson (2008); *Austerity Britain 1945–51* by David Kynaston (2007); and although I can vividly remember the warmth and neighbourliness of the old streets around where I grew up, I added *The Only Way is Essex*'s very own Nanny Pat's account of her East End childhood, *Penny Sweets and Cobbled Streets*, to my collection of East End memoirs this year, along with Shire Library's *British Family Cars of the 1950s and 1960s* and *Make Do and Mend*, which is a reproduction of the official Second World War leaflets. I've added a 1948 and 1951 copy of *Nursing Mirror*, and three 1948 editions of *Woman's Own*, plus several late 40s early 50s issues of *Housewife* to my collection.

I also used several post-war photographic books including *'Couldn't afford Eels' Memories of Wapping 1900–1960* Leigh (2010); *The Wartime Scrapbook* Opie (2010); *The Forties, Good Times Just Around the Corner* Maloney (2005); and, although it is slightly later than the period Connie's story is set in, *London's East End: A 1960s Album* Lewis (2010), as this documented wonderfully the sights and sounds I remember as a child.

You can read more about my East End childhood and some of the locations I used in the book on my website www.jeanfullerton.com.

I would also like to thank a few more people. Firstly, my very own Hero-at-Home, Kelvin, for his unwavering support, and my three daughters, Janet, Fiona and Amy, for not minding too much that they are literary orphans sometimes. My fellow author in the Romantic Novelist Association and great chum, Carole Matthews, with whom I've enjoyed several delicious lunches and hours of putting the world to rights. I'd also like to thank the Facebook group *Stepney and Wapping living in 60s early 70s,* who helped me search out an authentic boxing club for Charlie and filled in other 1940s and 50s local details I'd forgotten.

Once again my lovely agent, Laura Longrigg, whose encouragement and incisive editorial mind helped me to see the wood for the trees. Lastly, but by no means least, a big thank you to the editorial team at Orion, especially Laura Gerrard, for once again turning my 400-plus page manuscript into a beautiful book.